[REMNANTS OF LIGHT]

by

Mike Yost

Whaley Digital Press
www.WhaleyDigital.com

Remnants of Light

© 2011 Michael Yost

Published by
Whaley Digital Press, LLC
12 Broadway, Ste. 221
Denver, CO 80203
info@whaleydigital.com
permissions@whaleydigital.com

All rights reserved. No part of this book may be reproduced or transmitted in any form or by any means, electronic or mechanical, including photocopying, recording or by any information storage and retrieval system, without written permission from the publisher, except for the inclusion of brief quotations in a review.

This book is a work of fiction. Names, characters, places, and incidents are either a product of fiction or are used in a fictitious manner. Any resemblance to actual persons living or dead is entirely coincidental.

ISBN-10: 1-501-09725-3
ISBN-13: 978-1-501-09725-6

Released in North America.

For my older brother, Paul

[REMNANTS OF LIGHT]

"Stars were falling across the sky myriad and random, speeding along brief vectors from their origins in night to their destinies in dust and nothingness."

—**Cormac McCarthy,** *Blood Meridian*

[I]

[2009]

They seemed to hover high above him, mute witnesses burning through a dome of obsidian above the desert. There were millions of them—billions, actually. All unimaginable in size, yet seen only as small, innocuous pinpricks on black canvas. A few were long extinct, their light reaching Earth from now-extinguished stars. Echoes of light.

Mark blinked. He stared at the ancient voyeurs peeking back at him through a large opening in the upper corner of a decaying cinderblock wall. Like distant observers, the abundant members of this universal audience loitered with ambivalence, unconcerned for Mark's thin, pale body, curled in on itself opposite a pile of broken bricks resting at the base of the opening.

He rolled onto his back and slowly stretched out his body. Mark closed his eyes as he took a deep, painful breath, inhaling the dry, stagnant air into his lungs. He tried to ignore the pain in his knee. It would often strike like a lightning bolt, shocking him out of any sleep. Mark rubbed his forehead, unable to remember how long he and Kevin had been locked in this dusty room, the three gray walls illuminated faintly with moonlight—the fourth wall of metal bars remaining ominously dark.

Mark placed his hands on his chest, tapping his fingers on the dog tag under his brown t-shirt as he tried to add up each day in his head. Kevin was sleeping in the opposite corner, his malnourished body periodically flinching. Probably dreaming about the stale, moldy bread they shared two or three days ago, Mark thought. They hadn't eaten in days, but the green bread made them both vomit until there was nothing left but air belching out of their sore stomachs—the guards standing in the hallway, just beyond the bars of the cell, watching with mild amusement. Mark sighed and turned away from Kevin. He narrowed his eyes and tried to focus down the pitch-black hallway. He could hear occasional laughter trickling down the long, empty corridor—a corridor that seemed darker than space itself.

Mark looked back at the cracked cement ceiling. He gave up trying to count the days. Instead, he strained to remember the constellations, their names, their positions in the night sky. Mark knew they could give him hints to his location. Ever since capture, he had kept watch through the opening in the cell wall.

A few scrolled across the opening in the wall like actors in a play: Lepus. Orion. Canis Major. Monoceros. Canis Minor. Gemini. Cancer. Hydra. Leo. Lynx. Ursa Major. Mark knew that from their presence and orientation, he was still in the northern hemisphere. He also knew that the hole in the wall was facing southeast. Mark watched Orion, the powerful hunter, rise and fall, followed by Canis Major and the brightest star in the sky, Sirius. Orion's presence revealed that, despite the cruel, desert heat during the day, it was still winter. Mark breathed deeply again. Pain in his ribs. Pain from his knee. His body instinctively jerked against the rusted chains that ran from his wrists to large, steel anchors bolted into the wall behind him.

Scorpius. Ophiuchus. Scutum. Aquila. Hercules. Serpens Cauda. Lyra. Cygnus. Vulpecula Sagitta. Delphinus. They were some of the constellations hiding behind the veil of blue during the day, only showing themselves at night during the summer months. Mark knew they were watching him, too. Had been watching. Would be watching—long after his bones were buried beneath the earth

Mark had already tried to map out an escape through the same hole where the stars gazed back at him. This was when he wasn't bound with chains. Back then, Kevin was strong enough to help Mark up the wall, using his body as a ladder for Mark's naked feet. Back then, Mark's ribs didn't hurt when he reached up for the opening in the wall. Back then, Mark was able to bend his knee.

When Mark had crawled up into the opening and turned on his stomach to reach down for Kevin, a small portion of the crumbling cinderblock wall gave way. Mark fell out of the cell and onto his back, landing on the desert floor with a quiet thump. For a moment, he couldn't breathe. Air stubbornly refused to enter his lungs as a cloud of dust hovered around his body.

Silence followed. Orion sat high upon his throne, looking down at Mark from his sooty citadel.

"Run," Kevin whispered over the wall.

Mark rapidly shook his head as he slowly pulled himself up, grains of sand falling from his hair, sticking to his arms and feet. He bent down, wrapping his fingers tightly around a single cinderblock that lay half-buried in the sand. His weak muscles jerked and pulled against his skin as Mark lifted the block and struggled to walk forward, dropping it below the hole in the wall. Mark lifted his feet and stood on the block, toes curled around the edge. He jumped, sore fingers barely grabbing the edge of the hole above. The blisters on his hands popped open as Mark strained to pull himself back up the wall. His belly scraped against the jagged opening, and Mark leaned over into the cell, holding out his open hand, blood dripping from his fingertips. Somewhere in the distance, Mark could hear dogs barking.

"Fucking run!" Kevin yelled, standing below Mark in the cell, his face covered in sweat and indignation. Kevin heard the familiar voice of one of the guards from down the dark hallway yelling in Arabic, chastising the barking dogs. Kevin swung his head back to the cell door.

"Fucking jump!" Mark replied as he stretched his hand farther out, slapping the back of Kevin's head.

They made it several miles in the moonlight, following the trajectory of Orion as the three of them moved slowly toward the horizon. Mark behind Orion. Kevin behind Mark. But less than an hour later, the barking returned, distant at first, like an echo from a nightmare that grew louder as it crawled its way out from the deep wells of the subconscious. Then they heard the truck. The flat desert offered no place to hide.

Ten minutes later, a German Shepherd sunk its sharp teeth into the pale flesh of Kevin's left arm, dragging him down into the sand. The sudden rush of warm blood that shot into the dog's mouth fueled its ravenous instincts. It snapped its narrow head back and forth, as if it were trying to tear a small branch from a tree. A second German Shepherd went for Kevin's throat, but missed, its angry teeth snapping together in the cool air. The dog lunged again, this time its drooling jaws clamped down onto the side of Kevin's face.

Kevin yelled as he tried in vain to fight off the two dogs that were tugging him in opposite directions. One grew more vicious, almost tearing Kevin's cheek away from the bone. Mark leapt forward, wrapping his arms around the dog's neck, trying to drag it away. A bullet sped past Mark's ear; he looked up and saw a truck driving toward them, his face illuminated by the headlights. The silhouette of a man stood on the bed of the truck, aiming his Kalashnikov rifle. Bursts of dust kicked up into the air with each bullet. The dog Mark was holding suddenly released Kevin and jumped back with a loud yelp, a cloud of red mist spraying Mark in the face. Mark fell onto his back, still holding tightly onto the animal as it kicked a few more times before going limp. Warm blood from the bullet wound gushed onto Mark's chest as he pushed the dog off onto the sand.

Scorpius was rising, followed by the light of the sun slowly burning away the night sky—the mute witnesses now slowly sinking beneath a sea of blue. The other dog instinctively jumped back at the continuing rifle shots, ears clamped to the back of its skull. The man in the back of the truck jumped out before the vehicle even stopped. He ran with the rifle pointed at Mark's head. Mark didn't even try to stand. The tip of a steel-toed boot embedded itself into Mark's side, his floating rib now literally floating. Two more guards jumped out of the truck and cursed Mark and Kevin in Arabic. The sun was peeking over the horizon when the guards tied Mark and Kevin's hands and feet with greasy rope. One guard stood over the dead dog with his rifle slung over his shoulder, shaking his head, his long shadow falling across the desert floor. He bent down to pet the lifeless creature. The other canine whined, pacing back and forth. Kevin and Mark were thrown into the back of the pickup, its metal skin spotted with islands of rust. As they drove back, Kevin moaned, pushing his wounded face into Mark's shoulder. The bed of the truck lurched violently, the tires occasionally sinking deep into the soft sand. White smoke poured out of the exhaust pipe.

"You're burning oil," Mark said flatly to the guard who sat across from him. The man quietly stared back.

When they returned, the guards remained silent as they threw Kevin's unconscious body back into the cell. Mark was silent as they dragged him by the arms into a room with a single gas lamp on the floor in the corner. Sunlight had never penetrated the walls. The guard who had stood over the dead dog now stood over Mark, his shadow falling across Mark's face.

"That was my favorite dog," the guard said in English, his accent barely noticeable. A white turban was wrapped around his head and face, revealing dark, amber eyes. The guard swung his Kalashnikov behind his back and unzipped his pants. The urine stung Mark's wounds as he tried to turn his head away. His cracked lips burned. He could taste it in his mouth. The other guards in the room laughed, seated along the walls with their rifles resting across crossed legs. Their bearded faces were half-illuminated by the dim lamplight. Tobacco smoke filled the room. The guard finished, zipped his pants, and walked over to the lamp in the corner.

"The dog's name was *Saiph*," the guard said. "Do you know what that word means?"

Mark spat, "It's Arabic for 'sword.'"

"Very good," the guard replied as he leaned down next to the lamp and a wooden toolbox in the dirt. Mark heard him unfasten a latch. The guard opened the box, letting the lid fall open. "It's also the name of a star in the constellation Orion," the guard said, holding a power drill with a large bit in his left hand. "A fierce warrior." He walked back to Mark. The other men in the room stood. "Do you know Orion's fate?"

Now Mark had a hole in his left knee. He could hardly stand, much less walk. Kevin didn't fare much better. Small, red holes in the shape of a thin U ran down the right side of his swollen face—Kevin's eye hidden beneath small hills of swollen flesh. Mark continued to stare at the night sky, ignoring the waves of pain that rolled up his leg and crashed against the base of his skull, lapping up against his mind and cutting away his thoughts.

"Orion," Mark whispered to himself. "Made up of the stars Betelgeuse, Bellatrix, Mintaka, Meissa, Rigel... Rigel, then..." Mark cursed to himself and closed his eyes. "Rigel... Rigel..." Mark's eyes tightened until the names of the stars shouldered their way out of the darkness. "Alnitak! Alnitak, Alnilam... and, of course, Saiph." Mark whispered the names of the stars to himself again and again, dust from the cell floor coating his mouth. He turned his head toward Kevin, who hadn't moved in hours. He was chained to the wall as well, the slack in a small pile next to his unnaturally white legs.

"You still sleeping, you lazy bum?" Mark's chest hurt when he talked.

Kevin stirred. "Can't sleep on account of your smell." He looked up, trying to smile. "Making my eyes water."

"Eye," Mark replied.

Kevin smirked and reached up with one hand, lightly touching the wounded side of his face. The chain rattled quietly. Kevin's body shook. "It's cold."

Mark's eyes narrowed. "It's not that cold in here."

"Not to a cold-blooded son-of-a-bitch like you," Kevin replied. His voice was weak and hoarse.

Mark almost laughed, but coughed instead, his ribs protesting in pain. "Keep talking like that, and I might just leave your ass next time."

Kevin's head fell back against the wall. "You should have left me the first time." He looked out the opening; the stars were looking back. "They didn't seal it."

Mark reached forward and massaged the back of his knee, wincing as he tried to bend his leg. "They didn't need to."

A few faint voices from down the hall echoed off the cell walls and then retreated. The wind died down and left silence. A small, steel bucket sat in the corner of the room, feces running down the sides.

"My camera was in the truck," Kevin said quietly. Mark looked up. "I was looking through the pictures when the IED went off. I dropped it and grabbed my gun. Left it in the cab."

"All of the trucks were destroyed."

"No, they weren't."

"They won't find it."

"Yes, they will. Probably already have," replied Kevin, looking at the bite marks on his arm.

"They didn't find it, or they'd be in here by now."

"The camera could have been damaged, but not the memory card. All they need is a computer."

Mark leaned back, rubbing his ribs. "What was on it?"

"Another village hit by our drones." Kevin closed his eyes. "Dead kids. Charred bodies. Crying civilians—the usual."

Mark exhaled. "I told you to stop taking those fucking pictures." Kevin kept quiet. "But like I said, they would have asked by now," Mark added, trying not to sound too worried. He looked back out through the opening. "I'm sick of this waiting—and for what? Seems like we've been here for months. Just kill us already."

"Maybe they're trying to find a buyer," replied Kevin.

"That would be a bad thing."

"Yeah. But our guys will find us before that happens."

"Maybe." Mark looked back at Kevin. "If they're even looking."

"They're looking."

"Maybe we're considered MIA, and they've already sent notification officers to our families."

"Stop," Kevin said. "They'll find us." He held his arm loosely against his chest, slowly rubbing it like a small, injured animal, immobile and discolored.

"I've tried to imagine what my father's reaction will be," Mark said, "other than the textbook stages of grief: denial, anger, depression, bargaining, acceptance."

"I think it's bargaining, then depression," Kevin replied, coughing lightly. "I'll correct you once we get back to the States."

"It's hard to read psychology books when you're stuck in a coffin."

Kevin rubbed his cheek with his shoulder. "You know I'm right. Hell, you might even try to die on me to keep me from proving you wrong."

"Can't the order change from person to person? Regardless, my father will probably skip a few."

"Which ones?"

Mark cleared his throat. "All of them."

Kevin's good eye opened. "Are all you gays such drama queens?"

Mark laughed out loud before grabbing his side in pain. "You're the one bitching about the cold. It's whiny mama's boys like you we need to kick out of the military, not us gays."

"Is that what it was?"

"What *what* was?"

"Your old man. He found out, didn't he?"

"You really that curious?"

Kevin thought for a moment. "More like bored."

Mark raised his right hand against the chains and extended his middle finger.

"Besides," Kevin added, "you promised you would tell me, remember?"

Mark tilted his head, eyebrows together. "Was I drunk?"

"Drunk and sobbing all over yourself like a little fairy."

"A fairy that could kick your ass," Mark said with a short laugh. "And promises don't count when you're drunk."

"Sure they do. Think of how many relationships would fall apart without copious amounts of alcohol, followed by tearful admissions of infidelity, followed by promises to stay faithful."

"Followed by ravenous make-up sex."

"Exactly. So, drunken promises *do* count and you *do* owe me the story." Kevin smiled and leaned his head back against the cool wall, closing his eyes. Despite his shivers, beads of sweat rolled down the back of his neck. "And hurry up. I don't have all night, you know."

Mark leaned forward. He started to reply, but paused when he saw a camel spider crawling up his bare ankle. Mark's skin didn't register any sensation from the eight tiny legs. The spider faced him and moved up his leg in short bursts of speed. It would stop for a few seconds, lift its front legs, then leap forward, as if to appear intimidating. The spider stopped at the kneecap and studied the open wound, its head sinking briefly below the rim of the red-and-black hole. Mark watched it lean back, then become motionless. Suddenly, the spider leapt forward, its pincers sinking into the blackened flesh. Mark winced, even though he couldn't feel the fangs in his body. The spider jumped back, its front legs swinging wildly in the air like windmills caught in a strong gust. It sped off Mark's immobile leg and ran to the corner of the cell, next to the bucket of excrement.

Mark kept his gaze locked onto the new wound beginning to form over the old one. "My father is blindly religious and over-the-top patriotic—like some idealized American cartoon character. But he could take apart almost any engine. When he put them back together, they always ran better. Never charged to fix a car for anyone he knew." Mark looked over into the corner of the cell. The camel spider sat motionless, staring back at him.

"The night he called my older sister a Jezebel, she spit in his face. He swung at her. That was the first time our father ever tried to hit either of us. My mom had been dead for a decade by then. He broke three knuckles on a stud behind the wall. He later claimed he missed on purpose, that he only wanted to scare her. Shannon was seventeen and left right after that. Then he started drinking. I can't tell you how many mornings I had to wake him up for work. He'd be hung over and half-awake, brushing his teeth—me in the kitchen fixing his lunch. The only time he was sober was on Sunday mornings." Mark rubbed the back of his knee. "I found him one time curled up on the couch with an empty bottle of Jack dangling between his fingers. As I put a blanket over him, he mumbled that my sister had left for reasons only God knew, and my mom was dead for reasons only God could understand. Of course, he could never come up with actual fucking reasons."

The spider dug a small hole in the sand, its front legs frantically kicking away the dirt under its abdomen. Soon the top of its body was flush with the ground. The front legs then kicked the sand over its body, while its other six legs jerked their way under the loose dirt. Mark couldn't even see the outline of the arthropod's body, buried less than an inch under the sand.

"My father hid in a bottle and a Bible."

Mark looked back at the wound on his leg. He pinched the rim of the small hole with his fingers. A small chunk of flesh came loose without much resistance. Mark lifted the dead flesh closer to his face and narrowed his eyes. It looked like burnt paper. He flung it over to where he thought the spider was hiding, but nothing moved underneath the dirt. Mark sighed and looked up. A small cloud, reflecting the moonlight, began to float across the inky abyss. The stars shone through the silver, gossamer veil like the eyes of a doomed bride. Kevin's breathing was irregular and raspy.

Mark continued. "So, eventually he caught me with another guy. That was the day I realized my father was nothing more than a constellation. Lines without substance. A hovering void." Mark heard snoring and looked at his friend. Kevin's head hung against his chest as if it was being pulled from his shoulders. "And you're bored."

Mark felt his own head weigh heavily on his shoulders, and he let it fall back. He slid under the blanket of his memory, finding warm company with the mythical figures drawn into the sky by ancient stargazers. Mark's eyes tightened, moving back and forth behind closed lids. His lips kept repeating, "Northern hemisphere. Winter. Facing southeast: Lepus. Orion. Canis Major. Monoceros. Canis Minor. Gemini. Cancer. Hydra. Leo. Lynx. Ursa Major."

His bare knees poked through threadbare camouflage pants. He dug deeper into his mind, distracting himself from the hole in his leg, from Kevin's harsh breathing, from the feeling of his raw skin rubbing against iron rings and pants hardened with dried blood and urine. A breeze cut through Mark's body and sunk its teeth into his bones. His muscles jerked periodically, reacting to the dry cold that clung to his body like a famished leech, growing fat as it sucked away at his warmth.

Instantly, Mark could breathe fresh air. The walls of the cell were gone. It was dusk. Mark's bare feet fell firmly onto grass that still felt warm from the hot, summer day. Mark found himself in front of a small crowd of faces he recognized, faces he hadn't seen in years. They were all quiet and expressionless, staring ahead without blinking, standing in an open field bordered by distant mountains. The sky was darkening, the blue towed away by a receding sun. Mark looked down. He was still dressed in his brown t-shirt and tattered pants. He could see the red-and-black hole in his kneecap peeking through, but there was no pain. He shifted his weight, lifting his bare feet. Loose blades of freshly-cut grass stuck to his skin; the smell filled the air. Someone spoke, and Mark looked up.

A tall, skinny man wearing a white button-down shirt and a blue bow tie stood at the front of the small group. As he spoke, his thin arms gestured toward the great expanse that hung above his scraggly, red hair. The sun had now disappeared, the moon still hiding its pale face behind the distant

Remnants of Light — Mike Yost

mountains. Mark could see the man adjusting his black-rimmed glasses, made thick through years of research.

"Professor Blackburn," Mark said to himself. He remembered how back in his astronomy class everyone called him Mr. Burns, and the professor would laugh, never completely understanding why. Mark watched with a slight smile as the professor spoke quickly and fervently, like a preacher proselytizing to a congregation of stargazers. Out of his mouth rolled endless facts about stars, nebulae, star clusters, quasars, galaxies, and black holes—giant wells of gravity, unseen but not unknown.

"The universe is not only expanding," the professor continued, as if in the middle of lecture, "but accelerating in this process of expansion, propelled by the mysterious power of dark energy. We know this based on measuring the red shift of galaxies. However..." The professor jogged a few steps to his left, his eyes locked onto the darkness above. The unblinking eyes of the students followed the professor's shaking finger as it pointed to a distant speck of light. "... That small blur there—there! That small blur is Messier 31. Better known as the Andromeda galaxy—an entire galaxy! It's only two point five million light years away, and it's speeding its way *toward* us on a collision course with our own Milky Way." The professor closed his eyes. "Think about that distant blur. Think about how, within that small point of light, there are billions upon billions of stars warming the surfaces of billions and billions of orbiting planets!"

The professor opened his eyes as his head snapped forward. He ran to his small audience, almost colliding with Mark. The professor held up his index and middle fingers.

"And that is only *two* of the billions—no—hundreds of billions of galaxies speeding their way through the universe, most of them speeding away from us. All these gargantuan galaxies pulled and stretched into an incredible variation of sizes and shapes that never cease to amaze those who make it their life's work to study them."

The professor paced back and forth, his arms now locked behind his back and his face anchored toward the infinite black expanse. One of the students near the professor suddenly turned his head to Mark. Mark stepped back. Then the student's body suddenly shot into the air without a sound. No one but Mark seemed to notice. Mark tried to yell, but his voice was silent.

"There are galaxies out there with perfectly symmetrical spiral arms that reach 50,000 light years in length," continued the professor, as two more students fell headfirst into the night sky. "The shapes of these same spiral galaxies are scrawled onto the sides of cliffs by the ancient Fremont Indians who lived in Colorado 1,200 years before America even existed! And all of these billions of galaxies are full of wondrous stars that work to birth and forge nebulae and planets. And some of those planets have the chemical infrastructure to support life forms we cannot even imagine!" The professor turned his back and held out his arms, as if he were trying to gather the sky to his chest. "We are surrounded, class, completely *surrounded* by the very furnaces and forgers of the fundamental elements of our existence!"

The professor's face was flushed red. His glasses slid down the bridge of his nose that was made wet with perspiration. Mark watched six more bodies bolt into the blackness above.

"The Pueblo believed stars to be shimmering grains of maize flung into the heavens by the great hand of the sky god—those grains giving birth to new life." The professor lowered his arms. "Their belief is not far from the truth. Our own sun is a fusion reactor that smashes atoms of hydrogen into atoms of helium. The mass of one helium atom is less than the mass of two hydrogen atoms. What happens to the difference in mass? Converted into energy. Energy that sustains life here on Earth—all from an element made of a single proton!"

Dr. Blackburn pushed the glasses back to his face. Only five students remained, including Mark. "When the source of hydrogen is exhausted, the star begins to fuse helium atoms together, producing heavier elements, such as nitrogen, oxygen and carbon—the basic building blocks of life itself. We are encircled by our creators who, in our galaxy alone, far outnumber every person who has ever lived on Earth."

The professor stopped for a moment and let his arms drop to his sides. The wind blew across Mark's ears, and he felt his own body leave the ground, blades of grass falling from his bare feet and spinning wildly in the breeze. His four remaining classmates followed Mark's ascent with blank stares. The professor adjusted his glasses, ignoring Mark's abrupt departure.

"There are more stars than there are grains of sand on all the beaches of the world!"

Darkness consumed Mark's vision as the Earth below his feet swiftly faded into a small, blue marble spinning quickly, as if time itself was let loose from its methodical and predictable march. Mark could hear Dr. Blackburn continue the lecture as he passed effortlessly by the familiar planets of Jupiter and Saturn, their many moons orbiting rapidly around their monarchs.

"Some stars are unimaginably big and bright, like the blue-supergiant, Rigel—the foot of the constellation Orion. It's the seventh brightest star in the sky. Its luminosity is almost 15,000 times our own sun. The star's diameter is seventy times greater than the sun's. If you were to set Rigel in the middle of our solar system, its surface would reach the orbit of Mercury!"

Millions of stars stretched into bright strings of light, loose threads hanging off the fabric of space, torn away by momentum. Mark's body accelerated faster and faster as the foot of Orion grew larger.

"It takes roughly seven hundred and eighty light-years for the light from Rigel to reach your eye. The light from Rigel we see today began its journey about the same year the Mongol Empire was conquering Russia."

The professor paused in his speech. Silence lumbered in Mark's ears. He felt pain in his extremities. Mark pulled his eyes away from the blue-supergiant slowly filling his field of vision.

"That's more than seven hundred years the light from Rigel was making its way to your eye. Such a distance we can hardly imagine, especially when we realize that a single light-year is approximately equivalent to five point eight *trillion* miles."

Mark's arms and legs slowly began growing smaller, his fingers receding into his hands. Mark tried to scream, but his voice made no sound. Dr. Blackburn's voice, however, grew louder.

"Think about what that means! Visible light speeding its way through a vast nothingness. Trillions and trillions of individual photons, and only a few find their way to the surface of your retina. Only a few to illuminate the darkness."

Mark felt his body drawing in on itself, his skin pulling away from the muscles, his bones collapsing in short, painful breaks. His body still hurtling through space, Mark brought his hands up to his face—they were the hands of a child, curling in on themselves. Mark realized that he couldn't breathe. A cold shock ran through his body. Mark could feel ice beginning to form on his face, coating the inside of his mouth and throat.

"And Rigel, like our own sun, will one day use up its fuel and die—likely as a massive supernova."

Mark looked up and saw Rigel casting his now-childlike hands into a silhouette. The ice on his skin rapidly evaporated.

"Hydrogen into helium, helium into carbon, carbon into oxygen, oxygen into silicon—over billions of years this process will eventually produce an iron-nickel core: Elements too heavy for fusion. As a result,

Rigel will collapse and explode—a violent supernova flinging millions of tons of particles and elements into space, creating a nebula that will span hundreds of light-years. The nebula will house the elements made by the star: oxygen, nitrogen, hydrogen, and carbon—along with heavier-than-iron elements produced by the explosion, like copper, gold, and zirconium. Those same particles will collect over time, pulled together by the perpetual force of gravity, eventually forming planets. Some of those planets will contain the elements essential for life, the elements forged in Rigel's furnace."

The blue-supergiant grew larger in Mark's field of vision. The Witch Head Nebula burned brightly nearby, the massive cloud of dust reflecting Rigel's blue light, forty light-years distant. Mark closed his eyes, but the light burned through his eyelids. His face grew hot. His skin began to blister.

"These residual elements from dead stars might find the perfect conditions for life to flourish. And if you were to calculate the number of stars in the known universe that have exploded and given birth to new stars and new planets, life itself is not just probable—it's inevitable."

Unable to block out the piercing light, Mark opened his eyes. Rigel loomed ahead, completely enveloping his vision, an immense sphere of turbulent blue plasma that grew larger and larger as Mark fell toward it.

"Rigel could produce millions of planets with the same mass as Earth. That's a million possibilities from one star alone."

Thick coils of blue plasma erupted and twisted from Rigel's surface, the prominences growing into great arches of fire—the deformed fingers of Prometheus reaching into space. Some of the coils were held in place by the star's magnetic field, the plasma illuminating hundreds of magnetic loops before falling back to the surface. Other prominences merged and escaped Rigel's magnetic pull, forming a large coronal mass ejection, a bubble of plasma and charged particles flung into space at 350 miles per second.

The massive wall of blue plasma slammed into Mark, and his body caught fire. His clothes instantly disintegrated into cinders, leaving a trail of fireflies quickly extinguished. Mark locked his jaw open. This time his voice climbed its way out of his throat, the scream of a child. He knew he shouldn't be able to hear himself in the vacuum of space. He knew the fire consuming him should not be able to breathe, but it was now eating away, painfully consuming his flesh. Scorched ribbons of skin and muscle peeled away from his arms and legs, floating listlessly into oblivion. Mark closed his eyes, but his eyelids burned away.

"Every atom in your body was forged—the by-product of an elegant, chemical reaction taking place inside every star."

Mark screamed louder as he watched the tips of his small fingers turn to ash, dissolving backward to his knuckles like cigarettes burning down to the filter. X-rays and gamma rays cooked his organs. Dr. Blackburn's voice overpowered Mark's screams.

"Your mind, the very genesis of thought, is but an amalgamation of star-born elements and chemical reactions. Those elements will one day be converted into other forms of matter or energy—for neither can be created or destroyed. Consciousness, on the other hand, is finite."

Large, burnt chunks of muscle slipped off Mark's scapula and blackened ribs. His eyes melted into two small pools that quickly evaporated. Mark's bones snapped and shattered like glass rods thrown against the face of a cliff. His screams ended as his skull cracked and broke apart into small shards of burnt bone. Dr. Blackburn's voice calmly continued.

"We are nothing but the dust of stars. Life itself a mere remnant of extinguished light, expelled with ambivalence into a vacuous void by a violent explosion. We are the death of stars. We are the death of our own creators."

[II]

[1997]

    The flag in the yard snapped sharply in the February wind. The red stripes burned brightly against the large, white flakes throwing themselves against Mark's numb cheeks as he stepped off the school bus—crystal kamikazes. Mark's small boots landed quietly in the snow, and the bus pulled away, engine revving as its back tires spun in the snowpack. Mark saw the bright orange flag sticking up from the mailbox. He ran over to it, dropping his backpack in the snow and pushing down the metal flag. He popped open the lid and eagerly looked inside. A white package, the size of a small book, greeted Mark. His name was written in calligraphy on the top. Mark ignored the rest of the mail—bills addressed to his father—and slammed the mailbox shut. He tore open the package with his gloved hands. A black, leather-bound notebook and a white envelope were inside. Eleven candles were carefully drawn on the front of the envelope. Mark smiled and shoved the card and the notebook back into the package, then shoved the package into his backpack before slinging it over his shoulder and running up the driveway past the waving American flag.

    As Mark approached the front door, he could see candlelight flickering against the inside of the frosted windowpanes. He stomped his boots to rid them of the snow packed tightly in the tread. Mark removed his gloves and grasped the cold, brass handle with his small hands, excitedly turning the knob several times before timing the momentum of his shoulder against the front door. It flung open wildly, slamming hard against the foyer wall and bouncing back. Mark's father was standing next to the kitchen table, his arms crossed over his broad chest, looking at his child with a slight smile. Mark ran and lunged forward, hugging the lower half of his father's frame.

When Mark pulled his face away, he eyed a cake with white frosting that sat patiently on the dinner table, waiting to be devoured. Eleven flames on eleven birthday candles lit up Mark's lobster-red face.

"You're letting the snow in, Marcus," Steve said, jutting his chin at the entrance.

Mark released his dad and apologized. His backpack hit the floor as Mark ran back to shut the door. He took off his thick coat and flung it into a small closet near the front door. The coat was so large that without it, Mark seemed to have shrunk in size by half. One of his boots clattered onto the floor; the other fell to its side with its shoelaces running out the top like creeks of black water. A wool cap landed quietly next to the boot. Mark slid on the linoleum floor in his thick, gray socks as he bolted back into the kitchen. He kept his face toward the cake as his eyes looked up at his father.

"Go ahead," Steve replied to his son's non-verbal pleas.

Mark's numb cheeks bulged out as he craned forward to blow out the candles. The flames flickered briefly and went out. Thin threads of smoke coiled to the ceiling. The soft shadows Mark and Steve cast in the candlelight disappeared. Dull, white light from the winter storm filtered into the room, the dark corners of the kitchen untouched. Steve nodded and uncrossed his arms as he walked over to the counter, pulling a knife from a drawer. The wooden drawer squeaked when he shut it. Mark's eyes grew wide with excitement.

"A small slice before dinner," his father commented, looking carefully at the blade and taking note of a few water spots. Though he tried to contain his excitement, Mark could feel his own smile stretching up to his earlobes.

"We can bend the rules for today," Steve added, wiping water spots from the knife with a damp cloth. "But then you put away your boots and your coat, and it's straight to your room with homework until supper, understand?"

"Yes, Sir," Mark replied enthusiastically before jumping into a dining-room chair made of polished rubberwood. Steve's eyes narrowed as he wiped the blade a few more times, scanning for spots. Mark's chair groaned as his feet swung back and forth just above the kitchen floor, wool socks bunched up at the ankles. Mark leaned over and thrust both arms deep into his book bag, keeping his eyes on the cake. He pulled out the black, leather-bound book with one hand and a black pen with the other. Mark opened the notebook over his empty plate. He tried to write on the first page, but the pen only scratched into the parchment without leaving any ink marks—shallow canyons with dried-out riverbeds.

"What's that?"

"A birthday present from Shannon," Mark replied as he reached down again into his backpack; his arm sunk up to the bicep before pulling out another pen. "It's a dream journal. Like hers."

Steve's eyebrows shot up. "Your sister gave you that?"

"She sent it to me in the mail," Mark replied. He flipped to the front of the journal and began writing his name. Below it, Shannon had written, "Act without hope." — Jean-Paul Sartre. She had added, *Happy eleventh birthday, Little Brother.* Her name followed in perfect cursive. "I write down my dreams before I forget them."

"I see." Steve's face narrowed a bit. His chest rose and fell. He threw the small dishtowel into the sink and walked back to the table. "And why would you want to do that?"

Mark concentrated on writing his name, carefully flaring each letter, his face inches from the page, tongue between his teeth.

"To find out what they mean." Mark frowned. His penmanship looked like scratches on the wall made by an angry cat.

"I see," said Steve as he pulled out each extinguished birthday candle. Steve sunk the knife into the cake. Once. Twice. He pulled out a thin slice. It leaned precariously to its side, and Mark closed the journal and set it aside, watching as his father carefully set the slice on Mark's plate. A few crumbs rolled off onto the table. Steve pinched each one between his fingers and stood for a moment, contemplating whether he wanted his own slice. Mark kept his hands neatly folded on his lap, looking up at his father.

"It's just to keep track of my dreams, Dad. Sis says it's important to try to understand our dreams—to try and interpret them. She said that where they come from and why we have them are even more important than the dreams themselves."

Steve walked back to the sink, held his pinched fingers directly over the drain, and watched the crumbs fall into the darkness of the drain. For a moment, Steve didn't move. He set his hands on the edge of the sink, the knife clattering against the stainless steel. Mark reached for the fork next to his plate. He pushed it sideways into the moist, white sponge cake and tore away a large chunk. Mark's mouth watered as his lips parted, and his legs swung back and forth faster as the fork moved closer to his tongue.

"Marcus!"

Mark froze, looking sideways at his father, the cake shaking slightly on the fork. Steve looked over his shoulder disapprovingly, his hands still clutching the side of the sink. An antiquated clock that hung near the refrigerator clicked away the next few seconds with its large brass pendulum. For the first time since he got home, Mark realized how cold it was in the house. Steve's forehead creased like folds in a blanket, and he slowly turned and walked back to the table, the knife parallel to the floor, clumps of white frosting stuck to the edge.

"Aren't you forgetting something?" Steve asked forcefully.

Mark dropped the bite of cake, then the fork, and it clanked against the dinner plate, somehow amplifying his mistake. Mark bunched up his shoulders, as if they were trying to touch his temples.

Silence followed.

The sunlight grew dimmer, barely illuminating the checkered white-and-black wallpaper covering the kitchen walls. Steve stopped at the edge of the table and slowly cut out a piece of cake for himself, keeping his eyes on his son as the knife scraped against the glazed stoneware. He walked around the table across from Mark and let the plate fall hard onto the pinewood table. It fell slightly askew and rocked back and forth a few times before coming to a rest. A few crumbs jumped from the plate.

"Sorry, Sir," Mark whispered.

"This is what happens when nonsense like that dream journal distracts you. You become irresponsible. You become lazy. You forget your obligations." Still standing, Steve set the knife down and leaned forward, his hands now fists—the knuckles white against the table. Steve's faint shadow enveloped his son. "Your obligations to the One who provides you with this food."

Mark brought his hands together, interlocking his fingers and bringing them to his chest. He bowed his head and closed his eyes tightly. Steve waited a few minutes before sitting in his own chair.

"Lead," Steve ordered as he bowed his head.

Mark thanked God for the cake and asked for his father's safety at the water-treatment plant and for his sister's safety on the college campus; he asked for God to tell his mom that he loved her and missed her, and then he asked for it not to snow too much tonight so that everyone could get home safely.

"Amen," Steve whispered.

Mark opened his eyes. His father was sweeping crumbs into his cupped hand. Mark immediately grabbed his fork and shoved a large chunk of cake into his mouth. Icing stuck to the corners of his lips, and Steve looked up and shook his head slightly with a smile, digging his own fork into the cake. Steve kept his back straight and motioned with his free hand for Mark to do the same. Father and son ate quietly. Mark's lips smacked occasionally as he licked the frosting from his fork. Snowflakes fell against the kitchen window, their intricate arms melting, running down the glass in small, clear streams.

"Now," Steve said, pausing. "What are your homework assignments for tonight? Anything you need help with?"

"Juss some reeedin."

"Not with your mouth full, Marcus." Steve took a large jug of milk and filled one of two empty glasses next to the cake. "You know better than that."

Mark chewed hurriedly, pushing the cake down his throat with effort. He took the glass from his father and drained it almost completely. Mark's feet began to swing again, this time more swiftly. "I just have to finish reading a book and then work on a book report."

"What's the book?"

"*The Adventures of Tom Sawyer*," Mark replied, followed by more chewing.

Steve filled his own glass. "Who's the author?"

Mark didn't look up from his plate. "Mark Twain wrote it, Dad. But that was just his pen name. His real name was Samuel Clemens."

"I see," Steve replied. He took a single gulp and set the glass down without a sound.

Mark finished another bite. "He got his pen name from working on the Mississippi River. The leadsman on the riverboat would call out 'mark twain' to let the captain know it was deep enough for the boat to—"

"Do you have any other homework?"

Mark ate the last bite of cake. He pushed a few remaining crumbs in a circle, the fork scraping the plate. "Yes, Sir. I have another writing assignment. But it's not due until next week."

Steve pulled Mark's empty plate away, setting it on his own. "And what do you have to write?"

Mark cleared his throat and drained his glass. His father filled it back up.

"Just a short essay on some bacteria fossils," Mark mumbled.

Steve sighed heavily. He stood and took the plates to the kitchen, running hot water into the sink. Steam rolled onto the surface of the windows. Steve walked over and picked up Mark's backpack, rifling through the books. Mark sat quietly, staring at the empty spot where his plate had been. He kept his hands clamped around the base of his glass.

"I warned you this day would come, didn't I, Marcus?" Steve stood behind his son, flipping through the books. He pulled out a thick textbook: *Physical Science*. A picture of the Earth was featured on the green hardcover, North and South America facing the reader. A small, yellow sticker in the lower-left-hand corner read Leadville Public Schools. The ticking clock grew louder in Mark's ears.

"It's just about some fossils, Dad." Mark's feet stopped swinging below the chair. He turned the glass with his fingers. "There are just these old bacteria fossils they found in Australia. Cy…an…o bacteria, I think. I'm supposed to write about—"

Steve opened the book and let it drop to the table with a hard slam.

"And how old does this book say these fossils are?"

Mark's father leaned over his son's shoulder, flipping through the pages. Mark smelled motor oil on his father's hands and saw grease tucked up beneath the fingernails.

"Can I go to my room now?"

Steve wrapped one hand around the back of his son's chair. "How old does your teacher say these fossils are, Marcus?"

Mark kept his head bowed to the glass. "Billions of years old, Sir."

"And why isn't that possible?"

Mark locked his feet behind the legs of the chair and stopped turning his glass. "Because the Bible says the Earth isn't that old, Sir."

Steve nodded his head in agreement. "Good." Steve flipped through some more pages, his fingers leaving few bits of frosting on the edges. The water was still running in the sink.

Mark looked up at his father's narrowed face. "It's just a report, Dad. I—"

Steve turned Mark's chair toward him, the rubberwood legs scraping against the linoleum in protest. Mark's glass was knocked sideways, and a pool of milk formed on the table, constantly changing shape. Some of the milk snaked its way to the edge of the table and fell to the floor in small, round explosions of white. Mark was face-to-face with his father. His eyes watered.

"Lies, Marcus. Lies. You don't believe them, do you?"

Mark shook his head and responded in a cracked voice. "No, Sir."

Steve looked at his son for a long time, his eyes held steady. Mark's brown hair stood up on his head from when he took off his wool cap. Steve patted the hair down and said "Good." He then stood up straight and grabbed the jug of milk and glasses from the table. They clinked together when he dropped them into the sink. Steve scraped the bits of leftover cake into the garbage disposal and turned it on. It growled to life as Mark quietly wiped his eyes with the back of his·hand. The snowfall was now heavy. Steve set the glasses in the dishwasher and looked outside.

"I'm sorry, son. I didn't mean to frighten you."

Mark repeated the line he said almost every week. "It's okay, Dad. I know you didn't mean to scare me."

Steve stuck his hands under the still-running water. "It's time I took you out of that school."

Mark jumped out of his chair, almost falling over his backpack. "Please don't, Dad. I'll—"

"You will not argue with your father!" Steve kept his gaze forward. "You will also get rid of that journal. It's not our place to interpret dreams. You know better." Steve looked over his shoulder. Mark stared at his feet. He gripped the side of his pants, pinching the cloth. "Don't act surprised, Marcus. We spoke about this. I will not tolerate my son being taught this secular worldview—reducing man to mere animal. Nor will I tolerate your sister filling your head with dangerous New Age notions about the importance of dreams."

Mark looked down at the open textbook. "You weren't even looking at the right chapter," he said to himself. Mark shut the science book and set the dream journal on top. He shoved them both into his book bag and flung it over his shoulder, almost losing his balance.

Steve turned and walked forward, his hands dripping with soapy water. "What did you say to me?"

Mark walked out of the kitchen and down the hall without looking back. His bedroom door slammed shut. Steve followed. He grabbed the doorknob with his wet hands, but it didn't turn. He pounded hard, leaving the wet outline of his fist on the door's white surface.

"Unlock this door, now!" Steve said through clenched teeth. Mark responded with silence. The sound of the clock in the kitchen made its way down the hall. "I will not allow what happened to Shannon to happen to you!" Steve pounded a few more times, the door violently shaking against the doorframe. Steve waited, then turned on his heel.

Deep footprints were left in the snow as Steve crossed the front yard to a garage separate from the house. He wiped his hands on his pants and flung open the door to his workshop, smacking the light switch with the palm of his hand. He walked past a dismantled engine balanced precariously on a greasy workbench, kicking a broken distributor cap under the frame of a gutted '69 Chevrolet C10 Stepside. The paint had long ago faded into a dull echo of its once-red luster. The fluorescent tubes blinked over the center of the garage, unable to maintain a steady light. Steve yanked open a steel drawer, and the tools inside slammed forward. A pair of pliers jumped out and bounced at his feet. Steve pulled out a flathead screwdriver and a hammer, their handles cold against his skin. Snowflakes blew in from under the main garage door.

"Dad?"

Steve turned, and the hammer fell to the concrete floor, bouncing loudly to a stop. Steve could see his son standing outside the open door, hugging the science book against his shaking chest. Mark's wool socks were buried in the snow.

"I'm sorry, Dad."

Steve could see his son's breath and felt the cold on the wet skin of his hands. He pointed at Mark with the screwdriver. Steve walked forward and pulled the science book out of Mark's arms and threw it behind him. It smacked against the back wall and fell, its pages open and soaking in the residual oil on the concrete floor.

"I told you to wear your coat when you're outside."

"Yes, Sir."

Steve grabbed Mark by the shoulders and spun him around, pushing his son back to the house. The door to the garage slammed shut behind them, shaking against its hinges. The fluorescent lights above the gutted truck flickered quietly in the cold.

[III]

[2009]

The American flag dangled listlessly in the breeze, its once-bright colors now faded, the pale face of a fallen soldier. It was torn at the edges, collapsing into uneven folds against the metal pole in the still air. The pole was coated in brown rust that flaked away like dead skin near the base. The lieutenant stopped at the edge of the property and composed himself before walking forward, checking his uniform and snapping his shirt tight.

He had to lift his polished shoes over various parts of a dismantled engine scattered across the walkway to the front door. Alternator. Starter. A single piston coated in grease. Three worn-out brake pads. They littered the walkway and the dead grass, eviscerated from their bodies of metal. Once valued. Once useful. Now cold. Forgotten. Slowly returning to the earth.

The lieutenant stopped at the front door of the small house, glancing at the tarnished brass numbers bolted to the white vinyl siding: 469. The lieutenant's shoes sat unevenly on the warped planks of the front porch. He checked his uniform again, rubbing his palms against his perfectly creased pants.

An hour earlier, in the same town—Leadville, Colorado—the lieutenant had held a mother in his arms. She collapsed when he told her that her son was killed in action. He didn't tell her that he burned to death. That the inside of his throat was blistered from the heat. He didn't mention that her son's dog tag had melted into his sternum or that the rubber in his boots fused with the bones in his feet. The lieutenant simply told her that her son died bravely, carrying out his duty. When he had finished, she fell forward like an ancient statue released from a crumbling foundation. Words worked their way between gasping sobs. Single parent. Two jobs. Couldn't afford college. Her son had signed up for the G.I. Bill. He was only eighteen. Died before his pimples cleared. Died before he could buy a beer. The lieutenant knew he was never—under any circumstances—supposed to touch the family members being notified. She had wept in his arms for fifteen minutes, her fingernails leaving a red outline on his arm. He'd stayed silent as she cursed God, her tears and saliva staining his shirt. He had changed in the car. The lieutenant always carried extra shirts in his car—folded and pressed, warmed by the sun in the back seat.

The bare sky burned blue with a sun now past its meridian. The lieutenant balled up his right hand, knuckles rapping against the slightly warped wood veneer. No answer. He knocked again. The windows were closed and dark. A small aluminum box was stuffed full of mail. He waited exactly three minutes, turned, and walked back to the street. A rusted, hollowed-out, 1966 Stingray sat next to the garage. The windshield and windows had been removed, and its rotors were buried halfway into the mud. The lieutenant, looking at the Stingray as he walked, tripped over an alternator with wires hanging out of it like the entrails of a gutted animal. The tips of his polished shoes were now scuffed. He leaned down, trying in vain to brush away the marks with his palms. A dog with yellow, thick, shaggy hair and a curled tail walked slowly up to the lieutenant, sniffing the ground. The animal looked up as the officer reached out his arm. The dog jogged forward and began licking the back of the officer's hand.

"You live here, buddy?" the officer asked.

A screwdriver suddenly flew into view, spinning end-over-end, barely missing the upturned ears of the dog. The officer and the dog jumped back. The screwdriver impaled itself in the muddy lawn, the handle sticking out at a forty-five degree angle.

A voice bellowed from the garage. "Get off my property!" The dog ducked his head and bolted down the street, barking.

The lieutenant hadn't noticed the open garage door, the inside dark, facing the front yard, framed by white siding that burned brightly in the sunlight. Slowly, the lieutenant's eyes adjusted, and a figure appeared in the garage, bent over a blue 1958 Apache. The upper part of his body was buried under the open hood. The lieutenant stood at attention, careful not to bend the manila envelope in his left hand. His hand twitched when he realized that the voice from the garage had been watching him since he parked in front of the house.

"Mr. Steven T. Bradford?" The lieutenant asked, peering forward.

"I wasn't talking to the damn dog," Steve said without looking up, his hands tangled deep in the intestines of the engine. A ratchet was clicking away. It stopped and fell with a clatter, and Steve cursed: "Dammit!" He reached for the lost tool, the heels of his feet leaving the concrete floor. For a moment, it looked to the officer as if the truck was trying to consume Mr. Bradford.

The lieutenant took a few more steps toward the garage, which was suddenly lit by a bare bulb in a metal cage, hanging from an extension cord across a rafter. His scuffed shoes pushed two bolts deeper into the mud. A large clock made from a rusty hubcap hung on the back wall, stopped at 11:17. Along one side of the garage, wooden shelves held glass Mason jars and coffee cans full of screws and bolts. Empty beer bottles crowded in between the jars. The ratchet began its clicking again. The manila folder tightened against his leg; his right hand snapped to a salute, fingers straight, middle finger set firmly against the outside edge of his right eyebrow.

"First Lieutenant Carl Jacobson. Are you Steven T. Bradford, father of Private First Class Marcus Elijah Bradford?"

The clicking ceased, and Steve pulled himself out from the hood of the Apache. His clothes were black with grease, gray hair matted with sweat on his forehead. Deep lines ran from his eyes as he squinted into the sunlight, trying to focus on the lieutenant's silhouette. He hit the palm of his hand with the head of the ratchet. The flag above unfolded briefly, then collapsed.

"I have an important message to deliver from the Secretary of the Army."

Steve turned his head and spat. He wiped his mouth, leaving a streak of grease down his chin. "Stop yammering and tell me why the hell you won't get off my property."

The lieutenant kept his gaze forward, his salute locked against the side of his head, hand tilted slightly. "The Secretary of the Army has asked me to express his deep regret in informing you that your son, Private Marcus Elijah Bradford, has been reported missing in action."

Steve stared for a moment. A commercial plane flew overhead, the hiss of its engines filling the dead silence as it shot across the blue horizon, leaving a gossamer streak across the sky.

"His convoy came under heavy fire by insurgents," continued the lieutenant. "His body was never recovered, and his whereabouts are currently under investigation. In order to ensure accurate information, Mr.

Bradford, I must verify next of kin. The Army will keep you informed of any new developments concerning your son."

"Mark..." Steve cleared his throat. "Mark was in the Army?"

The lieutenant dropped his salute, shifting his feet. He looked at the envelope in his hand, needlessly checking the name written across the front, then back up at Steve. "Yes, Sir. Marcus Elijah Bradford. 12th infantry battalion. A-company."

Steve leaned back against the front of the Apache, folding his arms across his chest. "I didn't think that the United States Army allowed homos to wear our uniform." Steve turned and walked between the lieutenant and the garage, ignoring the envelope held out to him. Steve kicked a few loose screws out of his way. He stood at the tool bench and pulled open a metal drawer. His fingers sunk into a sea of sockets.

"Sir?"

"Why are you here by yourself, lieutenant?" Steve asked with his head lowered to the open drawer. "Notifying next of kin is a two-man job."

"There are many families to notify and few officers, Mr. Bradford."

"I'm sure." Steve looked over his shoulder. "When did Mark go missing?"

"Four weeks ago, Sir. The Army has been searching the surrounding area, but—"

"And you're just now getting around to telling me?" Steve shook his head and turned back to the drawer, sorting through the loose sockets. "Nothing changes," he said to himself. Steve looked up, facing the wall. "What year is it?"

"Year?"

"Yes, Lieutenant. The year?"

"2009, Mr. Bradford."

"So, for sixteen years they've been sneaking in, hiding behind that ridiculous 'Don't Ask' policy. In my day, we used to beat the perverts with bars of soap tucked into socks. That always straightened them out."

For the first time in years as a notification officer, the lieutenant didn't know how to respond.

Steve pulled out a three-quarter-inch socket with his oily fingers. He held the ratchet over the open drawer and hit the release. The half-inch socket fell with a clatter. "Marcus was gay, Lieutenant. A perversion of nature—a perversion of God's plan. And he was apparently allowed to disgrace our uniform and our country with it." Steve turned and leaned against the tool bench. He folded his arms and shook his head. "It's disgusting."

The lieutenant lowered the envelope. "Sir, there are a number of services—"

"Stop calling me Sir, Lieutenant."

Jacobson nodded his head as he opened the envelope. "I know this is a trying time for you, Mr. Bradford. There are a number of services the Army provides for next of kin. I can call for a chaplain, if you'd like."

Steve threw the ratchet across the garage. It slammed into the coffee cans, breaking one of the Mason jars. Bolts, screws, and shattered glass rained down onto the floor. "Dammit, Mark!" He yelled. "Of all the ways to…" Steve clamped his mouth shut, grinding his teeth. He turned back to the notification officer. "I don't need a chaplain to commune with God, Lieutenant."

Jacobson lowered the envelope. "I hope you will appreciate the gratitude this country has for his sacrifice, and the Army—"

"Homosexuals jeopardize the mission of the unit, and the lives of the men and women in uniform who protect the freedom these degenerates piss on with their unnatural behavior." Steve ran his greasy hand through his hair, scratching the scalp. "They are an embarrassment to the uniform—to the country. They spit in the face of the families you've spoken to today."

The lieutenant didn't respond. He stood at attention and held out the envelope again. Steve lurched from the tool bench and snatched it out of Jacobson's hand.

"So, you don't know if Mark is dead or alive?"

"The Army is currently investigating the incident, Mr. Bradford."

"So, he's dead." Steve responded, pulling out the various official forms and documents from the envelope. "I know what 'currently investigating' means. You should know who you're speaking to. I hope you did your homework before trespassing on my property." Steve looked up from the paperwork. "You people obviously didn't do that with Mark."

"Master Sergeant Steven T. Bradford. Retired," replied Jacobson. "Explosive Ordinance Disposal. Twenty-one years. Honorably discharged. Purple Heart. Bronze Star."

Steve began pacing back and forth, kicking at loose hardware, reading over the file. "Good. Don't bullshit a bullshitter, Lieutenant. Stop with the formalities and just tell me the military doesn't have the resources to search for…" Steve squinted, "…two missing privates in the middle of a big, empty desert. It's called war for a reason. People die. I can accept that."

Steve pointed the envelope at Jacobson. "What I won't accept is risking my life for twenty years dismantling bombs so that faggots like my son could—"

"There is an information sheet with contact numbers should you have any more questions or need additional assistance, Mr. Bradford."

Steve narrowed his eyes and walked forward, his footfalls forced and even. "I've known guys who were notification officers, like you. They were all alcoholics. All divorced. One of them killed himself, the coward. Most of them volunteered for the job. Some think it's an honorable thing to do for your country. But I know better. Notification officers want to be stateside so they can drive around in air-conditioned cars and yammer to civilians about the dead —too afraid to be in the trenches."

The lieutenant's eyes focused on the broken Mason jar on the shelf. Steve turned and walked back to the truck. "I once sunk a six-inch blade into the stomach of a Vietnamese kid who couldn't have been more than thirteen years old. He fired a mounted Degtyaryov into our unit. His eyes opened wide when I stabbed him." Jacobson looked back at Steve. "It was like sticking my hand into a drum of warm oil, the blood coating the skin, sinking into my pores. The kid screamed when I turned the blade in his gut. When his body went limp, I could hear the screaming soldiers he shot down. Private First Class Jackson, screaming for someone to help, half his arm reaching for me. Private Chase, gargling words from a hole in his neck. Everyone else was silent. Six total."

Steve threw the envelope and all the paperwork into the cab of the truck. "I killed a child, and I sleep fine at night. I sleep fine because he wasn't a kid; he was an enemy of the United States—a country founded by God himself. So, Lieutenant, for the sake of those who died serving this great nation so many take for granted, you will exercise some respect and not—fucking—interrupt me again."

Jacobson kept his mouth resolutely shut.

"Now. Faggots like my son cause deaths in the field. They're not soldiers to be honored, but weeds to be pulled out by the roots. And you can assure the Secretary of the Army, Lieutenant Jacobson, that if my son's body is found, he will not receive a military burial. I will not allow him to disgrace the Army or our country." Steve walked back over to the ratchet on the garage floor. He brushed away the broken glass before picking it up.

The lieutenant hesitated, then said, "The Army found no survivors in the attack. Two bodies from the convoy were never recovered, one of them your son's. Unfortunately the Army has no more information at this time."

"'Course not." Steve replied.

"Because of the remote location at the time of the attack, and the—"

"Yes, Lieutenant, I get it. MIA means presumed dead. You're just not allowed to say it." Jacobson didn't reply. Steve turned the socket in his hands. The ratchet clacked in protest. "Now, if you'll please get the hell off my property."

The lieutenant snapped to attention again with a salute. "On behalf of the Secretary of the Army, please accept the Army's deepest condolences."

Steve lowered himself back into the jaws of the Apache. "Good day, Lieutenant."

The afternoon sun warmed the back of his neck as Jacobson made his way to his car. Snow from the day before had melted into puddles, lining the sidewalks and the street. The lieutenant stepped through them without deviating, the cold water seeping through his socks, soaking his toes. The dog with the yellow hair chased the lieutenant's car down the street.

Steve walked to the passenger door of the truck and picked up a cell phone from the seat. He punched in the numbers with his thumb, wiping the grease from his chin with a rag as the phone rang on the other end.

"I need to leave a message for Shannon Livingstone... No, I don't want to be transferred. I said I want to leave a message." Steve wiped his forehead with the dirty rag and tossed it into the cab of the truck. "Tell her I know about her brother in the Army... Yes... Tell her Mark is dead...Yes. Mark, her brother. In Iraq... Yeah... No, that's it." Steve walked out onto the lawn, squinting in the sunlight. "Her father." Steve snapped the phone shut. He bent over and pulled the screwdriver out of the ground.

Jacobson's car slowed to a stop at an empty intersection, brakes squeaking. The light turned green, but the vehicle sat idling. His cell phone sprang to life, vibrating over the edge of the passenger seat and falling onto the floorboard. Jacobson leaned over and grabbed the phone. Behind him, a car horn began honking endlessly. Jacobson hit the speaker button with his thumb, looking in the rearview mirror.

"Hey, Kurt," Jacobson answered flatly.

"I know, I know. I'm not supposed to call you while you're working," the voice said on the other end. "But I got off early tonight and wanted to see you. Dinner at your place? I'll cook."

The lieutenant slowly pulled forward. The driver behind him extended his middle finger out the window as he passed by.

"Yeah. That's fine."

"I've never made my chicken, cheese, and broccoli casserole for you, have I?"

"No. It sounds great."

Silence.

"Honey, what's wrong?"

"Nothing."

"Nothing means something, sweetheart. Where are you?"

The lieutenant pulled into a parking lot and slowly moved the gearshift into park. The lot was empty, but for a delivery truck near the edge, the driver asleep in the cab. Another car behind him turned, honked the horn, and sped off.

"I'm in Leadville."

"Leadville?"

"Listen," Jacobson cleared his throat. "I'm fine. Long day, that's all. I'll tell you about it when I get back. It'll be late, though, and I'm already tired. You still have my key?"

"Of course. Dinner will be waiting," Kurt replied, adding, "I've missed you."

The lieutenant wedged the phone between his ear and his shoulder. He picked up another file and let it fall open in his hand. Private Andrew Kelly. Nineteen. Killed in action.

"Missed you too. And Kurt, I have nosy neighbors, so if anyone asks..."

"Yeah, yeah. I know. Don't ask, don't tell. I'm just an old friend from school."

Jacobson said goodbye, snapped the cell phone shut, and studied the open map on the passenger seat, his finger tracing the highway to Glenwood Springs.

[IV]

[2009]

The congregation's voices grew louder and louder, twisting together into a cacophony of sound, like a tidal wave gathering strength as it cast a shadow on the shore of worshipers. The song, amplified by the towering stone walls, rained back down from the vaulted ceiling and the angels of stone, motionless and stoic above the pews, their ambivalent, chipped faces an antithesis to the elation staring back. Most parishioners had their heads turned upward, some with tears on their cheeks, others with eyes closed tightly, as if God himself were hidden within their eyelids. Hands shot up into the air, palms up, the hymn reaching its apex. The tidal wave bellowed and fell, crashing down onto the people in the pews in a fury of spiritual elation.

The echoes from the final note ricocheted from wall to wall, sinking beneath the silence that followed. A few wiped their faces with tissues; others lowered their hands, closed their hymnals, and set them gently in the maple cases bolted to the backs of the pews. A few more coughed as the pastor stood, shaking the hand of the choir director. He buttoned his suit coat, adjusted his red tie, and reached down for his Bible, gilded pages bound in burgundy leather. Holding the tome against his chest, the pastor approached the pulpit and thanked the choir and thanked the congregation and thanked God and began to speak of Jesus and of forgiveness, his face still flushed with emotion.

No one but a few seemed to notice that Erin's lips failed to move throughout the entire canticle. Her hands were wrapped tightly around a faded, black, leather-bound Bible with tattered edges. Several pages had come loose, held in place only so long as the Bible remained closed. The name engraved on the cover had faded long ago. Three months earlier, Erin had pulled her deceased grandfather's Bible from the bottom drawer of an aging oak credenza. The name, now flush with the surface of the faded and cracked leather, was Everett Kevin Zuelke.

She had given her son the name Kevin, after his great-grandfather, more than two decades ago. This Bible had once sailed the Atlantic, tucked neatly away in a duffle bag with a pair of battered boots, a single change of threadbare clothes, and a picture of parents long dead in the Great War. A war that was to end all wars, but was only antecedent to even more wars. Everything he owned had swayed on his back as Erin's grandfather fought his way to the railing of the boat and watched the city of New York appear out of the gray fog, the towering buildings peering from behind small white clouds of his own breath. The same Bible now lay on Erin's lap and her white, flower-print dress. A few small pools of tears turned to streaks as she wiped them from the cover.

Erin failed to notice the communion of crackers and grape juice as worshipers in the same pew passed the tray along, not wanting to disturb her. The preacher lead the final prayer with his head bowed low to his chest and his hands folded neatly on the pulpit. She failed to notice the service coming to a close, the congregation rising to its feet, or the narrow eyes of several elderly churchgoers behind her, their nonverbal criticism cutting across the auditorium. Someone from behind nudged her, but she didn't stand. Instead, she clamped her hands tightly around her grandfather's Bible and prayed her own prayer, ignoring the shuffling of feet, the accusatory whispers, the looks of judgment and empathy. A few lingered nearby but held their breath, for it had been many months; what could be said, had been said, and words were now hollow and elusive and abrasive. Soon, people cleared the church, and the cars cleared the parking lot. The quiet heat from the sun burned through the stained glass, throwing sharp starbursts of red, green, blue, and yellow onto the uneven, gray stone walls. Dust swirled and settled, illuminated by thin sunbeams, then fell into shadows. Seen and then unseen.

Erin opened her eyes and stared at the abandoned pews. The pastor was sitting behind her with his own Bible open in his lap, his fingers passing slowly along each verse as his eyes scanned the passages. Erin wiped her cheeks and pulled out a small, black cotton cloth. She slowly wrapped the Bible like a child in a blanket and set it gently on top of her purse.

"I remember, not that long ago, a young girl walked into this auditorium ahead of her parents," the pastor began, his head still lowered to the Bible. "She walked right up to the front row, ignoring her mother's pleas to return to her seat. She pushed her hand out and shook the hand of the first person in the front pew. She told each person in the pew her name and asked their name in return and told each delighted congregant that she was new, but if there was anything they needed praying for, she would make sure to pray for it that night." The pastor turned a page in the Bible. "On down the line, shaking hands. Her mother was horrified, red with embarrassment." The pastor adjusted his tie, pulling the knot away from his neck as he smiled. "No pen. No paper. That little girl didn't take a single note. Sure enough, the next Sunday, that same little girl walked right back up to the front row, addressing each church member by name, asking if her prayers helped out. She always brought a smile to every member of the church. Her enthusiasm spread through the congregation like fire in a dry field."

Erin shifted in her seat. "Mr. Jenkins."

The pastor looked up from his Bible. "I'm sorry?"

"In the front row. The first person I spoke with—Mr. Jenkins. He asked me to pray for his wife sick in bed with bronchitis."

The pastor nodded his head with a smile. "That's right. Henry Jenkins from Alabama. He and Mrs. Jenkins ran a business renovating rooms. He hammered the nails, and she crunched the numbers."

The laughter of two children rolled into the auditorium from the open doors at the back of the church, then faded. The pastor looked back down at his Bible as he continued. "Not too many years later, that same little girl had a child of her own. The boy spent his first day shaking hands and talking to anyone who would listen, hugging the legs of those he somehow knew needed a kind gesture."

Erin remained silent for a few minutes. The pastor stayed quiet as well, the pages turning in his Bible the only sound. Erin turned her head to the pastor.

"I met Mrs. Jenkins two weeks later. She thanked me for praying for her and handed me a plate of brownies wrapped in a white napkin. She had made them night before. My mom let me eat one before lunch." Erin paused. "Mrs. Jenkins died the next spring. Mr. Jenkins followed that winter."

"Yes. I remember. I led both services."

An elderly woman appeared at the front of the church. Her wrinkled hands pushed a metal cart with large, black wheels down the center aisle. Short, determined steps. The soles of her feet dragged against the smooth marble floor. She walked the deserted pews, gradually gathering hymnals and settling them gently in the cart.

"I want to thank you for your kind words at Kevin's funeral, Pastor Knight."

The pastor nodded and closed his Bible. "I haven't seen you since then."

Erin remained silent for a moment. "They won't tell me how he died. No matter how many officers I speak with—they all smile uncomfortably and tell me they have no more information. Then they say what's important to know is that my son died in the service of his country. I keep awake at night imagining what his last moments were like—his last thoughts."

"Erin, you are not alone in your struggles. There are other parents who have lost their sons or daughters in the war. There's a support group that meets every week a few blocks from here. I can put you in touch."

Erin sat up straight, holding her back away from the hardwood back of the bench. "It's not other parents I need to hear." She turned her gaze to the pulpit. A wooden cross decorated the front, illuminated by a small light embedded in the floor, out of sight. "When I was young, I prayed for strangers because I sensed they were in need. Now that I'm older, I realize what I saw in Mr. Jenkins' eyes, and in the eyes of the others, was a constant yearning for something unfounded."

The pastor kept quiet. A few hymnals fell from the old woman's shaking hands. She hummed to herself as she gathered them up, one by one, wiping the face of each book before setting it carefully in the cart.

"I know now that their struggle was not from the suffering they endured," continued Erin, "but from the silence that followed." Erin picked up her purse. She set it down again. She cupped her hands over her knees, smoothing the dress with her palms. The pastor remained silent. "Mr. Jenkins told me that God spoke through others, like myself. But even as a child, I wondered why God never spoke for himself. I wondered why he needed others to comfort His own children, the ones He created, and who yearned to hear their Father's voice—but were denied."

"The Lord keeps close the brokenhearted, those crushed in spirit."

"I'm familiar with Psalms, Pastor." Erin lifted the tattered Bible. She opened it carefully to the back page, keeping her left hand tight against the binding. "Were you aware that my grandfather was a preacher?" Erin moved her eyes closer to the open pages. "His wife battled cancer for more than a year. He wrote here, two days after she died, that he couldn't find the strength to forgive God. Not because of her death. He wrote that being angry at death is like being angry at the sun because it rose in the east." Erin read the short passage to herself, then to the pastor. "'The silence of my Savior is unbearable.'"

Erin ran her thin fingers through her long, black hair, pushing it out of her face. She pulled a few tissues out of her purse, lightly dabbing her cheeks and chin.

"My grandfather wrote this passage in the same Bible that he used to preach about the importance of God's love and mercy." Erin closed the aging book. "I've never doubted before. I know He can hear my prayers and the prayers of others. I can't help but wonder why His children must endure such overwhelming silence." The wheels of the cart turned and squeaked and stopped. The pastor listened. "It pushes against my ears, Pastor. It clamps onto my head like a vice, tightening and tightening. Silence so great, I weep aloud to drown out the quiet."

"Faith, Erin, conquers our fears."

Erin paused, then spoke. "Maybe faith just distracts us from our fears." The cart moved past Erin's pew. She turned to face the pastor. "The night before Kevin left for his second tour in Iraq, I gave him one of those small travel Bibles, the kind you can stick in your pocket. It had a desert-camouflage cover, and I wrote his name on the inside. Kevin smiled and flipped through the Bible nervously, then handed it back to me. He told me that night he was leaving the church. He told me, if there was a God, He didn't need an institution or a book to communicate with us. '*If* there was a God...' Naturally, I was upset. We argued a bit, and I told him the importance of faith and belief in God's Word. I told him some of the things you're telling me, Pastor. Kevin said that perhaps God couldn't be explained with words or ideas. He said that maybe God existed as something undefined, something that... How did he put it?" Erin's eyes looked up, searching for the memory, "... something that manifested itself into the tangible world. 'What we witness in nature is an echo of the unknowable,' my own son told me. I'm not even sure what he was trying to say. Kevin was such an intelligent boy. Smarter than his mother. Always was." Erin wiped her cheeks. The pastor listened. "It seems, Pastor Knight, that faith is either the acceptance of things unseen, or willful blindness to an awful silence—to an awful truth." Erin turned in her seat, facing forward again. "In either case, I miss my son."

She wrapped the Bible again in the black, cotton cloth, placing the book under her arm as she stood. The pastor walked with her to the aisle. "God does not want the worship of those who ignore their doubts or their anger." The pastor held his Bible to his chest. "When you're ready, He will be waiting for you... as will I."

Erin nodded her head and looked at the pulpit and the cement angels, enduring for generations. She turned to walk to the open doors of the church when a pair of aged arms surrounded her torso and squeezed with surprising strength. The elderly woman buried her face in Erin's chest, pulling her close. Erin was silent and motionless. Without a word, the woman released her grasp and resumed gathering the hymnals, humming to herself as she stacked them neatly in the cart.

The warmth of the sun had dissipated by the time Erin stepped out of the church. Goose bumps rose on her ankles as she walked down the stairs with muted footsteps. A cold breeze shot across her bare arms as she tried to keep her dress from rising in the wind. Her black hair lifted off her thin shoulders. There were only a few vehicles left in the parking lot, dead leaves scraping the asphalt as they blew past her. Erin walked forward, head down, eyes squinting with the regret of forgotten sunglasses. She couldn't believe the air could be so cold with the sun burning so brightly. Before she could reach her car, a figure approached from the edge of the parking lot. He had been leaning against a wood fence with his hands deep in the pockets of a thick, green, camouflage coat. He was limping, keeping himself steady with a black cane in his right hand. His brown hair was cut almost to the scalp, his skull reflecting the bright sunlight. Erin's pace quickened as she dug her hands into her purse, wrapping her fingers around her keys. She kept her eyes straight ahead as she fingered the correct key and nervously tried to slide it into the lock.

"You Erin?" he asked.

Her hands jerked, the keys landing next to her feet. The young man pushed himself up and sat on the hood of Erin's car near the door, rubbing his knee. He leaned the cane against the vehicle and pulled a cigarette out of the inside pocket of his jacket. Erin could see herself squinting in the reflection in his sunglasses.

"You're Erin Zuelke, right?"

He cupped his hands over his lighter, but the wind kept extinguishing the flame.

"Can I help you with something?" Erin replied nervously.

"You know, when we were in the dirt, almost everyone had some horror story from their childhood they'd end up talking out." He gave up and stuck the lighter back in his pocket, the unlit cigarette dangling between his lips. "You spend twelve hours in a hole in the middle of a desert with the base at your back and an M-60 pointed at the horizon, you learn things about your battle buddy their wives don't even know. A crazy, drunk father who beat his son with dining chairs. A bitter grandmother who told her grandson he was a mistake, and that his mother should have aborted him. One guy told me he was fucked by a priest when he was ten."

Erin bent down, picking up the keys. She unlocked the car door and swung it open, throwing her purse in the passenger seat and setting her Bible gently in the back.

"Will you please get off my car?" Erin asked without looking at Mark.

"Kevin, on the other hand, never shut up about all the good goddamn things his mother did for him." Erin froze with one leg in the vehicle. "He always shared the care packages you sent him, because his mommy taught him to share. Those peanut-butter cookies you made were the best I ever ate." The keys in her hand dropped to the ground again. "Anyway, Kevin was a bit naive, bragging how great his mom was. Trying to rub it in, I guess. Naturally, this lead to the others calling him mama's boy, bitch boy, pussy boy, pansy ass—hell, the sergeant called him Private Whelp. I don't think the sergeant even knew Kevin's real name."

Erin stood back up. "Who are you?"

"Mark," he said flatly, "and I laughed right in his face when Kevin told me he joined the Army to help people. I watched him take pictures of bodies so shot up they looked like bloody sponges. He would snap photographs of children crying over the corpses of their families—you know, he was 'being helpful.' Kevin told me he was going to bring the war home—show Americans what they don't show on the news." The wind died down briefly. He pulled the lighter back out and lit the cigarette. "Like grisly pictures could fucking change anything."

"You...knew Kevin?"

He looked over at Erin, taking a long, deep drag on the cigarette. Thin wires of white smoke wrapped around his head and uncoiled. "I knew him being the correct tense. But it's still my turn to ask questions. Were you the one that put him up to such a stupid fucking idea? Joining the Army to take pictures of dead people?" Mark flicked some ash into the wind. "Were you the one who got him killed?"

Erin got into her car, slamming the door shut. She stared ahead without blinking, her hands gripping the steering wheel as tears fell onto her lap. Mark jumped off the hood, landing on one leg. He bent over next to the driver's-side door and then raised his body halfway, tapping on the glass with Erin's car keys. "I only ask because I was with him," Mark said, voice muffled. "They made me bury his body."

A strong wind blew across the parking lot, shaking the vehicle. Mark grabbed his cane and slowly limped around the front of Erin's car. He unlocked the passenger door and opened it, moving Erin's purse before slumping down into the seat. Erin remained motionless as Mark set his cane on the floorboard. He leaned out to close the door when Erin finally spoke. "Not in the car, please."

Mark took one last drag and flipped the cigarette out onto the asphalt, watching it bounce wildly in the wind. He shut the door. Erin could still smell the tobacco. The wind shook the car again. A small, wooden cross that hung from the rearview mirror swung back and forth. The warmth of the sun filled the inside of the vehicle. Mark set the keys on the dashboard and pushed them to Erin. She kept her hands on the wheel, looking past the hood of the car.

"Kevin wouldn't listen to me," Erin finally said. "I never understood. I begged him not to join the Army. He loved photography. He was a humanitarian. He could have been a reporter. He could have joined the Peace Corps or worked for the World Food Programme—anything. But he wouldn't listen to me. Kevin wouldn't listen to anyone."

"Very true," Mark replied as he rubbed his left knee. "And that's all I needed to know, Mrs. Zuelke."

Erin turned her head. "What happened to him out there? The Army...they only give me vague details."

Mark looked ahead, pointing at the exit of the empty parking lot. "Turn right. Take Broadway to Second Avenue. I need a drink." Erin hesitated for a moment, then grabbed the keys from the dashboard and started the car. White smoke poured out of the exhaust and wrapped around the vehicle. "You're burning oil, Mrs. Zuelke," Mark said, leaning forward, rubbing his hands together for warmth.

[V]

[2007]

"Explain."

Kevin stood at attention, looking at the captain seated across an untreated pine desk. The makeshift office was cramped and hot, a storage shed emptied of everything but a chair, a desk, and a few trinkets. Bare wood walls with exposed steel studs were the only protection from the blowing sand, the wind whistling through the cracks in the corners of the room. Sweat rolled down the back of Kevin's neck as he breathed heavily from the fifty pushups he just completed. He kept his feet firmly planted on the plywood floor, heels together, toes pointed out at a forty-five degree angle from the center.

"I'm waiting for a reply, Specialist."

Kevin looked at the screen of the laptop that was facing him. The solid white eyes of a dead soldier stared back at him. "Sir, I didn't—"

"Shut it," the captain said, before he slammed the laptop shut. "I don't want to hear any more of your excuses."

"Captain, I—"

"I thought I said to fucking shut it." The captain pushed the closed laptop to the side; it scraped loudly against the dry surface of the desk. The captain leaned forward. "Give it to me," he said, setting his elbow on the desk and motioning with his hand.

Kevin reached into the cargo pocket of his pants. He leaned forward and set a small, digital camera on the desk next to a framed picture of the captain's son. The boy was kneeling in the grass in a white-and-green baseball uniform, holding a bat in one hand; his other hand was deep in a baseball mitt.

"Memory cards, too."

Kevin set down a stack of three memory cards clacking together.

"You got any more?"

"No, Sir," Kevin replied.

"Empty your pockets."

Kevin rummaged through the rest of his pockets, setting the contents on the desk: a few crumpled Dinars, a small Tabasco bottle from a Meal-Ready to-Eat, a Leatherman Multi-Tool, a travel-sized bottle of hand sanitizer, sunglasses, a small, leather-bound journal, a black pen with the word ARMY written in camouflage on the side. Kevin set the items neatly on the desk next to the camera. The captain's son seemed to be staring at the journal. Kevin then pulled his pockets wrong-side out. Grains of sand fell onto the plywood floor. The captain looked over to the MP standing quietly at attention next to the door.

"Corporal, have your men search Specialist Zuelke's bunk." The captain stared at Kevin, still talking to the corporal. "You find any memory cards, another camera, pictures—anything—you report back to me immediately."

"Yes, Sir," the corporal responded, giving a quick salute before snapping around and walking out of the office, his heavy footsteps resonating under the plywood floor.

"Another fifty," the captain said sternly, as soon as the office door closed shut. Kevin dropped to the dusty floor and began doing more push-ups, the floor bowing slightly under his weight.

"One, two, three—one. One, two, three—two. One, two, three—three."

The captain stood and turned, locking his hands behind his back. He gazed out a small reinforced window behind his desk. He was watching a convoy of five deuces, three five-ton trucks, and a lead Humvee waiting just inside the entry control point. The convoy was parked next to a tall wall of sandbags covering barriers of concrete. The walls were topped with coils of concertina wire, like a huge slinky stretched out and fastened with hundreds of razors. The walls served as the only perimeter of the small Forward Operating Base—the only physical defense. Sentries were posted along the top at various points, their M-60s always pointed toward the distant hills. An officer walked down the line of vehicles, inspecting each one, pointing his finger and shouting orders at a few privates crawling over the equipment in the bed of each truck, double-checking the tautness of cargo straps and securing green polyethylene tarps to metal frames. Other sergeants were shouting out orders of their own, performing weapons checks with their men. A few men were standing in a circle next to the chaplain, heads bowed.

"One, two, three—eight. One, two, three—nine. One, two, three—ten."

"You used the only COM station on this FOB to post those pictures on the Internet, and you accomplished absolutely nothing," the captain continued, still talking to the window, "except pissing a lot of people off—including me."

"One, two, three—thirteen. One, two, three—fourteen."

The captain turned around and picked up the camera, shaking it as he spoke. "You used this to photograph dead American soldiers. That is fucking unacceptable." The captain slammed the camera down onto his desk over and over, like a judge banging his gavel. The memory cards bounced each time the camera hit the desk. The captain's son fell over; his father stood him back up.

"One, two, three—eighteen. One, two, three—nineteen."

The captain grabbed a large, marble paperweight next to his son's picture. It was a cube with the Department of the Army emblem carved into the top. He slammed it down three more times on the camera. Then he brought it down on the memory cards until they looked like a small pile of blue wood shavings.

"One, two, three—twenty-three. One, two, three—twenty-four."

The captain walked around his desk and knelt down next to Kevin, still holding the paperweight in his hand, pointing it at Kevin's head. "The Colonel ordered me to make it clear that if you ever pull this shit again—disgracing the sacrifice of one of our own—he'll see to it personally that you're stripped of rank and sent to Leavenworth breaking big rocks into small rocks for the rest of your life."

"One, two, three—thirty-two. One, two, three—thirty-three."

The captain leaned forward. "And if I ever catch you taking pictures again of dead American soldiers—if you embarrass me again in front of the Colonel—I'll see to it that you never even make it to Leavenworth. Do I make self clear, Specialist?"

"One, two, three—thirty-six. Yes, Sir. One, two, three—thirty-seven."

"Good." The captain stood and slowly walked back behind his desk, tossing the paperweight up and down in his left hand. He picked up the notebook. Kevin's body tensed.

"I didn't tell you to stop, Specialist," yelled the captain, dropping the paperweight to the desk.

"One, two, three—thirty-nine. One, two, three—forty."

The captain turned to the window, placing his hands behind his back, the journal dangling from his fingers. "Keep in mind the only reason you're still in uniform is because you didn't write anything with the pictures you posted." The captain turned and looked over his desk, slapping the palm of his hand with Kevin's journal. "No evidence of sedition. A technicality." The captain walked over to the other side of the desk. "And we happen to be in the middle of a soldier shortage," he added as he brushed the shards of silicon from his desk. "But it's no secret what you think about our mission—your insolent behavior preceded your transfer." The captain flung the journal across the room. It slapped against the door and fell to the floor.

"One, two, three—forty-four." Kevin slowed down. His arms felt like rubber bands.

The captain picked up the shattered camera. A few pieces from the cracked casing, along with the shattered glass screen, fell back to the desk. "Now, take all the pictures of dead hajjis you want." The captain tossed the broken camera over his desk. It fell to the floor next to Kevin, breaking apart into smaller pieces. "Print them up and leave them in the villages for all I care. It lets the enemy know what's waiting for them if they decide to fuck with the United States Army." The captain pushed the rest of Kevin's belongings off the desk with one large sweep of his arm. The Tabasco bottle bounced to a stop next to the pen. The Leatherman Multi-Tool fell and smacked Kevin on the back of the head.

The captain sat back down. He picked up the paperweight and leaned back. The metal chair groaned as he tossed the marble cube from one hand to the other. "What is our mission here, Specialist?"

"One, two, three—forty-six. To give the enemy a chance to die for their country."

"To die for Allah, Specialist. The hajji don't give a shit about their country, no pride in their community, or we wouldn't be here in the first place, would we?"

"One, two…three—forty-seven."

The captain stopped tossing the paperweight. "I said would we, Specialist?"

"No, Sir. One…two…three—forty-eight."

"They have no sense of patriotism or duty to their nation. They want to kill infidels, which is basically everybody who doesn't agree with them. There is no diplomacy. They won't listen to us. So, we have to kill them and let God explain it to them. Never forget that." The captain looked over his desk and pointed to the floor. "Clean that shit up."

"One...two...three...fifty." Kevin brought in his legs, leaning on his hands and knees as he slowly started to gather his things. The first thing he grabbed was his journal.

"You are banned from using the COM station. Don't let me catch you near a computer. You want to write mommy to let her know what a fuck-up her son is, you use snail mail. Furthermore, you will immediately report to Lieutenant Perry at the sandpit to begin remedial training. Three weeks. I believe he has everyone filling sandbags for twelve hours in this God-forsaken heat. Builds character." The captain leaned forward in his chair, pointing at Kevin with the paperweight. "In that time, if I receive any feedback from the LT stating that your participation in this training is anything less than exemplary, I'll make you wish you were one of those dead soldiers. Is that clear, Specialist Zuelke?"

Kevin stood at attention, breathing heavily. "Yes, Sir."

The captain set the marble cube down and pointed at the door. "Now get the fuck out of my office."

Kevin donned his sunglasses and tossed the broken camera into the trash bin behind the chow hall as he made his way to the sandpit. He looked up at the single star that burned brightly through a cloudless sky. Kevin took off his hat and wiped his forehead, glancing at a large, circular thermometer mounted next to the entrance of the building. The thermometer read 130 degrees. The smell of grease, eggs, and burnt sausage filled his nostrils. Kevin's stomach turned as he put his cover back on.

He walked past the chow hall and down a short line of green portable toilets. He stopped at the last one, took a deep breath, and held it. He opened the door and stepped into the latrine. The door slammed shut behind him and Kevin locked it. He kept his mouth shut tight as he rolled up his left sleeve past his elbow. He knelt down, turning his head sideways as he slowly reached down into the toilet, careful to keep his hand from touching the deep pool of feces and urine at the bottom. Several flies circled and landed on Kevin's face as he carefully moved his hand to the left. Kevin coughed and fought the urge to vomit, his eyes watering. He breathed through his mouth as he reached in further until his fingers touched the surface of a plastic bag duct-taped to the inside wall. He carefully pulled at the bag until it came loose. He quickly pulled his hand out of the toilet, examining the memory cards inside the bag. A few bits of excrement clung stubbornly to the surface of the clear plastic.

"Shit," Kevin said to himself, laughing at his own pun.

Kevin used the toilet paper to wipe away the small brown globs. Outside, the convoy rumbled off. A few loud soldiers stepped into the toilets next to him. Kevin untied his boot and pulled it off. He took out two more memory cards stuffed in the toe of the boot. He dropped them into the bag. He did the same with the other boot. There were three cards. Kevin cussed when he saw that one of them was broken in half. By the time he finished securing the bag back under the toilet, someone was pounding on the latrine door.

"You floggin' the dolphin in there or what? Hurry the hell up!"

Kevin tied the laces on his boots, securing each pant leg with blousing straps. He pulled out his bottle of sanitizer, drenching his hands and rubbing them together furiously. He did this more than once. He was so engrossed that he had forgotten about the smell. Kevin gagged as he flung open the door. His sergeant was standing there, eyes narrow in the bright sun.

"Well, if it isn't Private Whelp."

"Sergeant Murphy," Kevin said with a quick nod, clearing his throat and trying to walk past him. The sergeant grabbed his arm.

"Thought you should know. There are a few friends of the late Private Rakes looking for you. I suggest you find a way to make yourself unseen."

Kevin sighed. "It wasn't meant to be disrespectful, Sergeant."

The sergeant pushed down the chew in his lower lip with his tongue, then spat. "Well, they weren't too happy to find a picture of their friend online, shot full of holes and taking a dirt nap."

"I was only trying to—"

"I don't give a shit what you were trying to do, Whelp." The sergeant let go of Kevin's arm. "Private Rakes was a dumb son-of-a-bitch who would have gotten somebody killed if he hadn't done it to himself first. Not losin' any sleep over him. Just lettin' you know to watch your back."

"Thanks, Sergeant," Kevin said, a bit confused.

"Hey, anyone who can piss off that asshole captain as much as you did is a fuckin' hero," Murphy said, smacking Kevin hard on the shoulder. Then he pointed at Kevin. "But don't go pullin' that shit when you're back in the desert with me. Last thing I need is remedial training, got it?"

"Yes, Sergeant."

"Good. Stick to shooting the hajji with guns and not a goddamn camera." Kevin nodded. "Now, I gotta go piss," Murphy said. The sergeant kept the door open and stuck his head out. "See you in three weeks, Private Whelp."

The latrine door slammed shut, and Kevin could hear the sergeant laughing. Kevin walked past a line of barracks—tents with plywood floors. Generators and portable AC units whined as they pumped cold air into the barracks. He could see the corporal, who was sent by the captain, standing outside his dormitory tent. Kevin's cot, sheets, and pillows had been flung out into the sand. Kevin's footlocker sat sideways, the top open, books, papers, and everything else spilling out. A few other MPs were going though his duffle bags, throwing his clothes into a pile. Kevin ignored the corporal and moved on.

He walked past a large antenna field of two thirteen-foot, high-frequency antennas and an array of VHF and UHF antennas mounted to a thirty-foot tower. Kevin ended up near the back perimeter of the base where a large pile of sand sat ten feet high—almost as high as the perimeter wall. At the base of the sandpit, two pairs of privates were working together, filling sandbags. There was a fifth soldier working by himself. A lieutenant stood nearby, ensconced in the shade on the west side of a small brick building, once a latrine. The bricks were peppered with bullet holes.

"About time you got here, Specialist," the lieutenant said as he walked out of the shade. "I was about to declare you AWOL."

Kevin snapped to attention and saluted. "Specialist Kevin Zuelke reporting for duty, Sir."

The lieutenant knocked Kevin's arm down. "Don't salute me, dipshit."

"Yes, Sir."

"You're here 'cause you fucked up. I'm here to un-fuck you up. You do what I tell you, when I tell you. You eat when I tell you. You sleep when I tell you. You shit when I tell you. Clear?"

"Yes, Sir."

"You do that, and the next three weeks will only be the most miserable three weeks of your life. You fail to follow my orders, and I'll make sure those three weeks turn into ten. Clear?"

"Yes, Sir."

"I want five hundred sandbags by the time the sun hits the horizon. You'll be working with that private over there. You two are already behind, so get to work." The lieutenant bent down and grabbed a canteen half-buried in the sand. He threw it at Kevin's chest. "And stay hydrated. You get sent to the Doc because of heat stroke, I'll make it a thousand sandbags a day as soon as you're released."

Kevin walked over to the sand pile, taking off his outer shirt. His brown t-shirt was already soaked with sweat. The canteen full of water was hot in his hands. He could see the lone private struggling to tie the sandbag off. Kevin stopped and reached down to help.

"Fuck off," the private said without looking up.

"Never try to fill the sandbag more than halfway, or you'll—"

"Don't need your help with a fucking sandbag."

Kevin tossed the canteen into the sand at his feet. "Well, according to the lieutenant over there, I'm supposed to assist you with your fucking sandbag."

The private looked to the lieutenant, then back at Kevin. "Great."

Kevin stared at the hill of sand. "Ever wonder why everyone calls this big mountain of dirt a sandpit?"

"Because most people are fucking stupid."

Kevin smirked. "I'm Kevin."

"Don't care," replied the other soldier, scooping a few handfuls of sand out of the burlap bag.

Kevin looked to his side. The private's outer shirt was flung over the handle of a shovel stuck into the sand. He read the nametag. "Well, Private First Class Bradford, if we don't work together to finish our five hundred sandbags by sunset, the lieutenant's going to find other ways to make our lives even more miserable."

"Five hundred?" Mark stood and kicked the sandbag in frustration. It didn't move. "It was three hundred an hour ago, the prick." He looked over at Kevin, blocking the sunlight with his hand. "What the hell are you standing around for? Grab the shovel." Kevin pulled the small, collapsible spade out of the dirt. Mark grabbed an empty sandbag from a pile and held it open. Kevin began shoveling, the metal handle burning his hands.

"You got gloves?" Kevin asked.

"Nope."

"The LT didn't give you any?"

"Nope."

"Me either." Kevin shoveled in some dirt. "So, how did you end up here?"

"Listen, Kenton—"

"Kevin."

"Whatever. I'm not interesting in chatting with you to pass the time. I don't want to get to know you—I couldn't care less. I'm—"

"Good," Kevin replied, filling the burlap bag halfway with dirt. "I was about to tell you to shut the hell up."

Mark tilted his head. Kevin snatched the sandbag out of Mark's hands, holding the top with one hand while he twisted the bloated bottom with the other. He choked off the top of the bag with his fingers as he reached down for the rope from a large, plastic spool. He wrapped the rope tightly around the neck of the bag and dropped it to the ground. Kevin pulled out his Leatherman and, with his thumb, locked the knife in place. He cut the rope with one swipe and tied off the top of the bag. Kevin reached down and tossed the bag on a small pile of sandbags next to Mark.

"We'll want to start stacking those in a pyramid," Kevin said, leaning over with his hands on his knees, "or the pile will look like shit and eventually fall apart; the butter bar will make us restack them all."

"You've done this before," Mark said. Kevin remained silent, motioning for Mark to grab another empty sandbag. "Ah, right. My fucking yammering is getting to you."

"Listen," Kevin replied, "this lieutenant's new. I don't think he's ever been in charge of remedial training before. The last butter bar had us stacking six hundred sandbags before noon."

"Jesus."

"I can do fifty an hour." Kevin turned to look at the others around the pit. "Private Marshall over there can do sixty-five an hour." Kevin turned back to Mark. "But as you can see, they only have about forty. All we have to do is take our time. Look exhausted. Pour water over your head when he's not looking so it looks like you're drenched in sweat."

"Already am," Mark replied.

"You should also throw a few of the bags into the sandpit like they're defective."

"You mean the mountain of sand," Mark said.

"Pretend to have trouble tying the knots and cutting the rope."

"Mountain. Meaning the fucking opposite of a pit," Mark added.

"You need to play it up. Curse and kick the ground every now and then. It would be perfect if you could get him to yell at you to shut up. If he thinks we're suffering, he'll leave us alone for the most part. He might even let us go a little early, if he's one of those empathy types." Kevin started shoveling dirt into the newly opened bag.

"Don't count on it," Mark replied. "And how many times have you done this?"

"This is my second," Kevin said. "At this base, anyway. Three times at the base before this."

"Sounds like you're a pain in the Army's ass."

"I don't try to be. At least, that's not my intent." Kevin filled up the bag, tied it off, and tossed it over his shoulder. "A lot of people got angry for what I did."

"What? Did you execute a bunch of Iraqi civilians or something?" Mark opened another empty sandbag. "You wouldn't be the first."

"Pretend it has a hole in it."

Mark looked up. "What?"

"Hold on." Kevin stabbed the bottom of the bag with his Leatherman, cutting a large hole. Sand poured out the bottom. Mark smiled and stood.

"God fucking damnit!" Mark yelled, throwing the sandbag into the dirt pile and kicking the rest of the empty sandbags over. "Do all these fucking sandbags have holes? This is bullshit!"

The lieutenant, standing nearby in the shade, walked forward, pointing his finger at Mark. "Knock it off and get back to work, Private!"

Mark slumped back down and grabbed another bag. "Yes, Sir," he replied, his head bowed.

The lieutenant stood there, watching Kevin and Mark for a few minutes before returning to his shade.

"I told you to pretend," Kevin said quietly, "not act like an overdramatic pansy."

"It worked, didn't it?"

"You don't want to overplay it. If he catches on to what you're doing, you'll be cleaning the latrines with a toothbrush."

"Voice of experience?"

"It's not that bad if you seal your nose shut with duct tape."

Mark looked up. "You're kidding, right?"

"Or if you can get a hold of some Vaseline and rub a big glob under your nose. It helps—kind of."

"You're fucking nuts, Calvin."

"Kevin."

"Whatever." Mark snapped the sandbag open. "So," he asked as Kevin began to fill it.

"So, what?"

"What did you do?"

Kevin remained silent as he shoveled more sand, making sure most of it missed the open bag.

"Fine," Mark replied. "Reciprocity. I get it. I 'accidentally' poured a pint of oil into the radiator of a Humvee—the asshole captain's Humvee."

Giant clouds of white smoke out the hood." Mark looked at Kevin with a proud smile. "The colonel was in the passenger seat."

Kevin laughed. "Holy shit. How'd you get to the truck?"

"I'm Vehicle Maintenance, moron. I work on all the trucks. How else?" Kevin nodded. Mark looked at him expectantly.

"It was nothing, really," Kevin responded to Mark's non-verbal request.

"The Army doesn't send you to remedial training for doing 'nothing, really.'"

Kevin sighed. "I took some pictures."

Mark looked confused. "Of what? Naked chicks?"

"No."

"Naked men?"

"No."

"Then what?"

"Dead bodies." Kevin grabbed the sandbag from Mark and tied it off.

"Dead bodies... that were...naked?"

"No, idiot. Americans. I took pictures of dead soldiers and insurgents. I even have a few of dead civilians—some of them kids."

Mark looked confused. "And?"

"And what?"

"You took some pictures of—"

"More than some."

"You took a ton of—"

"More than a ton."

"Fine. But the Army has its panties in a twist 'cause you took a fucking shit-ton of pictures of dead people? I don't get it."

"I posted some of them online." Mark shrugged his shoulders. "I guess," Kevin continued, "they thought I was being disrespectful to the American soldiers who died."

Mark burst out in laughter, then tried to stifle it by holding his arm across his face. Kevin turned around to see if they'd attracted the lieutenant's attention. The officer was on the other side of the sandpit, pointing at a pile of sandbags next to another pair of privates. Kevin turned back around. Mark was wiping tears from his face, still chuckling.

"You don't look like you're suffering," Kevin said with a slight smirk.

"Disrespectful? It's war! The insurgents plant bombs in roads and kill us, and we drop missiles on their heads and kill them. You take photographs of the mangled, charred bodies and they're all pissed at you? What fucking hypocrites."

"Well, they—"

"And you," Mark said, pointing at him, "I thought you actually did something cool to get in trouble. You know, getting into a drunken fight with a sergeant, snorting a line of coke off the dash of a Humvee, fucking a camel in the ass—something interesting."

"Sorry to disappoint." Kevin walked over to the packed sandbags. "Let's start stacking these correctly." Kevin untied a few of them. "Let these fall open when you pick them up."

Mark stood, slowly, holding his hands to his lower back. "My fucking muscles."

Kevin looked over his shoulder, then back at Mark. "The lieutenant's not even looking at us. Stop being such a drama whore."

"Screw you. I've been at this for hours already." Mark walked over and began helping Kevin. "So, why the hell did you do it in the first place? To cause problems? Our captain is a complete ass, and it would be interesting if you did it to piss him off."

"I don't even know the captain that well," Kevin responded.

"So, you do it because you love filling sandbags in 120-degree heat?"

"130-degree heat. And I do it because I'm sick of people rationalizing what they never see."

"Oh, God. Let me guess," Mark added, shaking his head, "you have peace symbols tattooed on each ass cheek and daisies stashed away in your bunk."

"Peace lilies, actually."

"Fuck me. Of all the soldiers in the Army, I'm stuck with—"

"It's willful ignorance that I'm sick of," Kevin interjected. "That's why my pictures piss people off. That's why I'm filling sandbags. No one wants to see the reality of this shitty situation we created, calling it 'the defense of freedom'—nothing but a gold-covered turd. Do you realize the average American is more worried about what happens on *American Idol* than what happens over here? Most Americans couldn't tell you the difference between a Shiite and a Sunni. The government we set up here is just as corrupt as Saddam's, if not more so. At least with Saddam, Iraqis had electricity and running water."

Mark looked over at the lieutenant. The officer had his back to them. "Aren't we trying to be quiet?"

"There are government offices in Bagdad with toilets that don't even flush. Sewage inside the buildings! Then the kidnappings, the bombings, the executions. There's a morgue with tens of thousands of unidentified bodies in the city of Najaf. They have to show the faces of the dead on television screens for families to come and identify their loved ones. Imagine having to look through thousands of pictures of corpses to find your son or daughter!"

"Calm. Down." Mark said under his breath. "The LT is looking."

"The sanctions our government imposed made it hell for these people before we even arrived. Now we show up and make things worse! Why the hell would anyone here want to support a government we appointed?"

"Yeah. Life sucks for the people in Iraq. Life sucks for everyone else, too. It's going to suck even more for us if you don't shut up."

"We've spent billions of dollars on this war, so everyone wants to sugarcoat the shit that goes on here. Everyone wants to pretend we've made progress and made life better for these people."

Mark looked over. The lieutenant started to slowly walk toward them.

"It's fucking bullshit. No one wants to see the price we're paying because of our inept leaders. I don't care if they're Republican or Democrat—they're all guilty: Ignoring the fact there were no WMDs, or that Iraq had nothing to do with September 11th. And why? Because if politicians make a public statement, pointing out the hypocrisies of the system, they'd be voted out of office by the ignorant Americans who put them there."

"Kevin," Mark said loudly, staring at the approaching lieutenant, "I don't care. Neither should you. For the love of God, shut up!"

"Americans want to see the world in black and white. Us against them. Christianity versus Islam—forgetting there are American soldiers who practice Islam. They want to make quick, superficial judgments so they can go back to watching *Gossip Girl*, taking for granted that they don't have to work next to a goddamn toilet overflowing in shit!" Mark stood, shaking his head at Kevin. "I hope I make them uncomfortable. I want to shove my pictures in their ignorant faces and force them to understand the ugly truth—dead bodies on both sides of the line—and everyone wants to just keep on fighting."

"This is not a goddamn sewing circle, ladies," the lieutenant said sharply. "Shut the fuck up and get back to work. I want seven hundred sandbags by sunset."

"But you said—" Kevin kicked Mark in the ankle.

"Make that eight hundred sandbags." The lieutenant looked at Mark. "You were about to add something, Private?" Mark kept his mouth shut. "Excellent. I'm glad we have an understanding." The lieutenant turned and walked away.

"Good job," Kevin whispered.

"Hey, fuck you," Mark whispered back in response, picking up another empty sandbag and shaking his head. "If it wasn't for your whiny little tirade, we'd still be at five hundred."

Kevin reached down and picked up the shovel. "Sorry. I..."

"You get angry," Mark replied, "at stupid people who willfully remain ignorant—no matter how many pictures you shove in their faces."

"You know, I never did get your name."

"It's Mark, asshole."

"That's an unusual last name, Private Asshole. Nice to meet a willfully ignorant American."

"Not ignorant. I just don't give a fuck about a bunch of dumbass Americans back home who sit around justifying or criticizing a war they'll never fully understand in the first place."

"So, an apathetic American soldier. I'm not sure which is worse."

"What's worse is you thinking people really want to know what goes on here. People may be ignorant, but you're amazingly arrogant. Do you really think that pictures will matter? What about all the other reporters from all over the world who have been reporting on this shit war since it started? But you're going to make a difference. You're going to bring the fucking war home!"

"One thousand sandbags!" the lieutenant yelled.

Kevin shoveled into the sandbag, mouthing the words shut up. Mark held up his middle finger.

The sun had long disappeared by the time one thousand sandbags sat in four pyramids next to Mark and Kevin. The other four privates had finished hours ago and were undoubtedly in their bunks. The gibbous moon was floating like a white disc sinking into a black sea. Kevin and Mark stood at attention as the lieutenant inspected the pile of sandbags with a flashlight, one arm behind his back.

"These sandbags look like shit. Whose idiotic idea was it to pile them like that? We're not in fucking Egypt. Tomorrow you tear these down and build a wall."

Kevin kicked Mark's ankle before Mark could respond.

"But first," the lieutenant pulled out two toothbrushes out of his pocket, "it seems to me that there was a lack of communication on my part today. I didn't make it clear enough what shut-the-fuck-up meant. So, tomorrow morning you will be scrubbing the toilets with these." The lieutenant handed the toothbrushes to Mark and Kevin. "I truly hope that this exercise will effectively communicate the importance of shutting-the-fuck-up. And if that doesn't work, then I'm certain the latrines will be ready for cleaning the next day."

Kevin and Mark remained silent.

"Excellent. I see you're learning already. One more thing. The other four privates will be joining you. I took the liberty of informing them that it was the two of you who were responsible for our latrine duty tomorrow. I'm sure they'll also be more than eager to help you understand the importance of shutting-the-fuck-up. I'll see you two at 0500," the lieutenant pointed his flashlight in their faces. "Dismissed."

Kevin and Mark were past the antenna field before either of them spoke. "I've got to stop by the latrine."

"Don't fall in, fucker," Mark replied, walking toward the barracks.

"Wait. I need your help."

Mark stopped and turned. "I'm sure you can hold your own pecker without any help from me."

"No, asshole. There are some memory cards I have hidden there. I need to mail them home, tonight."

"Hidden where?"

"Inside the toilet."

"What?"

"I sealed them in a plastic bag and duct-taped it to the inside wall of the toilet."

Mark paused. "What the fuck is wrong with you, Kelvin?"

"It's Kevin."

Mark walked to Kevin, pointing his finger. "As far as I'm concerned, your name's Specialist Sack-of-shit Douche-bag who got us all cleaning latrines tomorrow and is probably going to have his ass kicked by the other four guys. And let's not forget your brilliant pile-the-bags-in-a-fucking-pyramid idea. Why the hell would I help you?" Kevin didn't respond. "And where the hell did you come up with the stupid idea of taping memory cards to a toilet? Seems like there are better places to hide things."

"I found a bag of weed one time in the same spot. It had been there for months. The guy was probably dead."

"Cleaning the toilets with a toothbrush?"

"Yep."

"The inside of the toilet?" Mark asked suspiciously.

"The LT was a detail-oriented sack-of-shit douche-bag."

"Like you!" Mark added.

"One of the other guys might find the cards."

"What a horrible fucking tragedy," Mark said, turning to walk away.

"I only need you to hide them in your bunk until I can mail them home."

Mark turned back around, shaking his head and laughing. "You do realize they've been doing random inspections of outgoing mail for weeks now."

"What?"

"Something the asshole captain started. The paranoid fucker doesn't want any security breaches."

"That's illegal."

Mark laughed again. "Like that matters. We're property of the U.S. government, Kelly."

"Kevin."

"They can do whatever the hell they want to us. And I'm sure anything you try to send home will be inspected by the captain personally."

"Shit." Kevin said. "Shit!"

"Now who's the drama whore?"

"What am I going to do?" Kevin said to himself, pacing back and forth. "I can't take them back to my bunk. I can't leave them in the latrine…"

"I guess you're S.O.L.," Mark said over his shoulder, walking back to the barracks.

"Wait." Kevin ran forward and jumped in front of Mark. "Where's your bunk?"

"D-block." Mark said, shaking his head. "And no."

"They might not check your mail. Can't you hold them a few weeks and then send them to my mom's address when this all blows over?"

"Your mom's? Really?"

"Yes," Kevin said defensively. "My mom's."

"Listen, this isn't going to blow over for you, Kepler."

"It's fucking Kevin!"

"Anything with your mom's address, regardless of who sends it, they're going to inspect—maybe even accidentally lose. So, forget it. Besides, what you're doing is pointless anyway. Nothing's going to change back home, and you're only going to end up getting kicked out of the Army or worse—Leavenworth."

"Let me worry about that."

"I might get kicked out along with you."

"You don't care about the Army, Mark. That much I already know. Do it because it will embarrass that asshole captain."

Mark thought for a moment. "You're still a douche-bag, remember?"

"Do it," Kevin continued, "because it will expose the hypocrisy of the Army, of those who run the Army, of the mainstream media, of willfully ignorant Americans who—"

"All right, all right. I'll do it if you shut-the-hell-up already."

Kevin looked surprised. "You'll help me?"

"Let's go before I change my mind," Mark said, walking toward the latrines.

It was past midnight by the time Kevin and Mark headed back to the barracks. Mark had all the memory cards stuffed in one of his cargo pockets. He was rubbing his hands down with sanitizer. Kevin walked ahead of Mark, writing an address on a blank page of his journal. They kicked up a thin cloud of dirt illuminated by the faint moonlight. Kevin ripped out the page and turned to give it to Mark, holding out his arm.

"Send the cards using my mom's maiden name. That way…" Kevin looked behind Mark and dropped his arm, shoving the journal into his pocket. "Shit."

Mark tilted his head. "What?"

A voice shot out from behind him.

"Private Whelp!"

Mark turned. Two men dressed in civilian clothes walked toward them. One was holding his hands behind his back. A chain rattled. The other held a two-by-four in his left hand.

"Jenkins," Kevin said, trying not to sound nervous. "How you been, man?"

"You don't get it, do ya?" Jenkins asked, swinging the lumber in his hand.

"Get what?" Kevin asked, shrugging his shoulders. The man standing next to Jenkins kept quiet, head tilted forward, his gaze locked on Kevin.

"Who the hell are these assholes?" Mark asked.

"You don't know what it's like unless you've been in battle," continued Jenkins.

Kevin walked forward holding his hands up in front of his chest. "How do you think I took that picture? I was there."

"Hiding under a truck, I'm sure," Jenkins replied.

"And I posted the pictures to show the people back home what's really going on—what they want to ignore."

"You don't have the fucking right to post those pictures—any pictures—much less use them to criticize the mission."

"I didn't write anything on that web page, Jenkins, and you know it. The pictures were there for people to judge for themselves."

"I'm surprised the captain didn't execute you in front of the entire base, you traitor," Jenkins replied.

Mark walked forward. "What the hell's your problem?"

"Fuck off, Private," Jenkins said, pointing the beam of wood at Mark. "This doesn't concern you."

Mark narrowed his eyes. "I don't see any bars on your lapels, dickweed. And even if I did, I'd still tell you to go fuck yourself."

Kevin walked between Mark and Jenkins, holding his arms out. "Calm down. Everyone. We're all on the same side here."

The man with his hands behind his back continued to stand motionless, quietly staring.

"You treat dead bodies like they're your trophies," Jenkins continued, knocking Kevin's outstretched arm out of the way. "Rakes pulled me to the ground one day on patrol before a sniper could get his shot off. There was a hole in the wall behind me. He deserved better than to have his shot-up body posted on the Internet by a cowardly fucking wannabe reporter."

"I'm not trying to be a reporter, Jenkins. People back in the States are ignorant of what's really going on over here. Did you know that—"

The man with his hands behind his back yelled, stepping forward as he brought out his arm. He was holding a 70-grade, stainless-steel chain with a large metal hook attached to the end. The chain became an extension of his arm, the hook now parallel to the ground. Kevin ducked, dropping to the dirt. Mark, who was standing directly behind Kevin, shot his arm up to block the chain. Mark's cover was knocked off as the metal hook smashed his wrist against his head. Mark felt a brief shock of pain right before he fell to the ground, limp and unconscious.

The next thing Mark saw was Kevin sitting in a folding chair next to his bed. There was a pair of old, wooden crutches leaning against the wall in the corner. Kevin was writing on a large, yellow notepad that sat balanced on his lap. Mark pulled at the thin gown. His right hand was in a cast. An IV trailed away from his arm. There were four other beds in the small recovery room, all of them occupied by sleeping soldiers in hospital gowns hooked up to IVs. Mark opened his eyes wider and tried to sit up. The pain in his skull, face, and hand brought him back down onto his thin pillow.

"What. The. Fuck. Happened?" he asked the ceiling.

Kevin looked up and smiled. "Morning, Private Asshole."

Mark tried to sit up again, but fell back onto the bed.

"Nope. You have to stay in bed at least another couple of days. I'm stuck here, too," Kevin added, grabbing his shin. "Doc's orders. Much to the chagrin of our friendly lieutenant."

Mark turned his head to his side, slowly. He was feeling the side of his swollen face and ear with his good hand. "We got out of work detail?" His jaw hurt when he spoke.

"Until the Doc releases us. Lieutenant Perry would like us to report to the sandpit at 0500 the morning after we're discharged."

"Fucker," Mark said, rubbing his head. "The last thing I remember was arguing with some jerk-off you called Jenkins."

"Yeah, Jenkins' friend smacked you in the head with a tow chain. It knocked you out flat. You're lucky it didn't kill you. When the guy with the chain saw you were unconscious, he bolted."

"Good thing. I would have kicked his ass."

Kevin laughed. "Yeah. I'm sure your unconscious body would have killed him. Anyway, after you hit the ground, Jenkins went after me with the two-by-four. Got me pretty good on the forearm and the shin before I was able to pull it away from him." Kevin looked up over Mark's bed. "He's the one over there in the last bed. Concussion and a few broken ribs."

Mark looked over, then back at Kevin. "Remind me never to try to kick your ass." Kevin smiled and went back to writing. "Why did that Jenkins guy call you Private Whelp?"

"Forget about it," Kevin said quickly.

A nurse in fatigues walked into the room, checking on a patient sleeping in the bed across from Mark and Kevin. Her blond hair was tied into a bun behind her head.

"Damn," Kevin whispered to Mark. "She's hot."

"Not interested," Mark replied.

Kevin tilted his head. "Why not?"

Mark ignored the question. "You're trying to change the subject. Some of the guys in the chow hall were talking about this new specialist who bragged to Sergeant Murphy about what a great mom he had." Kevin returned to writing on the large notepad. "They were talking about you, weren't they?"

"I've heard it all, okay?" Kevin said, anticipating Mark's insults. "Just because everyone else had bad parents doesn't mean they can take it out on a guy who has a great mother."

"Calm down there, Private Pansy. I'm sure this mother of yours is great."

"The best, Private Asshole."

Mark looked at the ceiling. "I never knew my mother."

Kevin looked up from the notepad. "Sorry to hear that."

"Shit happens," Mark replied. He snapped his head toward Kevin. "The memory cards?"

"I stashed them in your bunk." Mark looked confused. "When I went to get the Doc. It was on the way," Kevin quickly added. "Only two tents over."

"Let me get this straight. I'm on the ground, bleeding and unconscious, and you walk..." Mark looked at the crutches, "...you limp your way to the Doc's tent. But first, you stop by my bunk to hide a bunch of memory cards packed with photos of dead people."

"You were breathing and only bleeding a little bit," Kevin said, writing on the pad.

"Right," Mark replied.

"And there are a lot of bunks in D-block, by the way. Not to mention it hurt like hell trying to limp on my bruised shin."

"You're fucking nuts," Mark said with a wide smile. "Certifiable. I mean, I might not hate you as much as I do everyone else."

"Well, thanks. What an honor not to be hated by the local misanthrope."

Mark looked over at Kevin's notepad. "You writing a letter or something? Not to your mom, I hope."

Kevin looked up. "Listen. There's one more thing."

"What?"

"The captain will be here soon to debrief you. He'll want your version of what happened."

"You want me to lie for you?"

"Not exactly."

Mark threw up his hands, the cast almost hitting Kevin. "Then what?"

Kevin sighed. "Jenkins and Rakes. They went through Basic together. Friends for years before that. He didn't take Rakes' death very well."

Mark let his hands drop. "No shit," Mark replied, before letting his head drop back on the pillow.

"He's been through enough."

"Yeah, I get it," Mark replied. "I don't remember who hit me. I don't remember a thing." Kevin nodded and went back to writing. The nurse was on the other side of the room. Mark looked over at Kevin. "So, who are you writing? Some sexy, twenty-something blond back home?"

"Actually, I'm into older redheads."

"How much older?"

"And if you must know," Kevin continued, reading over his letter, "I'm writing a letter to my mom's friend, Victoria. Maybe she can—"

"Jesus fucking Christ. You really are a mama's boy."

"Screw you."

"You planning to ask her to come pick you up when the war's over?"

"Nope," replied Kevin. "I'm writing Victoria to send me another camera."

"You're going to make me hate you again with stupid comments like that."

Kevin looked up, and realization washed over his face. "They'll check my incoming mail, too."

"Of course they will, moron." Kevin's shoulders fell. "Maybe you could sketch the dead bodies," Mark added.

Kevin threw the pad of paper at the window next to the bed. It smacked the glass and fell to the floor with a clatter. The nurse looked over at them. Mark held up the hand in the cast to indicate everything was okay. She went back to checking a medical chart. Mark turned back to Kevin. "You're doing that whole drama whore thing again," he said with a slight smirk.

"I'm fucked," Kevin replied, holding his head with his hands.

"Jesus, calm down," Mark said, leaning over the bed and grabbing the notepad. The tubes in his IV stretched taut. Mark pulled the pen out from between Kevin's fingers. "What kind of camera was it?"

Kevin looked up, watching Mark write on the notepad. "What are you doing?"

"It's a good thing I'm left-handed," Mark said to himself. "A thin, lightweight, digital camera..." Mark said as he wrote, "...at least eight megapixels. You like black? What brand was it?"

Kevin spoke slowly, "It was a Panasonic Lumix."

"Panasonic piece-of-crap Lumix with extra batteries and some memory cards…got it." Mark looked over at Kevin. "I'll send your memory cards to my sister in New York. I'll have her send me a new camera—problem solved."

"I thought you said you weren't my friend," Kevin smirked.

"I'm not," Mark replied as he continued writing. "But I don't want to spend the next few years in remedial training listening to you brood and whine."

"Thanks, Mark."

"No problem, Keegan."

"Kevin."

"Whatever."

[VI]

[2010]

The late afternoon sun hung angrily, its heat penetrating the large windows along the wall of the restaurant. Erin's eyes watered. She left her sunglasses on, using the bright light as an excuse to hide her bloodshot eyes. Long shadows cut across the restaurant floor, the legs of each server extending like black stilts along the carpet. Erin sat across from Victoria, making an effort to listen. But her thoughts baked in the heat—as if they were suffering from heat stroke. An elderly woman two tables away fanned herself with a menu. Their server approached with a glass pitcher of water. Victoria waved him away without looking. She held a digital recorder to her mouth and started to speak into it. Her bleached-blond hair was pulled back into a ponytail, shaking as she emphasized certain words.

"It's 2010, and the feeble, so-called Universal Rights Coalition has infected our armed forces with homosexual ideals, attempting to turn an entire generation of soldiers against their country—and more disturbingly—against God. Don't Ask, Don't Tell was put in place to protect the unity and efficiency of our armed forces, yet the URC uses guilt and emotional blackmail to force homosexual assimilation into the ranks—demanding that soldiers accept the sordid behavior of gays in their platoons, in their barracks, in their showers. Imagine how that must feel, not only fighting to protect your country from terrorists, but also fighting to protect your sense of morality." Victoria paused. "We are at war. And the selfish URC is working hard to undermine that struggle. They see themselves as rebels, crying to the media that they are fighting for civil rights. But you know the truth: Their propaganda is a virus attacking this country, making America more vulnerable—a fact they refuse to acknowledge." She paused again.

"We will not sit silently and watch this happen." Victoria stopped the recorder with her thumb. "No, that's not it," she said to herself.

Erin looked at her water glass, the sunlight refracting through the ice cubes and cutting across the eggshell-white tablecloth—a mangled spider of color caught in its own web. Victoria closed her eyes and hit a button on the side of the recorder with her thumb. A small red LED shone on the side of her face, along with a few wrinkles hidden under a layer of foundation.

"We will no longer stand idly by to bear witness to this pandemic that is weakening our military and threatening the unity and the lives of those in uniform. With your prayers and your support, the Leviticus Alliance can inoculate the military against the URC's agenda—a selfish, corrosive, liberal paradigm." Victoria smiled, setting the recorder down next to a plate of crackers. She picked up a knife and sunk it into a small, white bowl of butter.

"Well, what do you think?"

Erin looked up from her glass. The elderly woman sitting behind Victoria was dabbing the back of her neck with a wet cloth napkin.

"It's far too hot for October."

"No, Erin, the speech." Victoria leaned forward, the knife still in her hand. A clump of butter clung to the edge. "Were you even listening?"

Erin pulled her sunglasses off, tossing them onto the table. "First of all, stop with the ten-cent words. You're not giving a lecture to college students; you're speaking to the base—and they don't walk around using words like assimilation and paradigm."

"What's with your eyes?" Victoria asked.

"You used the word selfish twice."

"Have you slept?"

"Also, there's nothing feeble about the URC. They've been around almost thirty years—longer than we have—with seven hundred thousand members. Their list of corporate sponsors reads like the stock exchange: American Airlines, Prudential, Nike, MetLife, Google, Microsoft—"

"It's called advertising, Erin. They don't care about the URC. Their sponsorship makes for great PR."

"Not to mention dozens of other organizations—the American Veterans for Equal Rights, Outserve, the Servicemembers Legal Defense Network—who, by the way, have been fighting DADT from the beginning."

"The URC is the public face of this repeal. I don't care about smaller—"

"You're making yourself sound uninformed."

"Not to the average American."

"And what's with the venomous language?" Erin asked. "It's no wonder we're losing support. Even our own church is distancing itself from the things you've said."

Victoria sighed, spreading the butter unevenly on a thin, toasted, sesame seed cracker. "How would you know? You don't even go to church anymore."

Erin picked up her glass of ice, realized there was no water, then set it back down. "A virus? Really? You don't think people are smart enough to see through that bullshit?"

Victoria's head snapped back. "Since when did you start cursing?" She set the knife back down on the table, the butter sticking to the tablecloth. "It doesn't matter if it's an exaggeration. In fact, the more overstated, the better. Hyperbole is the only way to get anyone's attention."

Erin picked up the glass of ice again. "What about being objective?"

"Overrated. Ineffective. In a word: Doesn't sell."

"That's two words. Three without the contraction."

"People are subjective, Erin," Victoria replied, spreading her fingers to examine the nails. "We're all fueled by emotion—we elect senators and presidents based on how we feel about them. They know it. Look at any political campaign. Sensation sells."

"You mean fear sells."

Victoria narrowed her eyes. "My cuticles are atrocious."

Erin sighed and examined her glass. An inch of water had formed around the melting ice. She tilted the glass to her mouth.

Victoria looked up. "You really shouldn't drink that. Bottled water is cleaner—fewer toxins."

Erin let an ice cube drop into her mouth. She pushed it aside with her tongue, letting it melt in her cheek. "Homosexuals are not a disease, Victoria. And thank you for proving my point."

"What point?"

Erin dangled the glass in her hand, the refracted shards of colored light moving back and forth across the table. "Show me the article published in a peer-reviewed medical journal that shows high levels of toxicity in Denver's tap water."

"Don't be stupid, Erin. Everyone knows that. And stop trying to twist my words. I said the homosexual agenda is a disease, not the homosexuals themselves. Those poor people are just confused." Victoria took a small bite from her cracker and let it fall from her hand. It clattered on her plate. "These crackers are stale, and this isn't even you talking."

"My point, Victoria, is that our audience is buried under an avalanche of hateful rhetoric meant to scare people into action." Victoria sighed and crossed her arms, staring across the table.

"What?" Erin asked.

"What happened?"

Erin look puzzled.

"We've known each other a long time. Do you remember when I first met you?"

"Twenty-eight years ago." Erin replied. "It was your first day at the church. I was in charge of welcoming newcomers. Why?"

"The first thing you asked me was if I needed you to pray for anything," Victoria responded with a grin. "After the service, you walked me around that beautiful building, introduced me to Pastor Knight and the deacons, and invited me to a potluck lunch you organized every month for new members and their families. You planned games for the kids, set up charity bake sales, arranged transportation for anyone who didn't have a vehicle—it was impressive. All this at eighteen."

"Your mother," Erin said. "You asked me to pray for your mother back east. In Boston."

Victoria smiled. "Your mind's a steel trap."

"I remember who you were back then, Victoria. You'd just finished graduate school and wanted to put your business degree to work. You used some money from your mother to open a tiny Christian bookstore two blocks from the church."

"Blessed Books," Victoria replied. "And that bookstore ended up expanding—twice. All because of this young, tenacious girl I hired, who, in less than a year, almost ran the store herself—while going to college."

"I never did like the name Blessed Books," Erin replied, rubbing her thumb on the tablecloth.

"That store could have been called Satan's Sanitarium, and you would have made it work. And what did we do with the money when I sold the store?"

"You started the Alliance."

"*We*, Erin. We started this. Together. Remember our first rally?"

Erin smirked to herself. "Wish I could forget. It snowed six inches the night before—in May. About twenty people showed up. You stood on a wooden crate so your feet wouldn't freeze."

"Then the megaphone died one minute into my speech," Victoria said with a short laugh.

"Pastor Knight ran across the street to buy batteries, then slipped on some ice and hit his head, and we spent the rest of the day in the waiting room of the ER."

"And now you're the Director of Operations of the Leviticus Alliance—a nationwide, million-dollar organization that strengthens family values and has influence in Congress." Victoria leaned forward. "You're family to me, Erin. Like my little sister. You were there for me when my mother died. I was there for you when your husband left—defended you against the women at church judging you." She leaned back in her chair. "I can't imagine what I would do without you. So I worry. I worry that my little sister no longer wants to be a part of this family, part of an organization we've worked so hard to build." Victoria paused. "You've changed."

Erin rubbed her temples.

"And for some blunt, sisterly advice," Victoria continued, "ever since you met up with that Mark kid, you've gotten worse. You've been distracted and unreliable. You need to get away from him. How can we run the Alliance if you keep hanging around homosexuals?"

Erin shook her head. "You talk about family. Mark was a POW. When he got back to the States, they kicked him out of the military for being gay—just like that."

"If he was honest from the beginning about being gay, he would have never been a POW in the first place."

"He's alone."

"He's taking advantage of you. Can't you see that? How many meals have you bought him? Clothes? I heard you're even helping him with his rent."

Erin looked away toward the windows. "It was only for a few months. Because of my help, Mark's finally starting to get his life back together. Got a new job at a gun range."

"Yeah. It only took him a year."

Erin turned her head and narrowed her eyes. "For some blunt, sisterly advice: What I do with Mark is my own business and no one else's." Erin paused, looking back down at the table. "Besides, it isn't Mark distracting me."

Victoria reached across the table, her hand touching Erin's elbow. "Kevin?" Erin didn't respond. "You need to share that loss—publicly. Kevin died defending this country. Talking about it with others will help you heal. And imagine how your story will resonate with our supporters."

Erin closed her eyes, shaking her head. "You promised you would stop asking."

Victoria squeezed Erin's elbow tighter. "This vicious circle of depression needs to stop, Erin. I can help." Erin yanked her arm away. "It's not good for you—not good for us. How long has it been since you had a decent night's sleep?" Erin didn't respond. Victoria leaned back in her chair. She picked up her knife and started tapping it on the table. "You know, Kevin's story would showcase the dangers of homosexuals in the military. This could be what we need to stop this ridiculous DADT repeal."

Erin knocked over her glass. Half-melted ice cubes tumbled across the table and onto the floor. The elderly lady at the next table pretended not notice. "Mark was not responsible for Kevin's death," Erin whispered angrily.

Victoria leaned forward. "Is that what he told you? He lied to the Army for years about being a homo—doing God-knows-what. How do you know he isn't lying to you, too? Didn't you say Mark was the only one with Kevin? How would anyone know what really happened? Maybe he's lying to cover his own ass."

"Now who's cursing?"

"He still won't tell you what happened to your son. Why?"

"He only needs some time to—"

"Twelve months? To do what? Get some more rent money out of you?"

"Enough."

"The only good thing to come out of this situation is that, if we go public with Kevin's death, Mark's silence will fuel what people think happened. Interpolation. The official story has enough gaps that people will apply their own theories about gays in the military—their own judgments. That's our advantage."

A waiter came to the table with a towel. "Let me get that for you, Ma'am."

Erin pushed her hands to her face, covering her eyes. "I'm sorry."

"Don't worry about it, Ma'am. I'll have another glass of water sent to your table right away."

"A bottle of water, please," Victoria demanded. "And I'd like to know what is taking our food so long. We ordered at least twenty minutes ago."

The server stood up, his hands cupped with a few ice cubes nestled inside the towel. "Yes, Ma'am. I'll find out right away. I apologize for the wait."

Victoria waved him away with her left hand—two swift swipes in the air. She leaned forward to Erin. "Listen. What happened to Kevin was awful. I can't even imagine what you're going through. But keeping all this to yourself is doing you absolutely no good—it's unhealthy."

"Please stop."

"Erin," Victoria said more forcefully, tapping her index finger on the table. "It's not just hurting you—it's hurting us. You have an obligation to this organization to help stop that repeal." Victoria leaned back again, crossing her arms over her chest. "And an obligation to God."

Erin moved her hands away from her face. Her cheeks were hot and wet. A bottle of water had appeared next to her plate.

"Look at me. They're on the verge of repeal, and our donations are dropping. We don't have the money to fund another national campaign. We're still feeling the effects of the recession and most of our volunteers are quitting because they can't afford to work for free. We're losing the fight," Victoria paused. "But you already know all this. You know we're not going to last much longer unless we can invigorate our base and add to it." Victoria leaned forward, lightly touching Erin's hand. "People need to be rejuvenated. They need to be reminded of their obligation to this country, and to protect it from moral decay—from those who mock our faith. Kevin's story can do all of that—and more. Let your loss be the catalyst in this fight." Victoria paused. "At the very least, you owe that to Kevin."

The room suddenly grew quiet as another server arrived and quickly placed the food on the table with a single fluid movement, like a perfectly tuned machine following its protocol. Erin failed to hear the server explain how her lentil purée was made with haystack mountain goat cheese, fried onions, and tomato oil. Victoria looked over, annoyed as the server explained that her *foie gras* was prepared with fresh mozzarella, arugula, and truffle oil, served with a toasted *bâtard*. Erin failed to notice Victoria waving the server away with her fork, saying, "I read the menu, thank you," as she stared suspiciously at her plate. Erin wrapped both hands around the base of her bowl, allowing the steam from the soup to roll over her face, like white, diaphanous wings evaporating over her head. Erin concentrated on the heat. She didn't hear Victoria ask if all she was having was soup. Erin failed to notice the old woman at the next table jump when she finally yelled out, "How dare you!"

"Calm down," Victoria whispered.

"You will not exploit my dead son."

"I'm not asking you to—"

"Yes, you are."

Victoria sighed. "I would never—"

"Yes, you would. You just did."

Victoria's cell phone jumped to life to "Count Your Blessings." Victoria picked it up at the end of the chorus.

"What is it? I'm eating... Yes... Yes, I know... Then call her office again. Keep calling until you get Musgrave herself on the phone... Because—obviously—a former Representative who co-sponsored the Federal Marriage Amendment will pull in thousands of people... I'm counting on it. The more protestors the better... She what? How much?" Victoria raised her hand, rubbing her thumb back and forth against her fingers. Erin shook her head and looked back down at her soup. "We don't have that kind of money... Okay, fine. I'll figure something out. Just set up the appointment. I've got to go—what? Threats?" Erin looked up. "Who from this time? I'd like to... Yeah, I doubt it. Listen, make the offer, text me the appointment details, and don't call me again. I'll be in the office in the morning." Victoria slammed the phone down on the table.

"Someone's threatening you?"

"Both of us. And what did that kid say to you to make you so obstinate?"

"I'm a target?"

"Of course you are. Your face is right next to mine on the flyers, the billboards, the website. It's happened before; you know it's nothing to worry about."

Erin sighed and let her spoon drop into the soup. "Listen. Mark was the last person to see Kevin alive. His mother is dead. His sister is in New York."

"Then why doesn't he move there?"

"His own father won't even speak to him."

"For good reason, Erin."

"His father abandoned him." Erin held her hands in the air. "I'm not about to abandon him, too."

"He's not your responsibility," Victoria replied.

"Well, I thought, for at least five seconds, I could put aside my personal objections to homosexuality and help someone in need. You know, be a good Christian."

"You're just using him to find out what happened to Kevin, and you know it."

"That's not fair."

Victoria smiled. "Certainly not to this Mark kid, but it's the truth."

"I'm not using him."

"No, you're only a shoulder to cry on," Victoria replied sarcastically, shaking her head.

"Why can't I be that?"

"Damnit, Erin. Mark represents everything we're fighting against. What about your responsibility to the Alliance? The staff around the office, maybe good Christians, but also a bunch of gossips. They talk to our donors and to the old ladies in the churches about your little outings with him—who talk to their husbands who talk to their pastors. It's embarrassing. My co-founder cares about homosexuals. Thinks we should allow—" Victoria paused. Her eyes widened. "You're not thinking of leaving the Alliance, are you?" Victoria's phone rang again. She answered and hung it up without taking her eyes off Erin.

"No, Victoria, I'm not leaving the Alliance." Erin leaned across the table. "But if you mention Kevin again, I'm pulling my support and my funding."

Victoria pursed her lips. "Fine."

"Do we have an understanding?"

"I get it. We'll find another way."

A busboy arrived to fill Erin's glass, the capped bottle of water next to it.

"Will you please stop pouring us your filthy tap water?" Victoria snarled without looking at the server.

"Thank you for the water," Erin corrected. She drank from her glass. The elderly woman behind Victoria shook her head. Erin looked around the restaurant. "We're barely staying afloat, and you ask to meet here."

"You don't want people seeing the founders of the Leviticus Alliance having a meeting at some greasy burger joint, do you?" Erin didn't respond. "So. You'll still be at the fundraiser?"

"Yes," Erin replied. "November twenty-first. Ten in the morning. Steps of the Capitol—in the middle of winter." Erin smiled slightly. "Just like our first one."

"There's no choice. The DADT repeal is—"

"Yes, I know. And apparently I get to hear Musgrave speak."

"That reminds me. I need you to arrange the transportation for her. Also, we'll have a tent behind the stage. You can sit back there and manage the schedules, food and beverage, you know. Terry said he can set up a link on your laptop to track phone and Internet traffic—donations. We'll know in real time how the rally is being perceived."

"In other words, you need me out of view and out of earshot." Victoria looked up as Erin continued, "But I told you I'd be there, and I will."

Victoria's penciled eyebrows pushed in toward the bridge of her nose. She leaned forward, staring closely at the small morsel of liver surrounded by a moat of truffle oil. She picked up her fork and stabbed at the meat, the tines not breaking through the delicate flesh.

"This *foie gras* is terrible. Just awful." Victoria looked around for a server, fingers snapping sharply.

Erin frowned. "You know they force-feed those poor animals."

"What animals?" Victoria asked, still searching for a server.

"Never mind."

[VII]

[2010]

Mark sat naked on the bed, thin elbows resting on thin knees, his head in his hands. Still a little drunk, he tried to clear the fog in his skull, tried to ignore the headache slowly growing in intensity—a ship about to slam into a rocky coastline. A young guy, almost as skinny, with short, black hair and gray eyes lay next to Mark on top of crumpled sheets. The back of his head rested against the headboard as he rolled a joint on his bare chest. His legs were crossed, covered sparsely in black hair. The young man was wearing only a brown leather bracelet around his wrist and a pair of white socks. It was early, the sky outside still black. The only light in the bedroom was a lamp with a red bulb on an end table, filling the room with a soft, red glow. Thin strings of smoke from burning sandalwood incense coiled in front of the lamp. Somewhere in the room a pair of speakers played trance music.

"You were really in Iraq?" the young man asked, concentrating on the work on his chest.

"Yep," Mark replied to the carpet, rubbing his scalp, trying to remember how he got there in the first place, or when he mentioned Iraq. Mark wasn't even sure where there was.

Mark only had short flashes: A bartender cutting him off from the bar. Limping through the parking lot. Lighting a cigarette for a tall blond guy next to a Lexus SUV. Black leather sticking to his ass while getting a blow job in the back of the Lexus. Getting kicked out of the vehicle after calling the tall blond guy a pretentious moron for buying an SUV made by Lexus. The taste of asphalt. The young guy with short, black hair helping him up. Feeling sick to his stomach. Riding in the passenger seat of an Altima. A cardboard rainbow dangling from the rearview mirror. A small living room lit by the blue screen of a flat-panel television. The smell of pot and red wine. The feel of sparse stubble and a tongue ring against his neck. Undoing the guy's belt in a hallway. The taste of pre-cum. Being pulled by his loosened belt into a bedroom lit in red. Tripping and falling next to the bed. Looking for condoms in the drawer of the end table, but finding none. Grabbing the back of the guy's head while being sucked off on the floor. Back and ass arching off of the floor while he came. Returning the favor. Finding condoms in the bottom drawer of the dresser opposite the bed. Finding lube in the top drawer. Knocking over a floor lamp. The knee aching as he topped on the bed. The headboard slamming against the wall. Collapsing on top of the guy after coming again. More pot. More wine. More fucking. Waking up hours later next to a skinny guy with short, black hair and gray eyes whose name he couldn't remember. Dry mouth. Swollen knee. Lingering hangover. Annoying trance music playing in the background. Smelly incense.

"Hey," said the guy without a name, lightly scratching Mark's back. "You okay?"

"Fine," Mark said, lifting his head and talking over his shoulder. "Tired, that's all."

"I bet," was the reply, framed in a smirk. "You said last night the Army kicked you out when you got back. Just like that?"

Mark wondered what else he'd said last night as he reached down and grabbed his jacket off the floor, fishing through the pockets for his cigarettes. "Just like that," he replied. All he found was a paperback of Bertrand Russell's *Why I Am Not a Christian* stuffed in the inside pocket. A gift from Shannon.

"That's so fucked up. You should fight it."

"Won't make a difference," Mark said, letting his coat drop to the floor.

"I mean, I bet you saw some crazy shit while you were over there," the guy with the tongue ring said, shaking his head before he licked the joint and sealed it. "I watched this news report once, where they—"

"It's nothing like the news."

"Maybe it was a documentary. Yeah, I think it was. Anyway, they—"

"It's nothing like any documentary," Mark interjected, still talking to the carpet.

The guy reached past Mark to grab a lighter sitting on the end table. "So, what was it like? Did you ever get shot at? Jesus, did you have to shoot anyone?"

Mark sighed and stood, scanning the floor, his bare feet kicking away a few condom wrappers, a wine glass stained red at the bottom, and a pair of blue jeans that weren't his.

"If you're looking for your boxers," the guy with the bony knees and ass said, lighting the joint and leaning back against the headboard, taking a long pull and holding it in, "they're in the bathroom next to the shower." Mark couldn't remember being in the bathroom. "Second door to the right," the guy added with a slight smile before he started coughing, face turning red, cirrus clouds of smoke rolling out of his mouth.

Mark limped over his boot and his cane to make his way down an unlit hallway, holding his arm against the wall for support as he kept the injured leg straight. He flipped on the light in the bathroom and squinted as the fluorescent bulb above blinked until it was steady. A gray shower curtain lay twisted and folded over itself on the tile floor, a white shower rod next to it in standing water. Mark stepped over the shower curtain and looked into the bathtub. A bent towel rack was surrounded by pieces of broken drywall. Mark's left boot sat sideways next to the drain, the laces wet from the dripping faucet. A dog collar with a leash next to the boot. Mark spotted his wet black boxers balled up on the tile floor next to the bathtub. He picked them up, water dripping onto the fallen shower curtain.

"Find 'em?" a voice yelled from down the hallway.

"Yeah," Mark yelled, dropping them back onto the floor, cold water splashing his ankles. He shut the bathroom door and stood over the toilet. Two used condoms swirled around on the surface of the water as he urinated. Mark flushed and washed his hands and turned, his fingers dripping with water, hovering in front of a wall with two holes where the towel rack should have been. As Mark shook his hands to dry them, he caught a glimpse of himself in a full-length mirror bolted to the back of the door. His skin was white, almost as white as the bathroom walls. His eyes were dilated and bloodshot, sunk into deep, dark circles. Long, bright-red scratch marks ran across his chest. Purple bite marks pocked his neck and shoulders. Another bite mark surrounded his right nipple. Mark turned around and looked over his shoulder. Deeper claw marks ran down his back and his ass. The alcohol was wearing off, and his knee was starting to ache again. Mark turned back, lightly touching the surgical scars on his leg— parentheses that surrounded a red, round period on his kneecap. Mark opened the door. "You got any aspirin?" he yelled.

"Help yourself to the medicine cabinet, hon," was the reply from down the hallway. "Anything you want." The trance music was now louder.

Mark opened the cabinet above the sink and rummaged through the various medicine bottles. His eye caught several orange prescription bottles. Vicodin. The name Ben Lawson was written on the sticker on the bottle. Mark opened the bottle and tilted his head back. He shook two pills onto his tongue and swallowed with effort, washing them down with handfuls of water from the sink. He thought about sticking more pills in his pocket until he remembered he wasn't wearing pants.

When Mark returned, the guy was slowly dancing next to the bed, eyes closed, and the joint burning in his left hand. His arms were outstretched, moving out of sync with the fast music.

"Thanks for the Vicodin, Ben," Mark said, limping forward and dropping his left boot next to his right boot. The guy suddenly stopped dancing and laughed. He fell on his back on the bed, the muscles in his abdomen tightening as he tried to breathe between giggles.

"My name's Derek, hon. Ben's my roommate." Derek held out the joint with a big grin. "You don't remember much from last night, do you—Mark?"

Mark smiled and shook his head. "Parts," he replied as he limped forward, his left arm holding his left leg while he took the joint.

"Don't worry about the bathroom. Ben's done far worse. He finds the craziest fucking women in the entire city, I swear." Mark took a long drag and held it. "One night, he and this red-headed chick tore down half the ceiling in the living room—they were swinging from some steel-and-leather jungle gym he tried to build. The crash woke me up, and I ran into the living room to see them still going at it—Ben and this girl screaming and fucking and moaning—legs and arms, tangled up in these leather straps and chains slapping into each other..." Derek laughed some more, holding his stomach. Then he looked at Mark mischievously. "You don't even remember what we did in there, do you?"

Mark blew the smoke out the side of his mouth and shook his head, handing the joint back.

"That's too bad," Derek replied. "I was the one wearing the dog collar. You had the leash wrapped around your wrist and you were... well... no one ever tried to flog me with a shower curtain before."

Mark turned his head, straining to remember any of it. He saw his pants hanging over the back of a wicker chair next to the dresser. He walked over and picked them up, sitting down heavily and stretching his leg out. The trance music slammed against Mark's skull like a hammer, knocking against aluminum siding with every beat.

"My first year of college," Derek began, setting the joint on the end table, "this recruiter came to the campus and gave this long speech about the importance of giving back to our country by serving in the military during a time of war…"

Mark cupped his hand around his ear. "Can't hear."

"Oh, sorry." Derek jumped up off the bed and walked over to a computer on a small desk next to the closet. The music stopped, and Mark thanked Derek under his breath. Even in the dim red light, Mark could see several deep scratches down Derek's back. Three distinct bite marks on his ass. "After the recruiter finished his speech," Derek continued, his face glowing in the light of the computer screen, "I walked right up to him and shook his hand. Told him I wanted to fight terrorists and defend freedom and… basically I repeated his speech back to him." Derek turned his head. "How about some goa?"

"Goa?"

Derek tuned back. The computer mouse clicked and more music began playing from two speakers on either side of the computer monitor. Derek turned it down—but not enough. Mark wasn't sure what goa was, but it sounded like the same crap he'd been hearing since he woke up. He repositioned himself in the chair, rubbing his head and waiting for the Vicodin to kick in. He felt something under his foot.

"Don't the recruiters have a quota to fill every month or something?" Derek asked standing up.

"Yep," Mark said, looking down. He saw his elastic knee brace under his foot, inside out.

Derek jumped back on the bed, locking his hands behind his head. "Because that recruiter got way too excited—pulling out all this paperwork for me to read and sign, talking real fast and telling me I was a courageous young man and that I was going to be part of something greater than myself. What crap. He sounded like a used-car salesman."

"All military recruiters are used-car salesmen," Mark replied.

Derek lifted his head. Mark was slowly pulling the brace up over his knee. "So, then I told him I was a great, big homo and asked if being a great, big homo was a problem. The guy freezes and goes silent, holding all those papers in mid-air. It was hilarious."

Mark held his pants in front of him, reaching into one of the pockets to pull out a box of cigarettes. The box, along with the three cigarettes inside, was soaked. Mark looked confused as he held up his pants. They were completely dry.

"If you need smokes, hon, there's some over there," Derek said, pointing at the end table. Mark tossed the wet box of cigarettes into a trash can near the desk as Derek continued. "Then I asked the guy, politely of course, why all the sudden I was less qualified and less capable to be in the military. He said, 'You can't join the Army. Talk to your senator.' Then he looked over my shoulder and asked for the next applicant—talk about a coward."

Mark limped across the room. Derek rolled over to his side, holding his head up with one hand. "How did you ever put up with all that military bullshit?"

"Never really did," Mark replied. He opened the drawer to the end table and found two boxes of Camel Lights.

"Take 'em both, hon, I don't even like Camels," Derek said. "I wouldn't last a week in the military. All those orders and procedures. All that discipline and being told what to do—and no sex. My God, what a horrible way to live. Worst of all, you're surrounded by idiots."

Mark pulled out a smoke from the open pack, then leaned down and stuck the two boxes of cigarettes into his jacket on the floor. "Not everyone in the military is an idiot."

"Well, not you, of course," Derek said with a smile.

Mark sighed heavily. "I really wish civilians would keep their mouths shut about the military. Grunts die or get hurt and then get fucked over by the government and you call them idiots."

"Hey. I'm sorry. I was just—"

"The real idiots are the assholes who start wars and write ridiculous homophobic policies, who profit from—" A sudden shock of pain made Mark's legs give out. He caught himself on the end table. The lamp with the red bulb shook. The cigarette fell from Mark's mouth as he turned and sat heavily on the bed, extending his leg. "Fuck."

Derek sat up. "Jesus, you okay?" Mark didn't respond. "Maybe I can find something stronger in Ben's room. He's got so many drugs, he won't miss it."

"I'll be fine," Mark replied flatly, rubbing his leg through the elastic brace. "Give me a minute."

Derek put his hand on Mark's shoulder. "Anything I can do to help?"

Mark shook his head. "Nothing. Happens every now and then. It won't last long."

"Nonsense," Derek said, scooting up behind Mark, slowly wrapping his arms and legs around Mark's body. "I bet I know something to help distract you." Derek said. He kissed the back of Mark's neck. Mark felt the warm breath, and goose bumps began populating the surface of his skin. Derek ran his tongue along the small ridges of Mark's spine, from the lower back up to Mark's tapered neckline. Mark closed his eyes, leaning back against the warm body behind him. Derek slowly ran his hands over the long scratch marks on Mark's chest and sides, gently pulling at the wounds with his thumb and index finger. Derek moved his mouth over Mark's shoulder—biting and pulling hard at the muscles under the skin with his teeth. Mark forgot about his knee. He felt the brown leather bracelet against his pubic hair as Derek slowly began to stroke his hardening cock. Derek's now-erect penis was pushing into Mark's back. Mark felt socked feet wrap tightly around his ankles, and Derek started to grind into him. Mark could already feel pre-cum on his back. Derek moved his other hand down Mark's left thigh. Mark tensed up.

"Relax," Derek said, biting Mark's ear lobe as he slowly moved his hand over the knee brace.

"Stop," Mark replied, opening his eyes and leaning forward.

"Relax," Derek added, pushing his fingers in between the elastic brace and Mark's skin, feeling the surgical scars.

Mark elbowed Derek out of the way and stood. "I said fucking stop!"

"Chill. Jesus," Derek replied, leaning back while holding his hands up. "I'm sorry."

Mark turned and stared at Derek for a moment. The music stopped between songs, then started up again. Mark turned and limped over to a wicker chair, picking his jeans up off the floor. "I have somewhere to be," Mark replied, hastily pulling his pants on.

"No. Don't. I'm sorry. You told me it was from the war. I shouldn't have... Don't be pissed."

Mark buttoned up his pants, careful not to catch his pubic hairs in the fly. He had to tuck his semi-stiff penis to the side.

"Does it have something to do with Kevin?" he asked. Mark's head snapped up. "You said his name while you were sleeping—you sounded really upset. You were grabbing your knee. Did he do that to you?"

"No," Mark replied flatly, scanning the floor for socks, but finding none.

"An ex-lover from the Army or something?"

"No," Mark replied with increasing annoyance. He grabbed his boots and limped to the opposite wall, leaning his back against it. Mark sighed, dropping the boots upright on the floor. "He was a friend."

Derek paused before responding. "Was a friend? What happened?" He asked carefully. Mark shoved his feet into the boots, not bothering to lace them up or to answer Derek. "Okay. Okay. You don't want to talk about it. But you don't have to leave," Derek said, leaning forward in the bed.

"I've got somewhere to be," Mark repeated, looking down the hallway.

"Listen, sometimes I do stupid shit when I'm stoned, okay?" Mark looked behind the door. "Let me at least give you a ride."

"I'll take the bus," Mark replied, looking behind the dresser.

"You're in the suburbs, hon. The nearest bus stop is miles away."

"I'll walk," Mark replied, looking under the bed.

"With your knee?" Derek asked with concern.

"It's fine," Mark responded, standing there shirtless, scanning the room for the rest of his clothes.

Derek watched Mark for a minute, then crawled out of the bed, smacking the off button on the computer speakers. The silence bounced off the walls. He went over to the closet and pulled out a long-sleeved, red-and-black t-shirt. It read South Carolina Cocks on the front in red letters. The last word was in bold. He tossed it to Mark. "Keep it," Derek said, slumping back down in the bed on his back.

Mark stood for a moment, then pulled the shirt on, then his jacket. He could smell Derek's cologne on the shirt. Mark laced up his boots in silence. A few birds chirped outside.

"I'd give you my number if I didn't think it would be a waste of time," Derek said to the ceiling, his hands behind his head.

Mark buttoned up his jacket. "I told you last night not to touch the scars. That I do remember."

Derek got back out of the bed, quickly walking up to Mark. "I know, I know. I shouldn't have. I just..." Derek reached out and grabbed Mark's hand. "Let me make it up to you, okay? I'll cook breakfast. Do you like omelets? I have fresh mushrooms and spinach in the fridge. I could..." Derek's voice trailed off. "Don't go."

Mark pulled his hand away and picked up his cane, leaning heavily on it. "I told you, I have somewhere to be." Mark paused. "Thanks for the shirt." He turned and left the room.

Derek stood in his socks, watching Mark limp down the hallway. He blinked his gray eyes a few times and turned his head, looking at the alarm clock next to the bed. The front door opened. "Where do you have to be at six o'clock on a Sunday morning?" Derek yelled. The front door slammed shut.

As soon as Erin walked into the bar, her nose reeled from the smell of stale beer, warmed-over coffee, and sweat. Small, opaque windows lined the east wall, filtering out the morning sun, the last remaining traces of light perishing on brick walls painted black. Erin let her eyes adjust to the dark, tucking her coat around her body. The lounge was claustrophobic, a single file of booths running along the wall on one side. A group of men sat in the booth at the back, talking loudly over Madonna's "Vogue," the Material Girl's voice braying out of blown speakers hanging precariously from the dark ceiling. The bar itself sat arm's length from the row of booths. A man with thick, gray hair and a yellow tie sat at the end of the bar, his face inches away from an electronic slot machine. A cherry, a 7, and a joker reflected in his glasses.

Mark sat near the exit, his camouflage jacket draped over a stool. His long-sleeved t-shirt had COCKS in bold, red letters across the back. He was hunched over an open copy of Bertrand Russell's *Why I Am Not a Christian*. His shoulders were sunk, like a sack of stones slung over his back. His cane hung from the edge of the bar, slowly swinging back and forth. Mark turned to Erin, who sat uneasily on a barstool next to him, crossing her arms, careful not to let the sleeves of her wool coat touch the sides of the bar.

"It's a gay bar, not a quarantine. Nobody here but dedicated alkies, broken-down queens, and every now and then, a harmless bum trying to stay warm."

Erin set her leather purse on her lap, the black strap dangling near her ankles.

"It's seven-thirty on a Sunday morning. Is meeting in a bar really necessary?"

"Nope," Mark responded, his eyes back on the open book as he lifted a brown bottle to his lips. "Nothing's really necessary, or even important if you think about it. Significance is chosen, then applied." Mark paused, holding the bottle in front of him. "I think it's important to drink—a lubricant that helps with conversation. Because discourse without alcohol is like fucking someone in the ass without lube."

"Language, Mark."

"I'm only saying. Too much friction—too painful."

Erin closed her eyes and rubbed her temples. The bartender cleared his throat, and she looked up. He stood with his arms twisted tightly across his broad chest. Blue-and-black scales were tattooed along the entire length of his arms, leading to the black jaws of a dragon around his neck, trying to swallow his head.

"A soda, please," Erin said. The bartender looked at Mark and mouthed yeah. Erin turned her head toward Mark, "Why can't we talk over breakfast in a restaurant?" She noticed several bite marks along the side of his neck.

"I hear the bags of pretzels here are excellent. Besides, breakfast is overrated. What great sage declared that breakfast was the most important meal of the day?"

"Mark..."

"Think about all those moronic, clichéd statements we hear every day, all of us assuming they have merit: Every vote counts. The rule of the majority is just. We are all equal. We all have inalienable rights. Life is precious. Everything happens for a reason. God loves you. Breakfast is the most important meal of the day. All steaming piles of manure shoveled into your mind by the blistered hands of uneducated teachers, charlatan preachers, and naive parents." Erin's fingers dug deeper into her temples as Mark continued. "'*The subjective perceiving subjective ideas as objective*,' I read once, as if lying will somehow make it true."

Erin sighed. "It's too early for you to be quoting dead authors of pseudo-philosophy."

"Actually, Mrs. Zuelke—"

"I told you to call me Erin."

"—it was Kevin who wrote that." Erin turned her head. "In one of his journals. Every time the military bombed a village to eliminate insurgents, killing children and old people, Kevin would get pissed and start ranting—especially when he read reports calling dead civilians 'collateral damage.' Every time our convoy returned to base, Kevin would sequester himself in his bunk and write, going through all the pictures he took on the trip—pictures he wasn't really allowed to take in the first place. I had to hide them from officers and nosy sergeants more than a few times." Mark took a pull from his beer. "In fact, they called Kevin's death an 'unfortunate incident,' right? And you go along with it like everybody else."

"You're being unfair. I'm not going along with it—it's why I'm sitting in a gay bar before church."

The bartender returned and threw down a napkin. His scale-covered arms set down a glass of soda. Erin pulled a perfectly-creased twenty from her purse and set it on the mottled bar.

"I'm sorry if I'm being an asshole," Mark replied, "but I can't help it. I have post traumatic stress disorder in conjunction with manic depressive disorder, topped off with a hint of abnormal, homosexual, man-on-man, lovin'-the-cock-instead-of-the-pussy sex disorder."

The bartender shook his head and pushed the bill back toward Erin. "Don't worry about it, Ma'am." He walked down the bar and grabbed a few dirty glasses from a tray, two in each hand. He sunk them into a mountain of dirty soap bubbles in the sink.

"You know that up until 1973, the American Psychiatric Association classified homosexuality as a mental disorder?"

"Yes, Mark. I know that. Even if you hadn't told me a hundred times."

"Treatments included electrical aversion therapy. They would, and in some places still do, show the patient male porn, shocking him in the balls with electrodes if he got hard. There was also covert sensitization where images of dead bodies, decaying animals, feces, or vomit were juxtaposed with pictures of naked males."

"Mark..."

"And my favorite, of course, was drug therapy. They would use apomorphine to induce vomiting while showing sufferers photos of erections. It's kind of like with alcoholics, when they poison their drinks and let them get completely plastered. The alkies spend the rest of the night projectile vomiting. The drinker's mind forever associates that horrible experience with having a cocktail."

Erin was about to respond, but she hesitated when she saw Mark hold up a small flyer. On the front, Erin and Victoria were holding a large American flag like a banner, standing next to each other in front of the Capitol building, gold dome blazing in the sunlight. On the bottom of the flyer, in bright red letters: Help Us Defend America's Defenders!

"You need a new graphic designer. This shit is cheesy as hell. You can tell the flag was Photoshopped in." Mark opened the flyer, examining it briefly before closing it and tossing it on the bar. "The Leviticus Alliance consistently vomits bigotry and intolerance, implying that gays have no ethics. I mean, I don't—but some homos out there are just as morally conscious as you breeders. So don't talk to me about being unfair." Mark reached over and tipped his beer bottle upward, then back down. The empty bottle hit the coaster hard, almost falling over. "If it wasn't for what happened to Kevin, if I hadn't been there in that cell with him, would you even be here—with me—in this shitty bar?"

"Enough, Mark. I've been meeting with you for a year now, and I've—"

"Would you?"

Erin paused for a moment. "No. I wouldn't." Erin leaned forward and took a sip from her soda. It was flat.

The elderly man with the yellow tie walked over to Mark holding two drinks in clear, plastic cups. His eyes were red and his eyelids heavy. "You're older than my dad," Mark laughed. "Fuck off." The elderly man stood for a moment, turned, and walked back to his stool.

Erin watched, concerned, as the elderly man sat back down. She turned back to Mark. "Breeders?"

"Straight people," Mark said, motioning for another beer. The bartender walked over slowly and reached into the refrigerator below the bar. He glared at Mark as he popped off the cap and set the beer down hard, his hand clamped tightly around the bottle, foam rolling down the brown glass neck.

"Five-fifty," the bartender growled at Mark.

Erin reached into her purse and pulled out the same neatly-folded bill from before, the open eye of Andrew Jackson gazing upward. "I've got it," Erin said.

The bartender looked at Erin, then back at Mark. "Two-fifty, Ma'am."

The door opened behind Mark and Erin, and white light gushed into the lounge. Everyone in the bar shielded their eyes. The barkeep quickly made change and walked around the bar. The door shut, and everyone took their hands away from their eyes. An old man wearing a tattered jacket stood near the door, shaking. His body was hunched over and his hands were cupped together, full of coins, a quaking money purse made of old leather. The bartender pushed the old man out the door. Dimes, nickels, and pennies spilled onto the floor.

Mark pulled out his cell phone and flipped it open. "You're going to that rally in November, right? What day is it again?"

"Of course I'm going to be there, Mark," Erin said. "I'm the Director of Operations."

"What the hell does that even mean?" Mark asked, holding down the power button on the phone. It remained off.

"You're fully aware that I'm going to be there, so stop asking obvious questions, trying to make me feel guilty."

"Stupid fucking battery," Mark said to himself.

"Language."

Mark shook his head and snapped the phone shut, shoving it back in his pocket. "I'm not trying to make you feel guilty at all. I just want you to look for me in the crowd. I'll be holding up a big sign that says: Fags Hate God."

"Cute, Mark." Erin stirred the ice cubes in her soda with a thin, red straw. "But I would expect more from you than some mindless witticism—a statement obviously meant to provoke."

"Ah, so will you admit that people provoked by this mindless witticism are equally mindless?"

"You shouldn't judge an entire group of people based on the actions of a few."

"Watch me."

"Not everyone in our organization vomits animosity."

"What about that bitch, Victoria Richman, standing next to you in that flyer?" Mark asked before downing half of his beer. "The diseased mouthpiece of your precious Alliance. You'd think her teeth would rot out from all the shit that rolls off her tongue."

Erin looked over again at Mark. "Please stop using my association with the Alliance as an excuse to lecture and insult me. Isn't that what homosexuals are fighting against? Superficial name-calling? Sweeping generalizations? Have I called you an abomination, Mark? Have I told you that you need to change your sexual preference or tried to convert you or save your soul?"

Mark stared ahead, slowly turning the bottle of beer with his hands. "It's fucking implied."

"Language, Mark. I'm here to listen; that's it. If you'd rather sit there and call me names and taunt me about my dead son, then…"

Erin's words trailed off. Mark remained silent. Ozzy Osborne's "Mama I'm Coming Home" played on the frayed speakers, the Prince of Darkness scratchy and distorted. One of the men in the corner booth slapped the palm of his hand down onto the table, laughing at his own joke, the rest of the table following suit. Erin gathered her purse.

"You ever been to a mountain town called Leadville?" Mark asked, looking straight ahead. "They like to brag about their elevation, like it's some sort of great accomplishment. It's 10,152 feet above sea level. But they'll be quick to tell you it's 10,200 feet."

Erin set her purse back down on the bar.

"Steve Bradford. A single parent of two—my sister and me. My mom died from an infection in her uterus after I was born. It was a C-section, and one of the surgical tools wasn't sterilized or something. Steve never talked about it with me or my sister, never explained why he didn't sue the crap out of the hospital for millions. To make things worse, his in-laws blamed him for her death. Something about a DNR. Steve responded by locking her body up in a mausoleum. Won't let anyone visit—not even her own children. Sis says it's from a broken heart; I say he went bat-shit crazy when she died. Anyway, Steve went on working at the local water-treatment plant. And when he wasn't saving the local trout population from lead poisoning, he worked as a mechanic at a friend's garage. He was gone more than fifty hours a week. But he kept food on the table, the house away from the bank, and himself away from his kids. Even when he was home, he was in the garage, working on some project vehicle."

Mark pulled a cigarette pack from his jacket pocket and shook it—empty. He crushed the pack in his hand and tossed it on the bar. "From what little my sister remembers, Steve rarely stepped foot into a church until my mom died. Overnight, he became obsessed with the Bible, Christianity, the afterlife—of course the afterlife. He made Shannon memorize and recite entire chapters, grounding her for weeks at a time if she got one word wrong. I can't tell you how many Bible drills I did in the kitchen after school. I couldn't eat dinner until I finished. Also, as a veteran, Steve was overly in love with America and American values and how America is the greatest fucking nation on the entire planet—hell, in the entire universe. He'd suck America's cock if he could. He raised the American flag every morning before breakfast, his two children standing in the yard, shaking in our coats from the cold."

Mark took a long drink from his beer.

"Fast forward past a bunch of boring, personal events to when I was fifteen. It was winter, and my sister was, reluctantly, visiting from Denver with her boyfriend. His name was Craig, a college student majoring in... Communications or something. I don't really remember. But I do remember his blond hair and dark eyes—Shannon had great taste. Steve and Sis left to get some lunch, have a little father-daughter time. Craig and I made out on the couch in the living room. I lost my virginity in the shower. My sister never knew we both fucked the same guy."

Erin closed her eyes. "Language. Please?"

"Two years later, there was an accident at the plant. Two workers killed. Safety violations. Accusations. Lawsuits. The plant was closed for weeks. Anyway, that day, Steve came home early. I had skipped school that day to fu—" Mark paused. "—to engage in sexual congress with the co-captain of the football team. Brown hair. Green eyes. He was bent over the side of the couch when my father walked in the front door. Steve ran at me, screaming, swinging so wildly that he never landed a punch. I fell to the floor, trying to cover myself with my hands, yelling *'Dad!'* over and over.

Finally, he stopped and walked down the hall to his bedroom. The football player grabbed his boxers and ran out of the house, his letter jacket and pants still in a pile next to the couch. It was snowing, and there must have been at least six inches of snow in the yard."

Mark laughed, then took another drink. Erin turned on her stool to face him.

"More than a little embarrassed and scared out of my mind, I pulled up my pants and reached down for my shirt. That's when I heard Steve coming back down the hallway—loud, heavy, rapid footsteps. In his right hand, he had his Benelli SuperSport twelve-gauge shotgun. Extended chrome chokes. A-grade walnut stock. I just stood there staring at the gun, shirtless and freezing from the open front door. Steve didn't say a word. He walked right up to me and swung the stock of the shotgun at my head. I still don't know why I didn't move. I didn't even raise my hands to protect my face. The walnut stock broke my nose with ease, like the sound you make when you step on a dry twig. I dropped to the floor, and everything went dark for a few seconds. I opened my watering eyes and looked up, trying to focus. When I wiped the blood and tears away, I saw the hollow end of a black barrel hovering inches from my face. Behind it was Steve, his expression framed in rage. Through clenched teeth, Steve just said, 'Abomination,' and pulled the trigger. Even though the gun only dry-fired, my whole body jerked back. Then he said, 'The shells are in the garage.' He walked out the front door toward the garage, shotgun over his shoulder, and I ran out the back door. That was the last time I ever saw him."

Erin's eyes were locked on Mark's profile. His right hand slowly turned the base of the beer bottle. His left hand was rubbing his bad knee.

"I moved in with Shannon here in Denver. Finished high school. Got a crap job stocking inventory at a warehouse. Went to community college off and on for a few years, but was getting tired of the cold winters. The snow. The ice. It reminded me of Leadville." Mark smiled and leaned back in his chair. "An Army recruiter showed up on campus—my ticket out of Denver. Fittingly, I ended up spending the next couple of years sweating my balls off in the desert. Careful what you fucking wish for, huh?"

Erin sighed. "You never told anyone? In the Army?"

"With the exception of Kevin, no."

"So, how did they find out?"

"Not sure. Some anonymous tip." Mark reached back into his jacket, pulling out a new box of cigarettes. The bartender said, "No smoking," as he walked past Mark and disappeared into a storage room next to the bar.

Mark scraped away the plastic wrap on the pack. "Shortly after I got back to the States, when I was in physical rehab, I was called into a room with the sergeant in charge of the hospital wing and some major I had never met before. Apparently, about a month earlier, the Army had opened an investigation—based on the tip they had received. I had been stuck in that damn hospital for what seemed like years, and my laptop was the only real access I had to the outside world. So, even though my computer was considered private property, the Internet servers I used were government property. They had gone through all my e-mails, the websites I visited—the gay porn was all they needed. And I had a hard drive full of it. Lack of sex leads to a lot—I mean, a lot—of jerkin' off."

Erin closed her eyes and shook her head.

"Celibacy sucks, by the way. Drives people insane—gay or straight. So, once I could actually get out of bed, I used my laptop to hook up with a guy..." Mark looked up, searching his memory. "Red hair with blue eyes. Lucas. Wore expensive cologne. He visited me several times as a 'family friend.' We fucked where we could. Janitor's closet. The bathroom."

Erin cringed. "The bathroom?"

"I was still on crutches. And they were monitoring me constantly." Mark kept tugging at the plastic wrap. It slowly pulled away. "It's not like I could just walk out of the hospital, jump in a taxi and go to his place for dinner and sex." Mark shook his head. "And I wasn't the only one with a 'family friend.' The straight guys just didn't have to be so secretive about it."

"So, someone saw you with Lucas?"

"Maybe. Who knows?" Mark pulled the plastic wrap from the cigarette pack, tossing it on the bar. "Anyway, they had all this evidence laid out on a table. Had I been screwing some blond bimbo in the bathroom, I probably would have gotten a slap on the wrist and a pat on the back. Maybe a month of remedial training and some lost pay. But instead, the major leaned forward and asked me outright if I was gay. I could tell he wanted me to say yes. Probably one of your supporters. So I told him. I told him everything. Even the conjugal visits. I was tired of lying to everyone." Mark took a drink, then began slapping the top of the cigarette pack against the palm of his hand. Erin remained quiet. "Keep in mind I wasn't the only one downloading porn. But downloading homosexual porn using government servers, along with homosexual sex in the base hospital, landed me an OTH Discharge—Other Than Honorable. Homosexual acts on base are considered 'aggravating factors' in a DADT discharge. Probably would have been a General Discharge if it wasn't for that asshole major. Of course, physical therapy was terminated once I was a civilian. No more mental health support either, not that the Army was any good at that. No more meds either. And with an OTH discharge, disability and medical benefits are cut." Mark took a drink. "At least I got to keep the stupid fucking cane."

"You're just cut off?"

"I can apply for a waiver through the VA Regional Office." Mark opened the pack and pulled out a single cigarette. "I would probably even get approved, being a former POW."

"So why don't you—"

"Apply?" Mark interrupted. "If the military is willing to kick out a POW for being a faggot—then fuck 'em!" A few of the men in the booth at the end of the bar looked over. Mark lit the cigarette; the tip glowed bright orange. "Fighter pilots, Arabic and Farsi translators, platoon leaders who took fire in the streets of Baghdad while rescuing civilians. All of them shoved out. All of them made irrelevant because of some homophobic compromise made into law—thank you, President Clinton." He let the lighter fall onto the bar with a loud clatter. The men in the booth went back to talking.

"But aren't the government and the military moving to repeal—"

"Too little, too late for the fourteen thousand military personal axed under Don't Ask, Don't Tell. No credit for time served. No reparations. Maybe we'll all get an apology letter or something signed by the President. I could use it to wipe my ass." Mark looked over at Erin. "By the way, your son didn't give a shit that I suck cock. I guess the whole God thing didn't rub off on him."

Erin turned forward. "What made you trust him?" she asked.

"Don't know. Maybe it was because he got into more trouble in the Army than I did—taking those damn pictures."

"Mark." Erin turned her head. "What happened out there in the desert? What happened in that cell?"

Mark kept his gaze forward. "You know that cigarettes are called fags in England?" He inhaled. "I do love to suck the butt of a good fag."

Erin reached forward, but Mark knocked her hand away. He blew out a cloud of smoke that surged across the bar. "Fuck the desert—that cell. Fuck the Army. Fuck Steve." Mark looked over at Erin. "Fuck your Alliance. And most of all—fuck your God."

Two large hands at the ends of tattooed arms landed from behind like vices on Mark's shoulders, lifting him up off the stool.

"Out!" The bartender yelled into Mark's ear.

The cigarette fell out of Mark's mouth as he was yanked away from the bar, the stool crashing to the floor. Mark asked if he could take his beer with him as he was dragged toward the exit. In a flash of blinding white light, the door burst open. The denizens covered their eyes. In one fluid motion, the bartender chucked Mark onto the sidewalk. The metal door slammed shut. The denizens dropped their hands. The elderly man with the yellow tie mumbled asshole to himself. Erin wiped her face with a balled-up napkin, set some money on the bar, and pushed her stool back. She stood and stuffed Mark's book into her purse and grabbed his coat and cane. The bartender crushed the still-burning cigarette under his foot, kicking it into the corner.

"Have a good day, Ma'am," he said to Erin with a slight nod as she walked past him to the exit.

The sun was tucked neatly away behind a blanket of white stretching from horizon to horizon. It took a few minutes for Erin's eyes to adjust to the dull light as she scanned the empty street. It was still early, and all the businesses were closed. A raven landed on the bare branch of a large Boxelder planted next to the sidewalk. Erin looked up when it cawed. A delivery truck drove by, kicking up black gutter slush onto her shoes. Erin stomped her feet and walked to the parking lot behind the bar, each breath a puff of white. She shivered and pulled on her gloves, Mark's cane and coat under her arm. Her purse dangled on her shoulder as she took out her keys. They jingled in her hand, and she tugged her green, wool coat tightly around her body, tapping the residual slush from her shoes on the asphalt. It was quiet outside the bar, and her footsteps echoed off the brick walls of the tavern. A few flakes of snow fell to the ground. She smiled a bit when she saw someone leaning against her car—the only car in the parking lot.

Erin froze.

The man had a black wool mask pulled over his head, and he wore a black leather jacket that reached the tops of his boots. The masked man's head jerked up as Erin ran back toward the bar. The cane fell with a clatter along with Mark's coat, followed by her purse and her keys. She tripped over an island of snow, but kept her balance. Erin was almost to the back door of the bar when an arm clamped tightly around her waist, lifting her feet from the ground. He wrapped his other hand around her mouth, crushing her lips against her teeth. Erin kicked at his shins, struggling for air. She desperately swung her elbows hard and landed a blow to the left side of his face. The masked man cursed and threw her down, landing on top of her and crushing her. She tasted blood mixed with dirty snow. His warm breath crawled onto the back of her neck. She started to scream, but the attacker reached around and clamped his arm around her throat; her eyes bulged, struggling for air. She clawed at his arm, her fingers slipping off the cold, leather sleeve. He whispered in her ear.

"I warned you, but you ignored me—you ignorant cunt. If you show up at that rally and say one word, I'll cut your fucking tongue out and nail it to the stage. I'll tie you to a goddamn stake and watch as the rest of us—yes, there are more—stone you to death… just like all the whores in your Bible."

The masked man grabbed Erin's long, black hair and pulled her head back, stretching her neck. "I dare you to scream," he said as he removed his arm from around Erin's throat.

Erin coughed as she gasped for air. She saw the flash of a blade. The cold, sharp metal pushed up against her reddened neck. Erin closed her mouth and her eyes.

"That's what I thought, ya bitch," the masked man said right before he flung Erin's head forward, smacking her forehead hard against the asphalt. He pulled her head back up by the hair and slammed it down again. Warm blood stung Erin's eyes; broken teeth fell forward like dominoes against the back of her closed lips.

Suddenly, he let go of her hair. The knife clattered on the asphalt as the weight of the attacker was flung from her body. Somewhere above her, a beer bottle shattered. The attacker yelped in pain. Erin gagged on her own front teeth, coughing violently. Mark stood with his back to her, holding his cane in one hand and a broken beer bottle in the other. Mark brought the cane over his shoulder like a bat. The attacker stood with a large gash running down the side of his face, blood soaking the wool mask. Mark swung the cane. It broke in half when it struck the assailant's skull, a loud crack echoing off the walls of the bar. Mark kicked him in the abdomen, and the attacker stumbled back and fell to the ground, holding his stomach. Mark dropped the broken bottle. It fell into an island of snow without a sound, speckling it in red. Mark leaned over and yanked the mask off. He spat in the attacker's face, "Fucking coward," kicking him in the ribs with each syllable. Erin pulled herself up from the ground, but the parking lot began to spin and tilt and lean; she reached for Mark, clamping down hard on his arm to pull him back.

Mark looked over his shoulder and dropped the broken cane. He helped Erin to the back door of the bar, pulling on the latch; it was locked. He banged hard with his fist and yelled for help, but there was no answer. Erin lurched forward and threw up, her bile running down the brick wall and melting the snow. Mark set her down gently against the wall.

"Erin? Erin!" Mark examined her head wounds. "Stay with me! Don't fall asleep!"

She only mumbled out a few incoherent words for a reply. Her body went slack. The attacker lay on the ground nearby, moaning and rocking from side to side while slowly kicking his black boots in the red snow. Erin closed her eyes.

The pain in her skull receded into a deafening silence and Erin was alone and Mark was gone and the attacker was gone as was her car in the parking lot and the parking lot itself and even the buildings and all the trees and the dirty snow-covered streets and the smell of blood and vomit all quietly faded away and Erin found herself standing on an endless flat field full of tall dead grass sticking out of a foot of freshly fallen snow with stalks bending to an unseen bitter breeze and only a few yards away Erin saw her son standing in his pressed Army dress uniform at the edge of a large precipice then Erin screamed her son's name and ran toward Kevin and he beamed back at his mother with that familiar smile and said he was sorry for leaving but he didn't have a choice and he snapped to attention and turned around sharply so that he was now facing the edge of the cliff with his toes in polished shoes sticking over the ledge and Erin tried to run faster but fell as she tried to pick up her legs through the deep powdery snow and she kept screaming his name and crawling forward on her hands and knees as tears ran hot down her cold cheeks and her fingers went numb from the snow and when she finally reached her son she leapt forward with open arms but Kevin's body dissolved into millions of snowflakes that scattered and tumbled and spun over the cavernous ravine leaving Erin in shock and silence as momentum carried her body forward into the mouth of the gorge and she felt the sudden rush of air as she plummeted into the void with the walls of the chasm rushing past her and consuming her until her vision went white and she snapped her eyes open and Mark was crouched over her with her cell phone in one hand holding his balled up shirt against her head with the other and Mark asked Erin what her name was and she shook her head as the pain flooded back into her skull and she heard Mark yell fucking battery as he shook her cell phone and Erin whispered back a single word: *Language.*

[VIII]

[1990]

"Vicky? Vicky, honey? Where are you?"

"Please stop calling me that, Mother," Victoria replied, walking into the small room, closing the door behind her.

"There you are, dear," Violet replied, staring out a window opposite the door. "I was worried."

"I was only at the cafeteria a few minutes," Victoria replied, unsuccessfully trying to hide her frustration. She was holding a plastic bowl of oatmeal. The white handle of a plastic spoon stuck out of the top. Steam rose from the surface. Victoria stopped. "What are you looking at?"

"Tommy used to run off all the time, remember?" Violet asked, her voice scratchy and uncertain. Her eyes red and swollen. The left side of her face was slack. "He'd be gone all day. Playing in the park with his friends. Worried his mother to death, that son of mine."

Victoria turned and set the oatmeal down on a small counter behind her. She stirred it with the plastic spoon. "Yes, Mom. I remember."

"Where is your little brother anyway?" Violet asked, sitting up in her wicker rocking chair and turning her head back toward the window. "It's almost time for supper. He should be back by now. The blue-and-white plaid blanket draped over her knees fell to the floor. Victoria sighed.

"It's morning, Mother," Victoria replied, gathering the blanket and folding it again. "And Tommy's not out there."

Violet squinted, holding her gaze on the eastern horizon. The other three white walls were bare, with the exception of a few crayon drawings framed and mounted to the wall opposite the window. There was a television in one corner with the volume turned down low—hushed voices and ambivalent, made-up faces reporting the latest tragedies around the world. Near the door, a short kitchen counter with a small sink ran along the rest of the wall. A few cupboards hung above, filled with plastic plates, bowls, and cups. The floor was linoleum, making it easy for the orderlies to clean up any messes. There was no stove for Violet to accidentally burn herself. No set of knives for Violet to accidentally cut herself. No uncovered outlet for Violet to accidentally electrocute herself. A small, black refrigerator hummed at the end of the counter. It held a few small boxes of orange juice and a bottle of water. An open box of cheese crackers sat on top.

"It's not safe out there after dark," Violet said. "You should go look for him, Vicky. Make sure he's okay. He could be getting into trouble with those gangs."

Victoria reached up and set her hand gently on Violet's shoulder, pulling her back into the rocking chair. "I said he's not out there, Mother. And Tommy was never in any gangs—you know that."

"Of course I do, Vicky. But they were always after him, trying to get his lunch money. I told him to hide it in his shoe, that way..." Violet's eyebrows pinched together as she looked down at her daughter. "Not out there? What do you mean?" Violet craned her head toward a doorway next to the window that led into a bedroom. She then turned her head toward the adjacent bathroom.

"Mother," Victoria said softly as she gently placed the blanket back onto her mother's legs, smoothing it out, "Tommy's gone, remember?"

"He's what?" Violet replied, shaking her head. "Nonsense. It was only a few minutes ago he went outside to play with his friends. He told me how much he loves his mother and kissed me on the forehead. But he didn't have his coat on, again." Violet shook her head. "I told him I don't know how many times to wear his coat outside—he'll catch an awful cold. Happens every winter. He..." Violet's voice trailed off.

Victoria gently squeezed her mother's wrinkled hand. "Mother, Tommy has been gone for more than twenty years."

Violet blinked a few times. Her hand shot to her forehead. "Oh, God. I'm so sorry, Vicky. I remember now."

"Nothing to be sorry about," Victoria replied, patting her mother's hand.

"My precious Tommy... that dreadful bus accident. All those children." Tears welled up in her eyes. "He was such a beautiful, gifted boy, Vicky."

Victoria closed her eyes. "No, Mother. That was your younger brother, Victor." Violet stared at her daughter blankly. "Victor died in a bus accident when he was eight. Tommy died when... when he was twelve."

"It wasn't a bus accident? But I remember so clearly."

"He was walking home from the science fair, remember?"

"Oh, yes. His science project! You should have seen it, Vicky. Mr. Thomason said Tommy's project was the best in the entire class." She tilted her head. "Something to do with bugs."

"He was studying ants and fungi, Mother." Victoria continued to run her hands across the blanket, smoothing out wrinkles no longer there. "He was cataloging their behaviors. Documenting their social structure and how they were affected by different types of fungi. I drove him to the park near the house to gather specimens."

"Ants?" Violet asked. "No, dear. It was spiders; I'm sure of it. Tommy collected spiders from the backyard and that cellar your father never cleaned." Violet lowered her head, looking at her daughter through the tops of her eyes. "You should have helped him with that science project, young lady. Tommy could have won first place. But you weren't even there that day. Always too busy to be a good sister."

Victoria sighed, squeezing the back of her neck. "I did help him, remember? And Tommy did win first place. The trophy is sitting on the dresser in your bedroom."

"You never supported your little brother like you should have," Violet added, looking at Victoria disapprovingly. "He was such a good, little boy, my Tommy." Victoria stood, biting her lower lip. "I told you to walk your brother to and from school every day," Violet snapped, looking straight ahead. "But you never listened to me... or your father for that matter." Victoria turned and set her hands on the counter, closing her eyes. "He disappeared on his way back from the science fair," Violet said quietly.

"Yes, Mother. I remember." Victoria reached over and grabbed a small, plastic shaker full of cinnamon that sat next to the sink. She sprinkled the spice into the bowl of oatmeal as she stirred it with the plastic spoon. "It's time for your breakfast."

Violet smiled. "Could you add some cinnamon to my oatmeal, honey? I can never eat oatmeal without cinnamon. It tastes too bland without it."

Victoria turned and opened a folding chair leaning against the wall behind the door. She pulled it up close to her mother. Victoria set a cloth napkin on her mother's knee and tucked another one into her mother's blouse. She sat in the chair, the warm bowl cradled in her hands. She spooned out a glob of oatmeal and began blowing on it.

"Mother," Victoria said between breaths.

Violet turned her head, smiled and leaned forward, taking the bite of oatmeal. Victoria cleaned the corners of Violet's mouth with the spoon. She waited until her mother swallowed before she spooned up some more.

"There's going to be a recital in the foyer today after lunch," Victoria said, wiping her mother's chin. "You should go. Let's get you out of this room for a few hours."

Violet shook her head. "Oh no, dear, I don't like loud music. It hurts these old ears."

"It's only a piano. Mrs. Mathis' granddaughter is going to play Beethoven for all the residents."

"Beethoven?"

"You once told me that 'Moonlight Sonata' was the greatest piece ever written for the piano."

Violet's eyes opened wide, nodding her head. "Ah, yes. *'Quasi una fantasia.'* C sharp minor. Did you know that the name 'Moonlight Sonata' was actually added after Beethoven's death? The music critic Ludwig Rellstab is responsible for its famous nomenclature." Victoria acted as if she didn't already know, as if she hadn't heard the story twice yesterday and three times the day before, nodding her head with a slight look of surprise. Violet continued, as if she were speaking to a college class. "Although the song is not a difficult piece from a technical standpoint, it's able to summon and cultivate deep emotions in the hearts of people from all cultures and of all ages. And what emotions?" She leaned forward with a smile. "The poor man dedicated the composition to Countess Giulietta Guicciardi—the woman who broke his heart."

Victoria nodded her head again, wondering how long her mother's sudden articulation would last. Violet held her hands out in front of her, her long crooked fingers moving in the air as if she were playing the song.

"The first movement is what most people are most familiar with— *adagio sostenuto*. It starts with a Phrygian progression of perpetual triplets coupled with a polyrhythmic motif." Violet closed her eyes. "It was written in 1801. Imagine that. Music that was composed almost two hundred years ago, on another continent, still possessing the power to evoke emotion—a sense of longing. A universal need for connectedness, and the sadness that follows when that need goes unfulfilled."

Victoria watched her mother play the song silently on an invisible piano, Violet humming the rest of the song. A lawyer on television asked if they'd ever been hurt in a car accident. The bowl of oatmeal grew cold.

Violet's hands dropped to her lap when she finished. She was still for a moment, then opened her eyes and turned her head. "Vicky!" she exclaimed with a smile, her eyes wide and bright. "It's so good to see you." Violet leaned forward, struggling to hug her daughter, her left arm stiff, resting on Victoria's shoulder. "When did you get here? I was practicing for my next performance. My students don't leave me time to practice."

Victoria dug her head into Violet's shoulder, then pulled away. "I just got here, Mother."

"You should visit your poor mother more often. I hardly see you anymore."

Victoria turned and set the half-empty bowl of oatmeal on the counter behind her. "I know. I'm very busy with the Alliance."

"The Alliance?"

"I started a non-profit foundation in Denver," Victoria continued, exhausted from telling her the same story for the tenth time that week. "A friend of mine named Erin is helping me get it on its feet. You met her last Christmas. We're—"

"Don't be silly, Vicky. It's not nice to lie to your poor mother about why you don't visit. You can tell me you're busy with other things and leave it at that. Besides, how can you run a foundation in Denver? That's too far away from Boston. Who will keep an eye on Tommy if you're in Denver?"

Victoria was about to respond, but didn't. She just stood, turned, and emptied the rest of the cold oatmeal into the trash. She set the bowl into the sink and turned on the water. "Yes, Denver is very far away," Victoria said to the wall in front of her.

Violet's attention went to the television. There was a commercial advertising the power of color-safe bleach—white sheets hanging from a clothesline over a bright green field, the sun shining through the cloth. "You have no business being in Denver when your brother and I are here in Boston, Vicky. Tommy sees me at least once a week. He makes the time to see me."

Victoria dropped her head, the water still running. Steam from the hot water rolled over a red emergency call box above the sink.

"He's a smart boy. You know he's working on a science experiment with spiders, don't you? You should take him to Ipswich River. He'd find some great spiders along the bank for sure."

"I'm sure he would," Victoria responded.

"And you should walk him to school, dear. It's dangerous for him to be out by himself at his age."

Victoria smacked down the handle to the faucet, turned, and leaned against the counter. Her mother stared out the window. The television was back to painted faces talking about a country called Kuwait and the threat of an invasion by a dictator named Saddam.

"I've got to fly back to Denver tonight, Mother. I won't be back for a while."

"Denver?" Violet responded, still looking out the window. "Why are you going to Denver?"

"I moved there years ago, Mother. I told you before…" Victoria paused, turning away and talking to the wall. "I sold the bookstore."

"Oh, yes. The Levity Alliance."

"Leviticus Alliance," she responded flatly. "And this isn't working."

"What is it that you do there, dear? I hope you wear your jacket when you're outside. These Boston winters get very cold."

Victoria's grip on the sink tightened. She jumped when a large mobile phone on the counter began to ring. It was as big as a brick, the battery larger than the phone itself. A simple electronic chirping filled the small room. Violet closed her eyes and began humming "Moonlight Sonata."

"What is it?" Victoria asked, wiping her face with a napkin.

"Victoria? It's Erin."

"I thought I told you not to call me this week—no matter what," Victoria said forcefully but quietly into the phone, keeping her back turned to her mother. "Calls on this phone are very expensive."

"Is that Tommy you're talking to?" Violet asked. "Tell him to come home and give his mother a hug."

Victoria walked past Violet into the bathroom, shutting the door slightly before sitting on a plastic stool with metal legs that sat in the bathtub. The name Richman was written on the shampoo and conditioner bottles with a black marker. She leaned her head forward against the metal railing along the white walls of the bathroom.

"I know, I know," replied Erin over the phone, her voice breaking up momentarily. "I'm really sorry to be calling you on your vacation. In fact,

I'm surprised I got through. I was going to leave a message with the hotel there in New York, but they didn't have you registered."

"I'm not," Victoria replied. "Now, what is it?"

There was a short pause. "There's a gentlemen here who insists on speaking with you right away. He was in the office all day yesterday and the day before; he's here again this morning pacing back and forth in the waiting room. I've stalled him as much as I can. He tells me it's extremely urgent he speak to you, and that it can't wait."

"Erin, you're the co-founder of this organization."

"I know. But I—"

"Which means you're also the boss. You need to tell whoever this guy is that he can talk to you or he can leave. Simple as that."

"If it was that simple, I wouldn't have called you."

"It is that simple, Erin. He's probably from the ALCU or the URC, trying to...wait. He's in the office? No one even knows about the Alliance yet, much less where it's located. How did he—"

"Victoria," Erin interrupted. "He says he wants to talk to you about your brother."

Victoria's head shot up. "What?"

"Didn't you tell me your brother ran away when he was twelve?"

Victoria stood quickly, knocking the stool over as she walked out of the bathroom. Violet jumped.

"Oh, my goodness, Vicky. You scared me," Violet said, holding her hands to her chest. "Where did you come from? I didn't see you come in." Violet was staring into the bathroom, eyes full of worry.

Victoria held the phone away from her mouth, covering the large mouthpiece with her hand. "I'll be right back, Mother."

Violet nodded, her face still fearful. "Okay, dear." She tried to get her daughter's attention. "Could you pick up some oatmeal at the store? I haven't eaten all day."

Victoria nodded her head. "Sure, Mother."

"And see if they have some cinnamon, dear. I can't eat my oatmeal without cinnamon."

"I will. I'll be right back." Victoria left the room and closed the door gently. "What the hell does he want to talk about?" Victoria yelled into her phone as she moved down the hall past two nurses.

"I'm not sure," Erin replied apprehensively. "He said he knows what really happened to Tommy." Victoria stopped. "Do you know what he's talking about?" Erin asked.

"Listen to me carefully. I want you to hang up the phone and call the security desk immediately. Do not talk to him. Do not give him any statements. Have security remove him from the building."

"Victoria, what's going on?"

"Call the police if you have to. Just get him out of that office."

The nurses stopped talking with each other and were looking in Victoria's direction.

"And if he tries to come back again, have him arrested for trespassing. Did they install the security cameras in the waiting area yet?"

"Not until next week. We don't even have any furniture in the waiting room. Victoria, is he a reporter or something? I don't think—"

"Get. Him. Out of there. You're the boss, remember? Get it done."

"Okay. Consider it done," replied Erin. "When do you get back from—"

Victoria hit the very large END button. She stood silently for a moment, shaking. She then screamed and threw the cell phone, which smacked the opposite wall and exploded. One of the nurses walked forward, then hesitated as Victoria dropped to her knees and continued to scream. Several residents opened their doors, including Violet. One of the nurses picked up a white phone mounted to the wall. Violet asked the other nurse what all the commotion was about. The nurse nodded toward Victoria.

"Oh dear," said Violet, looking down the hallway. Victoria was now quiet. "That's my daughter. I'm sorry. Vicky gets so terribly upset." She looked back at the nurse. "I'm very proud of her. She runs a bookstore, you see. But it's very stressful, the poor thing. Takes up all of her time. She can't even visit her lonely mother." Violet walked toward her daughter, the cracked skin of her bare feet scraping along the linoleum floor. Her right hand shook as she struggled to grip the railing. Two orderlies came running around the corner, heavy keys jingling from their belts. The nurse on the phone motioned for them to wait. Violet shuffled forward and stopped, setting a wrinkled hand on Victoria's shaking shoulder to keep her balance.

"Vicky? Vicky, are you okay, dear?"

Victoria's head dropped further. She reached up without looking and set her hand on top of her mother's. "I'm fine, Mother," Victoria said to the floor.

"You're worrying me," Violet added, now frightened.

Victoria turned her head and saw that Violet's eyes were red and tearful. "No. No, it's okay, Mother. Don't be upset." Victoria stood, holding her mother's arm. "Let's go back to your room," she added as she wiped away a few tears from her mother's cheeks, reassuring her with small pats on Violet's curved back. "You can catch a nap before the piano recital today."

"Recital? There's a recital today?" Violet asked, her steps quickening toward her room. The residents remained in the doorways, watching.

"Yes, Mother. Beethoven."

"Oh, I have the perfect dress. Something your father bought me years ago. Did you know that Beethoven dedicated his most popular composition to a young woman?"

Victoria looked up and saw the nurses leaving the hallway. "What was her name?"

"Countess Giulietta Guicciardi. She was one of his pupils."

Victoria nodded as she led her mother back into the room. A few minutes later, Victoria returned to speak to the young orderly shoveling up the remains of Victoria's phone into a metal dustpan, dumping the contents into a small trash bag.

"I must apologize for my behavior earlier," Victoria said. "I hope I didn't disturb the residents too much."

"No worries, ma'am," the orderly shrugged, smacking his gum. Headphones hung from his neck, and he spoke without looking at her.

"Well, as a Christian, I do worry about how one might interpret such ghastly behavior. I've seen you in the chapel and I didn't—"

"It's fine, Ma'am."

Victoria nodded her head. "Thank you for cleaning up my mess. Do you know if Doctor Bennett is in?"

The orderly grabbed the broom leaning against the wall. Kurt Cobain sung quietly out of headphones as he shrugged his shoulders. "Don't know." He pointed behind him. "But his office is down the hall, near the entrance." The orderly slid his music back over his ears.

"Thank you kindly for your help," Victoria said. She handed him a small tract: Do You Have Life Insurance? There was a Bible verse beneath the question, John 3:16, and a line drawing of a cross at the bottom. "God bless," Victoria said as she walked down the hallway. For the first time, the orderly looked up. He shook his head, turning up the volume to Kurt's singing before shoving the tract into the trash bag and whispering wacko to himself.

The long hallway was well lit, generic pictures of sunsets and blue lakes and open fields framed and mounted to the walls. Victoria pulled her long blond hair back into a ponytail as she walked, passing an elderly woman in a white bathrobe and blue slippers. The woman mumbled to herself as she stared at her feet. Victoria could hear muffled applause from a game show behind one of the closed doors. Someone in another room coughed violently.

Victoria walked into the doctor's empty waiting room, past the young, female assistant slowly typing on a large computer that took up half the desk. She stood as Victoria walked by. "Excuse me. Excuse me, ma'am. You can't go in there."

"Family friend," Victoria said without looking back, opening the door to Dr. Bennett's office. The doctor was on the phone. His eyes shot up, looking over his glasses at Victoria's abrupt entrance, followed by the assistant.

"I'm sorry, Doctor," the assistant exclaimed with a worried look. "She just barged in—"

The doctor sighed. "Yes, she just walked in," he said into the phone. "As I said, everything is fine. Get everyone back into their rooms." He hung up and nodded at his assistant. "It's okay, Cameron."

Cameron folded her arms and looked at Victoria, but Victoria stared straight ahead. Cameron walked out, closing the door behind her.

"My mother needs to be moved," Victoria said.

"How many times must we have this conversation?" the doctor asked, motioning for Victoria to sit as he stood.

"The window faces east. The window in the bedroom of her old house faced west—it confuses her."

"Victoria, sit," the doctor said forcefully, pointing again with his open palm at one of the two polyester chairs in front of his desk.

Victoria squeezed her hands, hesitated, then reluctantly took a chair.

"Water?" the doctor asked as he walked over to the corner of his office, opening a small refrigerator in a cabinet.

"Bottled, please. And a glass. No ice."

"Of course." The doctor shook his head. "So, how have you been? It was only... what... yesterday when I last saw you?"

"We need to find her a bigger room with a window that faces west. And it needs to be carpeted this time. The linoleum floors make her think she's sleeping in a hospital."

"She is sleeping in a hospital." Victoria's head shot up. "An assisted living facility surrounded by nurses and orderlies. The sooner you come to realize—"

"If I wasn't a God fearing-woman, Philip, I would..." Victoria's voice trailed off.

The doctor sighed and walked over to the front of the desk, setting down an empty glass and an unopened bottle of water in front of her. "Curse at me? Call me names like you did when we were kids?" Victoria pursed her lips.

Philip leaned back against the front of his desk, folding his arms across his chest. He took a long breath. "I was on the phone with one of the nurses. She told me what happened."

Victoria reached forward and grabbed the bottle, unscrewing the cap. "My mother is unhappy."

"So are you." Victoria didn't respond. Philip leaned down. "Your mother has had three mini-strokes in the past sixteen months, resulting in multi-infarct dementia. She's unhappy because her brain has been permanently damaged and she's no longer independent, not because her room isn't big enough. She gets confused because of memory loss, not because her window faces east."

"The damage is not permanent," Victoria replied as she filled the glass with water, taking a few sips to get rid of the lump in her throat.

Philip stood and walked over to the other side of his desk. "Sections of her brain tissue have been destroyed by blood vessel blockages. There's no way of repairing that."

"You don't know that for sure."

"Yes, I do. I also know that there's a strong possibility that it will happen again, despite any precautions we may take."

Victoria took another drink from her glass. "Well, you keep faith in medical science, and I'll keep faith in God, Doctor."

"We're back to being formal now, are we, Miss Richman?"

Victoria looked up from her glass. "How are the wife and kids, by the way?"

"Don't."

"Have you told your daughter yet that you got married because of her?"

"Okay." Philip sat down in the large, plush chair behind his desk, tossing his glasses on the desk. Victoria kept her eyes forward. "Every time I tell you what you don't want to hear, you come at me with these tired personal attacks."

"Perhaps you should speak to God about your iniquities," Victoria responded, adding more water to her glass.

"I've known you too long to take you seriously when it comes to belief in God."

"If you sought forgiveness for past sins, then perhaps our conversations wouldn't make you so uncomfortable, Philip."

Philip set his elbows on the desk and folded his hands. "I'm not having this conversation with you—again. You want to talk about uncomfortable conversations? How about I tell you to quit bringing up Tommy with your mother."

Victoria's eyes grew wide. "You know better than anyone what—"

"The nurse heard you screaming his name in the hallway. What happened?"

"That's none of your concern," Victoria replied.

"True. But the welfare of your mother is my concern, as is the welfare of all of the residents under my charge—half of whom you scared senseless this morning. And this is not your first outburst. There are nurses who want you banned from the residence."

"Well, they'll just have to learn to deal with my little outbursts," Victoria said, her voice starting to break. She took another drink of water. Philip leaned back and waited. Victoria kept her eyes forward as she spoke. "There was another reporter in the office this morning—asking about him."

"Ah, I see."

"They're not going to let this go. I've gotten a lot of attention since I started the Alliance."

"I've heard. And they're going to want a statement from you about what happened to Tommy." Victoria quietly set the glass down on the desk. "I'm sure you already know," continued the doctor, "that some will accuse you of starting the Alliance because of what happened to him."

"The truth doesn't matter to those people," Victoria replied. "They only want to smear anyone who disagrees with them, anyone who takes a stand against their propaganda."

"Personally, I think you're crazy to go through with this Alliance business." Victoria looked up. "But your craziness is why I left you in the first place," Philip added, closing his eyes and squeezing the bridge of his nose. "Along with the damn stubbornness." He looked at Victoria. "And if they're digging up information about Tommy, it's only a matter of time before they find out about us."

Victoria narrowed her eyes. "It won't come up, Philip. It was more than twenty years ago. We were teenagers."

"You're going to have to accept that as a possibility, too."

"They won't find out. The hospital doesn't even exist anymore. Any medical record is—"

"Listen. Bottom line. You're mother suffers from memory loss—loss, Victoria. Every time you bring up Tommy, every time you try to remind her of what happened to him, she relives that event—as if it happened yesterday."

"She needs to remember, Philip. Maybe, if I can jog her memory with an emotional event, she'll—"

"Jesus, Victoria. Listen to yourself. Do you remember what happened to you? I was at your house when the police came knocking on the door to tell your mother they found the body."

"Stop."

"You locked yourself up in your bedroom for days. Then, when the autopsy showed evidence of sexual trauma, you—"

"I said stop."

Philip paused, then continued. "And then they couldn't find the guy who did it. My parents and I took turns watching you so you wouldn't hurt yourself—your mother just sat in the living room; she couldn't even speak." Philip leaned forward. "Violet is a strong woman, but bringing up Tommy's molestation and death isn't going to bring back the person she was."

Victoria picked up the glass and threw it at the wall behind Philip. It shattered and fell in pieces to the carpeted floor. "I said stop!"

Silence. A knock at the door.

"It's fine, Cameron," Philip called out, just before lowering his voice. "That, right there, is what you're putting Violet through every time you bring Tommy up."

Victoria stood up. "You're a horrible, evil person. I can't believe I ever agreed to have you care for her."

"Throw all the glasses at me you want. Call me all the names you want. I have an obligation to my patients for their wellbeing... and your persistence in trying to jog her memory is not helping her—or you."

Victoria took in a deep breath, closed her eyes. Her voice became calm and collected. "I'm not listening to a man who's been divorced twice and is probably screwing his secretary."

Philip leaned back, bringing his folded hands to his chin. "There you go again."

"I'm taking my mother away from you... away from a prideful man who mocks God with his sexual proclivities."

"Your mother is cared for *pro bono*, Victoria. A personal favor for all she's done for me and my family. My daughter got into Juilliard because of her." Philip shook his head. "And I know for a fact you can't afford to put her anywhere else, especially with all your assets tied up in this ludicrous Alliance of yours."

"*Leviticus* Alliance. And I'm sorry if you find God's Law ludicrous."

"I read and follow same Bible you do, Victoria. What you're doing has nothing to do with God's law."

"I can't believe you would defend those homosexuals."

Philip sighed. "Your mother stays here, and you're going to stop bringing up your brother."

"An adulterer who is nothing more than a hypocr—"

"We're done here," Philip said, opening up a folder that sat on his desk. He donned his glasses, adding, "I have work to do."

Victoria turned toward the door. She opened the door slightly, then slammed it shut. "You'll be sure one of the nurses gets her to the recital today?" Victoria asked, her back to him.

Philip began scribbling his name on a stack of forms. "I'll be sure to seat her in the front row, as always." Victoria opened the door. But before she walked out, the doctor called out her name. Victoria stopped. "One last thing," Philip said, closing the folder on his desk and reaching for another one. "The next time you want to speak with me about your mother, you make an appointment with Cameron like everyone else."

"So, I'll just call your house when the wife is away?" Victoria asked before she walked out, the door shutting behind her. Cameron sat behind her desk, letting the phone ring as she eyed Victoria.

"God bless," Victoria said with a smile. She walked back down the hall to Violet's room. The same elderly woman was standing in the hallway, mumbling to her feet. One of the nurses was standing next to her, trying to coax her back into her room. When Victoria opened the door to Violet's room, her mother was out of bed, sitting in the rocking chair and pretending to play the piano, her crooked fingers moving in the air.

"Mother," Victoria said, kneeling down next to Violet. "I have to go now. I have to fly back to Denver. But I'll be back next month." Violet kept her eyes closed, humming to herself. "Mother," Victoria said more forcefully.

Violet opened her eyes and turned her head. "Well, hello, little girl," she said. "Are you here for a lesson?"

Victoria grabbed her mother's arm. "It's me, Mother. Victoria."

"I'm afraid I only give piano lessons by appointment." Violet turned away from Victoria, staring into the bathroom, then into the bedroom. "You need to speak with my daughter first. She can set up a weekly time for lessons. Vicky!" Violet said toward the empty bedroom. "We have a young lady here who would like to set up a time for some lessons." Violet turned toward Victoria. "Now, you must be a very disciplined player to be one of my students. I expect you to practice every day. I do not tolerate slothfulness."

Victoria stood. "I know." She turned and used a damp cloth to wipe down the counter, putting the cinnamon shaker and the box of cheese crackers in the cupboard. She set the quilt across Violet's legs and lowered the blinds in the window, so the sun wouldn't warm the room too much. She went into the bathroom and set up the fallen stool, making sure nothing else was out of place. In the bedroom, she laid out the green dress Violet wore every week for the recital, pushing out a few wrinkles and pinching off two small balls of lint, flicking them to the floor. When she walked back into the main room, Violet was leaning back in her rocking chair, eyes closed, breathing steadily. A different painted face on the television, wearing a red tie and a blue suit, was pointing at a computer-generated map of Boston with virtual clouds dumping virtual snowflakes on a virtual city. Victoria quietly grabbed her purse and flung it over her shoulder. She briefly looked for her cell phone before remembering it was in pieces. Victoria leaned down and kissed her sleeping mother on the forehead, then turned and left the room, careful to shut the door gently behind her.

[IX]

[2010]

    Parallel metal barricades cut across Lincoln Street and ran up to a stage built at the base of the Capitol steps. The gold dome over Colorado's Congress was drab under an overcast sky. The barriers were like a metal ribcage bulging against the crowds of opposing demonstrators. The swarms pushed toward each other, fists slamming hard against the cold air. Cardboard signs swung back and forth, swirling the newborn snow flurries just before they perished on the pavement. On one side, the signs read: *Let Us Serve Openly; Marriage is a Right; Remember Matthew Shepard*. The other side: *No Faggots in my Foxhole; Marriage = One Man + One Woman; Matt is in Hell*. On occasion, a plastic bottle arced over the barren space between the two crowds—a grenade of water, the casualties wiping the spray from their red cheeks, curses dripping from their lips. The asphalt was wet with snow; a few patches of ice pulled both protestors and supporters of the rally to the ground without prejudice. A sparse line of riot police ran like a dotted line between the two trembling barriers. Their rigid faces were hidden behind black helmets and clear plastic visors.

    Victoria examined the crowd through the open wall of a large, white tent functioning as the temporary headquarters behind the main stage. The oscillating heaters on the floor blew her blond hair slightly off her shoulders as the walls of the tent swelled with each gust of cold wind.

    "We did this on purpose, you know," Victoria said, sliding leather gloves over her slender fingers. "Lining up our supporters directly across from the protestors, all the way up to the stage." One of the protestors swung his sign at the line of police. He was yanked up over the barrier and slammed to the ground, his arms pulled tightly behind his back. "It will make for excellent sound bites on the news tonight," Victoria added.

"Hurry up and get this over with before someone gets hurt," Erin commented, shifting in her folding chair, rubbing the white bandages on her forehead, and staring at her laptop.

"Are you sure you're up for this? It's been less than a month since the incident. You were in the hospital for four days. Aren't you still on painkillers?"

"Stop calling it an *incident*. I had my head bashed into a parking lot."

"The parking lot of a *gay bar*, Erin. The *incident* is a PR nightmare. I don't know what the hell you were thinking."

"I'll be fine, Victoria. Thank you for your concern about my health and well-being." Erin monitored the screen, tracking the donations already starting to trickle in. She clicked to another window—a live video feed: the tent they were sitting in behind the stage, and hundreds of people. "The video is streaming."

"Any volunteer can stare at that computer screen. You're just here to see if he'll show up."

Another gust of cold wind blew into the tent, bulging the canvas walls. A police officer walked up from the stage and told Victoria they were ready.

"Thank you, Officer."

Erin leaned in close to the screen, rubbing her bare hands together for warmth. "He saved my life. And you said you wanted me here."

"How do you know the kid didn't set up the attack himself?"

"Victoria, please."

"To embarrass you—the Alliance."

"Go give your speech."

"Deflecting," Victoria replied in a high pitch.

Erin's cell phone lit up, vibrating next to the laptop. The table set up for her computer wobbled in the wind. Victoria shook her head as she examined her full-length leather coat for lint, running her hands through her hair.

"You know, Erin, it's not really two opposing groups out there. They're not even people, really, just concepts." Erin held her other hand to her ear and turned away as she argued with someone on the cell phone. "Two ideas," Victoria continued, looking over the crowd. "Two perspectives fighting for control. Ideas are parasites of the mind." Victoria thumbed through her notes. Erin's leaned into her laptop as she gave orders over the phone. "There is a fungus," Victoria continued to no one in particular, "called *Ophiocordyceps*. It infects the brain of a carpenter ant, taking control of its bodily functions as it grows. It directs the ant's body to the colony." Victoria pulled her hair back into a ponytail. "Then it forces the ant to clamp onto something secure, like the end of a twig or a rock, and the ant dies. The fungus continues to grow out of the ant's body until it rains down spores on more unsuspecting ants, infecting even more hosts. Its only purpose? Propagation." Victoria crossed her arms as she looked at the crowd. "Creatures existing as hosts for the proliferation of ideas. It's an intriguing thought."

Erin looked up and pulled her phone away from her face, covering it with her hand. "What?"

"Nothing. Is Musgrave on the way?"

"Twenty minutes," Erin replied, looking back at the computer screen, snapping her phone shut. "The driver was standing there holding a damn sign with her name on it. She was upset that he didn't recognize her."

Victoria stifled a laugh.

"What were you saying?"

The police officer returned before Victoria could respond. "Ma'am, we can't wait any longer."

Victoria nodded. "If you know how the fungus works, you can manipulate the ant's behavior. Make it go anywhere."

Erin's phone began to vibrate again. She ignored it. "What are you talking about?"

Victoria grabbed her notes and smiled. "Time to charm potential contributors."

"Again about the money," Erin sighed.

Victoria turned her head over her shoulder. "Grow up, Erin. It's very expensive to uphold God's values—especially in America." Victoria made her way down to the stage. A few flakes of snow circled her head. As she approached, the cheers and jeers of the two crowds grew louder. Victoria stepped up to the podium, a slender smile tucked into the corners of her mouth. A sign ran the length of the podium in bold, red letters: *God's Word Does Not Compromise!* Below the statement was a phone number: *1-800-LEV1822*. Below that was an Internet address: *www.LeviticusAlliance.org*. Victoria tightened her white leather coat and raised both gloved hands. Some of the police officers turned their reflective masks toward the stage.

"Welcome, my friends, to the Leviticus Alliance campaign against the repeal of Don't Ask, Don't Tell!" She paused, allowing the applause and condemnation to blend together into a cacophony of white noise. "In the spirit of fairness, I have invited our opponents here today, so that they may witness our fortitude. We are resolute in the cold and snow of November, to fight legislation of personal agendas, to fight against a minority who try to force their special rights onto our military and our great nation. We are here to fight those trying to rewrite the laws of God!" Victoria's words boomed from speakers on each end of the stage. Her supporters cheered and waved small American flags. The protestors' slightly smaller numbers couldn't break through the surfeit of cheers. They waved American flags, too, interspersed with rainbows and pink triangles. A cardboard sign swung into the gap between the two groups, and a cop yanked it away from a woman with a shaved head and nose rings riveted through both nostrils, almost pulling her over the barricade.

Victoria moved closer to the microphone. A silver cross dangled loosely from her neck. "The so-called Universal Rights Coalition has infiltrated our military like an infectious disease, confusing privileges with rights, attempting to turn an entire generation against their parents, against their government, and—most disturbingly—against God. Our country was founded on Christian values—on Christian morality. Yet the URC—"

"Wrong!" a voice thundered from the crowd of Victoria's supporters, much louder than Victoria.

Victoria turned her head toward the source of the interruption. The noise subsided, leaving only puzzled faces. Mark stood in their midst in his camouflage jacket. A cardboard sign thin, plywood handle was tucked between Mark's arm and his body. On the upper end of the handle was a cardboard sign that read: *Fags Hate God.* He held a large megaphone.

"Thomas Jefferson in his *Notes on the State of Virginia...*" Mark held up a small book with a portrait of Jefferson on the cover. A few of the Alliance followers surrounding Mark tried to yell over him, but he continued, "*'Millions of innocent men, women, and children, since the introduction of Christianity, have been burnt, tortured, fined, imprisoned; yet we have not advanced one inch toward uniformity. What has been the effect of coercion? To make one half the world fools, and the other half hypocrites.'*" A few of Victoria's supporters clapped, confused as to why so few were cheering. A couple of others grabbed at Mark's arms. "So who are the fools and who are the hypocrites, Victoria?" The protestors on the other side of the barriers began to applaud and laugh. Someone yanked the book out of Mark's hands. Some were laughing.

"It seems we have a wolf in our midst, ladies and gentlemen," Victoria said calmly, but her voice was drowned out by Mark's.

"*'Question with boldness even the existence of a God; because, if there be one, he must more approve of the homage of reason than that of blindfolded fear!'* Jefferson's letter to Peter Carr!"

A gloved hand from the crowd lunged forward and tried to slap the megaphone out of Mark's hands. Victoria looked over her shoulder, waving at the audio engineer, directing him with her thumbs to turn up the volume. She saw Erin standing next to the tent, one hand over her mouth. Mark fought his way to the edge of the stage, the throng behind him pulling at his jacket.

Victoria turned back to the crowd. "So, you must be Mark." Several people near the stage covered their ears against the suddenly loud volume. Shrill feedback cut through the air before she continued. "And you certainly seem to be playing the part of the fool." The Alliance faction laughed.

Two police officers moved toward Mark, batons held horizontally across their chests, but Victoria waved them away. "No, don't arrest him. Stop. I want everyone to witness the horrible pain this young man is going through. Do you see what the absence of God's love drives him to?" She looked in his direction. "Mark, you are the very person that we at the Leviticus Alliance are trying to reach—are trying to help."

Mark leaned over the barrier, snapping his shoulders forward to keep the crowd from pulling at his arms. "*'Christianity neither is, nor ever was, a part of Common Law!'*" Mark yelled into the megaphone, "Jefferson's letter to Dr. Thomas Cooper!" The protestors on the other side erupted in adulation, yelling for Mark to continue. Mark's sign was ripped away, and he watched someone fling it at the protestors. It arched over the cops, the pinewood handle hitting a young man in the face. Mark turned and swung his fist at the supporter who threw the sign. The injured protester jumped over the barricade, his hand held to his bloody nose as he tried to bolt across the gap between the two crowds. He was immediately tackled by the police. More officers began moving toward the stage.

"You are a frightened and confused young man," Victoria continued, ignoring the accelerating deterioration of the crowd. "He needs God's love, everyone! He needs our prayers and the help of the Leviticus Foundation. Call or go to our website to find out how you can help people like him find salvation."

"Tyranny of the majority!" Mark yelled. An officer jumped down from the stage and pulled the megaphone from Mark's hands; it fell to the ground with a clatter. Someone behind Mark pushed him forward, his body slamming hard against the metal barrier and the cop. Cameramen pushed their way to the stage, filming with their unblinking eyes. Others captured the event with cell phones. Erin ran down the stairs and tried to jump onto to the street, but a policeman held her back.

Victoria stretched out her arms. "Look at the pain caused by this homosexual's separation from God." Despite her voice blaring from the speakers, Victoria's words hardly broke through the noise of the now-chaotic crowd. "Witness! This is where his rejection of God's love and forgiveness has brought him."

A second cop reached Mark; both officers grabbed him by the shoulders and tried to lift him over the barrier, but Mark jerked his body to the side, hitting one of the cops in the jaw with his shoulder. A few people were still trying to pull him back into the crowd. The barriers leaned forward from all the weight and finally collapsed. Mark, the two police officers, and several supporters tumbled onto the ground in a tangle of legs and arms and metal and screams. Protestors jumped the barriers and charged across the gap; the other side stormed their barricades as well. The two sides collided, the police caught in the middle. The officers swung their batons, hitting both sides indiscriminately. Handles from signs became bats. Cups of hot coffee and tea became grenades. Canisters of tear gas spewed clouds of caustic white smoke. Scores of riot police lined up on the street.

Mark tried to stand, but turned when he heard someone yell, "Cocksucker!" behind him. A man with wide eyes and bulging biceps brought the megaphone down with both hands onto his head. When it hit Mark, the white cone shattered into pieces. Mark fell back and laughed, holding the top of his head with both hands, blood seeping through his fingers. A gay-rights advocate tackled Mark's attacker before he could hit Mark again with the broken, jagged megaphone. One of the police officers jumped on Mark, rolling him over onto his stomach.

"You're under arrest for assault on a police officer!" he yelled into Mark's ear. "Not to mention inciting a riot." The other cop drew his gun and yelled for everyone to get back, coughing between the words. Mark continued to laugh as the crowd around him cleared, crouching to avoid the hovering, white smoke.

Victoria held one hand to her chest. "This is why I'm here, ladies and gentlemen! This is why I have sacrificed so much of my time—so much of my life—for this organization! It's to help these lost—"

Victoria's microphone went dead. The officer holding Erin grabbed Victoria's arm with his other hand, and Erin slipped away into the crowd.

The policeman couldn't see her in the confusion. "Time to go, Miss Richman."

Victoria stepped forward, almost walking into the officer. "I'm not finished! You don't have the authority to shut us down!"

"We're clearing the area, Ma'am," the officer said with annoyance. "Let's go. Now." Victoria hesitated, looking over what was left of the rally. Almost all of the barricades were down, a few broken legs and arms still twisted in the mangled metal. A group of malcontents stood in the midst of the tear gas, bandanas or t-shirts wrapped tightly over their faces. Some were holding broken handles of cardboard signs, swinging them wildly at each other, slicing the air. Some were wrestling on the ground or throwing knuckle-bruising, teeth-breaking punches. A few were standing face-to-face, yelling hoarsely at each other with bloodshot eyes and clenched fists.

"This is not a request, Miss Richman."

"Fine," Victoria said, staring at the cop's chest. "I want your name and badge number. I'm friends with the Chief of Police."

"It's for your safety, Miss Richman," the officer replied wearily. Victoria turned her back to the crowd and followed the cop to the tent. She scanned for Erin but didn't see her. She reached down to pick up the laptop, but hesitated.

"Now, Miss Richman! I will have to place you under arrest if you don't leave the area."

Victoria smiled at the computer screen. She closed the laptop, tucking it under her arm as the officer pulled her away.

A voice boomed from a megaphone mounted onto a black-and-white police SUV. "This event is over!" A line of police in riot gear banged their batons in unison against their shields as they walked forward. "Clear the area immediately! You will be arrested if you do not comply! Clear the area immediately!"

Three more black canisters of tear gas shot through the air, landing and rolling amid the fallen barriers and abandoned protest signs. Plumes of white smoke added to the already acrid air. The remaining fighters in the crowd saw the advancing line of police and began to run. They stumbled, covering their mouths, coughing heavily, long strings of mucus swinging from their noses. A few crouched down, vomit splashing between their legs.

Erin held a black wool scarf over her mouth, squinting as she tried to wave the gas out of her face with her other hand. She wove through the now-thinning crowd. Two police officers pushed their knees into Mark's back, yelling at him to stop resisting. His hands were tied behind his back with a nylon zip-tie. But Mark kept trying futilely to knock the two officers off-balance. One of the cops pulled out a large, black cylinder from his belt and held it in front of Mark's face.

"If you keep resisting, I will mace you!"

"Fuck you!" Mark yelled out.

The officer flipped up the thumb latch on the canister.

"Wait," Erin said, leaning down next to Mark. She dropped the scarf.

"Ma'am, you need to leave!"

"I know him; please let me talk to him. He'll cooperate."

"Like fuck I will," Mark replied, eyes reddened by the tear gas. He was coughing and choking on his own saliva. Blood and phlegm drained out of his nose, smeared across his cheeks. "Did you like my sign?" Mark asked.

"Ma'am! Leave now, or you will be arrested, too!"

"Three minutes!" Erin pleaded. "Just give me three minutes."

The officer dug his knee a little deeper into Mark's back. "Two."

Erin knelt down. "You have to stop resisting, Mark. I can get you out of jail, but you need to cooperate."

"I'll stop resisting when you stop objectifying homosexuals."

"Mark, please!"

He could see that Erin was crying, but not from the tear gas.

"You're not going to win the fight this way!" Erin exclaimed.

"You don't fucking get it, do you?" Mark yelled, turning his head away from her. "There is no winning this fight—ever. We're all swirling in a shit-stained toilet bowl, and I'm dragging down as many people as I can with me."

Erin swayed slightly and held her head. "I can't lose you, too." Mark's eyes snapped up. Erin turned away, pushing her black hair out of her face.

"One minute," the officer said, staring at his watch as he pushed his knee deeper into Mark's back.

"You were the last person to see Kevin alive," Erin said quietly. Mark lowered his head. "Please don't take that away from me."

Mark's body went limp. The two officers stood slowly, pulling him to his feet, their arms locked under his shoulders. "My leg hurts," Mark said with a smirk, right before they turned him around and marched him toward a waiting police van. Its back doors were open, swallowing cuffed prisoners from both sides of the debate. Erin watched Mark limp forward and struggle into the van. Her eyes stung from the tear gas. She looked down for her scarf.

"You're under arrest," an officer from behind said forcefully, grabbing Erin's wrists and tying them behind her with a nylon strap.

"Wait," Erin said over her shoulder. "I'm with the Alliance. I'm—"

"You ignored repeated instructions to leave the area."

"But I'm—"

The officer pushed Erin forward, leaning in and lowering his voice. "I know exactly who you are, you fucking hypocrite. You feel sorry for the faggots, hang around with them in gay bars." The officer raised his voice again. "You were told to clear the area. Come with me."

Erin was silent as she was pushed forward. She ducked, almost hitting her head as the officer pushed her into the back of the police van. The doors slammed shut, locking out the sunlight. The officer hit the back door twice with the palm of his open hand. Mark sat across from Erin and looked up with a broad smile framed in phlegm, blood, and dirt.

"You still gonna post bail for me?" he asked as the van jerked forward.

[X]

[2008]

Kevin watched out of the corner of his eye as Mark lifted the beer to his lips, gulping as bubbles shot back up into the bottle. Kevin shook his head as he looked at a small digital camera cradled between his hands.

"You and your beer need a room?" Kevin asked, his own beer sitting next to him untouched, beads of condensation rolling down the sides. The whine of a commercial plane backing away from a nearby gate filled the small lounge. Mark and Kevin sat at the bar in their civilian clothes, duffle bags on either side of them, slumped over in their stools as if they had too much to drink. A man sat at a small table behind them; his gray suit hung loosely over his thin frame. A red tie was looped tightly around his neck, almost choking him. He typed forcefully on his laptop. The rest of the chairs in the lounge were vacant. A female voice from somewhere overhead welcomed everyone to Denver International Airport and reminded travelers not to leave their bags unattended. She repeated herself. Kevin held his digital camera a few inches from his face, thumbs tapping on the touch-screen, scanning through each photograph at an uneven pace.

Mark slammed his empty bottle onto the bar as he gestured for another. "I never thought cheap, piss-flavored beer could taste so damn good."

Kevin smirked, his face glued to the camera. "Well, enforced prohibition in a Muslim country will do that."

The server was staring out the floor-to-ceiling windows of the lounge at the distant Rocky Mountains cutting into a cloudy horizon. A passenger plane crawled toward the main runway and came to a stop. Another five planes were waiting behind it, waves of heat and exhaust distorting their shapes. A large, gray thunderhead hovered above the distant, jagged peaks, a few thin ropes of rain uncoiling onto the unseen pines, aspens, and fir trees.

"What the hell is she looking at?" Mark said, staring at the server.

Kevin shook his head and mocked, "Iraqi civilians gunned down by the Taliban or blown up by suicide bombers, killed accidentally by our Predators. But the biggest tragedy on the planet is that Mark Bradford can't get a goddamn beer." Kevin tapped the screen. "Woe is you."

A male voice from somewhere overhead announced that United Flight 310 to New York was now departing from Gate B10. He repeated himself.

Mark looked back toward the window. The server was gone. "Shit." Kevin flipped to the next picture. "Give it a rest, will you?" Mark said as he reached over and grabbed Kevin's untouched bottle. "We're supposed to be on leave. Get drunk. Find a hooker. Hell, find a *male* hooker. Try to forget for one night that we have to go back to that blistering, spider-infested sandbox."

"I don't need a hooker—not where I'm going."

"Why *are* you going to Aspen? It's nothing but a yuppie-infested mountain town full of condescending blowhards."

"My mom's friend has a house up there, and we were invited for the weekend. I think my mom wants to take me hiking up by the Maroon Bells. She says they're beautiful at sunrise. Make for some great pictures."

"I hate those fucking Maroon Bells. We passed three pictures of those mountains on the way to this bar, all of them advertising *The Great State of Colorado*. The most photographed pile of rocks in the state."

"Well then, I'll be sure to snap a few for you," replied Kevin.

"And hiking? You're on leave and you want to go *hiking?*"

"Not the whole time. In fact, I plan to stay in town as much as possible. Aspen's full of rich, lonely wives and widows who want to feel young again."

"Ah! Now that makes more sense. What about your mom's friend?" Mark asked.

Kevin's face became contorted. "Victoria? God no. She's a complete bitch—definitely one of the blowhards."

"But she's a rich blowhard," Mark said encouragingly.

Kevin shook his head. "I've always wondered why my mom is friends with that awful woman." He looked back at his camera. "Speaking of mountain towns…" Kevin's left thumb tapped on his camera. A picture of a burned-out car filled the screen, twisted, charred metal, peppered with bullet holes. An ashen skull rested against the back of the driver's seat. The teeth somehow remained white. "... Are you going to Leadville to visit your dad?"

"Fuck that. He doesn't even know I'm in the Army. I want to catch up with a few of my GLBT buddies from the community college. I'll crash with them. Go to clubs. Get trashed. Get laid. Get trashed some more. Get laid some more. Then I'm flying out to New York to see my sister and her insufferable husband."

Kevin was looking at Mark with a puzzled expression.

"Gay, Lesbian, Bisexual, and Transgender," Mark said condescendingly. "GLBT."

Kevin lurched back on his stool in mock horror. "You're a homo!?"

Mark shook his head and leaned forward, his elbows resting on the bar. "Fuck you."

"My God! I'm sitting next to a cock holster!"

"I'm a top, actually. I fuck the cock holsters."

"I've gotta turn you in." Kevin pulled out his cell phone and pretended to dial numbers. "What's Senator McCain's number?" Kevin looked up. "Don't Ask, Don't Tell, Mark."

"Fuck. You."

"What if you try to boink me in the barracks?"

"Don't flatter yourself, Kev. You're not even rape-worthy."

Kevin laughed. "Ouch."

"And speaking of unspeakable sex acts," Mark added, "what is it with you and the cougars?"

"Simple," Kevin replied. "No games. No drama. No awkward phone calls the next day. They only want cock. I'm more than happy to provide."

"Straight sex with old women," Mark replied. "*That's* the abomination."

Kevin watched Mark stare at a television in the corner of the lounge. The bartender had his back to them, flipping though channels.

"You never answered my question," Kevin said to the back of Mark's head.

"What question?" Mark said to the distant television.

"The question I asked in Richmond before we boarded the plane—sitting in the *other* airport bar."

"I already told you. He's a pathetic fuck." Mark brought the bottle to his lips, then paused. "In fact, I take great comfort in the fact that he's rotting away—alone—in that house. He built his own little coffin up in the mountains, and I hope he fucking rots in it."

Kevin turned back to his camera and flipped to another picture, turning it vertically. *"'Men in rage strike those that wish them best.'"*

Mark took a long pull, breathing through his nose as he drained the rest of Kevin's beer. "My father—I mean, Steve—doesn't wish me anything but misfortune."

"I doubt that."

"Stop making assumptions about who you think he is." There was a short pause. "And stop quoting books at me."

"It's from a play, dipshit. *Othello*. Didn't you take any Lit classes at your community college?"

"Weren't all of Shakespeare's children illiterate?"

"Great writer, bad father," Kevin replied. "And I'd stop making assumptions if you'd stop being so cryptic about your dad—sorry, Steve. Saying he's a pathetic fuck doesn't tell me much."

"Some other day," Mark said, the neck of the empty beer bottle swinging precariously between his fingers as he motioned to the bartender for another. "And just so you know, quoting passages from books—or *plays*—only increases your dickishness."

"As does consuming copious amounts of alcohol," Kevin quipped. His eyes scanned a picture he had taken of a young girl. She was standing barefoot in sand blackened by an explosion, dwarfed by a pile of broken adobe and splintered wood. Black snakes of smoke slid out from between cracks in the fallen walls. The little girl's hands were at her sides, eyes full of tears, face wrinkled with anguish.

"Where was that?" Mark asked, looking over Kevin's shoulder.

Kevin reached for his bottle without looking, his hand grasping at empty air. "Somewhere near Al Kut. Our Predator mistakenly bombed their village. Faulty intelligence. So, no insurgents, just ten dead civilians. The kid's family was under the rubble."

Mark placed the empty bottle into Kevin's hand.

"I know why you take those pictures," Mark said.

Kevin looked at the bottle in his hand and set it down with a sigh. "Please, enlighten me, oh wise one, oh, sage of thought and reason."

"You could take a million pictures of a million children crying over the dead, bloated bodies of a million parents, and you could plaster all those pictures onto the walls of a million schools, memorials, and museums, so millions of school children would see them—every day—as a reminder of the horrors of war. The kids could go to bed thinking about those maggot-filled, black-and-blue broken bodies, even have nightmares about rotting corpses dragging them into the ground—millions of children screaming and crying with tears rolling out of their eyes as their parents frantically attempt to wake them up, trying to tell them it was only a dream. And their hearts will bleed while they're still immature. They'll be idealistic and imagine a world without conflict, and then grow up to listen to anti-war music and smoke pot and think they can change the world."

"But then?" Kevin asked wearily, looking at his camera.

"But then, they become adults. And as adults, they have to live in the *actual* world, teeming with conflict. Before you know it, those children will be shooting each other with more efficient rifles than we have, designed for greater range and accuracy. They'll push big, red, flashy buttons that launch self-guided missiles into buildings and factories and storage depots thousands of miles away, blowing other humans apart in a macabre orgy of violence."

"Orgy?"

"All of this in the name of land or freedom or religion or God or because their government told them to—"

"Like we do."

"—or because dad told them that to be a man, they had to kill other men. Or maybe because they get off on it."

"I'm not an idiot, Mark. I know these pictures aren't going to end the war."

"Pictures aren't going to end—prevent—*any* war. Ever."

"I suppose you're going to tell me why?"

"War is progress. Look how it brought America out of the Great Depression. It plays an essential part of every society that has ever existed—keeps it strong. Civilization would dissolve without it. And it grinds weaker cultures into powder, their ashes blowing away in the wind—soon forgotten."

"You sound like the end of a bad poem," Kevin replied.

A male voice from above announced a gate change for United Flight 744 to Boston.

"But people like you want to stop this process of social evolution, demanding peace with pictures, like your insignificant voice could ever hope to stop this machine. '*War is over if we want it.*' Really? John Lennon forgot the essential role that war plays in the development of societies, not to mention that people *do* want war and always will. Why, you ask?"

"I didn't," Kevin replied, looking for the bartender.

"People are eager to construct reasons to live, and they are equally eager to create reasons to kill. Consciousness engages—"

"I'm eager not to listen to your crap," Kevin said, giving up on the bartender and looking back at his camera.

"Consciousness engages the meaningless chaos that is existence, finds patterns that exist only in the mind, and then attempts to apply those patterns to the outside world."

"You took two philosophy classes in a community college. Just because you fuck guys, too, doesn't mean you're a Greek philosopher."

"It was *five* classes, dickweed."

"Stop being so abstract," Kevin added, setting his camera on the bar next to a brass divider. "That's the source of *your* dickishness. Always talking in abstractions, never giving concrete examples of what you're trying to say."

"Okay. Let's pretend I'm a Christian."

"That's a lot of pretending."

"*As a Christian*, my faith is intangible. It's a pattern I have integrated into my perspective, turning it into an absolute truth that *must* exist for everyone else." A cell phone behind them rang. Kevin turned around. The man in the business suit flipped it open and began relaying numbers to some distant assistant, his left shoulder covering his ear. "Are you listening?"

"Or course. Blah, blah, blah, *patterns*. Blah, blah, blah, *absolute truth*," Kevin replied.

"Christians have declared a war on drugs," Mark continued, "on homosexuality and gay marriage, on premarital sex—anything they don't agree with, right?"

Kevin turned back around. "Not just Christians."

"Exactly! The mind constructs ethics out of nothing and tries to codify those ethics through religion or government, attempting to project and force that perspective onto everyone else, as if values are somehow universal—their origins somehow external."

"So, what the fuck does that have to do with war?"

"People, especially fucking religious crazies, justify war because it's the best way their artificial beliefs can be tested, solidified, and used as a hammer to knock down any other contradictory way of thinking—consciousness creating meaning out of nothingness through conflict."

"Okay. For the sake of argument, let's imagine you're right. Explain, then, how meaning, if it's being constructed internally by the mind, is somehow rendered meaningless because it didn't come from an absolute external source like Zeus or Jesus or space aliens."

A Boeing 747 taxied by the windows of the lounge, its loud drone of its four bulky engines forcing Mark to raise his voice.

"Because the source of all meaning comes from a couple of pounds of gray matter locked away in the skull. That's it. A couple billion chemical and electrical reactions in the brain. Yet people believe good and evil exist outside the mind."

"Not everyone believes that," Kevin said. The server set down two napkins, followed by two more perspiring bottles of beer. "Thank *God!*" Kevin said, grabbing his beer before Mark could. The server walked over to the man in the gray suit, who held up his finger. A few seconds later, he set his phone down, staring at a short woman walking in, her long, red hair resting neatly over the contours of her small shoulders. Her tight, black pantsuit snapped with every step; her cell phone stuck to the side of her face like a parasite made of plastic and light. She clumsily dragged a single piece of luggage with no wheels, knocking into the bar stools. Mark and Kevin leaned forward as she walked past them. She was speaking French insistently into her phone. When she reached an empty table near the windows, she let her bag fall hard onto the floor like a dead body. She then walked to the windows, clamping her forehead with her free hand, her hair bouncing as she emphasized every other word with a violent shake of her head.

"That woman…" Mark started again, turning on his barstool.

"… is fucking beautiful," replied Kevin, "not that you care."

"She's obviously angry at whoever's on the other end—a lover? A friend? Who knows and who cares? What does it mean to us? Nothing. An observation. Nothing more." He turned back around to Kevin. "We project absolutely no value on what she sees as important."

"She's arguing with someone about a kid. Her son, I think. He died."

Mark stared. "You speak French?"

"Some." Kevin waved his hand back and forth. "Never mind the woman. You're trying to argue that bombing a village and killing civilians is somehow meaningless. Try telling that to the orphan crying over her dead parents. Try convincing her that her loss is somehow morally ambivalent." Mark took a pull on his beer as Kevin continued. "War has a tragic effect on the civilian population. Those who start wars rarely see the consequences. If I can reach a few future leaders, I've helped prevent future bloodshed."

"The only thing you're going to accomplish is getting yourself kicked out of the Army."

"You're one to talk—Mr. Don't Ask, Don't Tell."

"Do you really think people who support wars are that naive about your gruesome pictures?"

"Yep. They're elected by ignorant voters, the same ignorant voters who keep them in office year after year."

"Maybe they understand more than you think." Kevin shook his head. "Not to mention, it doesn't say much about humanity when you have to shove macabre pictures in their faces so they think twice about killing strangers."

The female voice from above asked Sarah-Michelle Thompson to please report to the nearest white courtesy telephone. She repeated herself.

"'*Every man is guilty of all the good he didn't do,*'" Kevin replied before taking a quick gulp of his beer.

"Dickishness."

"Voltaire had a point, and that's what I want to change with these photographs. Expose individuals to the horror, so they *do* care. Even if it's only one person, it's worth it."

"So you taking pictures is the result of a guilt trip?"

"Beats sitting on your ass in a bar, yammering away with your shitty pseudo-philosophy and offering no solutions to problems you can't seem to help deconstructing."

Mark rolled his eyes. "At least I'm not living my life based on a cliché: 'Changing the world, one person at a time!'"

"No, you're basing your life on the cliché that nothing matters—so let's get drunk and bitch about it in an airport bar."

"And at least I don't take bad photographs and use them as guilt tactics to motivate people into action."

"What the hell do you know about photography?"

"Okay, fine. They're not *bad* pictures. You have an eye for photography. You utilize lines and framing, the Rule of Thirds—all that shit you learn in photography class. But what you're doing is no different from people who project their values of Christianity, Islam, Judaism—even Secular Humanism. All just different patterns of thinking and engaging the world. Different tools for projecting a specific pattern of 'truth,' applying a particular value system onto everyone else. The idea that every single individual life is of equal value is merely a fabricated moral platitude modern society only recently pulled out of its smelly ass."

"Sure. Of course. Everything is relative. There are no absolute truths. Let's all commit suicide and be done with it."

"That's not what I'm saying."

"I should record this shit and play it back for you. Hell, forget waterboarding. We'll lock terrorists in a room with you and feed you caffeine and cocaine and let you rant endlessly. They'll do anything to get away. The War on Terror would be over in a month."

The businessman stood and looked at his reflection in a mirror running the length of the bar. Mark and Kevin watched as he combed back his curly, black hair with his hands before he turned and walked nervously toward the French woman, the reflection of his head bouncing slightly above rows of backlit vodka and gin bottles. The French woman pulled the plastic parasite from her head and set it down on the table. It was dormant next to her Gucci purse. The businessman flicked a small ball of lint from the knee of his pressed gray slacks just before he cleared his throat to get her attention. "*Pardon, Madame,*" he said. "*Je m'appelle Brian.*"

"*Fous-moi le camp,*" she replied calmly without looking up from her menu.

Mark turned to Kevin. "Fuck off," Kevin whispered. Mark laughed, and Kevin told him to stop staring.

"You know," Mark said as he turned, watching the businessman in the mirror, "we see stars that form constellations, man-made patterns somehow bolted onto the night sky for all of us to gawk at."

"You mean there are no gods in the sky?" Kevin replied. "Heretic!"

The man in the business suit was still standing next to the table. The French woman ignored him. He slowly slid a folded napkin onto the table, then turned back to his table.

"The stars have no true relation with each other, except those patterns we associate in our minds. And those alignments are constantly changing. The retarded zodiac signs are already an entire month off because of the wobble of the Earth, not that anyone who follows a horoscope would care, even if they knew."

"But *my* horoscope is always *so* accurate," Kevin laughed.

Mark ignored him. "Two thousand years ago, Ptolemy catalogued the eighty-eight constellation patterns we know today. And in a hundred thousand years, all of those patterns will be gone."

"It's called stellar drift," Kevin replied. Mark looked up. "I took Astronomy, too. The stars are all moving away from or toward each other."

The man in the business suit gathered his laptop and his briefcase and left. The chair at his table stood askew. The glass that held his whiskey sour was left untouched.

"Right. Take two stars in Orion: Betelgeuse and Rigel. They're moving at unimaginable speeds, but they seem fixed, somehow permanently significant. But in a hundred thousand years, Betelgeuse and Rigel will be in completely different positions in the sky. Orion will no longer exist—the constellation consumed by movement and time."

The server cleaned the table where the businessman had been sitting, wiping it clean with a single swipe of a damp, white cloth. She straightened the chair, picked up the full glass, and set it on the bar. The bartender took his attention away from the game on the television and slowly walked over, pointing with his chin at the lonely glass. "You want that?" he asked. "I'm just gonna dump it."

Mark nodded and thanked him, and the bartender set it next to Mark's beer bottle. The server took the French woman's order, the pen in her hand flying furiously across the pad. Kevin kicked the base of Mark's stool.

"What?" Mark asked, annoyed.

"Did you have a point?"

"Origin."

"Origin?"

"This planet. Humans. Life itself. The atoms that make up the body, the mind, everything we see and use. All of it was forged from stars long dead. We are their fading memory. All meaning, value, purpose—as impermanent as those constellations."

"You were one of those goth kids with black lipstick and eyeliner in high school, weren't you?"

"Fuck off."

"I've got a better idea." Kevin set the camera on the bar and turned toward Mark. "If you don't mind relinquishing the floor for a rebuttal, I'd like to demonstrate how you and your conclusions are full of shit."

The server walked swiftly by with a glass of red wine on an oval tray. As she approached the French woman's table, she tripped and stumbled over the luggage on the floor. The glass lunged forward, then backward, as she frantically shifted her arm to keep the tray balanced, her legs awkwardly askew.

"I'm full of shit?" Mark asked, watching as the server recovered the glass, long veins of red wine clinging to the inside of the glass.

"Origin is irrelevant," Kevin replied as he joined the rest of the bar in quick applause, the server smiling with relief and taking a quick bow after setting the glass down on the table.

Mark turned his head. "Irrelevant?"

"You're assuming that the origin of something somehow defines the value of its meaning for all eternity. Like how some Christians would define meaning as coming from the origin of their existence in God's image."

"Did you just accuse me of thinking like a Christian?"

Kevin smirked. "What if the value of meaning comes, not from its genesis, but from the very act of its continual construction—how it lives and breathes in the world?"

Mark's head tilted a bit. "And did you use the word *genesis*?"

"It's the act itself, the choices we make, assembling and constructing meaning out of existence. This *meaninglessness*, as you call it. Choice defines our future, not our origins. True, we are stardust, but that fact doesn't somehow make life permanently idle and mindless."

"Choice is irrelevant."

"No. It's through choice that meaning *means* anything, Mark. We choose to value ethics, or—like you—we choose to ignore them completely. But the value we apply is no less legitimate than if ethics were handed to us by space aliens, if morals were external to the human mind—external to our choices. In fact, I might argue they're more valid, because we are constantly refining them."

The French woman sipped her wine and set the glass on the folded napkin, burning a dark purple ring onto the white paper.

"But our choices are still temporary," Mark argued. "The consequences of bombing a village are a blink of geological time, soon fading into the oblivion from which it came."

"Sophomorically poetic, but still bullshit. You and I don't experience time that way, so I would argue that those consequences *do* resonate into something meaningful, because of the way the mind engages the world—regardless of whether the universe will eventually erase the events."

The French woman lifted the glass again to her lips. The napkin clung to its base, then fell away, fluttering toward her feet. It landed without a sound on the floor.

"Meaning?" Mark asked.

"Just because the stars don't give a shit about what happens to you or me or the kid in the picture, doesn't somehow eliminate any possible significance to the events. Just because we are born into this world without purpose doesn't mean we can't create one. It's how events influence each individual perspective—each individual's *internal* universe—that matters to the person experiencing them."

Mark turned the whiskey sour in his fingers, watching the ice cubes knock into each other. The female voice from above asked Samuel Henson to please report to the nearest white courtesy telephone. She then repeated herself.

"No badass comeback?" Kevin asked.

"You're making the assumption—"

A hand clamped down onto Mark's shoulder, polished, red nails digging deep into his shirt. A large diamond glared loudly in Kevin's eyes. Mark jumped, almost bringing a closed fist over his left shoulder. The French woman was standing behind them. Streaks of black mascara ran like dirty creeks down her swollen, red cheeks.

"Who was that man?" she asked Mark, sobbing.

The server stood frozen near the end of the bar with her pen lodged behind her ear, a bowl of salad with grilled chicken balanced on the tray—ranch dressing on the side. The bartender picked up the phone.

"Who?" Mark asked, as puzzled as Kevin.

"That man who gave me this!" She released Mark's shoulder and slapped the folded napkin down on the bar. Black ink bled through the white surface. "The man who wrote this!" The napkin fell to the floor.

Kevin stood, pushing his stool back. "You okay, Ma'am?"

She turned to Kevin, her face contorting and twisting as she yelled even louder, "NO!"

Silence followed as she looked back at Mark's confused expression. She turned and walked out of the lounge, dragging her bag behind her and knocking over empty bar stools. She plunged into the river of moving bodies that carved its way through the canyon walls of the busy terminal. She stood motionless, a reluctant island refusing to succumb to the currents of the water. She moved her head from side to side, peering over the bobbing heads. The female server walked over to Kevin, who was still standing, watching the French woman. Mark looked down at his glass, now on its side, contents spilled on the bar. The ice cubes were melting in their own growing puddles of water.

"The bitch didn't pay her tab," the server said, still holding the bowl of salad as she reached between Mark and Kevin, wiping up the spill with one swipe of a bar rag. "You guys want her salad?" Mark and Kevin shook their heads. She walked back over to the French woman's table. Mark was staring into the mirror behind the bar.

Kevin looked over at Mark, shrugging his shoulders and mouthing *What the fuck?*

"Something must be wrong with her *internal universe*," Mark scoffed.

Two men arrived outside the lounge in black bullet-proof vests, POLICE printed across their backs. They tried to pick up the woman, whose limp body was now curled up on the floor of the busy terminal. She wept and cursed at the cops in French as they tried again to get her onto her feet.

"Jesus..." Kevin whispered.

"He had nothing to do with it," Mark added, picking up the fallen glass and draining the few remaining drops. "And you're late."

Kevin pulled his phone out of his pocket and tapped the surface. It reflected his panicked face. "Shit! I'm going miss my flight."

Mark turned the empty beer bottle in his hands. "Have fun in Aspen. Give my love to your mom for me. Give your own love to her elderly friend."

The server walked past, righting the fallen stools. Kevin reached over, grabbed his duffle bag, and flung it over his back, the camouflage shoulder straps pulling his shirt tight across his chest.

"I'll ignore the sarcastic tone and end with 'Later, chicken fucker!'" Kevin plunged his thumbs up under the straps and jerked the pack forward, adjusting it to the small of his back. "We'll finish our discussion later, so enjoy leave while you can. Soon it's back to losing arguments with me in the sand pit." Kevin smiled. "And endless sobriety."

Mark turned his head. "Try not to fuck too many rich cougars; one of them might give you some ancient form of crabs."

"Only if I'm lucky," Kevin said as he swung around. His pack bounced against his back, and he turned his head back. "And don't get caught sucking cock. Hate to see you kicked out of the military. You'd just start torturing innocent civilians with your banal babble."

Mark smiled and held up his middle finger, watching Kevin and his camouflage pack sink into the river of people. Two paramedics with orange vests and blue gloves were now kneeling next to the French woman. A crowd began to gather. The two police officers kept pushing people back, waving them away like flying insects. The bartender replaced the spilled whiskey sour, telling him he had to pay for that one.

By the time the sun had fallen into the horizon, Mark had finished three more whiskey sours and was working on his fourth. Through heavy eyelids, he watched planes take off behind the dirty windows. Curt Smith from Tears for Fears began singing "Mad World" from Mark's cell phone. He pulled it out of his pocket; it said *Shannon* on the glass surface. Mark's thumb hit the *answer* button right after Curt Smith sang: "The dreams in which I'm dying are the best I've ever had."

"Hey, big sis," Mark said. "How's it hanging?"

"Where the hell are you?" Shannon asked.

"Nice to talk to you, too. I'm fine, thank you. No bullet holes. No missing limbs. Grateful to be alive. How've you been?"

"I've been waiting here forever. Your plane landed two hours ago."

"Oh. Yeah. About that…"

"I got a parking ticket and my car was almost towed. I had to park out in the middle of—" Shannon paused. "You're drunk. Again. Did you miss your plane?"

"No, I didn't miss the plane. And, yes, I'm drunk. Again."

"Where? I went to the bar in the main terminal. You're not there."

"Well, I *am* at an airport bar," Mark replied, looking around the empty lounge. The server had long disappeared. Even the bartender was missing. "I'm just not at a La Guardia airport bar."

"Are you at an airport somewhere on the planet?"

"Yep."

"Goddamn it, Mark. You're in Denver, aren't you?"

Mark stood, pushing his stool back and walking slowly to the bathroom, running into an empty chair on his way. "DIA has many exceptional airport bars. World-renowned. I just drank the world's best whiskey sour."

"I'm really tired of your shit, Mark," Shannon snarled. "You know that?"

"How did you know I was in Denver?"

"I paid for your ticket to New York. Took time off from work to be with you while you're on leave…" Shannon trailed off, too angry to continue. Mark could hear an overhead voice on the other end tell Shannon not to leave her luggage unattended. "How long are you going do this to me, Mark?"

"Jesus, Sis. Calm down. Who pissed in your cornflakes?"

"I know you're in Denver because you're there to see *her*. He's not going to let you; you know that. He's never let either of us—"

"I didn't plan on asking," Mark said as he pushed the bathroom door open with too much force. It slammed hard against the tile wall, the sound echoing. The bartender looked up from washing his hands. "And doing what to you?" Mark asked, walking past the sinks. "What possible past event would I ever hold over your head for years and years?"

"Don't be an ass," she snapped.

"Don't be such a drama queen."

"Cute. This coming from my queer brother."

"Fu—nny," Mark replied, standing over the urinal. The bartender briefly examined the wall where the door hit the tiles, checking for damage, then left. Mark held the cell phone to his ear with his shoulder and unzipped his pants. He urinated as he spoke. "I only made a small change to the ticket. I'll be in New York tomorrow. Didn't you get my text message?"

"You didn't leave me a goddamn text message, Mark. You never answer your phone, much less return my messages. You don't even have an email address. Now you expect me to—" Shannon paused. "Are you taking a piss while you're talking to me on the goddamn phone?"

"Actually, to be technical, I'm leaving a piss. Taking a piss would be rather unsanitary, don't you think?"

"You. Are. Disgusting."

"Hard to believe we're related, huh, Sis?"

"You know what? I don't even care." Mark could now hear wind blowing into Shannon's phone. "Promise me you're not planning on driving up to Leadville to confront him. Dad will never apologize. He'll never back down."

"Neither will I."

Shannon paused. "That's what scares me."

"Listen, I'd fuck a girl before I'd ever speak to him again. *Steve* is an ignorant asshole who doesn't deserve to have children."

"One of the very few times you and I are in agreement," Shannon replied.

Mark shook and zipped up his pants. "I'm positive that's the only time," he said, just before he flushed the urinal.

"Asshole."

"So, I'll see you tomorrow then?"

Shannon sighed. "Do you at least have someplace to stay tonight?" she asked worriedly.

"The cushy benches at airports make great beds."

"Doesn't that friend of yours, Kevin, live in Denver? Why don't you stay with him?"

Mark started washing his hands. "I told you already." He smacked the soap dispenser with his hand, but it didn't produce any soap. "Kevin's a friend. A *friend*. Can't a gay guy have a straight friend without everyone thinking he wants to fuck him?"

"I never said you wanted to fuck him."

"Besides, Kevin likes sex with old women," Mark added. He waved his wet hands in front of the sensor of the automatic paper-towel dispenser. It remained inert. "You want me to give him your number?"

"Fu—nny."

Mark walked out of the bathroom and made his way back to the bar, wiping his hands on his pants. His last whiskey sour was missing, and a glass of ice water sat in its place. Mark sat down, cursing to himself.

"It's twenty goddamn degrees out here," Shannon said, her voice shaking.

"Probably colder with the wind chill," Mark added, stirring the water with a thin, black straw. A single ice cube knocked against the side of the glass.

"And now I have to walk fifty miles back to my parked car."

"Uphill in the snow, right?" Mark asked, looking over at the bartender. His back was to Mark. "It sounds really windy there. I hope you're wearing a thick coat."

"You can take a cab here when you get here. Which is when?"

"Around noon," Mark said. "And I really did send you a text. Don't blame me for your crappy phone. You'd think your sugar-daddy husband would set you up with decent cell service."

"You owe me for gas, parking, and the ticket I got waiting for your ass."

"You take checks? I can put one in the mail."

"And try to stay sober this time. My *sugar-daddy husband* is cooking dinner for you tomorrow night. And paying for your hotel room, jackass."

"Only because he doesn't want me around the house," Mark replied, taking a sip of his water through the straw. The single ice cube was half-melted, and the water was lukewarm. "Does he think cocksucking is contagious or something?"

"Mark, I thought we were past this," Shannon said, her voice barely audible above the sound of the wind.

"He hasn't thrown you out of his million-dollar home in SoHo because his wife has a faggot for a brother?"

"Get over yourself. He couldn't care less who you screw." Mark rolled his eyes as Shannon continued. "He's never wanted anything more than to be a friend to you, so stop being such a dick."

"I didn't know rich assholes could cook for themselves. Doesn't he have servants that cook for him and feed him at the table?" Mark searched his pockets for cigarettes.

"Mark. I love you, but you're being a fucking baby. You always act like this when you're drunk. And you were drunk all the time when you lived with me in Denver."

"I'm always drunk no matter what city I'm in. But tomorrow, for you, I'll be as sober as an Irish priest on Sunday morning."

"That's not very sober."

"Exactly," Mark replied. He pulled his hands out of his empty pockets and began looking through his duffle bag. "Helps me forget the past."

Shannon sighed. "You're never going to let it go, are you Mark? No matter what I do for you, no matter what I say..." Shannon's voice trailed off.

Mark couldn't find any cigarettes in the bag. He stirred the water with the straw, remaining silent. A tall man wearing white sunglasses, a white t-shirt, and a black suit coat walked in and ordered a shot of vodka. Mark pulled the phone away from his mouth.

"Hey, man. You smoke?"

"People who smoke disgust me," the man said. He drank his shot in one swift gulp, slamming the shot glass on the counter.

"Me too," Mark replied. "I was making sure you were only a regular asshole in white sunglasses, and not a *disgusting* one."

The man sneered at Mark as he left. He didn't tip the bartender.

"Mark? You there?"

Mark brought the phone back to his ear. "Yeah."

"What was I supposed to do?" asked Shannon.

"Not leave," Mark responded. The bartender pulled the empty shot glass off the bar, shaking his head.

"So, tell my fiancé to go to New York without me because my little brother wants me to stay in Denver and keep paying his rent?"

"I'm not talking about Denver. You left me with *him*." Shannon didn't reply. The female voice in the ceiling informed Mark that the terrorist threat level was yellow, elevated, and that all carry-on liquids must be in a container no larger than 3.4 ounces. "You still there, Sis?"

"What do you want me to say?"

"I don't know. Ask me about Iraq."

"How was Iraq?" she asked flatly.

"It fucking sucked. We spent ninety percent of the time bored out of our minds, and the other ten percent being shot at or blown up."

"Mark..."

"I watched people die. Then I drove away. 'Keep following the vehicle in front of you. Keep the convoy tight.' Driving, driving, driving—but never getting anywhere. Destinations only rest stops between anxious tedium and brief bouts of brutality."

"Dad tried to hit me, Mark."

Mark took a slow sip of his water. "I could have protected you."

"You were ten. He would have gone after you."

Mark set down the glass. "He did. But you knew that."

The woman's voice welcomed Mark again to Denver International Airport and told him that his bags should not be left unattended in the terminal. The bartender walked up and threw a few cigarettes on the bar. He pointed his finger at Mark. "Not 'til you're outside."

"I'll see you tomorrow, Sis," Mark said, nodding his head and sticking one of the smokes behind his ear.

"I'll be there to pick you up," Shannon replied. "What's your flight number?"

"I'll text you," Mark said. He hung up the phone and dropped it onto the bar, rubbing his eyes, rubbing his knee. The bartender filled Mark's glass with more water. Mark thanked him and took another sip. When the bartender walked to the end of the bar and turned his back, Mark reached into his pocket and pulled out a tiny bottle of vodka he had bought on the plane, dumping the contents into the glass of water. He stirred it with the straw and took a sip.

The sky burned red and yellow and purple as a few solitary clouds hung stubbornly against the wind. Mark slowly finished his drink. The earlier storm had disappeared, and soon the sky burned black with the soft lights above the bar illuminating empty chairs and solitary tables. The bartender stayed near the end of the bar, watching a baseball game without the sound. He shook his head every time a strike was silently called by the umpire. Soon the terminal grew completely empty as Mark's head began to wobble. He looked down at his feet through glassy, red eyes and noticed the napkin on the floor. It had a purple ring just off-center.

"We're closing, kid," the bartender said as he flipped on the lights. Mark squinted and blinked. The television was dark; the lounge was quiet.

Mark stood and set a few twenties on the black lacquer surface of the bar. After securing his duffle bag to his back, Mark knelt down and picked up the napkin, swaying slightly as he unfolded it. The penmanship was perfectly aligned across the surface of the napkin, each word written carefully so as not to tear the surface. Mark read it to himself.

'*Agir sans espoir*' — *Jean-Paul Sartre*. Mark blinked and read the next line. *Moi aussi, j'ai enterré un enfant.*

He held the napkin as he turned his head, looking over his shoulder at the table behind him, as if the man in the gray suit would still be sitting there. It was spotless. The barkeep was setting chairs upside-down on tables. Mark asked the bartender if he knew French.

"Go home, kid," was his reply, shaking his head.

Mark turned his gaze to the table where the French woman had been sitting. Vacant. Clean. Sterile. Void of any evidence that it was ever occupied. Mark looked past the huge windows and the red, blinking lights on the wingtips of planes lumbering slowly toward takeoff. Orion was falling toward the dark horizon, a black cloak stretched behind him stained with a streak of milky white.

Mark turned and staggered through the empty terminal, past closed coffee shops, unlit bookstores, and rows of unoccupied chairs, taking note of a few places he could sleep without being bothered. A few weary flight attendants walked in front of him, dragging their luggage behind them, heads bent down as if they were sleepwalking. Mark made his way past the unmoving metal carousels in baggage claim and the empty, lineless ticket counters, and stumbled outside to the cab stand. There were three taxis in the waiting area. The cold air shocked Mark's senses, but woke him up only slightly. He leaned against a large cement pillar, and grabbed the cigarette from behind his ear, forgetting he didn't have matches or a lighter. Instead, he pulled a boarding pass out of his back pocket.

It read *Depart: Denver, Co (DEN) 6:30 A.M. Arrive: New York, NY (LGA) 11:45 A.M.*

Mark looked up at a large red LED clock that hung above the sliding glass doors of the terminal: *1:49 A.M.* A shuttle driver stood nearby, smoking a cigarette.

"Hey, can I borrow some fire?" Mark asked.

"Don't smoke," the driver replied, staring at Mark as he blew smoke out the side of his mouth.

Mark slurred, "Asshole," under his breath and trembled in the cold as he walked over to one of the taxis. The car was running, and the cabbie was reclined in the driver's seat, sleeping, mouth slightly open. He jumped when Mark rapped on the passenger-side window.

"Need a ride. Alameda and Quebec. Then a ride back," Mark said, sticking the smoke back behind his ear and shoving his hands deep into the pockets of his camouflage jacket.

The cabbie took a close look at Mark, rolling the window down only slightly. "You're drunk," he said. "Pay me now, or no ride."

"How much?" Mark asked. The cabbie turned his head, hesitating. "And don't screw with me. I know the city."

"Sixty-five dollars," the cabbie said.

"Fifty," Mark replied.

"Fifty-five," the cabbie said. "But we come straight back."

"I won't be long," Mark said, pulling out his wallet and shoving folded bills through the window. The cabbie popped the trunk but stayed inside the taxi as Mark stowed his duffle bag. Before he slammed the trunk shut, he opened his bag and pulled out a flashlight, a pair of gloves, and a small teddy bear, shoving them all into the various pockets of his coat. Mark jumped into the back of the vehicle, rubbing his hands together and placing them over his ears.

"You cold?" the cabbie asked, shoving the money into his pocket and putting the car in drive. "It's fifty-eight degrees, my friend. You wear thick coat and you shake. Yet you say you're from the city."

"I just came from the desert. A hundred degrees would be cold."

"You're military, yes?" the cabbie said, flipping on the turn signal and speeding out onto the roadway.

"Can I smoke?" Mark asked, ignoring the question.

"No," the cabbie replied, shaking his head.

Mark sat up and pulled the napkin out of his pocket, trying to read it again. "You speak French?"

"I'm from Ghana my friend, why would you think I speak French?"

Mark sighed. He carefully folded the napkin and stuck it in his wallet. He pulled out his cell phone and texted the flight information to Shannon. He then turned his phone off and let his head fall back against the window, closing his eyes. "Wake me up when we get there."

"There is not much there but a cemetery and a mausoleum. You know someone there?" Mark didn't respond. "You know it will be closed at this hour, yes?" he asked, looking at Mark in the rearview mirror.

"With locked doors and a single, lazy security guard that takes a fifteen-minute break every night at 0230 when he's supposed to be watching the doors." Mark replied, sinking his hands deeper into his jacket pockets.

"Who you go to visit in a mausoleum at two in the morning in the dark?"

Mark kept his eyes closed. "Dead people." Yellow light from the passing street lamps flashed across his face.

"Fine, fine," the cabbie said, shaking his head and looking straight ahead. The engine hummed as they increased speed. The car slowly swayed up and down on its worn-out shocks. Mark heard something bounce to a stop next to him on the seat. He opened his eyes and saw a blue lighter. "I understand," the cabbie added. "No more questions. I take you there. I take you back. Just crack the window, my friend."

Mark pulled the cigarette out from behind his ear and rolled down the window slightly. "I'm visiting someone I never knew," he said, picking up the lighter.

The cabbie nodded his head. "Those are the people I miss the most."

Mark didn't respond as he lit the cigarette, staring out the window past the highway, the stars blinded by distant city lights.

[XI]

[2010]

"Schedule it," Victoria said, rubbing her hands together for warmth, sitting in the backseat of a town car. She motioned for the driver to turn up the heat. "I'd love to help out some cancer kids. We need the PR."

"That's not why I asked," Erin replied, and Victoria turned down the speaker phone.

"Of course it's not."

"And don't call them 'cancer kids' while you're there," added Erin.

"Of course not," she answered, rolling her eyes.

"And thank you for this. I know this type of charity work falls outside of the Alliance's usual outreach."

Victoria checked herself in a hand-held mirror, pushing away a few stray hairs from her eyes. "The Leviticus Alliance always helps those in need. Plus, the volunteers will welcome the distraction from all the work for the next convention. It will remind us why we're doing all of this in the first place."

"For the kids?"

"PR, Erin."

There was a short pause. "Okay, well, I'll let the staff know, organize the transportation, the food. The zoo will give us a discount on the tickets, and I have a few sponsors who will—"

"I'll trust you with all the details. I've got to run."

"Where are you, by the way? You've been out of the office all day. Terry came in asking—"

"Taking care of some things for the next rally. I'll see you in the office tomorrow." Victoria reached down and hit *End* on her phone.

"Keep the engine running," she said to the driver. "I won't be long." She stuffed the cell phone into her purse and stepped out of the town car into the burning cold.

A tattered American flag hung loosely from the side of a rusted pole, its white and red stripes torn and threadbare, dusty stars barely visible against the faded blue. Victoria stood at the boundary of the yard, its edges lined with tall weeds trembling in the cold mountain air. Pockets of snow littered the frozen mud and dead grass. The windows of the house were black, the panes cracked. The paint was peeling, leaving blotches, like diseased skin.

Victoria walked up the cracked walkway, stepping over a rusted wrench and a pair of orphaned screws. The sky hung low overhead—a thick blanket of white, pregnant with snow, hiding the noonday sun. She reached the door and knocked three times, her eyes passing over the doorbell. It hung by two green wires and jiggled in the wind.

She waited.

Across the street, a yellow dog barked at a passing truck, its yelps echoing down the quiet street. Victoria turned and saw the driver of the truck slow down as he rolled down his window. The dog grew more aggressive, trying to jump over the chain-link fence that bordered the sidewalk. Its shaggy, yellow hair came off in clumps and stuck to the fence. The driver tossed a small paper bag out the passenger-side window. It cartwheeled through the air and landed behind the jumping animal. Chunks of dog feces shot out of the top of the bag.

"Keep your shit in your own yard!" the driver yelled, honking his horn and accelerating away, the dog barking and chasing the car, slamming into the wooden panels of a second fence that lined the neighbor's yard. Victoria turned back to knock again, but Steve was already holding the door open. She jerked back, almost dropping her purse.

"Can't you read, Lady?"

Steve's body filled the entire door frame, his eyes angry, hanging over a chin carpeted with gray stubble. A dark-blue robe, matted with dirt and grease, was tied at the waist. Steve's gray hair stood high on his scalp.

Victoria smiled nervously. "I'm sorry?"

Steve stepped back and pointed his index finger to the open door. There was a small, brass plaque bolted below the peephole: *No Solicitors*.

"Are you Mr. Bradford?"

The door slammed shut. A gust of wind blew Victoria's blond hair back from her shoulders. She heard the deadbolt slam hard into the cylinder. Victoria stood there a few minutes, closing her eyes and breathing out slowly. She reached into her purse and took out a black scrunchie, pulling her hair back with both hands. Victoria knocked again with three hard raps, rolling her sleeves up past her elbows. "Mr. Bradford? I'm here about your son, Mark."

Victoria waited. The dog across the street had stopped barking. He was now pacing up and down the perimeter of the fence, beating down a trail in the snow and frozen mud, drool hanging from his open jaw. Victoria reached back into her purse.

"I'm Victoria Richman from the Leviticus Alliance." She bent over, her long legs pushing against her black pantsuit, stretching it at the knees. She tried to slide a small, white business card with gold lettering under the door. "I'm sure you saw the news. Your son was arrested at our rally last week." The bottom of the door was insulated, and the corner of the card folded and wrinkled against it. She put it back in her purse and pulled out a fresh one. "He started a riot that garnered national coverage." She paused. "I know about your loss. We—those of us at the Alliance—are asking you to share your side of the story with us and the rest of the country."

Victoria waited.

The deadbolt latch slammed against the lock, and the door swung open. Steve took one step forward, but Victoria didn't step back. His naked, calloused feet landed hard on the weathered wood of the porch. "Share what? I have no son. And what the hell do you know about loss..." Steve reached over and snatched the business card out of her hand, squinting, "...Victoria Richman of the Leviticus Alliance?"

"I'm here to share the Alliance's mission."

"What mission?"

"I did, however, lose my own son in the war. I know about loss, Mr. Bradford."

The weathered flag snapped loosely behind Victoria. Steve cleared his throat. "Then he died serving his country. You should be proud."

Victoria turned and stared up at the white sky until her eyes watered. "Yes, of course I am—we all are." She looked back toward Steve. Her eyes sat behind small pools, but she didn't wipe them with her hand. "I mourned for many months, Mr. Bradford. And only with God's help did I learn to accept his death and find closure. I'm able to move on because I know I will see him again." Victoria blinked and gently wiped away a single tear from her cheek. "But with Mark, Mr. Bradford... I can't imagine the pain you must endure—your son alive in body but not in spirit."

Steve stuck his hands in the pockets of his robe, shifting his weight back and forth, the floorboards creaking in sync. "I told you," he said softly, "I have no son."

"After the incident with your... with Mark, at our rally, I did some research of my own to try to understand why this angry young man would attack our group so unjustly. I discovered he was in the Army—as was his father." Victoria stepped forward. "It must have been heartbreaking to find out he was discharged for being a homosexual." Steve looked down at his feet as she continued. "The Universal Rights Coalition is trying to use his story to gain sympathy and generate more support. They're fighting to repeal Don't Ask, Don't Tell, but they're going to want more—reparations, perhaps, for those discharged while the policy was in place."

"Please, leave, Miss Richman," Steve said, slowly closing the door.

Victoria put up her hand, stopping the door with little effort. "Mr. Bradford," Victoria said calmly, "this is important. More important than you or me. The nation must be made aware of the danger. They also need to hear about the suffering you've endured—a father abandoned by his own child." Victoria paused. "Luke fifteen, verses eleven through thirty-two."

Steve looked up. His eyes widened behind a thin film of tears. "The prodigal son," he whispered.

Victoria stepped forward, grabbing the door handle. "Your son is lost. But with your help, we can prevent this from happening to other fathers, other veterans—like yourself—who have sacrificed so much for this country."

The dog across the street began barking again as another vehicle passed by. Steve turned and disappeared into the living room and down a hallway.

"Close the door behind you," Victoria heard from the hallway. "I'll be only a minute."

Victoria shut the door behind her quietly, as if someone were asleep in the same room. She walked forward, her eyes adjusting to the darkness. A fan blew idly in the corner of the living room, oscillating back and forth. It circulated heat from the portable heater directly behind it. An orange glow emanated from the back of the heating unit, partially illuminating the once-white walls. The carpet was matted down and littered with nuts and washers. A pair of black snow boots lay sideways next to the entrance. Five sets of car keys hung on nails pounded into the wall next to the door frame. Despite the fan, the air was stale and thick with the smell of motor oil.

Steve's voice rolled down the empty hallway. "You should know, first off, that I wasn't aware Mark was in the military. Not until he went missing. I would have kept him from joining, had I known."

A small television sat across from the couch, the word *Mute* in green letters flickering in the lower corner. On the screen, an elderly man with thick glasses and a bolo tie stood behind an oak pulpit with a cross carved into the front, his short, gray hair slicked back against his scalp. The preacher's words scrolled silently across the bottom of the screen—white words against a black background. The preacher held a Bible in one hand, smacking it into the open palm of his other hand to emphasize every sentence, eyes closed. The camera zoomed in closer to his face. Several empty beer bottles lined the top of the television.

Steve's voice continued from the back of the house. "It makes me angry to think of all those homosexuals in our military, hiding their immorality among our troops—the cowards." Victoria looked up when she heard something slam against a wall. "They are purposely deceiving their commanders," Steve continued, "their sergeants, their own friends—the people who depend on them for survival. Soon they'll be able to flaunt it. Civilians will pat them on the back for lying to everyone about their perversion. How can that do anything but disrupt the unity of the platoon?"

"That is one of our goals, Mr. Bradford," Victoria responded to the dark hallway. "One of our aims is to maintain the integrity of the Armed Forces." She walked closer to the heater, holding out her hands and spreading her fingers in the welcoming heat. A disassembled alternator sat in pieces on an oil-stained plywood table in front of the couch, each corner of the table propped up with cinderblocks. Screwdrivers and pliers littered the floor near Victoria's feet. A few pictures in cheap, black frames hung above the television.

"Mark," Steve said, clearing his throat, "purposely dishonored both me and this country."

Victoria glanced down the hallway, then back at the pictures along the wall. One showed a young woman standing with a younger Steve, next to a black 1966 Corvette Stingray. Both of her arms were wrapped around her swollen belly, and his right arm was draped around her shoulders. They were both smiling. It took a minute for Victoria to realize that the picture had been taken in front of this house, when it was new and had no blotches of peeling paint. Steve was holding a sign in his left hand that read: SOLD. Their wedding bands glittered.

The photograph next to it was faded, edges curled against the glass of the picture frame. In it, Steve stood stiffly in his army dress uniform, his face free of facial hair, and his arms wrapped tightly around the thin waist of a much younger version of the same woman. She stood in front of him, the back of her head resting against his chest. The woman's straight, brown hair fell past her shoulders and down to her waist. They stood on the shoulder of a blacktop highway, stretching in a single line toward distant mountains hovering in a haze of blue. Directly behind them, a wooden sign read *Welcome to Colorful Colorado*. The letters were all in white. The same black Stingray was parked on the shoulder of the road.

Another frame showed Steve holding the hand of a little girl, her fingers wrapped around his index finger. She was carrying a large ball of pink cotton candy in her other hand. Her wide smile proudly revealed a few missing teeth, and her left shoe was untied. A large sign of colored light bulbs hung over them: *Elitch Gardens* written in yellow, green, blue, and red.

Victoria pulled her gaze away from the pictures as Steve walked back into the living room. He was wearing jeans torn at the knees and a wrinkled white t-shirt. He was rubbing his hands with a small, blue towel that he tossed onto the plywood table, grease still showing under his fingernails.

"To be honest, Miss Richman, I can't help but wonder if I'm responsible," Steve said, trying to mash his gray mane down onto his scalp. "It was my duty to raise him right, and I failed—which means I failed God." Steve hesitated, then walked across the living room, rubbing the back of his neck. "I can't sleep, wondering what I could have done differently, something that would have kept him from becoming a homosexual."

"I'm sure you tried your best, Mr. Bradford," Victoria responded. "It couldn't have been easy," she added, looking at the pictures above the television, "raising two children on your own." She didn't see Mark in any of the photographs, but she noticed blank rectangles on the wall where pictures had once hung.

"God doesn't always make it easy to do what's expected of us," Steve said, almost to himself, as he walked into the kitchen. "Nor should we expect Him to."

Victoria followed. She was going to sit, but saw only a single chair. It sat askew from a small, rickety table littered with spark plugs. A few bowls, with bits of dried oatmeal stuck to the sides, were piled near the kitchen sink. A clock ticked away the passing seconds dutifully. Victoria glanced at her watch, the silver strap reflecting the dim light from the bare windows of the kitchen.

"It doesn't keep accurate time," Steve said, looking at Victoria over the open refrigerator door. "My grandfather built it. Back then, my grandmother would set the rest of the clocks in the house to it." Steve looked up at the clock. "But now... now it just inaccurately counts away the seconds." Steve paused, then looked back at Victoria. "How did you know about my wife?"

"It came up in my research, Mr. Bradford."

Steve nodded. "She was an amazing woman, especially with Shannon." He stared blankly into the open refrigerator. The compressor kicked on. "It's Steve, by the way. And have a seat."

"I only need a minute of your time, Steve. I have a very hectic schedule, as you might imagine. God keeps the Leviticus Alliance very busy these days."

"I insist," Steve said. He sniffed the containers of milk and orange juice, then put them back. He ignored the last remaining bottles of beer. Victoria slowly walked back into the living room and sat apprehensively on the edge of the sofa, keeping her back straight and her arms folded over the purse in her lap.

Steve closed the fridge and stood at the entrance of the kitchen, gesturing behind him with his thumb. "I'm afraid I don't have anything to offer but tap water."

"No. No tap water. I'm fine, thank you."

Steve walked past the couch and fell into a dusty old chair next to the television, facing Victoria. "I knew about your group before it made the news," Steve said, reaching forward and gathering the parts of the alternator, pushing them into a small pile. "I've even donated a few times, when I had the money. You do good work. Though, I think you could do more."

"Well, that's why I'm here."

Steve cupped his hand and swept a few loose screws onto his palm, dropping them in his shirt pocket. "I'm not sure how much help I can be. I'm just a mechanic and a weary veteran. I'm not the speaker type."

Victoria cleared her throat. "You're more than just a mechanic." Steve tilted his head slightly. "Won't you consider speaking at our next rally? It would be completely informal. Put a face on the tragedy Mark has created—risking the lives of his fellow soldiers by eroding unit cohesion." She leaned forward. "And betraying and dishonoring you and other veterans by flouting, even bragging, about serving as a homosexual."

"I'm not going to yammer away to a bunch of strangers, looking for their pity."

"It's important for others to hear your story."

"I'll be frank with you, Miss Richman. Talk is cheap, used by cowards to fool the foolish—this potential repeal of Don't Ask, Don't Tell is evidence of that. The fact that the appalling law exists at all is proof that propaganda can convince anyone of anything." Steve reached over and hit the power button on the television. The preacher in the bolo tie disappeared. "No offense to you and how you run your organization, of course."

Victoria interlaced her fingers and placed her hands on her lap. "The repeal may pass, but we can still slow it down, perhaps even reverse it. And may I be candid as well, Steve?"

"I wouldn't expect anything different."

"God wants all of us to utilize the gifts and strengths he has given us. Perhaps you're right. Perhaps we have come to a juncture where words are no longer as effective against the opposition as they once were."

"Meaning what?"

The clock ticked away a few more seconds. Victoria shifted on the edge of the sofa. "Now that we have this opportunity to make an impact on a national level..." She trailed off.

He looked at her blankly, and she leaned forward. "What was your job in the Army?"

"Don't insult the both of us by asking questions you already know the answer to."

"Yes, of course, Steve. I shouldn't have. I was only—"

"And it's called MOS, Miss Richman, not a *job*. Military Occupation Specialty. I was an EOD specialist." Victoria sat quietly. "Explosive Ordinance Disposal." Victoria nodded her head. "But you already know all this," Steve added.

"About what you said... a few minutes ago."

"About what?"

"About your duty."

Steve narrowed his eyes. "What about my duty?"

"Your duty—not only to Mark," Victoria continued, "but to this nation, to God... and how you might have failed in that regard."

Steve sat up in the chair. "It's not polite, Miss Richman, to accuse veterans in their own homes of failing in their duty to this country." Steve leaned forward. "Not very smart either."

Victoria sat motionless, locking her eyes with Steve's. "We all fail at one time or another, Steve. Does not Isaiah write that our righteousness is as filthy rags?"

"Indeed it does," replied Steve, leaning back. He sighed heavily. "But I didn't fail in my duty to this country. I was the one who turned him in."

Victoria struggled to hide her surprise. "Turned who in?"

"Mark. I informed an old friend of mine, the commander of the base Mark was sent to for rehabilitation. I fulfilled my duty, as I always have." Steve narrowed his eyes. "So what about your own righteousness, Victoria? What about your duty as an American to keep this country free of the enemies of God? All I've ever seen you do is stand behind pulpits and flap your mouth to your supporters to get more money."

"Mr. Bradford..."

"And who the hell are you," Steve continued calmly, "to come into my home and lecture me on duty?"

"I didn't come here, Steve. I was sent."

Steve sat back in his chair. "Sent, huh? Sent by God, right?"

"I, too, have grown tired of empty words. I, too, feel that I have failed in my duty to God, my duty to my son."

"And why do you think God sent you here?"

"Mark, your son, has given us the opportunity to reach out to the entire nation at this next rally. The riot he started made national news."

"I have no son."

Victoria leaned forward. "God is offering you—and me—a chance for redemption. Mark disrupted my last rally for a reason." Steve remained quiet. "God doesn't want you to spend sleepless nights contemplating what might have been. Rather, God works to give us every opportunity to receive His mercy and His blessings, even His forgiveness. You simply have to recognize the opportunities God provides and seize them before they vanish." Victoria opened her purse and sunk her long, manicured fingers into the black leather folds, pulling out two cell phones. "As I said, you're much more than just a mechanic, Steve. God has blessed you with so much more potential." Victoria tapped on the screen of her own cell phone, typed a short text message and sent it before putting it back in her purse. "Mark abandoned God. He abandoned his country. He abandoned you. You now have the opportunity to demonstrate the consequences of turning your back on God—on your duty. Help us show others that one cannot so easily mock His laws."

Steve interlocked his fingers and brought his hands to his forehead. "I told you; I don't do speeches."

"You have other talents, Steve, which can be much more useful." Victoria flipped opened the second, smaller phone and hit the power button. It lit up, and she snapped it shut, setting the phone on the plywood table next to a pair of needle-nose pliers.

"By assisting the Alliance in a way no one else can, you are demonstrating your faith, Steve. You are fulfilling your duty, defending God's law against its enemies."

"You're yammering again, Victoria. Tell me what you wa—"

The phone jumped to life, the cheap, plastic casing vibrating violently against the surface of the table. A few stainless steel bolts shook in sync with each ring. Steve looked at the dancing, rectangular box as it moved toward him in short bursts.

Victoria snapped her purse shut. "I believe we all have a purpose, a destiny God created for us to fulfill. All we need is the courage to embrace our role—and act on it" Steve looked up as Victoria stood. She swung her purse over her shoulder and walked to the front door. The phone stopped, then started up again, vibrating in short bursts. Victoria opened the door and turned. "Working toward forgiveness, Steve, is a call God gives to all of his children. All we have to do is answer."

The front door slammed shut. Steve leaned forward and grabbed the phone before it fell off the edge of the table. It vibrated in his hand, the lights glowing against his skin. Steve flipped it open and held it to his ear.

"We need a compact, concealed device," a male voice said on the other end, "with a blast radius of less than fifteen meters. Minimal frag. Remote detonation." There was a pause. "Can you build it?" the voice asked.

Steve cleared his throat, looking at the wall of pictures above the television.

[XII]

[2010]

    The cerulean sky cut sharply across the horizon, accented by a few clouds hanging languidly in the atmosphere. The moon obstinately hovered midway in the sky, refusing to fully relinquish the night to the source of its light. Two gunshots rang out, ripping across the range, quickly fading. Another shot rang out. A small ring of sand and snow arced into the air against the deep blue, forming a temporary, transparent semi-circle that hovered and then instantly descended. Despite the nude sun burning against the almost naked sky, the cold air remained fixed against Erin's coat, chapping her lips.
    Mark shook his head and stepped forward. "No, no. Stop anticipating the recoil." He took the Glock from Erin, held it in front of him, pointing the gun downrange. Erin pulled her ear protection back from her right ear as Mark continued. "Remember, how you hold the gun is everything. Wrap your right hand around the grip, then wrap your left hand over the fingers of your right hand. Be sure to keep the index finger straight, off the trigger, until you're ready to shoot. Keep the pistol level and on target as you pull the trigger—all the way through. The bullet will be out of the barrel before the gun kicks back."
    Erin squinted. "I get anxious."
    "Nothing to be anxious about." Mark handed the Glock back to Erin, motioning to her to try again. "Unless, of course, you're on the other end of the barrel."
    Erin pushed the ear protection back on with her shoulder and held the gun at eye level, remembering to bend her elbows only slightly. She kept her feet shoulder-length apart, her left foot slightly ahead of the right. She

slowed her breathing, concentrating on the bright orange targets dug into the weed-covered berm twenty-five yards away. Another cold gust of wind kicked up swirls of snow. She blinked. "Squeeze, don't pull," Erin whispered to herself.

The gun kicked back, and an orange disc exploded. Shards flew into the air, spinning as they fell back to the firmament without a sound.

"Yes!" Erin yelled out.

"Good," Mark said as he leaned heavily on his cane. "Next target." Erin fired and missed. "Don't rush," Mark said.

Erin blinked, concentrating on the discs. Mark looked up and down the cracked cement walkway that ran the length of the gun range. There were only a few other shooters present. One was a man with a large belly poking out between his pants and his t-shirt. He sat in a folding chair, cleaning a shotgun that rested across his lap. A plywood wall separated the shooters from the parking lot. A single door had been cut into the plywood wall, the word *EXIT* spray-painted onto it with neon-orange paint. A corrugated aluminum overhang barely hid everyone from the sunlight.

"Can I ask you something?" Erin said, still aiming the pistol.

Mark turned back to Erin. "What?"

"You said you told Kevin." Erin lowered the gun and looked at Mark, pulling off the ear protection. "How did he react?"

Mark looked relieved. "Oh. That. I thought it was something important." He smiled. "It was all very anti-climatic. I wanted to tell him for weeks after we met, but I'd made enough enemies on the FOB. Anyway, Kevin and I were on twelve-hour guard duty in a DFP, and we—" Erin look confused. "Forward Operating Base and Defensive Fighting Position. DFP is also known as a Deep Fucking Pit." Mark paused. Erin didn't even bother saying *language* anymore. "Kevin was droning on and on and on about some Irish redhead he met between tours. He wouldn't shut up. So, I told him I was a homo. Interrupted him, just like that. Kevin shrugged his shoulders and said, 'So? Did I mention she's Irish?'" Mark smirked. "Kevin told me later that he'd suspected. He also told me most of the other guys wouldn't care if they knew. I told him he was full of…" Mark paused. Erin was looking down range.

"He never told me he met a woman between tours."

Mark laughed. "Kevin met a lot of women." Erin tuned to Mark. "I mean… not so many as… Kevin liked to exaggerate… sometimes… you know…"

Erin smiled, pushing her ear protection back on. "I know Kevin didn't tell me everything. I'm happy to hear he wasn't lonely." She aimed the gun down range. "And that he didn't—"

"Take after his mother?"

Erin sighed heavily. "Not exactly what I was going to say."

"Which is what I don't understand," Mark said, raising his voice so Erin could hear him through her protective earmuffs.

"What don't you understand?" Erin asked before she fired again.

Mark held his hand to his forehead, shielding his eyes from the sunlight. Small, rectangle bandages littered his forehead. One of his eyes was partially black. "Why you work with those morons at the Alliance. Hell, you co-founded it. Kevin hated them, you know."

"Yes, Mark. He told me his dislike for it many times."

"Not as much of a mama's boy as I thought."

"Get to the point."

"It's a compliment, really. You've never struck me as the type of idiot who would work at a place like that."

Erin dropped the gun slightly, eyeing the next target. "Thanks for the accolade. But we've been through this before."

"I was drunk last time."

"You're drunk all the time," Erin replied.

"Not today."

"No, today, you're hung over."

"Only slightly. Beer and vodka and rum and whiskey don't mix well."

Erin looked over at Mark. "Do you think it's smart to be hung over at work?"

"I worked at a different gun range, not this one."

"Oh." Erin looked downrange, then back at Mark. "Worked? You lost your job?"

"It's also not smart to show up to work intoxicated to give a lesson on gun safety." Erin shook her head. "I didn't handle any live ammo, Erin. It's a *safety* class, and I'm not that stupid. So stop changing the subject. I think I deserve an answer. After all, we've been in jail together. We're both victims of the machine and we've bonded through that experience, ready to ascend to the next level of friendship and trust."

"We were in an overcrowded cell with a hundred other protestors for less than a day. Speaking of which, isn't your court date next week?"

"I'm only saying, I think I'm due a rational, logical explanation as to why I'm so unfit to serve in the military. Me—the one teaching you how to properly handle and fire a Glock 21, big bore, .45 caliber pistol with a magazine capacity of thirteen rounds and right-hand, octagonal barrel rifling that—"

"Okay, okay. I get it."

Mark spat and turned his head. "Didn't that last rally, that last so-called *speech* by your friend Victoria, make it obvious to you that the Leviticus Alliance is full of shit? Victoria, in particular, uses fear to perpetuate misunderstanding and animosity toward a group of people I doubt she's ever really met." The gun kicked back again. The second orange disc jumped high, as if it were trying to escape. It fell on its side, rolling down the berm and circling to rest near a small patch of snow-covered dirt. "And yes, my court date is next week. I really pissed off that cop… he was mostly pissed off that he didn't get a chance to beat the hell out of me. They're going to make an example out of me in that courtroom. You watch."

"I'll go with you if you want me to."

"It'll only be another example of a bullshit justice system in a country run by corrupt judges, lawyers and politicians—all put in place to protect the interests of the elite who run this country—America's most precious offspring: corporations."

"You do realize that donations, some coming from those corporations, have gone up since your little demonstration of defiance?" Erin replied, lowering her aim slightly. "Victoria couldn't be happier. And that protestor you hit—"

"The little fucker hit me first."

"—he was the son of a prominent deacon. His father dragged him to three of those megachurches, even the one down in Colorado Springs, preaching to more and more people about how dangerous the opponents of the Alliance are, showing pictures of his son's bruised face."

"I bet that kid will think twice the next time he tries to punch a fairy in the face."

"The deacon has raised hundreds of thousands of dollars, Mark, all because of what you did."

"I'm flattered. And I'm sure all the little sycophants at those churches confirmed their misguided perceptions of us silly faggots."

"Plus," Erin replied, ignoring him, "Victoria is using my attack as a sign that gay rights supporters are getting desperate—losing the fight."

"Please. The guy who attacked you was some random nutjob using civil rights as an excuse to hurt someone—just like religious nutjobs do. And we homos lost the fight a long time ago, when Christians started legislating their bigotry in Congress. We'll never be seen as equal, or even human, as long as men and women in power continue to beat everyone over the head with their Bibles." Mark squinted. "And you won't need to worry about being attacked again if you keep shooting like that."

"Victoria has a plan to duct tape Bibles to bats."

Mark laughed. "Well, we homos are gathering our forces in the north, near Laramie, armed with fairy-dust cannons and glitter grenades that blind straight people. The invasion begins next Sunday at dawn." Mark kept his eyes downrange. "But now that you've coerced our secret plans out of me, I have no choice but to kidnap you and take you up to Laramie with me."

Erin fired. A plume of dirt rose from the ground and disappeared. The target sat nervously. "You have to get the gun back from me first," Erin replied.

Mark lifted his eyebrows and nodded. "True."

"And I'm just trying to point out that your stunt galvanized support that was slipping away a few months ago."

Mark dropped his hand to his side. "About seventy-seven percent of this country believes in a Christian God—ergo—seventy-seven percent of the country perceives homos as evil, sinful people who don't deserve rights, much less respect—ergo—we faggots are forever fucked—and not in the good way."

Erin shook her head. "Not all Christians hate gays, Mark."

"Save it. I'm not like those credulous idealists at the Universal Rights Coalition who think that their organization is going to someday create some huge paradigm shift in America and magically establish equal rights for gays. It doesn't matter what I do, or what any other homo does—we will always be seen as less than human."

Erin fired. The target spun into the air, missing a small section at its edge. It wobbled awkwardly before crashing back down under a blanket of dirt. "So why'd you even show up at the rally?" Erin asked, as she tilted her head and the gun in opposite directions. The slide was locked back.

"You're out," replied Mark. "Move your left hand under the magazine and use your right thumb to hit the release."

The empty clip fell into Erin's hand. She set it on a short, rusty table with the rest of the ammunition and the empty gun case. The four legs of the table were buried halfway into the dirt in front of the walkway.

"Keep the gun and your eyes pointed downrange," Mark said, massaging his knee. "Practice reloading the weapon without taking your eyes off the target."

Erin reached behind her and pulled out a full clip from her belt, sliding the magazine into the handgun. She wrapped her left hand around her right hand. Her thumb pushed down the catch lever. The slide snapped forward.

"I thought you were trying to educate people," Erin said. "Isn't educating people the key to change?" The gun clicked but didn't fire. The wind blew Erin's black hair into her face. Mark took the gun from her, keeping the barrel downrange.

"Probably a faulty primer," Mark said. "And why the hell are you giving me advice on how to fight the Leviticus Alliance?"

Erin pushed her long hair out of her eyes. "Those quotes… at the rally. I never knew Jefferson wrote things like that. I don't think most people do. But I only listened because I knew you. Everyone else thought you were just an angry lunatic."

"I am an angry lunatic," Mark replied, pulling the slide back. A single bullet spun into the air, bouncing off the metal table. It buried itself in the loose dirt. A small dimple was visible on the back of the shell. "An angry, alcoholic, half-psychotic fucking lunatic with PTSD and a solid knowledge of firearms, who doesn't feel like wasting his time trying to educate narrow-minded zealots when he can embarrass them instead. Not that the URC is much better—pissing about how every human is *special* and *equal*, as if it's some secret, unwritten, universal law. If the URC had the power you Christians do, they'd have fed people like you and Victoria to the lions a long time ago. You'd be the ones fighting for *straight* marriage and the right to be openly heterosexual in the military. The world is nothing more than groups of people in power fucking over those without—and then finding a way to call it just."

"I'm a zealot?"

"I'm sorry, I meant delusional morons who think that some invisible, all-powerful deity actually created the world in six days, and—get this—had to rest on the seventh!" Mark slapped the Glock down onto the metal table. A few spent shells rolled off the side of the table and fell quietly into the dirt. "An omniscient entity that gets winded! Fucking priceless!"

"What's priceless is you calling other people zealots while you harangue me—foaming at the mouth."

"There was a Greek philosopher named Epicurus who wrote that if God is willing to prevent evil, but not able, He can't be omnipotent. However, if God is able to prevent evil, but is just unwilling, then He must be malevolent. If God is both willing and able, then why does evil exist?"

A few rifle shots echoed off the berm farther down the gun range. A tall man sporting a long, brown beard and a red-and-white plaid flannel shirt fired off a few more rounds.

"It's man that brings evil into the world, Mark. You've read the Bible. It's our free will that brings about suffering." Erin took her ear protection off and set it on the table. Another shell rolled into the dirt. "We choose to separate ourselves from God, and that separation causes suffering."

"Isaiah 45:7: 'I make peace and create evil. I the Lord do all these things.' I the Lord. Sounds to me like he's taking credit. Of course, that's just the King James version. The word changes from evil to calamity in other versions." Mark bent over to pick up the disobedient slug. Erin closed her eyes, rubbing her temples. The stitches that ran from her hairline to her eyebrow stretched and pulled against her sore skin. Mark stopped and watched as a lone black ant crawled up the casing of the unfired bullet. The back legs anchored its body as it slowly swung its upper body into the wind—its antennae swinging frantically and erratically.

"There was a girl in our neighborhood," Mark started, as he observed the ant. "Her name was Samantha, but everyone called her Sam. She was a few years younger, the only child of this nice God-fearing, Christian couple that lived a few houses down the street. She was sick, very sick. My sister would sometimes babysit her, read to her at night. Sam loved Dr. Seuss books and would quote them back to Shannon, giggling at all the silly rhymes and constantly chanting, 'I am Sam. Sam I am, I am.' Anyway, Sam's mother had to stay home to take care of her daughter. The father was always working, trying to pay for all the medical bills.

My sister wanted to help out, so Sam's mom taught her how to wrap and repair the bandages around Sam's arms and legs. They had to be really tight, to the point where Sam could hardly bend her elbows or knees. Without the wrappings, her skin would blister and scar from the slightest touch. *Epidermolysis Bullosa.* Exposed skin can literally come right off, like pulling the skin from fried chicken. To keep the blisters from infecting, Sam had to take a bath—twice a week—in an antibacterial solution. It was, more or less, bleach water. My sister told me how Sam would shake, her freckled face contorted, crying like a leaky faucet. But Sam never yelled. She never complained. She never whimpered. She would cry without making a sound, silently shaking in a tub of bleach."

A few lark sparrows flew overhead, silhouetted against the deep blue sky. Their songs faded as they grew small and distant. Erin kept her eyes downrange.

"When she got older, the blisters on her right foot got so bad that her toes fused."

"Mark," Erin said quietly.

"The blisters lead to other complications, of course. Muscular dystrophy. Pyloric atresia." Mark caught the end of his index finger on the edge of his thumb and flicked the ant from its lead-and-brass tower. It went tumbling into the air and out of sight. "One day, the passage to Sam's small intestine swelled shut from blistering." Mark picked up the bullet and brought it to his mouth. A quick puff of air blew the remaining grains of sand off the casing. He set the rebellious bullet with the dimpled primer upright on the rusty table. "She was on a feeding tube for three weeks before her body finally gave out. Her mom prayed constantly by her bed, but I guess God was too busy with other things."

Erin used one hand to wipe both eyes.

"Sam was never really hugged or kissed by her parents. She never felt her mother's arms around her. She was never thrown giggling into the air by her father. She never played tag with the other kids in the neighborhood. Never went swimming or biking. Never took a bubble bath. She never grew up to have a boyfriend—or a girlfriend, for that matter. Her life was complete, physical isolation, no human contact."

Mark eyed the chamber of the gun, making sure the next round was in the correct position. His thumb hit the release. The slide shot forward. He pointed the Glock at an orange disc stuck horizontally into the berm. "Most children diagnosed with *Epidermolysis Bullosa* never survive to adolescence."

Erin remained silent.

Mark breathed out, then halfway back in. The gun came alive in his hands, like a volcano spewing lead. He emptied the entire clip. The remaining discs disintegrated as puffs of dust rose into the air and dissipated. The slide locked back, and Mark released the empty clip into his left hand, holding the gun in his right. His thumb moved up from the magazine and hit the release for the slide. It punched forward with a sharp snap.

"What the fuck did Sam ever do to deserve that?"

"I can't explain why God does what he does."

"That's a cop-out, Erin, and you know it."

"But the suffering of the innocent doesn't disprove the existence of God."

"No. It demonstrates that He's an uncaring, evil son-of-a bitch—assuming there even is a God."

Three sharp blasts rang out from their left. The bulky man with the large belly was rubbing his right shoulder, a 10-guage Remington gripped in his right hand.

"That's not fair."

Mark turned back around. "Why do people always say that when they're losing an argument?" Mark set the Glock down. He started picking up the empty brass around his feet. Hollowed-out soldiers of a brief and pointless conflict.

Erin picked up the empty magazine. "To Sam. It's not fair to Sam… or to the other children." Mark stopped. The brass casings burned his palms. "But there must be a reason behind it," Erin added. "Reasons we can't even begin to understand."

"Do you hear to yourself? Is that what you tell yourself to feel better? There must be a fucking reason? Not much comfort to Sam's mom."

"Mark, stop it. I'm not your enemy."

Mark spat on the ground. "Don't you get it? We make up the reasons! Sam's mom told everyone that her daughter was meant to be with the Lord. Her father quit his jobs and started a fund for children suffering from the same disease. He claimed he'd found his purpose in life. We apply useless 'reasons' to everything—to make us feel better as we swim and drown and die in this pointless existence." Mark paused. "Just because you believe in something, doesn't make it true."

"Your position is no different," Erin said as she filled the magazine, pushing each bullet into the casing with her thumb. "Just because you deny something, or see no evidence for belief, doesn't mean it doesn't exist."

Mark looked over. "There is no free will with your God—or any God for that matter. In fact, the very idea of God limits your choices."

"You mean the freedom to do harm?" Erin pushed the last bullet into the clip. She tapped the back of the magazine against her leg and handed it to Mark. "If there were no God, you could do whatever you wanted—hurt and kill the innocent—and there would be no justice."

"Yeah, 'cause God is doing such a great job right now at protecting the innocent. Have you ever seen your son's pictures?"

Erin looked up at Mark, then back downrange. "The Army confiscated most of his things."

"Big surprise! We killed—are killing—a lot of the wrong people over there, Erin. Americans can't stomach the fact that to win a war, people—

innocent people, and a lot of them, have to die. And doing what's morally right out of fear of punishment from a cruel, tyrannical God, by the way, is not being moral."

"Yes, we've been over this. But tell me again how belief in God limits my freedom of choice?"

"How about Marx? *'The more man puts into God, the less he retains in himself.'"*

"Stop quoting other people, Mark, and tell me in your own words."

"God is innately part of an institution established and created by man. Man limiting himself with the creation of morals, of absolutes—all codified by institutions."

"The church?"

"That's one. The Leviticus Alliance certainly qualifies. Any institution that works at trying to define how you should live your life."

"Even the URC?"

"Them, too," Mark replied. "The opposite side of the same fucking coin."

"So, these institutions limit freedom how?" Erin asked.

"By default, the Christian church says to the parishioner, 'You are a sinner—therefore incomplete.' In fact, you aren't complete without the church or without Jesus or God or baptism or communion or a fucking cross around your neck." Mark held his hand outstretched, as if addressing a congregation. "From childhood, individuals are indoctrinated to believe they can never think for themselves, that they are never whole without the institution—that they are fragments of a broken vase. And don't get me started with the other religions."

"And how is your perspective any different? Isn't your pseudo-philosophy—"

"Pseudo?"

"Isn't it also an institution, created by man, telling others how they should and shouldn't live their lives?"

Mark leaned over and began stacking the boxes of ammunition. "Most philosophers don't damn people to a physical hell of perpetual torment if they reject an idea."

"No. They only call people who don't agree with them delusional idiots who live in ignorance."

Mark shook his head and smiled. "Now you're getting it. Ignorance is bliss! And the first step to recovery is admitting that you are an idiot, Erin.

Are you ready to overcome your denial? Let me be your guide through this difficult transition."

Erin rubbed the scar on her forehead, the stitches like a zipper trying to hold in her frustration. "You have all the answers, don't you?"

"More than most, but only because I think for myself and question anyone who claims to know the truth."

Erin continued. "Don't philosophers and their followers damn those who reject their philosophies to a *mental* hell? The rejection of *their* truth results in the torment of self-deceit, brought on by the refutation of a specific, philosophical paradigm."

Mark looked over with a slight smirk. "I'm rubbing off on you."

"I read books, too," she snapped.

"Not the right ones. Neither did Kevin." Mark opened a black case with foam lining cut into the shape of the Glock.

"And you're the authority on what books should be read?"

"Nope," replied Mark. "But certain books should be read for what they are. The Bible is an incredibly violent, sexist historical narrative of a single, specific culture whose traditions and practices have almost no relevance in today's society."

"Tell that to the millions of followers. And stop with the insults."

"Like mother, like son."

Erin turned her head. "What?"

"Kevin could have been anything, yet he chose to join the Army—the Army! He became a bullet sponge for his country. How fucking heroic."

"So did you," replied Erin.

"To get the fuck away from here. And I wasn't brainwashed by a religion that told Kevin he could somehow quell suffering with photographs and love and forgiveness and happy thoughts and God, as if injustice is some external, evil force that overcomes the weak and can be conquered."

"I told you, Kevin left the church."

"But not his stupid belief in God. And you're the one who read him bedtime stories from the goddamn Bible."

Erin's eyes widened. "How did you know that?"

"Though I'm sure you skipped parts, like the passage in Numbers where Moses commits genocide—in the name of God, of course, which makes it acceptable."

"What else did Kevin tell you?"

"Malevolence emanates from our culture—from people. It's something *humans* create every day. And until humanity ceases to exist, there will always be suffering as a result. I've seen evil, Erin, and it's unmistakably human." Mark tucked a few boxes of ammunition under his arm. He grabbed the Glock and shoved it into the case, snapping it shut. He gripped the cane in his left hand. "And if there is a God—if I'm wrong—then he abandoned this clusterfuck of an existence a long time ago."

Erin didn't move. "Mark, what happened to my son?" Mark ignored her, grabbing the gun case and turning on his heel. His cane left small circles in the dusty concrete as he slowly limped away. "Enough, Mark! Stop walking away from me every time I ask about Kevin! What happened over there?"

"What happens to all of us, Mrs. Zuelke," Mark said over his shoulder. "Eviscerated by the world and left to slowly die in our own entrails."

Erin ran forward and grabbed the gun case, pulling it out of Mark's hand. It fell to the ground with a loud clatter, bouncing to a stop. Mark stopped and turned, keeping himself balanced with his cane.

"Have you ever lost a son, Mark?" Erin yelled, her face turning red. "What the hell do you know about loss?"

"Don't do that! Don't ask me fucking rhetorical questions to get sympathy. He wasn't just your son, you know. He was my friend." Mark held his hand to his face, pretending to wipe away tears, his cane dangling from his fingers. "Woe is me! Something bad happened *to me,* so now I can feel sorry for myself and help run a foundation that hates gays in the name of God. I can take my anger out on strangers and hide behind superstition. Now I have meaning and purpose in life, and I can lie to myself and cower behind the false idea that my son died for a fucking reason!"

Erin reached forward and yanked Mark's arm. The boxes of ammunition fell and hit the concrete floor. The bullets in the top box jumped out, rolling in all directions.

"Stop it!" yelled Erin, tears welling up in her eyes. "You're no different—spreading your own *fucking* hate because of what they did to you."

"Language!" Mark said loudly, shaking his finger and leaning forward. "Now that you're realizing your hypocrisy, I respect you enough to waste my time with you." Mark stood straight. "But your son was too indoctrinated to know better. And now Kevin, the one person in that entire desert who treated me like a human fucking being, is dead because of an *ideal.*"

"Shut the hell up about my son!"

"It took the death of your only child to make you realize how full of shit your insipid belief in God is—how full of shit that *Alliance* is. But despite all you've been through, you still desperately cling to those beliefs—it's pathetic." Mark pointed at Erin. "You should really ask yourself this: What if the mother who reared Kevin in such a narrow-minded environment, filling his head with supernatural nonsense, is the one responsible for him being worm food."

Erin slapped Mark hard, the white outline of her fingers slowly fading from his cheek. For a brief moment, they didn't say anything. Even the gunfire from the others at the range had ceased. Erin covered her mouth with her hands.

"Excuse me." Both Erin and Mark turned their heads. A tall man with a flattop haircut stood next to them. He was wearing a gray t-shirt with ARMY written across his chest in bold black letters. "Mark?" he asked hesitantly, "Are you Mark Bradford, son of Steven Bradford?"

Erin dropped to her knees and began picking up the bullets from the ground, trying to hide her tears. Mark leaned forward on his cane.

"Yeah. So who the fuck are you? And why can't you mind your own business?"

"I'm Lieutenant Carl Jacobson."

"Well, good for you, Lieutenant Carl Jacobson. You'll excuse me if I forget the proper salute." Mark grabbed his crotch, yanked on it, and then began to walk away, kicking some of the derelict bullets out of the way.

"Your father was the anonymous tip," the lieutenant said suddenly. Mark stopped. Erin was still crouched on the floor. She was no longer picking up the bullets. "He contacted the commander of the rehabilitation program shortly after your arrival. He knew several officers there in the chain-of-command at the base—got them to open an investigation."

Mark stood quietly for a moment, then spoke. "How do you know that?"

"I was the notification officer who told your father you were MIA." The lieutenant paused. "I was also the notification officer who informed him of your return." Mark was silent. "I thought you had a right to know." The lieutenant turned to walk away, then paused. "All you had to do was make up an excuse or deny it outright. They wouldn't have kicked you out if you'd told them you were straight."

"Integrity," Mark replied. "It's a core fucking value of the military, right?" Mark limped forward. "It's all sickeningly ironic."

The lieutenant paused, then spoke. "For what it's worth, I'm sorry."

Mark stopped and turned, tilting his head. "I know one when I see one, Lieutenant. You're worse than the fuckers who kick us out." Mark slapped his cane down. "A closeted faggot, worried about his military career. I'll bet you won't even come out if they repeal it, will you? Afraid it might ruin your career."

The lieutenant turned without a word and walked past Mark, disappearing out the plywood door. Mark started to follow but stopped. Erin was holding her hands to her face.

"You knew, didn't you?" Mark said, still facing away from her.

Erin stood, her eyes rimmed with red. "I was waiting for the right time to—"

Mark turned and limped back. He stopped and kicked the boxes of ammunition on the floor. Erin jumped. The bullets flew in all directions, gleaming in the sunlight as they spun helplessly in the air. "Right time for what? For me to hear from a stranger that my piece-of-shit father got me kicked out of the Army? Why did you contact *Steve* in the first place?"

"It was Victoria. I only found out after—"

"Of all people. This whole time you've been fucking lying to me. Why?"

Erin tried to speak calmly, but her words were disconnected as she tried to catch her breath. "Please listen, Mark. I… I don't know why… except… Victoria wanted your father… to speak at the next rally."

Mark's eyes widened. He pointed his cane at Erin and pushed it into her shoulder. "Stay the *fuck* away from me!"

"I didn't tell you because…" Tears were now burning down her red cheeks as she continued. "… because I was afraid you would leave."

Mark pushed on the cane, shoving Erin back. She tripped and fell, landing hard on the ground. She pushed herself up. "You're just like the rest of them." Mark said.

"No."

"You used me so you could get to my father for your fucking *Alliance*."

"Please…" Erin managed to mumble, "… you know that's not true."

Mark turned toward the exit. The bearded man was standing near the door, the rifle slung over his shoulder. Another person entered, a 9mm holstered at his side. Mark recognized him as the range master. The two men began talking quietly, the one with the beard pointing toward Mark.

"Something horrible happened in that desert," Erin said, crying softly. "You can't bring yourself to tell me, but I saw it on your face the first day we met. What did they do to you? What did they do to my son?"

The two men started walking toward Mark. He turned away from them. Erin was on her elbows, strands of black hair matted to her face. Mark leaned over. "You want to know what happened to your precious child?" Mark asked through clenched teeth. "He screamed for them to stop—yelled until his throat bled—and I could have stopped it. I could have saved your son." Mark stood straight. "But I didn't. I did fucking nothing as they ran a knife across Kevin's throat—"

Erin quickly covered her ears and closed her eyes, yelling the word *'No!'*

"—slicing open the carotid arteries on either side of his neck." Erin went quiet, slowly shaking her head back and forth. "He was dead in minutes." Mark paused. "I was the one who killed him."

"Out!" yelled the range master, one hand pointing at the exit, the other tightly gripping his holstered handgun. The man in the flannel shirt stood near the range master, his bolt-action rifle now held across his chest. Mark turned and picked up the Glock case. He limped toward the exit without another word. The door slammed behind him.

"She all right?" the rifleman asked.

The range master knelt down next to Erin. She stared straight ahead, rocking back and forth on the balls of her feet, her arms crossed over her stomach, clutching at her abdomen.

"Ma'am, did he hurt you?" Erin didn't respond. The range master looked over and shrugged his shoulders at the rifleman. He looked back down. "Ma'am?"

Erin didn't respond.

[XIII]

[2009]

"Mark. Wake up, Mark!"

Mark jerked his arms against the restraints, snapping his head forward. He felt the cold metal dig deeper into the red rings on his sore wrists. The pain from his leg shocked him out of his stupor as the sound of Kevin's voice kicked him in the back of the head. Sweat dripped from his forehead. Mark closed his eyes and breathed slowly, trying to keep his muscles slack.

"I'm up," he whispered, almost frightened by the weak sound of his voice.

"You okay?" Kevin's voice was hoarse, tongue swollen.

"Yeah."

"You sure?"

"I'm fine."

Mark opened his eyes and looked toward the ominous opening in the wall. Rigel was looking back. Distant. Quiet. Innocuous. Mark coughed and shook his head violently. He looked at his hands, pulling against the chains as he stretched his arms out in front of him. He curled his fingers into the palms of his hands, digging uncut nails into the skin. Sand blew into his mouth. He tried to wipe his lips on his shoulder.

"You were screaming—again."

"Weird dream, that's all."

Mark lay down and felt the weight of his body push against the cool dirt of the floor. He looked at the bucket but couldn't find any sign of the camel spider. He knew it was there, watching him through the vibrations in the ground. "Screaming like a little girl," Kevin added. Mark stifled a short burst of laughter. The stench of urine and mold invaded his nostrils, coating his tongue like layers of ice on limestone. He felt stomach acid climb up his esophagus, but he clenched his throat, fighting back the urge to vomit.

Kevin's chains rattled slightly as he scratched the back of his neck. "So, what was the dream about?"

"Seventy-two virgins. All of them female."

"Hence the screaming?"

"Exactly."

Silence.

"What was the dream really about?"

"Don't remember. I think I was back in college or something."

"You remember," Kevin replied. "Your hands are still shaking."

Mark looked up, tucking his hands between his legs. "I'm fine."

"Bullshit."

"Fucking drop it, will you?" Mark spat toward the bucket, unable to scare the spider out of hiding.

Silence.

Kevin tilted his head back, leaning it against the cool cinderblocks. "I've been having weird dreams, too."

"Seventy-two male virgins?"

"No," Kevin replied with a slight smile, cracking his lips. "It starts with me sitting in my mom's kitchen, eating breakfast—scrambled eggs and toast. I can still smell the butter. Anyway, my mom walks into the room wearing these same restraints." Kevin held up his hands. "And she just stands there in her pink robe, watching the sun rise through the window above the sink. I jump up and try to pull the restraints off. Then I notice, for the first time, that the kitchen table is covered with old, rusty keys. And it's not only the table. There are keys in the sink, in the dishwasher, in the cupboards, all over the floor. Even my bare feet are ankle-deep in keys. I start frantically picking them up, one by one, telling my mother it will be okay as I try to unlock her restraints one key at a time. But she just stands there, her face expressionless, like granite."

Mark pushed himself up from the floor, leaning his sweat-covered back against the wall.

"The keys keep falling through my fingers. The ones I do manage to hold on to don't open the locks. Some break in half or dissolve into dust. The whole time, my mother is staring out the window, oblivious to the chains, oblivious to me. I start yelling at her, screaming *Mom*, grabbing her shoulders and shaking her. But her face is blank, eyes sunken into her skull—her mouth a small slit above her jaw. She doesn't even blink, her eyes watering from staring at the sun."

Kevin coughed, then cleared his dry throat. "I finally turn her body away from the window, pleading with her to acknowledge me... look at me... anything. All the sudden, her eyes open and her body tenses up. She opens her mouth and starts screaming—jaw locked open. I cover my ears and yell for her to stop, but she keeps screaming, without taking a breath, looking straight through me. I drop to my knees from the pain in my ears. I look up and she's standing there, screaming, with the same blank expression on her face. Blood starts streaming from her nose, her eyes, her ears. I reach for more keys, but I keep dropping them, blood on the back of my head, my neck." Kevin paused. "Then I wake up."

Mark pulled his head up slightly, looking at Kevin's thin body. He looked like a partially melted wax sculpture, twisting and falling away from its supports. "I'm sure she's fine."

Kevin's head tilted back. "She always worries too much about me."

"Moms always do, at least that's what I've been told."

"Yeah, I guess."

"Look. It's just a fucking dream, okay?"

"Maybe."

"There's no maybe, Kevin. Dreams are nothing but the random firing of neurons in the brain while you're asleep. It's the brain trying to assimilate and process the events of a day, mingling them with your memory—like defragging a computer. They don't—"

"I can't remember," Kevin said flatly.

"What? Your dream? You just told me—"

"How we got here. I can't remember anymore how we ended up in this damn cell."

Mark sat silently, looking carefully at his friend. Kevin rubbed the temples of his forehead. Then he asked, "What do you remember?"

Kevin dropped his hands and sighed. "We were in a convoy, on our way to Samarra, right? I was riding shotgun in a deuce three trucks behind the lead. I was joking around with Doc when the IED went off."

"I was in the truck in front of you, remember?"

Kevin nodded his head. "Then what?"

"I never heard it," Mark continued. "The floorboard launched me up and slammed me against the door. Fire filled the driver side of the cab. We were right on top of the damn thing. But it must have malfunctioned."

"Why do you say that?"

"I was still alive," Mark replied. "The heat was instant. My gun burned my hands. I could smell burning flesh. No oxygen. I tried to breath, but the heat seared my mouth and throat. I couldn't hear anything. And the driver—Private Wicker. I could tell he was screaming, clawing at his face with his hands, trying to pull the fire away from his body. I kicked open my door and reached across the cab, trying to yank Wicker out, but he was stuck. That's when the rest of the IED went off. I woke up on my back. It was muffled, but I could hear gunfire. Screaming. Someone shouting orders. My eyes burned. I tried to pull myself up. I didn't understand how I wasn't hurt. I looked down. My hands were sunk into mud—blood mixed with the dirt. I grabbed a rifle and tried to stand. More gunfire from the hills. Large caliber. RPGs hitting some of the trucks. There was a severed arm lying near me, the fingers clutched into a fist. I think it belonged to Wicker. That's when you grabbed me from behind, dragging me by my collar." Mark rubbed his leg, looking at Kevin. "Do you remember dragging me into that ditch with the others?" Kevin didn't respond. "One was that baby-faced private—Private Bricksen."

"Yeah." Kevin responded. "He hadn't shaved a day in his life."

"He had multiple chest wounds. The holes kept making these sucking noises as I tried to stop the bleeding, fucking bullets flying everywhere. He kept opening his mouth, trying to breathe, but he didn't make a sound. Sergeant Murphy was with us, yelling as he fired on the hills, the hot shells falling onto my back. I kept lying to Bricksen, telling him it would be okay, to hold on. He grabbed my hand. There was something behind those eyes, then it was gone—no last words, no dramatic exit, just his body shutting down. You went to look for other survivors as we fired into the hills." Mark turned his head and spat. "You didn't find any."

Kevin closed his eyes. "It was an ambush."

"They were waiting for us. Better firepower. And you're remembering."

"Sergeant Murphy had burns on his back from an explosion," Kevin replied.

"He was giving us orders, trying to spot for us, telling us which direction to fire. But by then, all the vehicles in the convoy were on fire or full of holes. Then we heard trucks coming from the other side of the road, down a ridge. For some reason, they were driving white Chevys. I wondered how American cars would somehow end up here, used to kill Americans. Anyway, we exhausted all of our ammo. Murphy looked at us and reluctantly told us to raise our hands. We walked out of the ditch as they pulled up in the trucks, shooting their rifles into the air, some of them praising Allah for their victory. Murphy walked between us and the vehicles when—"

"They shot him."

"Yeah. He spun. His arms flung out from his sides, and he collapsed. Eyes locked open, staring back at us as the insurgents drove their truck over his body. Then they started arguing with each other when one of them pointed his Kalashnikov at us. All I could see were their eyes, turbans wrapped around their faces. They made us get down on our knees as they searched for other survivors. They found a few under a burned-out vehicle. Too injured to run or fight or even move. The insurgents pushed the rifle barrels against their foreheads. One of the soldiers didn't say a word. The other one spat in the guy's face before the back of his head exploded—a cloud of pink fucking mist. And the sound of the skull cracking open... I can still hear it when I sleep—like shooting a watermelon."

"Who were they?"

"Not sure. One of them might have been Doc."

Kevin coughed violently. The chains rattled as he covered his mouth. Mark saw movement in his peripheral vision and looked to his side. The camel spider had launched itself out from under its blanket of sand. A small, black beetle struggled in its fangs, legs kicking and twisting in the air. Mark wondered if the insect could feel the fangs in its body, the saliva slowly dissolving its organs, its life being sucked up through the holes in its back. Then he continued. "Not much else. We were the only ones left. They tied us up and brought us here. I don't know why they didn't just kill us like the others. I don't even know how long we've been in this cell."

"'*A man is the sum of his misfortunes,*'" Kevin said quietly. "'*One day you'd think misfortune would get tired, but then time is your misfortune.*'" Kevin coughed again, struggling against his restraints to cover his mouth.

"Dickishness, remember?"

"It's from Faulkner. *The Sound and the Fury.*"

"How do you remember exact passages like that?"

Kevin wiped his mouth on his shoulder. "I don't know. My mom read to me constantly when I was a kid. She would tuck me away in a blanket and read to me all night."

"Is that so, Private Pansy?"

Kevin ignored Mark and continued. "I'd fall asleep to her voice reading Frost, Faulkner, Poe—even the Bible."

"Poe? So, you had a lot of nightmares as a kid?"

"One or two," Kevin replied with a slight smile.

Mark glanced over to the corner of the cell. Both the beetle and the spider were gone. "Misfortune is all we have to define us, huh?" Mark asked. "Well, the limited time it takes for us to understand that misfortune, so as to avoid it, is never enough."

Kevin licked his chapped lips, scraping the sand from his teeth. "Or maybe time gives us limitless possibilities we choose to ignore, out of fear or apathy. Maybe it's limited time that gives choice meaning."

Mark stifled his laughter, trying to subvert the pain from his chest, his knee—his whole body. "Are we continuing our discussion?"

Kevin looked around. "It's the perfect place."

"And we have plenty of time," Mark added, sitting forward.

"It's the knowledge of our limited time to create a finite future that makes life valuable." Kevin continued, "We are aware of our finitude, bringing weight to each choice we make."

"Well then, I choose to get out of this cell." Mark held his hands up in front of his face, holding his wrists against the chains. "Lot of fucking good that did."

"Don't be a prick."

"I choose wrists without restraints," Mark said loudly. "A knee without a hole. Bricksen to be alive again. Humanity without war—all equally worthless." Mark looked around the cell, then at his knee, then at his wrists. "Maybe humans choose to live in misery because that's all we really know. Our choices prolong our suffering. It's an addiction. We wouldn't know what to do with never-ending peace. Hell, we'd find a way to fuck it up."

"Okay, yes, there are circumstances we can't escape," Kevin replied, looking around the cell. "But we have the capacity to adapt to shitty circumstances and choose how we react."

"How? Does it really matter in the entire history of this planet?" Mark leaned forward against his chains, trying to stretch his sore muscles.

"I know the analogy," Kevin replied wearily. "If Earth's history were reduced to a single, twenty-four hour period, humanity would only occupy the last four seconds." Kevin began rubbing his bloodshot eye. A few grains of sand were stuck in the eyelid. He tilted his head, his eye watering as he tried to dislodge the culprits.

"Those pictures you take of the dead," continued Mark, "are pictures you choose to believe will make a difference—out of faith, I might add, since you can never really know for sure what, if any, impact you'll make."

"And maybe you choose to do nothing because it's easier," Kevin replied, kicking his legs out.

"Well, fuck you too."

"You accuse the religious of preaching to everyone while you do the very same thing. Worst of all, you contribute zilch on how to resolve it."

"Because there is no way to resolve it."

"Says the wounded animal shaking his fist at the sky."

"Says the credulous philanthropist with a camera and an M-16."

"Maybe," Kevin replied, "if you can force yourself to believe that this world is worth nothing, you can choose not to choose—thereby avoiding risk, disappointment, or failure."

"Free will is a delusion we create to avoid the truth."

"And what *truth* is that?" Kevin asked. The slamming of a large metal door echoed down the long, dusty hallway. Voices followed. Kevin peered down the dark hallway.

"Shit. The other knee," Mark said quietly, lying back down on the dirt.

"What?" Kevin asked.

"They said they were going to drill the other knee." Mark's eyes sunk down into his face as he lay down on his side. He spoke to himself, the words kicked up clouds of dust. "We try to avoid the truth that we are like the stars, burning silently into oblivion."

"Shut up," Kevin said through gritted teeth, "and pretend to be sleeping."

"An improbable cosmic accident waiting to be corrected," Mark whispered, staring back at Rigel. The footsteps of two pairs of boots made their way down the long corridor, growing louder and louder. Mark lay motionless. Kevin tensed up. He laid his chin back onto his chest, closing his eyes, struggling to release his rigid shoulders. The barrel of a Kalashnikov slid its way past the bars, scraping metal against metal. The guard stood for a moment and cursed in Arabic. Both were wearing turbans. One was wearing the camouflage pants of an American soldier, with blood stains down the left pant leg. Several dog tags clattered about his chest—one had a hole in its center. The guard pointed the barrel of his rifle at Kevin as a second guard pulled a set of large, black keys from his pocket. He shoved one of the keys into the lock, slamming the bolt and flinging the gate open. It groaned on its hinges. The second guard stepped in, grabbing the back of Kevin's neck with one hand and pulling him up to his feet. Kevin's legs gave out and he fell back to the ground.

"No." Mark shot up. "No! The escape was my idea!"

The guard with the camouflage pants walked slowly into the cell. He stood above Kevin's collapsed body. The dog tags clinked together as he slowly took his turban off, looking down with amber eyes. His hair was black and peppered with grains of sand. He reached into his side pocket, staring at Kevin as he pulled out a small digital camera. He bent down onto one knee and held the camera by the wrist strap, swinging it back and forth in front of Kevin's one bloodshot eye. Mark fell silent.

"We found this among the wreckage," the guard with perfect English began. "Somehow, it wasn't damaged in the attack on your convoy." The guard turned the camera on. "It took a week to get fresh batteries. It takes weeks to get anything out here." The guard looked over at Mark, then back at Kevin. "I wanted to kill you, you know, when we first found you. I was the one pointing my rifle at your head. But I was ordered not to. There were others who thought you two might be more valuable alive. I thought them foolish." The glow from the camera's faceplate illuminated the guard's face. "So, imagine my surprise when I found you in the first picture, standing next to the same trucks we destroyed." The guard began flipping through each photograph. "You made a record of your own atrocities," the guard added, "along with a record of each stop your convoy made." He turned the camera display toward Kevin. "Others are sure to follow a similar route—there being so few alternatives. Where was this first picture taken? Where did your convoy originate? How frequent are they? What supplies do they carry, and who do they carry them to?" Kevin remained silent. The guard flipped to another picture. "This information is, obviously, more valuable to me than you two could ever be." Kevin lowered his head. "You're asking yourself how long you will last—how long you will be able to tolerate the pain before you tell me what I want to know, aren't you?" the guard asked, rubbing his chin, his hand scraping against stubble.

"Specialist Zuelke, Kevin. United States Army. Service Number 523-56-9284."

"I'm curious about that myself," the guard said, standing up.

Kevin kept repeating the same line, over and over, his voice flat. The guard with perfect English waited a few minutes, staring at Kevin before nodding his head. The second guard nodded back and walked over toward Mark, aiming the gun at his head.

"Go ahead! Shoot me, you fucking coward!" Mark yelled, pulling against his restraints, kicking up dirt as he leaned his head toward the barrel. Kevin stopped his mantra and looked over at Mark, then back at the guard.

"It's your choice," the guard said, tilting his head toward Mark.

Kevin sighed as he slowly tried to stand. He struggled as he pulled himself to his feet, holding his injured arm to his side, splintered fingers scraping against the cinderblock wall for support. The guards ignored Mark's protests as they released the locks around Kevin's wrists, the restraints falling to the floor in a cloud of dust. Mark kicked forward with his one good leg, cursing, straining his throat, jumping forward against the chains and falling flat on his face. Mark could taste his own blood as he struggled to stand.

"Keep an eye on my mom for me?" Kevin asked over his shoulder as the second guard pushed him out of the cell, digging the barrel of the gun into his back.

"Fuck all of you! Fuck Allah!" Mark yelled, trying to pull himself up again, yanking his body against the bloody restraints. The remaining guard chuckled to himself, shaking his head as he held his rifle loosely in his hands. He bent down to one knee, facing Mark, rubbing a few of the dog tags together with his fingers.

"I'm not Muslim. In fact, most Muslims I know would condemn what I'm doing—would condemn me. Don't get me wrong, there are those in this compound who would burn you alive in the name of Allah. But I hate you for a different reason." The guard spat on Mark. Mark spat back. The guard grabbed Mark by the throat and shoved him back against the cell wall. "I studied in America. New York City. I thought myself lucky at the time." The guard let go of Mark's throat. Mark grabbed at his neck, coughing. "I was traveling to the wealthiest nation on earth. Anything was possible. The first week I was there, I saw a man—a citizen of your own country— starving on a street corner less than a block away from a restaurant. He ate out of trash bins. A month later, a Muslim friend of mine—also a citizen of your country—was beaten because he visited Ground Zero. They called him a terrorist as they hit him in the face with bricks. He now struggles to raise his little girl, unable to find any work without the use of his eyesight—a result of the beating." The guard leaned forward. "I witnessed the invasion of other countries by a people who claim freedom as a right." Mark turned his head to one side, breathing heavily from the pain in his leg. "Then I see you Americans judge us for *our* iniquities—telling us that we need their democracy, their religion, their Coca-Cola."

The guard grabbed Mark's left ankle, below the injured knee, and yanked him away from the wall. Mark screamed, trying in vain to swing his arms. The guard slowly walked backward, pulling Mark with him. Mark's body was stretched taut, inches above the cell floor. The guard pulled at his ankle violently.

"We never did finish our conversation last time, did we?" he said, pulling harder. Mark screamed. "I must apologize for urinating on you. It was rather crude and uncivil. But, as I said before, *Saiph* was my favorite dog. I was... upset." The guard stopped pulling Mark's leg and knelt down, his rifle held by the barrel in the other hand. The chains holding Mark's wrists slackened. Mark stopped yelling to catch his breath.

"I asked if you knew what happened to Orion. Remember?" Mark closed his eyes, trying to slow his raspy breathing. "There are many versions of the myth, of course, but my favorite comes from the Greco-Romans. According to them, Orion was once a great and powerful warrior. None in the entire world could match his strength as a fighter or his skill as a hunter. Orion constantly boasted of this greatness to the gods, claiming that no beast could ever kill him." Mark tried to pull his leg away, and the guard tightened his grip and pulled back. "Ah, but Zeus' wife, Hera, grew tired of listening to Orion's arrogant declarations; she grew weary of his pride. So, she sent a small, innocuous scorpion into his chambers. It stung Orion in the ankle, fatally wounding him." The guard smacked Mark's wounded knee with the butt of his Kalashnikov. Mark yelled, shaking his head back and forth, pulling at his restraints. "And just like that, the greatest warrior on the Earth was killed by a little insect." The guard finally released his grip on Mark's ankle and stood. "Orion was then cast into the sky to be forever chased by Scorpius, the beast that killed him."

"You're forgetting," Mark said slowly with half-open eyes, barely conscious from the pain, "that Orion smashed that fucking scorpion after he was stung."

The guard smiled. "Only to die soon after." He threw his rifle around his back, turned, and left without another word. Mark stayed on the dusty floor, unable to move his left leg. He listened to footsteps fade down the corridor.

Silence.

Kevin's distant screams followed.

More silence. A few hours passed before the butt of a rifle nudged Mark in the ribs. The guard with perfect English stood over him, his face sprinkled with blood and sweat. "Your friend is resilient," the guard said, wiping his face with a dirty rag. He tossed a handful of severed fingers onto the dusty ground next to Mark's face. "What happens to him next is up to you."

Before Mark could respond with more cursing, the stock of a rifle came crashing down on the back of his head. Two other guards dragged his unconscious body out of the cell and down the dark corridor. The guard with perfect English remained. He lit a match on the underside of a fingernail, lighting an unfiltered cigarette. He stood for a few minutes, staring out the opening in the wall, smoke wrapping around his head. The stars were hidden behind a black wall of clouds that flashed white with lighting. He couldn't hear any thunder. A camel spider crawled across the cell floor. The guard walked forward and slammed his boot down on the arachnid's body. He took another drag and flicked the cigarette out the opening. The spider was still stuck to the sole of the guard's boot as he left the empty cell.

[XIV]

[2011]

"I told you to stay away from him."

"Victoria, stop."

"You know he jumped bail, don't you? Never showed up for court, the coward."

"I know. I was there."

"I can't believe you're friends with a homosexual fugitive. Spin that one to our supporters."

"Let them think what they want."

"He doesn't respect you, Erin. He never did. Can't you see that? And now..." Victoria snapped her head away from Erin, locking her gaze out of the tinted window of the idling limousine. "Jesus, Erin. You've been shut up in your house for weeks. What the hell did that kid say to you before he disappeared?"

Erin paused before answering. "It doesn't matter."

Victoria sighed and ran her hands through her hair. She turned back toward Erin. "Listen, I know you were trying to help him, but—"

"Mark doesn't want help, especially not from me." Erin cleared her throat. "He never did."

Victoria nodded her head. "Well, I'm glad that you're finally starting to come to your senses. So here's your chance to move on. *I* need your help—especially today."

"Victoria..."

"Have you even been watching the news? It's only been a few weeks since they repealed Don't Ask, Don't Tell, and the donors aren't happy. A major victory for the URC that I have to address today, with no speechwriter, no one to even manage this event. The girl who's substituting for you is absolutely horrible—just awful. She couldn't plan her own funeral. It's a miracle this rally even happened." Victoria leaned over and grabbed Erin's hand, holding it tight. "And we've missed you. I've missed you. These events are a train wreck without you. We all miss your contagious enthusiasm. We need you back, today. Right now."

Erin pulled her hand away. "I was naive, Victoria, not enthusiastic."

Victoria straightened her back. She turned her head again, staring out the tinted window, her gaze falling on the waiting crowd. They held the usual small American flags that waved in the wind. "So, you've made up your mind without even talking with me about it? The Alliance has momentum now. We're launching a new campaign—"

"Yes, I know, Victoria. I was the one organizing it."

"So, you're going to jump ship?"

"No. I just... I need a few more weeks."

"To do what? Sit around and sulk? Do nothing?" Victoria shook her head. "I don't care what that Mark kid said to you, it's no excuse to ignore your responsibilities."

"I wish you would trust me."

"How can I trust you? You're dumping all of your work onto me and the others—and you won't even tell us why." Warm air blew through vents in the ceiling and floor of the limo. A small fly emerged and hovered near the back window, its wings beating rapidly as it continuously slammed its tiny body against the tinted glass, finding no escape.

"Fine," Erin said. She turned in her seat and leaned toward Victoria. "Let's talk about trust, Victoria. Why did you contact his father?"

"Whose father?"

"Don't play stupid."

"Don't you care about the Alliance anymore? About our work? Our mission?" Victoria pulled her gaze away from the cheering crowd.

"Stop dodging questions with questions." Erin reached over and turned off the heater. "Why did you contact Mark's father?" The noise from the crowd was now bleeding into the vehicle. They chanted slogans and quoted Bible verses and sang hymns. The afternoon sun hung precariously in the sky, framed between skyscrapers in the crowded, downtown streets. A cold wind blew across the red faces of the crowd and shook the limousine. A young woman with a clipboard ran up to Victoria's window and rapped harshly on the glass, yelling the muffled words *'Ten minutes.'* Victoria watched as she ran back toward the stage and tripped. The clipboard fell to the ground. Papers flew in all directions.

"You'll notice," Victoria continued, staring out the tinted windows, "that the stage is not only in front of our headquarters this time, but we put all the protestors across the street and out of ear shot." Victoria pulled her gaze away and looked back at Erin. "That was your suggestion. Almost everyone else disagreed, but I defended you because I *do* respect your judgment. But it wasn't until now that I realized you asked me to do it simply because you're afraid of them, aren't you? You're afraid of what they represent. Are you doubting your commitment to the Alliance? Your commitment to God? Hell, you might even agree with those protestors, for all I know."

Erin said quietly, "You still didn't answer."

"This rally is twice as big as the last one. Reporters from all the major networks are here—CNN, MSNBC, FOX, even that liberal soapbox, NPR. Journalists from *The New York Times, Newsweek, USA Today. The Denver Post* and *Westword* are nothing now. Live webcasts and blogs. Facebook and Twitter…" Victoria glanced up through the sunroof. "We've even got news helicopters circling overhead." Victoria shook her head and looked at Erin. "And you're brooding in the back of this limousine, trying to avoid confrontation—telling me you need a leave of absence. You weren't like this before you met Mark."

Erin sat back, crossing her arms. "You're hiding something from me, and it has to do with Mark's father."

Victoria sighed heavily and reached down by her legs. She wrapped her manicured fingers carefully around a thin, black folder sticking out of an open briefcase on the floorboard. "I asked Steve to speak at today's rally, that's all. I wanted him to share his story. His own son abandoned him, after all. Left him alone in that house, the poor man. You should have seen it."

"Is that what Steve told you happened? That Mark abandoned him?"

Victoria slammed the briefcase closed with her foot. "Let me guess, Mark told you some dramatic story that plucked away at your heartstrings."

"And Steve didn't do the same with you?"

"Steve refused to cooperate," Victoria continued. "Apparently his shame is too much to bear."

"Oh, for Christ's sake, will you stop with the bullshit."

Victoria's head snapped back. "Yeah, that Mark kid hasn't influenced you at all."

"I'm not one of your donors. Stop trying to convince me Steve is somehow a victim."

"We are all victims, Erin, victims of this small group of people who constitute less than two percent of the entire population of this country. Yet here we are, bowing down to their demands for special protection as they force their perverted perspective down our throats—it's disgusting."

"Two percent of gays who are gay-identified, Victoria—you're manipulating stats. I doubt you even care what people do in their own bedrooms."

Victoria put her hand to her chest. "Meaning what? Where is this coming from?"

"Meaning… you don't care about the mission of the Alliance as much as you do its methods—your methods."

"I'm not listening to this." Victoria reached for the handle and pushed the door open. Erin reached across Victoria's lap and pulled it closed.

"Speaking of avoiding conflict," Erin said, grabbing onto Victoria's wrist. "You'll use it to manipulate others into a frenzy, but God forbid someone should challenge you directly."

Victoria snapped her arm forward, yanking it from Erin's grip. "We have to defend ourselves against those who want to destroy our culture. *They* are the enemy, Erin." Victoria pulled her hair back into a ponytail as she looked pointedly at Erin's scar. "You, of all people, should be aware of that." Victoria rolled up her sleeves. "These people are working to systematically dismantle America's moral foundation. God doesn't hesitate to destroy those who oppose him. Neither will I."

Erin stifled a small laugh. She looked up briefly at the fly now trying to escape through the sunroof. "You're reciting parts of a speech I helped you write two years ago." She looked back at Victoria. "I don't know why I never saw it before. It's all a game to you. You don't believe in all of this—I doubt you ever did."

"How do you know what I believe?" Victoria asked, opening the folder and flipping through her speech, the pages falling lightly through her fingers. "I can hardly look at you anymore, these things you say to me—the big sister who hired you to run my store when you were only eighteen. The person who helped you become the successful woman you are today."

"I don't owe my successes to you, Victoria," Erin replied. "So don't try to guilt me into submission."

"I'm not trying to—"

"You live in your small, self-contained bubble of subterfuge, spouting your rhetoric to convince others, unable to fully convince yourself."

"Rhetoric you helped write!"

The fly buzzed between Erin and Victoria, briefly circling their heads before retreating to the back window. Neither tried to swat it away.

"When was the last time you actually went to a church service?" Erin asked. "When's the last time you even spoke to Pastor Knight?"

"I run this organization seven days a week."

"And you enjoy creating this façade. You enjoy manipulating others in believing what you don't."

"The Leviticus Alliance is now a façade?" Victoria shook her head, adjusting a thick, red wool scarf around her neck.

"This—what you're doing," Erin continued, "has nothing to do with upholding family values or protecting anything but your own opportunism."

"Kevin's death has made you a weak Christian, Erin. A test from God I'm sorry to say you failed."

Erin shook her head. "Nope. It's not going to work. There you go again, trying to use the death of my child as a tool to manipulate me, to control every conversation. You used to do the same thing with my divorce."

"Getting defensive," Victoria said, underlining a few lines in her speech with a red pen. "And it's because you know I'm right."

"You're deflecting, because you know you're full of shit."

Victoria slammed the folder shut. "Stop!" She tucked the pen into her inside coat pocket. "You know, people come to me—donors, reporters, even homosexuals—all of them asking why the co-founder of one of the largest foundations for family values is spending so much time with a goddamn homo. Why she was found unconscious in the parking lot of a damn gay bar. I try to tell them it's because you lost Kevin, or that you want to tell Mark about Jesus." Victoria adjusted her white leather coat, pulling it tightly around her body. "But now I know it's because you're selfish. You miss your son so much that you're trying to be a mother again with Mark—make up for all the mistakes you made with Kevin. And it's destroying the Alliance and our friendship along with it."

Erin looked forward, rubbing her scar. "I'm done. You and the Alliance can go to hell."

Victoria opened her door. A blast of cold wind shot into the limo as she pulled herself out of the vehicle. When the crowd saw Victoria emerge from the parked limousine, they started cheering. Banners waved more frantically, American flags swinging viciously back and forth in the cold air. Victoria stood and waved and smiled and waved some more. Then she turned back around and stuck her head inside the limo, raising her voice over the wind.

"Look at that crowd. After today, I won't need you or your money." Victoria started to close the door, then stopped. "You know, Erin, maybe it's a good thing you were a single child. I'd hate to see how you would treat an actual sister."

The door slammed shut. It was quiet. Victoria said something to the driver waiting outside. The driver's door opened, and he slumped into his seat.

"Where to, Ma'am?"

Erin looked down at her lap, closing her red eyes and rubbing her temples. "Can we sit here for a minute?"

"I was told to take you out of the area immediately, Ma'am."

"Just wait a minute, please."

"Your dime," replied the driver with a shrug, just before raising the tinted glass barrier between them.

Victoria bolted up to the podium, waving vigorously as the crowd grew more energized. Behind her, a large building with glass for skin stretched skyward, the sun burning as a reflection, an island of yellow fire floating in a sea of black glass. She stood behind the lectern and opened her folder, looking over the faces of the crowd as she held the flapping pages down with her gloved hand. She pointed at the protestors across the street. They were lined up behind thick, metal barricades, their voices dying in the wind.

"They speak of rights and individuality, while simultaneously deriding ours! They try to tell us that we don't have a right to say to them, 'You are wrong! You are immoral! You are an offense against God!'" Victoria paused, the crowd cheering and nodding and clapping. "They speak of tolerance, while trying to push their own distorted morality onto your lives, your country, *your children*!"

The police stood next to the barriers on both sides, batons across their chests. On either side of the empty street, large police vans with mounted water hoses stood at the ready. Officers in riot gear stood on either side of the trucks, tear gas guns cradled in their arms. At least two dozen cops patrolled the crowds.

"They may have repealed Don't Ask, Don't Tell, but the Leviticus Alliance is here to say 'No more!' We will continue to fight this repeal. And as they turn to attack the sacred institution of marriage, let us pray for strength, strength from God to hold our resolve! Together, we can proclaim what we know for certain is morally true: One man, one woman!"

The crowd began chanting the same slogan. A large white banner with bright blue letters ran the length of the stage behind Victoria, secured to the glass building. It read *www.LeviticusAlliance.org*. Victoria turned slightly, one hand holding her speech to the podium, the other pointing behind her.

"You can help us stomp out those who dare to redefine morality, God's supreme law! We will go to D.C., we will stand on the steps of the Capitol, and your voice *will* be heard. By calling or donating online, you take a stand against those who have the audacity to claim man's law somehow supersedes God's!"

Erin sat in the limousine, shaking her head as she listened to Victoria's words. Her cell phone vibrated in her purse. She pulled it out and read the name on the display: *Mark*. She set it down on the leather seat. It turned slowly with each ring, like the large hand of a clock. A few minutes later, the display lit up with the word *Voicemail*. The phone rang again, and she picked it up. *Mark*. It vibrated in her hand a few more times until she pushed the *Ignore* button. It rang again. She hit the *Ignore* button and then turned the phone off. Erin could hear Victoria's words seeping into the quiet limo. A pause. The crowd cheering. The fly had disappeared.

She hit the buzzer for the driver, and the window separating them rolled down with a mechanical buzz. "Fort Logan National Cemetery, please," Erin said.

"We are here to put an end to this tyranny, to the erosion of family values!" A few strands of Victoria's ponytail had escaped and were dancing wildly in the wind, whipping across her face. She used one hand to push them out of her narrowed eyes. She leaned forward and opened her mouth to continue, but she suddenly lost her breath as a bright flash of light and heat slammed against her body.

Victoria and the lectern were launched from the stage. Like dancing partners in mid-air, they slowly spun together before landing hard on the sidewalk immediately in front of the building of black glass, the lectern splintering apart on impact. The banner fell to the ground, half of it on fire. Victoria lifted her head, thin streams of red trickling out of each ear. There was a deep hole directly in front of where she had been standing only a few seconds earlier. The remaining metal supports to the stage were bent upward and the wooden beams were scorched black. She tried to lift herself, but a second explosion went off near the stunned crowd of supporters, knocking her back down.

Mangled arms and legs arced through the smoke-filled air, dragging behind them threads of liquid red like strands of crimson dangling from a threadbare quilt. Thousands of glass shards descended from the building above, showering the injured and the dazed and a few who didn't move at all. The sharp pieces of glass twisted and spun in furious flashes of reflected sunlight, bouncing to a stop on the ground. The stage and the parking lot were now carpeted with broken glass reflecting a shattered, blue sky above. Columns of black smoke mingled with the screams of those who held wounds vomiting blood, their lives escaping onto grass and asphalt, rolling into thirsty gutters. A few stood motionless, their clothes and hair burned away—naked, charred bodies draped with burnt skin hanging loosely like dirty rags from broken towel racks. Other bodies became fuel for the fire that licked the sky.

Victoria worked again to hold her head up. Pain shot through her body. She looked down and saw her left arm bent at an awkward angle, the ulna jutting out past the skin. She looked up and blinked, then blinked again. She could see unfocused figures close to her. They were walking toward the street with outstretched arms black as soot. She couldn't hear the screams.

Erin tripped over broken planks and shards of glass as she ran toward the destroyed stage. Sirens echoed off the city's tall canyon walls. A large column of smoke slithered against the buildings, snaking its way upward, a great transparent python with beams of sunlight shooting through its massive body.

Two craters now sat in front of the headquarters of the Leviticus Alliance, littered with bodies, some attempting to pull themselves out from the rubble. Erin stopped and covered her nose and mouth with her arm, scanning the ground for Victoria. Her eyes burned. She turned and saw Victoria's body, her white coat stained with blood and soot, her blond hair matted to the sidewalk with blood.

"Victoria?" Erin coughed as she said the name, the smoke burning her throat and lungs. Victoria slowly opened her eyes halfway.

"I told... you... to go home," Victoria said weakly.

Erin looked up, tears dripping from her shaking chin. "Somebody help me!" Her voice was drowned out by sirens. "Please! Someone!"

Cops and medics were spilling into the periphery of the explosion, bending over broken bodies. Erin could smell burnt flesh, and it pulled at her stomach. A hand, warm and wet, wrapped around her wrist. Victoria pulled her head up.

"...too close," Victoria whispered, her head slowly moving from side to side as she swallowed hard. Her face was black with smoke, contrasting with the red in the whites of her eyes as they moved languidly, trying to focus on Erin. "I can't... can't hear anything." Victoria erupted into a violent cough that sprayed blood onto Erin's pants.

"I'm getting some help." Erin, said, pointing to a fire truck in the distance. When she tried to stand, Victoria's grip tightened around her wrist.

"He put them..." Victoria whispered, each word contracting her face. "... too close... to stage... to the people."

Erin looked back down, trying to pry Victoria's hand from her wrist, wondering where such a broken body got the strength. The paramedics were getting closer. There were now two more helicopters circling overhead. The sun burned through the swirls of black smoke.

"I'm sorry... little sister..." Victoria's head wobbled forward toward her chest, as if it were trying to fall off.

Erin reached down and supported her head and leaned in, Victoria's trembling mouth only inches away from Erin's ear. "Just be quiet, Victoria. Stop trying to move."

"Away from... the crowds," Victoria coughed out, her eyes closed. "I told... told him." Victoria closed her eyes.

"Stop talking. You'll be fine."

Victoria's grip tightened. "I never meant... never meant... for..." Victoria's body curled in on itself as she leaned forward, the contents of her stomach spilling out onto the sidewalk, mixing with the already-darkening blood.

Erin's knees scraped against the cement as she pulled the black wool scarf off from around her neck and pressed it hard against a large wound on Victoria's side. Erin pushed. Victoria screamed in pain, eyes clamped shut. "I have to stop the bleeding." The smoke was somehow thicker, veiling any help coming their way.

"I wanted us..." Victoria said quietly, "to be... on BBC." Her body began to shake. "You... you were leaving us..."

"You're in shock, Victoria." Erin placed both hands over the scarf. A fire truck blasted its horn so loudly that Erin tried to cover her ears with her shoulders. The helicopters were lower, the vibration of their blades slapping against the walls of the buildings. Erin could feel a sharp pain in her knee and realized she was kneeling on a shard of glass, now deep beneath her skin.

Suddenly lucid, Victoria grabbed Erin by her lapels, pulling her close. "It was Steve."

"What?" Erin asked, the sounds of the sirens and the helicopters fading away. Victoria slowly let her head fall back against the concrete, her red eyes staring up at the sky.

"... Steve put the... the bombs... too close..." Victoria was breathing heavily, her chest heaving.

Erin fell back from her knees, holding herself up with her arms stretched out behind her. The glass shard was still sticking out of her knee. Erin didn't notice. "You did this," she whispered, her face full of disbelief.

"No one... gets... hurt." Victoria closed her eyes. "We'll be on... BBC."

Erin brought her knees to her chest. "My God, Victoria."

A few paramedics appeared, shamans covered in soot and dressed in stained, white shirts and blue gloves and clear plastic glasses clamped to their faces, emerging from walls of smoke with tools of healing dangling from their necks and shoulders. "Over here!" one of them yelled, pointing in Victoria's direction.

Erin wrapped her arms around her legs as the paramedics sprinted and knelt and huddled over Victoria. She was now lying motionless. One paramedic ripped off his glove, holding two bare fingers over Victoria's limp wrist. "Ma'am. Ma'am, can you hear me?" he asked, as another paramedic opened Victoria's eyes with two gloved fingers, shining a small flashlight into her pupils.

A third paramedic knelt down next to Erin. "Ma'am, are you hurt?" he asked in a calm voice that seemed muffled and distant. Erin's eyes were locked straight ahead, blinking slowly. Her body shook. The paramedic took a thin blanket from his bag and draped it over Erin's shoulders. "You'll be fine," he said as he examined the shard of glass sticking out of her knee. Police officers stormed by, faces flushed as they scanned for more bodies. A few firefighters held their helmets on their heads, looking for fires and damage in the building above. The paramedics who knelt over Victoria pulled out two small white panels from an orange bag. One yelled *"Clear!"* in a raspy voice. Victoria's body jerked upward with each shock, then fell limp. Jerk. Limp. Jerk. Limp. Erin's black scarf was crumpled up in a ball near Victoria's feet. Someone from behind yelled for a paramedic, and one of the men crouched over Victoria jumped up and ran past Erin. The remaining EMT closed Victoria's eyes with his gloved hands. Erin looked at her knee and saw that the glass shard was gone. A blue-gloved hand was holding gauze to her wound.

[XV]

[1986]

Shannon leaned forward with her short arms locked behind her back, pushing herself up by her toes so she could gaze into the crib, her eyes barely reaching over the top railing. The newborn smiled, kicking his legs, eyes opened wide as he gazed back at her.

"Hi, Mark," she said in her soft voice. "I'm your big sister, Shannon."

The baby cooed, his small arms stretching toward her. Shannon reached over, pushing her hand out of the floppy sleeve of a green sweater that was too big for her. She extended her small finger, and Mark reached up and swatted at it. Above the crib, a dozen multicolored balloons hovered near the ceiling, knocking into each other. They were tied with white string to the arm of a large, brown teddy bear that smiled ceaselessly. The stuffed animal held a white card between its furry paws that read *Congratulations on your new baby boy!* The bed next to the bear was empty.

"Grab it," Shannon said excitedly, wiggling her finger. "You can do it."

Mark blinked and reached up again, this time wrapping his tiny fingers around Shannon's index finger. She smiled and turned her head.

"He got my finger, Daddy!"

Steve was pacing in front of the hospital bed where his wife had been sleeping an hour earlier. He hadn't shaved and was still wearing his work shirt from the day before, untucked and wrinkled. The words *Leadville Water Treatment Facility* were written on the back. The name *Bradford* was on a patch above the breast pocket. Steve kept glancing into the small, empty bathroom where Laura had collapsed, smacking her head against the rim of the toilet. When Steve found Laura, she hadn't remembered falling. Then she had trouble breathing. Then she vomited. The nurses wheeled her away on a gurney. The doctor told him not to follow, to stay with his children. A single nurse remained to clean up the blood and the bile. Steve tried to help, but the nurse shooed him away. After she left, Steve washed his hands, the water turning red before swirling down the drain. He was wiping his hands on the sides of his jeans when he nodded his head at Shannon. "That's great, honey."

"Does he know?" Shannon asked as she turned back around. Mark's large, round eyes stared back as his small arm pulled on her finger. "Does he know who I am?" Mark kicked both legs again. His small, bare feet peeked out from under a blue blanket. The crib jiggled slightly as Shannon leaned forward.

"He probably does," Steve responded, forcing himself to stop pacing. "Don't lean on the crib, honey," Steve said as he walked over to Shannon, pulling a chair away from the wall, welcoming the distraction. He picked up his daughter and sat her in the chair. Shannon leaned over, careful not to touch the sides of the crib.

"His feet are all flaky, Daddy."

"That's normal," Steve replied, pulling up a second chair next to his daughter. He carefully re-wrapped the blanket over his son's feet. Mark closed his eyes and turned his head, coughing.

"And what's that?" Shannon asked, pointing at Mark's belly.

"It's a clamp for the umbilical stump."

"The what?"

"That's where they cut the umbilical cord."

"Did it hurt?" Shannon asked with concern.

"Not at all," Steve said, pointing at Shannon's belly. "You had one, too."

Shannon looked surprised. She pulled her shirt up and stared at her stomach. "That's just my belly-button, Daddy."

"But there was a stump there, just like on your brother."

"A stump?" Shannon asked, still staring at her stomach.

"When you were in Mommy's belly, you were connected to her with a cord that fed you."

"Really?" Shannon asked, looking back up at her father skeptically. "Where is it?"

"It fell off," Steve responded, "leaving a belly-button. I have one from my own mommy." Steve pulled up his shirt and poked at his belly. Shannon giggled, revealing a missing tooth. Mark started crying.

Shannon dropped her sweater. The excess material folded on her lap. She looked back into the crib, worried. "Is he okay?"

"He's fine. Babies cry a lot," Steve said.

"Did I cry a lot?"

"You did," Steve replied, standing and reaching for the pacifier next to the teddy bear. "More than your brother," Steve added with a slight smile.

"Did not," Shannon replied, shaking her head, her long, brown hair shaking with it.

"You were the loudest little girl in the entire nursery," Steve continued.

"Was not," Shannon replied defiantly.

"Was too. But you were also the prettiest," Steve added, kissing his daughter on the forehead before sitting back down. Shannon shyly shrugged her shoulders and giggled again, still watching her brother. Steve stuck the pacifier in Mark's mouth, and the baby immediately stopped crying. Steve looked back at the door of the room. A large window allowed him to see down the hallway. He looked at the empty spot near the door where the doctor had stood, telling Steve they weren't sure what was wrong, that they needed to run some tests. That they would find out why she passed out, why she looked so pale, why she was still so weak. The doctor had said they would take care of Laura—that there was nothing to worry about. The doctor had said he would be back soon; he had said it twenty minutes ago.

"Now he looks sleepy." Shannon observed. "How much do babies sleep?"

"A lot," Steve responded.

"Do they sleep more than they cry?"

"Yes, they do."

"How much is a lot?" Shannon asked, tilting her head.

"At least eighteen hours a day."

"Eighteen hours?"

"But not all at once," Steve replied, wiping his dry hands on his pants.

"How long is that?"

Steve smiled. "A long time, sweetheart." Steve looked at the door, then back at Shannon. She was carefully studying her new brother. His small face scrunched up as he sneezed. Shannon smiled and dutifully said, "God bless you." The blue hat on Mark's head came loose on one side. Steve reached into the crib and pulled it back in place. Mark cooed.

"Daddy?" Shannon asked, her voice suddenly serious. "Is Mommy okay?"

"She'll be back soon, honey," Steve replied, trying to sound reassuring.

"She said she wasn't feeling good." Shannon stuck her finger out again. Mark smiled and reached up to grab it. "Just before she fell."

"Mommy's tired, that's all." Steve looked over his shoulder. Through the window, he could see the doctor approaching. A nurse followed behind.

Steve turned to his daughter. "Shannon, I want you to stay here with your brother, okay?"

"Okay," Shannon replied, slowly moving her finger up and down. Mark tried to grab it, but it slipped away.

Steve stood and kissed Shannon on the top of the head. "And let your brother sleep. I'll be right back."

"Okay," Shannon said, pulling her arm away from the crib. She stuck it back in as soon as her father walked away.

Steve opened the door before the doctor arrived. The nurse squeezed by between Steve and the doctor. She walked straight to Shannon sitting next to the crib. She immediately removed Mark's blanket and lifted his shirt. Steve ignored the doctor at first, watching the nurse as she examined Mark's skin, holding her thumb against his chest and checking for a change in skin color when she lifted her thumb. The pacifier fell out, and Mark cried. Shannon's eyebrows turned down. The nurse smiled and asked Shannon's name as she examined Mark's eyes with a small, dim flashlight. Shannon shrugged her shoulders and looked away.

"Shannon," Steve said firmly from across the room, "she asked you a question."

"I'm Shannon, Ma'am," she replied quietly.

"That's a beautiful name," the nurse replied, checking Mark's lips and mouth for any blue coloration. "Is this your baby brother?"

"Mr. Bradford?" the doctor started. Steve ignored him.

Shannon nodded her head, looking into the crib. "His name's Mark. He sleeps eighteen hours every day and he cries a lot. But not as much as I did," Shannon added proudly.

The nurse smiled and looked over at the doctor and Steve, giving them a quick nod. "He's fine."

"Mr. Bradford," the doctor said again, more forcefully.

Steve turned back toward the doctor. "My son is hungry."

"Nurse Flores will take care of your son. We have formula on the way. But I need to speak to you. In the hall." The doctor held the door open, his other hand tucked away in one of the pockets of his white coat. Steve turned toward his children for a moment. Shannon was talking to the nurse, pointing at her belly button. "They'll be fine," the doctor said, walking out into the hallway. Steve turned and followed. "Do you have family on the way?"

Steve shut the door softly. "I called Laura's parents before we left the house." Steve was talking more to himself than the doctor. Steve squinted in the bright hallway. White floors and white walls reflecting white fluorescent lights. "But they're driving from Denver. The storm will slow them down."

"Mr. Bradford," the doctor began, "I want to let you know, first of all, that we will—"

"What's wrong with my wife, Dr. Harper?" Steve asked, staring the doctor in the eye.

The doctor pulled his hand out of his pocket, gesturing with both hands. "She's septic," the doctor said, walking down the hallway and motioning for Steve to follow.

"Septic?" Steve asked.

"Your wife is fighting a severe infection that's spread into her bloodstream."

"Infection from what?" Steve asked loudly, refusing to move.

"We're not sure, Mr. Bradford." the doctor responded, trying to pull Steve away from the room.

Steve jerked his arm away. "Not sure? What *are* you sure about? What the hell is going on?"

"Mr. Bradford," the doctor responded firmly, "your wife has been given an aggressive course of antibiotics to help fight the infection, but her body is already weak from the delivery and the surgery."

"Meaning what?"

"She has hypotension, she's lethargic, and her breathing is shallow. We might need to put her on a ventilator." The doctor stuck his hands back into his pockets. "And there is a strong possibility that her body will be too weak to fight the infection."

Steve's face was slack and white. A few men in blue scrubs ran by. Doctor Lawrence was paged overhead to the emergency room.

Steve shook his head. "And Mark?" he said almost in a whisper.

"Your son is fine. His blood tests have come back negative. Nurse Flores is performing a visual inspection to verify those results. It seems the infection originated after the caesarean." Steve looked back at the door to the room. "Mr. Bradford, your wife is asking to see you." Steve continued to stare at the closed door. He could hear Shannon laughing. "Mr. Bradford," the doctor said firmly, "once we put her on a ventilator, she will not be able to speak."

Steve turned back toward the doctor. "How the hell did this happen?"

"There are a number of possibilities for infection, as with any surgery. But for now, I need to get you to your wife. If you'll follow me, Sir."

"Don't call me 'Sir,' Doctor."

Doctor Harper led Steve down a hallway, then another, then another. Steve heard a siren from an ambulance scream, then suddenly stop. A phone rang at a nurse's station. When they reached the ICU, the doctor stopped at the door and turned. "Mr. Bradford, there's one more thing. Have you and your wife ever discussed a Do Not Resuscitate order?"

Steve narrowed his eyes. "Yes."

The doctor waited patiently before asking. "And?"

"You keep her alive, no matter what."

"We will do everything we can, Mr. Bradford. But if she signed—"

"Excuse me," Steve interjected, pushing past the doctor.

The Intensive Care Unit was darker than the hallway, but warmer. Laura's bed was near the back of the room, next to a window. Snow fell silently outside. Steve walked past several unconscious patients, a few with machines breathing for them. They all had clear, plastic hoses running out of their arms, their mouths, their noses. Bags of urine hung from the lower railings of the beds. The cardiac machine that monitored Laura's heart rate beeped steadily, but slowly. A male nurse in blue scrubs stood nearby, setting up a breathing machine at the foot of her bed. He looked over at Steve.

"I'm Aaron. I'll be right over there if you need anything." Aaron walked to one of the other beds, looking over a patient chart. Steve stared at his wife. Laura's face was pale and perspiring, but she smiled when she saw her husband standing next to her bed. A small gold cross hung from a chain around her neck.

"How's the baby?" Laura asked, taking a short breath. "They told me his blood tests were clean. And Shannon? She's worried, isn't she?"

Steve sat down next to her on a short, stainless steel stool with wheels. He grabbed Laura's hand with both of his, careful not to disturb the needles in her forearm. "Shannon's fine," Steve said. "She's playing with Mark. Won't let him sleep."

"You did the same with Shannon after she was born," Laura replied with a smile.

"Mark already recognizes her."

Laura turned on her side and slowly lifted her other arm, rubbing Steve's cheek and the dark stubble pushing through his skin. His cheeks were wet.

"He has your smile," Steve added.

"Already his mama's boy," Laura replied. "And what about you?" Laura asked, stroking her husband's thick, black hair, stretching the plastic tubes in her arms.

"Don't worry about me and the kids." Steve lifted Laura's hand and kissed her palm. "You just worry about getting better."

Laura smiled and closed her eyes as she fell back, trying to take a deep breath. "You're not fine. I know how you get when things don't go according to plan." She opened her eyes and looked at him without moving her head. "And I'm not going to be here anymore to calm you down and tell you it'll be all right."

Steve squeezed his wife's hand. "You're going to be fine."

"Promise me something?"

Steve leaned forward. "Anything."

"Don't be angry."

Steve's head dropped. "They made you sick," Steve said forcefully through clenched teeth.

"Everything happens for a reason—even this." Steve shook his head. Laura closed her eyes, working hard to breathe. "I know you've never believed as I have. I knew that when I married you."

Steve looked up, his eyes in tears. "I can't do this without you."

"Yes, you can. If anyone can raise those two beautiful children, it's you." Steve shook his head. "You refuse to see the man I've loved all these years. The man who drove his two-year-old daughter around town at three in the morning because the only place Shannon could sleep was in a moving car. The man who worked nights for four years without a vacation so that his family could have a home." Laura tried to lean forward, barely lifting her head from the pillow. "The man who brought me a dozen roses for every anniversary—never forgot. Who quit drinking, even though it was the hardest thing he ever did." She let her head fall back to the pillow. "The man who drove two towns away to buy his pregnant wife a pint of white-chocolate raspberry truffle ice cream."

Steve's head dropped again. "You were asleep when I got back. It stayed in the freezer for weeks."

Laura smiled. She pulled on the cross around her neck. "Help me with this," she asked, trying to sit up. Steve looked up and reached over, unhooking the chain. Laura pulled it from her neck, setting the cross in Steve's palm. "Promise me you'll keep the faith." She closed Steve's hand. "Raise our children in the church—"

"Please, don't ask me that," Steve replied.

"—so that someday, we'll be together again—all of us. As a family. As God intended. Just promise me..." Steve squeezed his wife's hand. "I know the nightmares that kept you up almost every night," Laura continued. "About that child solider. God helped you overcome those horrible experiences."

"*You* were the reason they stopped."

"They stopped because we had faith in God. And that same faith can hold our family together until we... until we are together..." Laura's breath was shallow. Her eyes rolled back into her head and her back arched.

Steve yelled over his shoulder. "Nurse!"

The nurse ran to the bed, dragging the ventilator behind him. "Sir, I need you to leave," he said, slipping in between them, slapping a large, red button on the wall. Three more nurses flooded into the room, followed by Doctor Harper. Nurse Aaron tried to pull Steve away, but he held on tightly to his wife's hand.

"Laura, don't leave me," Steve pleaded.

"She can't breathe!" Nurse Aaron yelled at Steve, trying to pry his hand loose. The cross fell to the floor. The gold chain curled on itself like a coiled snake.

"I can't do this alone," Steve choked. The electronic beats from Laura's heart monitor sped up. Another nurse ran to the other side of the bed. She stuck a long, plastic tube down Laura's throat. Laura gagged and turned her head, her chest lifting higher up into the air. Steve knocked the nurse's hands away. Doctor Harper grabbed Steve's arms and yanked him back. Steve kicked the stool away and swung his elbow back, smacking the doctor in the jaw. Doctor Harper stumbled back, his clipboard clattering to the ground next to him. Nurse Aaron reached over and locked his hands around Steve's wrists, pulling hard. Steve immediately turned and clamped his hands around the nurse's throat. He pushed Aaron back and slammed him hard against the wall. The other two nurses stood defiantly between Steve and his wife. Only one woman remained on the other side of the bed, monitoring the ventilator.

"Leave her alone," Steve pleaded, his voice cracking. His hands began to let go of Aaron's throat. The nurse knocked them away, coughing as he pushed past Steve.

"She's stable, Doctor," the nurse on the other side of the bed said calmly. Doctor Harper nodded, picking up the clipboard from the floor. Steve stood facing the wall, breathing heavily. Two security guards came running into the room. Harper turned and waved them away with the clipboard.

"Mr. Bradford," the doctor said, walking up to Steve, keeping his arms at his sides. "If you don't let us help your wife, she will die here, right now." Steve looked over his shoulder at the doctor, then at his wife. "Mr. Bradford," the doctor insisted, holding his arm out toward the exit. "If you'll come with me, please."

"I'm sorry," Steve said, first to Laura. Her eyes were closed, but she was breathing normally. Steve turned to Nurse Aaron. "I'm sorry." The nurse was rubbing his neck, standing at the foot of Laura's bed. He didn't respond.

"Mr. Bradford," Dr. Harper continued calmly, "Your wife is stabilized. Let the nurses do their jobs." Doctor Harper held out his arm again, pointing toward the exit. Steve bent down slowly and picked up the cross. The gold chain dangled from his hand as he followed Doctor Harper out of the room. The security guards watched cautiously. The doctor told them to remain in the ICU. Once again, the bright lights of the hallway made Steve squint. He walked over and leaned forward, holding his head against the wall. Dr. Harper stood nearby. "You were in the Army, weren't you?" Steve stood straight, turned, and looked at the doctor suspiciously. He nodded his head. "Then all of that in there was purely instinctual. Nothing but a trained reaction to a hostile environment."

"I didn't mean to—"

"Your wife is sick. You're upset." The doctor motioned for Steve to walk down the hallway with him. "When my older brother came back from Vietnam... He had only been there a year, but he wasn't the same. Jittery. Apprehensive. Paranoid. He never sat with his back to a door. He slept on the couch in the living room. One morning, I woke up early, eager to talk to him about what he had seen, about what he had been through. I was sure he would tell me things he couldn't say in front of our mother." Steve looked over his shoulder at the receding ICU, but his feet continued to carry him toward the room where his children were waiting. Doctor Harper continued. "I stood next to the couch, leaned down, and shook his shoulder, whispering his name. His arms shot out and clamped onto my shoulders. In an instant, my feet left the ground. He flung me into the air, up over the couch. I slammed into a china cabinet that had been in the family for years. Broke almost every plate, bowl, and glass in that cabinet—along with my left arm. The crash woke up the whole family. Everyone came rushing into the living room. My dad had an old baseball bat held high over his shoulder."

They turned down another hallway. The doctor rubbed his jaw as he continued.

"My brother was asleep through the whole thing. Didn't remember any of it. From then on, if we had to wake him, we did it with a broom handle." The doctor looked over his shoulder, making sure Steve was following. "He's now married with three kids. He sleeps in a separate bed."

They reached the room where Laura had been holding Mark only a few hours before. Steve looked in through the window in the door. Shannon sat talking quietly to the nurse, her small legs swinging. The nurse whispered something in Shannon's ear and Shannon laughed, quickly covering her mouth and looking into Mark's crib. His eyes remained closed.

"Did your brother ever talk to you about the war?" Steve asked, his breath fogging the window.

"No. Not to me. Not even to his wife, as far as I know."

"Was he a religious man?"

The doctor shook his head, holding the clipboard to his chest. "Not after he came back. Never set foot in a church, no matter how much our mother scolded him."

"Neither did I," Steve said, pinching the gold cross in his hand. "But it seems I may not have a choice." He secured the chain around his neck, tucking the cross under his shirt.

The doctor was silent for a moment. "We'll let Laura rest for the night, keep a close eye on her."

"I'd like to be with my children now, Doctor."

"Of course. But there still is the matter of the DNR." Steve straightened his back. "Should your wife's condition get to the point where—"

"She signed one years ago," Steve interrupted, turning and facing the doctor. "Her grandmother was in a coma for six months. Laura never wanted to put her family through the same experience."

"I understand," replied the doctor. "We'll need documentation, so that when the time comes—"

"Please apologize again to the nurse."

"Certainly. We'll let you know if there is any change in your wife's condition."

"Thank you, Doctor," Steve replied, walking into the room quietly.

Nurse Flores was wrapping the blanket tightly over Mark's small feet. She looked up at Steve. "He keeps kicking the blanket away. Already a troublemaker."

"Hi, Daddy," Shannon whispered. "I think Mark said his first word."

Steve smiled, took a deep breath, and cleared his throat. "Did he say 'Shannon?'"

"Nooo," Shannon giggled, wildly shaking her head.

"Did he say, 'big sister?'"

"No, Dad," Shannon replied, rolling her eyes. She leaned forward in her chair. The green sleeves of her sweatshirt covered her hands as she tried to cup them over her mouth. She whispered, "He said 'hi.'" The nurse smiled.

"Did he?" Steve asked.

Shannon nodded, then looked up at her father as she tilted her head. "What was my first word?"

"Hobgoblin."

Shannon giggled, then held her hands to her mouth. The missing front tooth was again briefly visible between her lips. She looked into Mark's crib. He was still sleeping. She then looked back at her father. "No it wasn't," she whispered.

"No, you're right. It was gobbledygook," replied Steve with a slight smile.

"That's not a word, Daddy," Shannon frowned.

The nurse stood. "I'll leave you with your children. If you need anything—"

"Actually, Nurse Flores—"

"Her name is Mariel, Daddy," Shannon said. "It means be-lov-ed. And she said my name means little wise one." Shannon looked over at the nurse. "What does be-lov-ed mean?"

"Close to the heart," the nurse replied.

"Nurse Flores," Steve said, "would you mind staying a few more minutes with my son? I'd like to take my daughter to the chapel."

The nurse nodded her head sympathetically. "Of course, Mr. Bradford. It's on the first floor to the right of the main entrance."

"Thank you." Steve's large hand dwarfed Shannon's small one as he held it. "Come with me, honey."

"Where we going?" Shannon asked, jumping off the chair. "What about Mark? What if he wakes up and we're not here?"

"He'll be fine, sweetheart. Nurse Flores is here to keep an eye on him. We won't be gone long. We're going to say a prayer for Mommy."

Shannon cocked her head. "But it's not Sunday. And you don't go with me and mom to church."

"Come on, Shannon. We'll talk about it on the way."

The nurse remained silent as Steve led Shannon toward the door, his daughter's small feet shuffling quickly with every step Steve took. Steve noticed her left shoe was untied. "Tie your shoe, honey," Steve said when they got to the door, pointing at his daughter's foot.

Shannon held her hands to her mouth, her eyes filling with tears. "What's wrong with Mommy?"

Steve bent down on one knee and tied the laces, not responding to Shannon's question. "Let's go," Steve said when he finished, leading his daughter out of the room. He closed the door softly behind them.

Nurse Flores crossed herself and held her hands to her chest. "*Pobres niños*," she whispered to herself. The nurse sat back down next to the crib, staring at Mark. "*Qué Dios esté con tu madre.*"

Mark opened his eyes and started to cry. The nurse reached over to the end table that held the teddy bear. There was a small bottle of formula sitting next to the stuffed animal. She pulled Mark out of the crib and held him close. The baby reached up, grabbing at the bottle. He sucked on the latex nipple.

"You miss your mommy, don't you?" the nurse whispered. "Don't you worry. God has given you a beautiful big sister and a good papa to take care of you." Mark kicked his legs, turning away from the bottle. A few drops of formula landed on his cheek. He began to cry again.

"Shhh," the nurse replied, gently wiping the formula from Mark's cheek. She rocked him in her arms. "It's all going to be okay," the nurse said. Mark continued to cry.

[XVI]

[2011]

On the fourth try, the call went straight to Erin's voicemail. Mark snapped his phone shut, cursing to himself as he looked out the car window, the glass now fogged over with his own breath. He muttered, *"Fuck it,"* as he pushed the door open and stepped outside. The road was still covered with a few inches of snow, a layer of ice beneath. Mark had to hold himself steady against the car as he looked down the empty street where he'd grown up—it hadn't been plowed in days, possibly weeks. Most of the houses were abandoned. Yards without fences. Windows broken or boarded up. Mark's old, black Honda Accord was the only car parked on the street. No laughing children. No snowball fights. No scolding parents. Not even the sound of a barking dog.

Mark leaned into the car when his phone rang. He answered it without looking at the display. "Erin?"

There was a short pause. "Is this Mark?" asked a male voice on the other end. Mark looked at the display. *Unknown Number.*

"Yeah?" Mark asked suspiciously.

"It's Derek."

Mark grinned briefly and stood. "Oh. Derek." Mark leaned forward against the vehicle. "Yeah. How are things?"

"Things are fine. I'm fine." Pause. "I got your package yesterday."

"So you got your shirt back?" Mark asked, ducking back down into the car and pulling out a heavy backpack, swinging it over his shoulders.

"I was surprised you sent your number with it."

"Sorry it took so long to get the shirt back to you." Mark pulled his cane out of the car, setting it on the hood. "I had to wash out the blood."

"The *what?*"

"Long story."

"Did you say *blood?*"

"It wasn't mine."

"Whose blood was it?" Derek's voice was more apprehensive by the minute.

"Listen, Derek, I can't really talk right now, but..." Mark looked over his shoulder, staring at his father's house. "... I'd like to see you again." Mark paused. "Can I take you up on the omelets?"

"Really?"

"Yeah," Mark replied, turning back. "I mean, if you—"

"Sure! That's... that's great. I just..."

"Is that alright? Or—"

"Of course! I just thought... when you left... you were pretty pissed at me."

"I'm always pissed." Mark held the phone to his ear with his shoulder. "But I wasn't angry at you."

"I'm just surprised to hear from you, much less see you again. Why would you—"

"Act without hope," Mark replied, rubbing his shoulders and arms for warmth.

"What does that mean?" Derek asked.

"Listen, there's something I need to take care of today." Mark leaned into the car and pulled his Glock out from between the seats. "But if you're free tomorrow night, I can—"

"I'll go buy the eggs," Derek replied, clearly excited by the prospect.

"Don't forget the lube. I'll see you tomorrow."

He snapped the phone shut, sticking it in his pocket. He then tucked the gun into his jeans, handle bulging out the front of his shirt. He grabbed his cane, shut the car door, and limped toward his father's house, making his own path past a snow-covered Stingray.

The sky filtered the waning sunlight into a dull gray. The faint whistle of a distant train was the only sound accompanying the crunch of snow beneath his steps. A few remnants of the American flag were hanging from the pole next to the porch. It was at half-mast, brass rings clinking lightly against the metal pole. Mark reached up, stretching his body, and tore the faded and decaying cloth from the lanyard, wrapping it around the knuckles of his right hand. He walked slowly up the stairs and stopped in front of the door, closing his eyes and breathing in deeply, the cold mountain air cutting deep into his lungs. Mark breathed out; a white cloud hung for a moment between him and the front door, then dissipated. The wind stung his face and ears. The tips of his fingers were already numb.

Mark tried to turn the door handle, but it refused to move. He stepped back and tightened the tattered flag around his hand, looking up and down the empty street. Mark punched his fist through one of glass panels on the upper side of the door, the shattering glass breaking the silence. Mark shoved his arm through the opening and unlocked the deadbolt and the door handle from the inside. He heard someone yell, followed by footsteps falling fast toward the front door. Mark pulled his arm out and opened the door slightly. Balancing himself with his cane, Mark kicked the door—hard—just as his father reached it. The heavy door flung open, the edge slamming against Steve's face. A few lines of blood shot onto the dirty, white doorframe. Steve fell back, slamming down on the living room floor, shaking a few empty beer bottles nestled together on the plywood table in front of the couch. The glass bottles reflected Mark's silhouette as he stood in the empty doorframe. Strands of the flag dangled from Mark's hand, drops of blood falling from the threadbare ends. Mark faced forward as he shut the door. Steve mouthed the word *Mark*, but the sound never left his throat. Steve balled up the bottom of his white t-shirt and held it to his nose, now bent to one side; his other arm stretched back, holding up the weight of his body. Mark said nothing as he reached under his shirt, eyes unblinking. The Glock hung between father and son, like a black rapier cutting straight to the purpose of Mark's presence.

"Well, this brings back memories," Mark said with almost a smile, staring at the small, red stream that fell from Steve's chin. "Only you're the one on the floor with the broken nose this time, and I'm the one with the gun."

Steve let his hand drop from his face. Blood rolled out of his nose, splashing down his mouth, his chin. Mark leaned in close, pushing the barrel of the gun against his father's forehead. Steve coughed, choking on the blood that fell without resistance down his throat. Mark was about to speak again, but a face in the periphery caught his attention. He turned his head and saw Victoria Richman on the television, standing behind a lectern. She pointed to the banner behind her, stretched across the headquarters for the Leviticus Alliance. The word *Mute* was on the bottom left corner of the television. Victoria's words scrolled along the bottom of the screen, out of sync with the movements of her mouth. It read *They speak of tolerance, while trying to push their own distorted morality onto your lives, your country, your children!*

Mark turned back to his father. "Figures." He stepped back and leaned his cane against the door, the cold air seeping through the broken pane of glass. "Faggots can serve openly now, Steve. Everything you believe in is rotting away, like this house."

Breathing heavily, Steve turned his head and spat out a mouthful of coagulated blood. "You cut your hand," Steve said, flecks of red landing on Mark's boots.

Mark looked down, smiled, and unwrapped the bloodstained flag from around his hand. He tossed it on the floor. "You're losing it, Steve. The flag's in pieces and hanging at half-mast."

Steve's face was indignant as he stared at the torn flag lying in a bloody pile on the floor. "It will remain at half-mast as long as homosexuals can serve without consequence."

Mark laughed. "A bit overdramatic don't you think?" He limped around behind his father, keeping the gun at Steve's head. "And I thought I was the fairy." With his other hand, Mark grabbed the back of Steve's collar and began pulling him down the hallway. "You got fat." Steve tried to get up, but remained limp when the barrel of the gun was pushed into the back of his neck. Mark dragged his father down the dark hallway into the bathroom, flicking on the light and leaving a smear of red on the switch. Steve held his shirt up to his nose again. "Jesus, haven't you ever heard of air freshener?" Mark asked, as he pushed his father's frame up against the bathroom wall. Steve didn't respond. The glass that covered the overhead light was opaque and full of dead bugs, casting a yellowish hue over the dingy white surfaces of the bathroom.

Mark stepped over his father and pushed the shower curtain open. "You're making a mess, Steve. Get in the bathtub." Mark limped back to the doorway of the bathroom, pointing his gun toward the bathtub with one hand as he held his leg with the other. "Hurry up. Haven't got all day for this whole father-son bonding shit."

Steve lifted himself into the bathtub, crawling like an abused animal. His body fell into the tub, and Steve leaned his back and head against the once-white tiles, now black with mold. His bare feet lay spread apart under the spigot, toenails long and dirty. A few drops of cold water fell from the faucet and splashed between his bare ankles.

"Don't run off," Mark said before he left the bathroom, tucking the gun behind his back. Steve reached over and pulled the toilet paper from the dispenser. He tore off a few pieces and held the balled-up tissue to his nose. The single bulb made the four walls appear sick with cirrhosis. A moth circled the light fixture, its body beating lightly against the glass. Mark returned with his cane tucked under his arm, dragging a folding chair from the kitchen, which he placed in the doorway. He held an opened bottle of beer in his left hand; it was already half-empty. Mark swung the backpack from around his shoulder and dropped it at his feet. "You're not a very good host, Steve. Nothing but cheap beer and sour milk. You don't even have a clean glass. The entire house is a shit hole." Mark sat down and slowly extended his left leg, keeping one hand under the knee. He unzipped his backpack and rummaged through the contents. "I tripped over an entire fucking crankshaft in the kitchen. You always said a cluttered room was the reflection of a cluttered mind."

Steve kept his head back, stuffing toilet paper into his nose. Blood, now black, clotted around his mouth and chin like Rorschach inkblots on a canvas of skin. "Your room was always clean," Steve said quietly. "Until you got older."

"You mean before I started thinking for myself?" Mark asked. He drank the rest of the beer and tossed the empty bottle over his shoulder into the hallway. It landed on the carpet with barely a sound. Mark reached down and pulled a few large, hardback textbooks out of his backpack, setting them next to the sink. A cockroach scurried out from behind the sink and hid behind the toilet. "Of course, I know now that independent thought is the enemy of any religious perspective." Mark pulled out his old science book, the green cover now faded. He held it in Steve's face. "Certain books even bring to light the limitations and fallacies of one's own beliefs."

Steve spat between his legs. "Belief in God is not a fallacy," he said flatly.

"Yeah," Mark snorted, as he set the book on top of the others. "Do you remember, *Steve*, when Shannon came home with that tattoo?" Mark looked up from his backpack. "A small, blue butterfly outlined in black on the back of her neck, hidden below her collar." Mark reached behind him, pulled the pistol from his waistband, and placed the Glock on top of the books. He searched through the bag with both hands. "You locked her in her room and kept her in there like a dangerous mental patient. She cried for you to let her out. She told you she was hungry. You spent hours on the phone trying to find someone who could medically remove a tattoo."

Steve pulled a wad of tissue away from his crooked nose. It began to bleed again. "The body is a temple. You know that, Mark."

"'*What? Know ye not that your body is the temple of the Holy Ghost which is in you, which ye have of God, and ye are not your own?*' First Corinthians six, verse nineteen." Mark shook his head.

"I did what I knew to be right."

"And when she got pregnant?"

Steve swallowed hard. The clotted blood started breaking apart around his mouth as he spoke. He leaned his head forward. "Don't."

Mark picked up the gun. He leaned forward in the chair, holding the Glock loosely with both hands between his knees. The chair groaned under his weight. "Do you remember what you called her?"

"She chose to ignore what I taught her. She chose to ignore God's law." Steve turned his head. "She abandoned both of us—remember?" A few flecks of dried blood flew through the air.

Mark wiped his forehead with the back of his hand. He leaned back, pointing the gun at his father. "Funny. I remember it differently."

"She's a murderer of the unborn!" Tears ran down his face, forming small gulches in the dried blood. "God does not compromise. Neither do I." Steve spat between his legs, throwing the used tissues into the toilet. The moth landed on the ceiling next to the light fixture. It rubbed its head with its front legs then leapt into the air, circling the light.

"Yes, you do, Steve. Every Christian compromises—especially you." Mark set the Glock back on top of the books and reached back into his backpack, pulling out a large, cordless drill. The casing was yellow and black, like some oversized mechanical bumblebee. A black battery was attached to the base; yellow letters on the side read *Dewalt 18V*. "It's the only reason I'm here. To show you what you really are—deep down inside that thick skull of yours."

Mark pulled a small, gray metal case out of his backpack. He reached over and closed the toilet lid, setting the box on top. Steve watched Mark unsnap the latch and open the case, letting the metal lid fall open onto the grimy white surface. There was an assortment of drill bits in various sizes, running in ascending order. Mark pulled the fourth-largest bit out of the case.

The cockroach scurried out from behind the toilet, as if curious about Mark's intent. Mark rolled up his left pant leg past the knee, and rolled down the black elastic brace to reveal a large, red oval on the kneecap—Jupiter's great red spot. He picked up the drill bit and placed it perpendicular to the wound, comparing the diameter of the bit to the diameter of the scar. Steve watched his son silently.

"As I'm sure you know, I was a POW. After a failed escape attempt, they dragged me back into a small room with no windows." Mark pulled up the elastic brace and pulled down his pant leg. He picked up the drill, wedging it between his legs, the chuck pointing toward the ceiling. He turned the chuck with one hand until it opened enough for him to drop in the bit. "To make sure I wouldn't try to escape again, they drilled a hole into my knee." Mark tightened the chuck and held the drill in his right hand, pointing it at the floor. "The pain was, well, remarkable. I couldn't even breathe. It was only when bits of bone from my kneecap hit me in the face that I started to scream."

"I had a duty to turn you in," Steve said, looking straight ahead.

Mark pulled the trigger on the drill. The chuck spun the bit, filling the small bathroom with noise. The cockroach bolted back behind the toilet. Mark released the trigger. The bit stopped spinning instantly. "Battery's charged." Mark said, looking at the drill, then back at Steve. "You know what happens to soldiers discharged for being faggots?"

Steve remained silent. The moth landed on the sink next to a few short, black hairs stuck to the porcelain. The moth walked down into the bottom of the sink and started drinking from a small pool of water near the drain. "Nothing. We fade away. And until recently, we were conveniently forgotten. Fourteen thousand of us shoved under the rug. The irony is blinding—the American government stripping away the rights of men and women responsible for protecting the rights of other Americans. Even after the repeal, some don't consider us veterans." Mark set the drill on the tiled floor of the bathroom.

Steve spat a clump of blood, staring straight ahead. It stuck to the side of the bathtub and slowly slid down toward the drain. "The Army has rules—"

"Rules that have changed."

"Rules that must be followed, must be reinstated—or soldiers die. We must all take responsibility for our choices."

"No, Steve. Soldiers died because our government invaded a country that was absolutely no threat to America. Soldiers continue to die because a bunch of Islamic lunatics think we're the enemies of Allah. Me sucking cock had nothing to do with it." Steve cringed, keeping his gaze forward. "But I didn't come here to talk about my shit life." Mark sat back and reached into his pocket, pulling out a pack of Marlboro Reds. "I came here to talk about *your* shit life." Mark pulled out a cigarette and tossed the pack onto the edge of the sink. "So, speaking of responsibility, Steve, have you taken responsibility for how your children turned out?"

Steve looked over at his son. Mark lit his cigarette. "I was a good father," Steve said defensively.

Mark reached over to the pile of books and pulled out a large Bible. "Of course you were." He let the thick book drop at his feet. The cockroach ran behind the sink. Mark leaned forward, cigarette dangling between his lips. "I mean, look at me."

"You always had food on the table."

"Yep."

"A roof over your head."

"I always did have a dry head."

"A warm bed."

"With sheets and a pillow!"

"Forty-five hours a week at the plant. Night shift for the extra pay. Weekends at the garage."

Mark blew a large cloud of smoke at his father. "Oh, such sacrifice!"

"I did it all for you and your sister." Steve coughed.

"You worked all those hours because you were afraid of your children. And now you're all alone," Mark said with feigned empathy. "You got your wish."

"I have God to talk to."

Mark took a long pull on his cigarette. Ash floated to the floor. "I find it pathetic when adults talk to imaginary friends for comfort."

"You left this house, Mark."

"Left?" Mark asked, leaning back in the metal chair. He flicked the half-smoked cigarette at the mirror. It bounced off and landed in the sink. The moth flew back up toward the light fixture. "Do you remember smacking me in the face with the stock of a 12-gauge shotgun?" Mark rubbed his nose, looking at his father's. "It's going to hurt like hell for months, just so you know—especially when you sneeze. Might want to get your hands on a big bottle of Vicodin."

"You left this house the day you decided—the day you chose—your immorality."

"You mean fucking other men in the ass?"

"I was a good father."

"You keep saying that," Mark said before he picked up the Bible and threw it at Steve. It opened in the air and smacked hard against the tile wall of the shower before falling with a loud thump onto Steve's legs. "'*Thou shalt not bear false witness!'"* Mark yelled, his hands raised. "Exodus twenty, verse sixteen."

Steve carefully picked up the Bible, turning it over so the spine of the book rested along his stomach. He let it fall open, gently brushing the pages with his hands. He moved his fingers to the bent edges and pushed them flush with the rest of the book. "I gave this to you when you turned thirteen."

Mark stood and limped forward, leaning his hand against the bathroom wall as he walked. He bent over his father, blocking the dim light from the bulb above. "*'Lying lips are an abomination to the Lord!'* Proverbs twelve, twenty-two." Mark tilted his head. "It seems we're both abominations to God—*Steve.*"

Steve let his hands fall back into his lap as Mark took the Bible. Mark held it open and began flipping through the pages. The dim sunlight from the living room had receded toward the darkening horizon. Mark turned and lifted the Bible toward the yellow light fixture.

Steve kept his gaze forward as he spoke. "I don't expect you to understand. When does a lost sheep realize he is lost?"

Mark chuckled under his breath, sticking his index finger into the Bible before closing it. He turned on his good leg and reached down, picking up the drill from the floor.

"It is the shepherd," Steve continued, "who sees his folly, who understands the danger he is in and tries to point him toward the righteous path."

Mark set the Bible on the rim of the tub, letting it fall open to a passage he had marked with a blue highlighter. Mark winced as he slowly lowered himself to his knees. He set the drill upright next to the open Bible. "You're not a fucking shepherd, Steve."

Mark picked up the Bible. He leaned over his father and held the book sideways, allowing it to fall open to the passage highlighted in blue. Mark pushed the open Bible flush against the shower wall with one hand. He reached back and picked up the drill on the rim of the tub with his other, pointing the bit at the open Bible

Mark looked down. "You might want to cover your eyes."

Mark pulled the trigger, and the chuck spun to life. Steve's eyes followed the drill as Mark moved toward the Bible, the drill bit parallel to the bathroom floor. He rammed the spinning bit into the open pages. His left hand tightened around the grip as the Bible tried to spin with the bit. Scraps of paper flew violently into the air. Mark pushed hard, rocking the drill deeper into the pages, leaning his whole body forward until the bit broke through the tough, leather cover, hitting the grimy tiles of the shower wall. Steve covered his eyes as ceramic shards flew in all directions, one hitting Mark in the forehead, another getting stuck in his short, brown hair. Mark pushed one last time against the drill, and it sank up to the chuck, flush against the open Bible, pinning it to the wall. He then released the trigger and leaned back. Steve was still covering his face. The drill remained in place, the Bible open and suspended above the bathtub. Mark was breathing hard as he limped back and sat on the folding chair. He placed his hands under his knee.

"Well," Mark said, slowly stretching his leg. "I'd make a joke about that being a holey Bible, but you probably wouldn't laugh."

Steve brushed broken tile from his chest, waving away the white dust that hovered in the room. He reached up and gently touched the hanging Bible. "There is no morality, no purpose without God's Word... God's Word made flesh." He let his hand fall.

"You sound like a computer spitting out a programmed response, Steve. What makes that God's Word and not, say, the Qur'an? I'd bet you wouldn't give a shit if I did that to the Qur'an—a book considered sacred by over a billion-and-a-half people."

"The Qur'an is blasphemous. Jesus was the Son of God, not a prophet."

"And as for your so-called morality, have you ever read the thirty-first chapter of Numbers? God orders the slaughter of the Midianites, and Moses gets angry when his soldiers spare the women and children." Mark closed his eyes, searching his memory. "*Now therefore kill every male among the little ones, and kill every woman that has known a man by lying with him, but all the woman children, that have not known a man... keep alive for yourselves.*" Mark opened his eyes and spat on the Bible that hung against the wall. "Moses condones—no, commands—genocide, pedophilia, and rape. Your source of so-called morality is repulsive."

Steve tried to push himself up out of the tub, his bloodshot eyes locked on his son. "You can't create your own morality, Mark."

"Been doing it my entire life," Mark said, reaching over for the Glock, motioning for Steve to sit down.

"There must be a center to define the circumference."

"Which center should I use, Steve?" Mark said as he slowly stood and leaned forward, reaching out and lightly tapping the top of Steve's head with the barrel of the Glock. "Of which *Word of God* do you speak? The entire Bible or only the Torah? What about the Apocrypha? What about all the books that were never canonized? Or maybe God does speak through the Qur'an. Or maybe the Christians, Muslims, and Jews all got it wrong, and God speaks through the Gita or the Dhammapada or the Tao Te Ching or through Harry fucking Potter." Mark rubbed the back of his neck with the gun. Sweat dripped from his forehead. "Don't you see it, Steve? The irony? These books were all written by fallible humans! The ethical codes written in those books come from mindless, delusional religious fanatics—" Mark pointed the gun at Steve. "—just like you. You're the one who gives this insipid book its supernatural authority."

"Man cannot create his own morality."

"Again with the robotic responses." Mark threw up his hands. "Haven't you been listening to me? Man *does* create his own morality—he codified it in that book."

"The Bible was inspired," Steve coughed out. "Written through men by God."

"Yes, of course. And how do you know this? Because the goddamn Bible says that it is." Mark raised his hands in frustration. "Do you not see the circular fucking flaw in that logic?"

"Both faith and God transcend logic."

"For fuck's sake!" Mark yelled. "Faith is the surrender of critical thinking. It's the result of a lazy man claiming to be blind when he's not."

Steve rubbed the back of his head. "I don't have all the answers, Mark. I leave that to God, as should you. My trust in Him is all I have." Steve paused. "All I have left."

"So, like Abraham, you willingly lead your children to slaughter, allowing this construct to define your actions and override your responsibility as a father." Mark held out a thumbs-up. "Then, like the coward you are, you hide behind the church or the Leviticus Alliance—any institution that will choose for you. No different from those fucking insurgents who kill American soldiers in the name of *their* God."

"Enough!" Steve yelled. He turned his head, wiping away a few tears as he quieted his voice. "I've endured emptiness only a father who has lost his children can understand."

"Except that your children are still alive, Steve." Mark slammed the Glock down on the pile of books in frustration. He grimaced as he rubbed his knee. The moth began circling the fixture again. "And don't ask me to pity you," Mark added. "I'm only alive because the shells to that shotgun were in the garage and not in the gun."

"I didn't have any." Mark looked up from his leg. "I cleared the gun before I came into the living room. There were no shells in the garage. I wanted to scare you." The moth flew out of the room. "I was angry."

Mark cocked his head. "Obedience through fear and violence. Forced prostration at the feet of a tyrant." Mark stood slowly, pushing himself up with much effort. "You take after the God you worship."

Steve sat up. "I will not listen to this anymore."

"And I can prove it." Mark picked up the Glock and pulled the slide back. He checked the chamber and watched the bullet kick forward as he released the slide.

Steve's face went from surprise to acceptance. "It wasn't loaded," he said to himself.

"Like father, like son." Mark smirked as he pointed the loaded gun at the Bible still hanging from the wall. "Now read." Steve looked at his son and remained motionless, sitting straight up. His eyes were locked on the gun. "The highlighted passage. It's open to it. Read it." Mark gestured with the gun toward the open Bible. The blue mark ran over a single verse. Steve turned toward the Bible and remained silent. "Out loud!" Steve's hands gripped the rim of the bathtub, keeping his head straight forward. "You can't possibly be afraid to read a single passage from your divine book in front of me."

Steve leaned forward and turned his head, keeping his hands on the rim of the tub. "'*If a man lie with*—'"

"Chapter and verse, first. Follow the drill!" Mark said, followed by a quick laugh. "Pardon the pun."

"Leviticus twenty, verse thirteen." Steve paused. His voice was shaky, like a schoolchild reading poetry before a class. "'*If a man also lie with mankind, as he lieth with a woman...*'"

"*Go on...*" Mark replied, turning his head to one side and cupping his hand behind his ear.

"'*Both of them have committed an abomination: They shall surely be put to death; their blood shall be upon them.*'"

Suddenly, Mark leapt forward, grabbing a fistful of his father's white t-shirt, now stained with sweat and blood. Steve didn't react.

"You have your instructions from God, Steve!" Mark was yelling into his father's left ear as he slapped the gun into his father's hands. Steve remained limp, staring down at the pistol. "I suck off other men! I fuck men in the ass. I drink their cum and I like it!"

"Stop, Mark!" Steve yelled, shaking his head back and forth.

"You have to kill me! According to your own moral law, you must put me to death!"

"The new covenant, it—"

"Romans. Chapter one, verses thirty-one and thirty-two. The New Testament wants those with 'unnatural affection' dead, too."

Steve didn't respond.

"What? Jesus made the Old Testament irrelevant? So, for thousands of years it was fine to murder faggots in the name of God? Then Jesus showed up and said, 'Verily, I say unto you, that verse was a typo.'" Steve didn't respond.

Mark let go of the bloody t-shirt. He reached up and gripped the drill in his hand, hitting the reverse button with his thumb, pulling it out of the wall. The Bible fell into the bathtub next to Steve's legs. Mark tossed the drill behind him. It hit the wall in the hallway and fell to the carpet with a few broken pieces of drywall. "Look at you. A drunk. A failed father who abandoned his children because a book told him to. Who turned in his son because a now-defunct military policy told him to. And now you're a hypocrite. Loyal to a God who couldn't even save mom from a goddamn infection."

Instantly, Steve bolted up and clamped his hands around Mark's throat. Mark's eyes widened as he struggled for air, trying in vain to pull his father's hands away. The cockroach ran out of the room, dodging Mark's kicking feet. Steve slowly stood, pulling his son up with him. Mark's eyes watered; his vision began to grow dark. Steve opened his mouth, about to speak. Then closed it. Steve flung Mark backward. Mark's arms reached out as he stumbled and hit the back of his head on the metal chair. Steve picked up the gun, holding it loosely in his right hand while rubbing the back of his neck with his left.

"Jesus taught us to love our enemies," Steve said. He pulled the slide back on the gun and locked it in place. The bullet popped out of the Glock's chamber, spinning rapidly in the air before clanking into the bathtub. "To hate the sin and not the sinner."

Mark was coughing, rubbing his leg. He reached behind his head. Blood ran down the back of his skull. He smiled as he rubbed it between his fingers. "Pointless platitudes that have no relevance in the real world." Mark spat as he looked up from the floor. "And as long as I'm alive, you're a hypocrite."

Steve didn't respond, his hands dangling at his sides. Mark slowly pulled himself up from the floor and grabbed his cane, his knee sending shocks of pain up his leg. Steve leaned back against the shower wall and closed his eyes. Mark coughed some more as he shook his head. He stepped over the collapsed chair, leaning heavily on his cane. As he limped down the dark hallway, Mark turned his head and spoke over his shoulder. "Your duty to God is clear. Letting me live is a violation of that duty."

Silence was the only response.

The living room was now hidden in shadows; the only light reflecting off the walls was from the television blinking in the corner. Mark limped into the room, then stopped. Flashing red-and-blue emergency vehicles filled the television screen. In the foreground, a reporter was talking into a microphone, his face weary and smudged with soot. He was standing in front of a skyscraper, the windows blown out ten stories up. Below the reporter, a caption scrolled across the screen: *Two bombs. Thirteen dead. Hundreds injured.*

"Holy shit," Mark said to himself. He dug his hand into his pocket and pulled out his cell phone, dialing Erin's number. "We'll have to finish our father-son bonding another night," Mark yelled down the hallway. "I need to call a frie—"

Mark heard the slide of the Glock lock into place. His eyes snapped up in time to see the muzzle flash—his father's frame briefly illuminated in the dark hallway. Mark's cane fell to the floor, followed by his phone, bouncing lightly on the matted carpet. Mark's hands instinctively reached toward his neck, trying to cover the hole in his throat as thick streams of blood shot out like water from a pressurized hose, arcing onto the couch, the starter to a Chrysler, the television. Mark stumbled back and fell hard against the front door, breaking a few more windowpanes. His mouth opened and closed over and over in a vain attempt to breathe. Red bubbles formed between his fingers, the blood warming his hands as his body grew cold. Steve walked slowly into the living room, his eyes wet, the gun pointed steadily on his son. Mark held his gaze on his father until his knees gave out, and he collapsed on the floor. Mark fought to keep his eyes open as he crawled into the kitchen.

His father followed, steadying the gun with both hands, cupping his left hand over the right. Steve slowed his breathing to steady the gun. Mark's coughing became more subdued, less frequent. When he was near the refrigerator, Mark rolled onto his back and looked out the window above the kitchen sink. A thick sheet of clouds reflected the lights of Leadville, blocking out the stars. Mark's hands fell away from his throat. He blinked. The clock in the kitchen ticked away six more seconds before the Glock kicked again. An empty shell bounced to a stop next to Mark's motionless body, followed by the Glock itself.

An hour passed before a SWAT team kicked open the door, masks over their faces, MP5s scanning each corner of the room, bright flashlights with small, red points of laser light roaming over the pictures on the wall. Steve remained seated on the couch, staring at the live footage of the blast site, the same reporter talking into his microphone. A red banner now ran across the bottom of the screen: *Downtown Denver Destruction*. The officers pointed their weapons at Steve, yelling at him to get on the floor. Steve kept his hands on his lap as he looked up. "They were set too close to the crowd," Steve said quietly. He stood and raised his hands over his head. The officers immediately rushed him, leaping over the couch and tackling him, the coffee table breaking under their weight, car parts spinning into the corners of the room.

"Sergeant!" one of the officers yelled. "We've got a body!"

Mark's corpse lay in the kitchen. A section of his skull was missing, and a mass of black-and-gray brain matter unfolded onto the linoleum. Steve lay on the carpet near the entrance to the kitchen with his arms pulled back in handcuffs. He could see the half-head of his dead son staring back at him.

"I had no choice," Steve said quietly as they lifted him up from the floor.

[XVII]

[2011]

Erin sat motionless on the white, leather couch, bare feet curled underneath her. The cell phone rang—again. An electronic jingle echoed off the vaulted ceilings of the living room. A calico cat on the opposite end of the sofa lifted his furry head toward the phone on the glass coffee table. His yellow eyes narrowed, and his ears pulled back, annoyed at the third interruption of his nap.

"Go back to sleep, Gabriel," Erin said, reaching over and running her fingers between the cat's ears. The calico closed his eyes and purred, pushing his head into Erin's fingers. Gabriel slowly stood and moved languidly toward her, rubbing his whiskers against the couch and her legs. Erin waited until the phone stopped ringing before picking it up. She tapped the volume button on the side until the word *Silent* appeared on the display. There was a prompt on the screen: *3 new messages*. She set the phone down and looked back at the open book in her lap. She realized she had been on the same page for at least thirty minutes. Erin jumped when the doorbell rang, almost dropping Faulkner on his head. The cat jumped too, running under the coffee table, ears flat against his head. Erin snapped the hardcover shut and tossed it on the table. It slammed loudly against the glass, and Gabriel bolted into the kitchen.

"It's been three months!" Erin yelled at the front door as she got up off the couch. "Why can't you people leave me alone!?" She walked down a long hallway past dozens of pictures of Kevin. One was with him in a Boy Scout uniform. In another he was wearing black robes at his high school graduation. The last picture was with him in uniform. Erin swung the door open wide and held up her hand against a falling sun sinking behind an advancing storm. A woman stood in the doorway, her brown hair hanging above her shoulders. She wore blue jeans, a dark green turtleneck, and a long gray overcoat, a few beads of water on the shoulders. A tattered package was tucked neatly under her arm.

"Erin Zuelke?"

Erin narrowed her eyes, trying to make out the face in front of her. "You're not a reporter..."

"I should have given this to you sooner." She held out the package in front of her. "I'm sorry."

Erin dropped her hand. She could see the woman's thin film of tears. "Who are you?"

"It's been very difficult," she replied. "With Steve's trial and my brother..."

"You're Shannon," Erin stated, without asking.

"These are Kevin's journals... his photographs."

Erin looked at the package, then back at Shannon. "How did—"

"Mark had been sending them to me," Shannon replied. "I didn't realize who they belonged to until after the funeral, and I started going through his things." Erin took the package from Shannon, studying it closely. "There's one extra journal in there—Mark's last before he came home. Some of the entries are about your son. I thought..." Shannon paused, clearing her throat, "...I thought you had a right to know."

"To know what?" Erin asked, looking at the box, then back up at Shannon. "Please, come inside. We can talk—"

"I'm truly sorry for what happened to Kevin, Mrs. Zuelke. From what I've read in Mark's journals, Kevin was a good friend to him—his only friend. And I'm sure you know that Mark was a difficult person to be friends with." Shannon turned and walked back toward a taxi idling next to the curb.

"Wait!" Erin yelled. She gently set the package just inside the doorway and followed Shannon across a green lawn, grass still wet from a morning rain.

"I can't," said Shannon as she opened the taxi door and got inside. She didn't shut the car door. "I have to fly back to New York tonight."

"If you have a few minutes, please," Erin said, jogging up to the taxi. "Come inside."

"Mark kept his distance from me," Shannon said flatly, her outstretched arm holding the car door open. The driver looked annoyed. "I was very angry at him for that. After everything that happened to him in Iraq, I knew

Mark needed someone—though he would never admit it. I begged him over and over to come and stay with me in New York. But he refused to leave Colorado." Shannon shook her head and smiled. "The stubborn prick. More like his father than he'd ever admit." Shannon looked up at Erin. "Every time I insisted, Mark told me he had to stay in Denver to keep a promise." Shannon paused. "It's not fair, I know, but when I found out that the promise was to keep an eye on Kevin's mother, I was angry at you, too."

"I was angry at everyone after Kevin died," Erin replied softly.

"I'm still angry."

"So am I," Erin replied. She asked the driver for a pen. She wrote her phone number on the back of a taxi receipt, forcing it into Shannon's hand. "Day or night."

Shannon smiled, looking at the number. She folded the receipt and stuck it in her pocket. "You're as stubborn as Mark. I can see why he liked you."

"I wouldn't go so far as to say *liked* as much as tolerated," Erin responded with a small smile.

Shannon nodded, closing the door. The window was still down. The driver asked if she was ready to go. "One more thing," Shannon said to Erin. She reached over and grabbed her handbag. She pulled out a folded paper napkin tucked neatly into one of the pockets. Shannon held it out the car window.

"What is it?" Erin asked.

"I'm not sure, exactly," Shannon responded. "It was in Mark's wallet when... when they found him. I think it's something you should have."

Erin took the folded napkin from Shannon just before the window rolled up. A few beads of water clung to the side of the glass, overlapping Erin's reflection in the window, as if they were her own tears. She stood motionless and watched the cab drive down the quiet suburban street, and then turn out of sight. Thunder, distant and foreboding, whispered in Erin's ears as she walked back to the house. Gabriel was in the doorway, sniffing the corner of the cardboard box Shannon had brought. Looking down, Erin slowly unfolded the napkin. It was stained with a red ring in the corner, two lines of text were written in French on the paper in black ink. Below it, someone translated the two lines into English with a blue ballpoint: *"Act without hope." —Jean-Paul Sartre. I, too, buried a child.* Erin's eyes widened when she realized the blue ink was in her son's handwriting.

Erin opened the small box on the gray, granite kitchen counter. Gabriel jumped up next to it, rubbing his face against the open cardboard panels.

Erin sat next to the counter on a metal stool, her bare feet locked in the rungs. A few minutes later, thirteen black, leather-bound notebooks were stacked neatly beside the box. The notebooks were worn at the corners, the leather dry and cracked, covered in dust. A few grains of obstinate sand were tucked between the pages like random bookmarks. Some of the notebooks were stuffed with water-warped pages. A few faded green rubber bands kept them shut. Other notebooks were crammed with photographs, their edges peeking out from between the worn covers. Erin stared at the stack for twenty minutes before she picked up the top one, removing the rubber bands. They snapped against her hand. She closed her eyes and slowly opened it, the binding creaking in protest as she let it fall open in her lap. She opened her eyes and looked down.

Thin slats of dying sunlight pushed past the darkening clouds and fell through the vertical window blinds onto the pages, creating the illusion of black bars holding in the words. She slapped the book shut and set it back on the pile of notebooks, pushing them away.

She sighed and looked back into the open box. It was almost empty. There was a small plastic container stuffed full of memory cards. Sitting under it, a smaller journal with a green cover. Scrawled handwriting on the cover read *Fuck Off!*

She opened it. There was a picture stuck between the cover and the first page. Erin saw her son facing her, standing in front of a Humvee. Mark stood next to him. They were wearing fatigues, and the desert stretched out behind them. Kevin was holding his M-16 with one hand, flashing the peace sign with the other. Mark was holding up his middle finger. Erin flipped the picture over and saw her son's writing: *To Mark, the King of Dickishness. Kevin.* Erin carefully placed the picture back into the journal. She flipped to the next page. It was dated three weeks after Kevin's death.

It's April... nightmares again... fitting... feels like I haven't slept for weeks but I know that's not possible. Not at all. Can't be. I have these dreams... floating above the surface of this huge desert, and I was alone with a solitude that seeped into my skin and clamped onto my bones, shaking me with a penetrating stillness because all was silent and isolated and mute and then I looked to the ground and saw my own pale body curled up into the fetal position, halfway buried in the sand with my arms wrapped around my chest and my knees touching my chin, but my body wasn't moving or breathing or sleeping—no—it just lay there, silently reflecting the moonlight with its naked skin until the wind, which I knew somehow was coming from the west, grew stronger and stronger, pushing me away like a parade balloon, so I had to fight to stay above my body as the sand began to roll across the desert like a thin, partially-transparent floor of tiny, sharp rocks that slowly peeled away layers from the motionless body below me—my motionless body below me—and I watched as the skin on my dead body began to roll away in layers, leaving bright, red patches of muscle that became loose flaps of dead flesh that snapped in the gusts like torn pages from an ancient book laid open in the wind, and the muscles arced and fell and ballooned and began to fold back on themselves, so I tried to turn away but the wind grew stronger, filling my ears with its howl and soon whole sections of flesh—of my flesh—were being ripped away, forever lost in the perpetual desert and I continued to float and observe and watch as my body disintegrated layer by layer by layer until nothing remained of myself except bare bones burning white under the moonlight, and I looked up and I saw... I saw more bodies—countless bodies lying in the fetal position in various levels of decomposition, all stretching to the horizon like the desert itself—they were all me, all of these bodies—these selves—these possible selves—were all me, all in the same position, all stripped of their flesh, naked bones exposed beneath the celestial canopy and the black sky—a sky without stars—pushed itself down onto the desert as it gathered up and consumed all that belonged to its bosom, and soon the moon was swallowed up in the pitch and then the dunes in the distance fell upward with the wind into the blackness followed by the wind itself which was sucked away into the great nothingness above pulling me at last into its gaping mouth as I stared at all the skeletons of me, all the numerous deaths that were me, then I woke up and remembered he was dead... he was dead because of me and the nurse shook me for what they said was thirty minutes before they stuck long, drug-filled needles into my arms, making the waking world fade away again and I tried to tell them I didn't want to sleep and I didn't want to be awake but I want to be in that wonderful blackness between the two that was darker than space itself—it was the empty space between galaxies... devoid of everything.

Gabriel meowed for attention, wrapping his body around Erin's legs and the legs of the stool. Erin closed her eyes and rubbed her temples, scratching Gabriel's back with her curled toes. She flipped to the next page and opened her eyes.

It's May... they've moved me back to the States. I need to find her. Kevin's mom. Erin. But I'm not fucking giving her Kevin's journals until I've met her. This Erin. She runs some kind of fag-bashing group. Kevin was in the desert because of his fucking mother. I'm not sure if she should even have them. I need to meet her. Erin. Her name is Erin. Erin fucking gay-bashing Kevin-killing Zuelke. But first, I need to get out of this goddamn hospital. My mangled leg has been in a metal brace for weeks, like an arthropod with a steel exoskeleton, but it's in constant pain, and I want to saw it off with a chainsaw like some bad horror movie, laughing as blood sprays onto my face and the chain sinks effortlessly into my flesh, hitting the tibia and jerking the leg toward the blade, ripping the leg away and flinging it into the corner of the room like a piece of wood. I'm surrounded. Never alone. Never fucking alone. They're even watching me—right now—as I write this. Doctors. Nurses. Counselors. Officers. Spend most of my time in a room with four white walls and those fucking cameras with unblinking eyes mounted in the corners and not a single window but a single white door sunk into the wall below a bright, migraine-inducing florescent tube that hums—no—screams loudly and reflects off a single, steel table which in turn reflects the blinding light in all directions, off chairs that creak and groan as the counselor and the officer lean forward with voice recorders and microphones and bad breath asking me again what exactly happened so I tell them the same fucking story over and over and over until I'm sick to my stomach and vomit onto the floor making the doctor frown but the nurse empathizes as she holds my head and the counselor scratches notes—that damn scratching!—but the officer's face stays chiseled in stone as he tells me I can't tell anyone what happened for reasons of national security but I ignore him and pay attention to the needles they're sticking in my arms, filling me full of ineffective drugs and tepid advice and they try to tell me I'm lucky to be alive and that it's a miracle I survived and I tell them to tell that to Kevin and Murphy and Bricksen and Wicker and all the other soldiers who died and I ask them where was their fucking miracle and they tell me it's just survivor's guilt and I should live my life and that's what Kevin would have wanted so I ask them how the fuck would they know what Kevin wants—he's fucking dead! He's gone! You can't ask him anything because he's nothing... he's the lack of nothing and they don't answer... just more scratching as they fill me full of drugs and tell me I need to rest—

Erin jumped when Gabriel landed on her lap. She winced as the cat's claws dug into her legs, trying to keep his balance. He pushed his face into the corners of the notebook, purring. Erin pulled the notebook to her chest and picked up Gabriel with her other hand.

"Not now," Erin said, as she set the cat on the counter. Gabriel walked in a circle and reluctantly slumped down, setting his head between his outstretched legs. Distant thunder grew louder in the background. Erin rubbed Gabriel's head, and the cat turned to lightly bite Erin's fingers without leaving a mark. Erin pulled her hand away and went back to reading the journal.

—but not even drugs can keep Kevin's screams away, screams that echoed down that long, dark corridor for hours and hours before the guards came back and dragged me into the same room and now every night I see Kevin's thin body pulling against those restraints in a wooden chair that was falling apart, his muscles pushing through skin stained red and black and his left hand just a stump of flesh without fingers and then Kevin's good eye locks onto me and he doesn't say anything but I can see that he's asking for help—without words—without words—without fucking words Kevin's asking me to help him to save him but I do nothing but watch as they cut the index finger off his other hand with a pair of rusty tin snips and toss it at me while the guard with perfect English stands behind Kevin and brings a thick, serrated knife to Kevin's throat and asks me the same fucking questions about those pictures and convoy routes and patrols and I lie and tell him I don't know anything about where our convoy was going and that no one knows where the convoy is going but the captain in the lead vehicle and then I tell him my name, my rank, my social security number and he asks four more times and Kevin is still asking for

help without words shaking his head violently as they cut each finger off so that both hands are just stumps of flesh and the guard says something about a scorpion that killed a great warrior and buries the knife deep into Kevin's neck like a snake burrowing itself beneath the surface of a sandy beach with red waves lapping at the shore... so I cover my ears but can hear Kevin trying to scream but it sounds like he's gargling so I open my eyes and his eye is wide with fright then almost too quickly his body goes limp and quiet and he's gone... then later my hands are blistered and full of splinters from the wooden handle of a shovel and I dig, I dig for hours and they make me drag his body into a deep, cool pit in the desert floor behind the cell just below the opening we crawled out of days before while the guards point their rifles and laugh and smoke cigarettes then the one with perfect English asks me if I liked the taste of his urine so I throw the shovel at him and call him a fucking hajji and it almost hits him in the head so he stands and points his rifle at me and I close my eyes and lift my arms waiting to hear the gunshots and feel the bullets tear through my body but instead I hear another truck pull up out of the desert and the guard with perfect English is arguing with the new arrivals in Arabic and they're pointing at me and they're pointing at Kevin's body and one of the new arrivals shoots the guard with perfect English in the head and just like that his body slumps over and suddenly there's more gunfire so I hit the deck next to Kevin's body and cover my head until the gunfire stops, then I pull myself out of the hole and almost all of them are motionless except for a few who are still moaning with flies circling overhead and the sun is almost gone so even though I can hardly bend my knee I pull Kevin out of the hole I dug and struggle to lie him down in the back of a Chevy truck... then... then I wake up in this infernal hospital again and my face is warm and wet and the nurse tells me it was only a dream and I yell back that it wasn't a fucking dream and hours later the psych officer tells me again that I shouldn't feel guilty and I tell him to fuck off then he tells me I possibly saved the lives of hundreds and I say fuck them too then the officer says I need to rest and calm down so I tell him I am fucking calm and they send me back to my bed but I refuse to sleep so the nurse for some reason sits by my bed—she just sits there by my bed at night and holds my hand and *she doesn't say anything—she's the only one who's truthful, who's honest—who doesn't tell me it's all going to be okay...*

Erin let a few tears fall off her chin. She blinked and looked out the kitchen window at the sky turning dark gray. The wind was knocking the thin branches of an Aspen tree against the house. The storm was rolling down the distant mountain range like a cavalry of clouds charging into the city. The hooves of powerful horses clapping against the floor of the sky, shaking the windows in their white, wooden frames. The cat slept uneasily next to Kevin's journals, his paw over his head. Erin rubbed the scar on her forehead and turned the page.

... millions of voices bleeding from their lips into my ears that fill and swell and rupture from throats swollen with hearts hollowed and minds sinking into stagnant ponds pooled with tenacity thwarted and skewed and sculpted by the wrinkled timeless hands of false beliefs that finger fuck the individual and the mind and the imagination so that each and every new perspective quickly fades into an ubiquitous shrill that resembles mere echoes of what the past has now consumed, feeding with feces stuck to its teeth and its gums as it cries for more never to realize that it's not feeding... it's being fed... we are being fed... and famished, by the imaginary gods who are feasting on our labors, we sink our teeth into the flesh of our own kind, tearing away skin and muscle and bone as hope weeps from her sanctuary high above the city she abandoned long ago, watching the creatures below her ingest and bulge with their very own, knowing we have no one to blame but ourselves and sending for Apophis to crash his fist deep into the crust of this planet and wipe away this infection from Earth's skin for the only way to cure an invalid this badly inundated with madness is to kill the patient—

"Enough!" Erin yelled. She flung Mark's journal back into the empty cardboard box.

The blue tiled walls of the kitchen exploded out of the darkness with the flash of lightning, followed by the thunder of two angry armies now clashing in the sky above—the warriors on horses now slapping their steel broadswords against large, metal shields.

Gabriel jumped down from the counter. The kitchen lit up again, and the startled cat wrapped his open paws around Erin's leg, sinking his claws into her skin. Erin jerked and knocked one of Kevin's notebooks to the floor. She sighed and reached down, calmly stroking the hair sticking straight out of Gabriel's back. Erin slowly removed the claws with her hand, talking to the cat in a calm voice.

"It's only lighting and thunder, silly," Erin said, as she rubbed the back of Gabriel's neck. The cat relaxed and walked over to a photograph that had fallen out of Kevin's notebook. Erin looked closer at the picture. A small girl with sunken, green eyes was looking back at her. Her face was dirt-coated and contorted like a crumpled piece of sandpaper. The cat leaned itself against Erin's leg as she got off the stool and bent over to pick up the photograph. She studied the child and examined the fire in the background that was licking a blue sky, lashing whips of black smoke up out of the edges of the picture. Erin flipped the picture over. The words *Our Bombs* sat next to a date and the word *Delaram*.

Erin glanced back at the floor and saw the words *Their Bombs* on the back of another photograph that had fallen out of the notebook. She picked up the picture and flipped it over in her hand. The glossy reflection of a dead solider stared back with black holes where eyes once been, windows to the soul melted away, jaw askew, teeth charred black. His arms were broken in several places and twisted around his chest like collapsed tent poles. Erin leaned down and picked up the leather notebook and opened to the last page, flipping backwards through the blank pages until she found her son's handwriting. It was the last entry, dated two months before she was told by a young lieutenant to accept the Secretary of the Army's deepest condolences.

I can't understand how anyone who has seen war firsthand would ever engage with enthusiasm in such an enterprise. I've had to keep the pictures I take hidden from everyone except Mark (who derides them anyway). But, ironically, he's the only one I can trust. I've already made myself unpopular by voicing my opinion of the war. There are those who agree with me, but they keep quiet. And the captain watches me all the time. I asked Mark to hold some of the memory cards, too—I'm afraid to keep them in my own bunk. They might turn up missing—hell, I might turn up missing along with them. Mark gives me shit for it, but hides them for me anyway. I've tried to make him see the importance of this work, but he doesn't think anything is important. A lesson I suspect he learned from his father.

I took a picture last week of a little girl, Delaram. She was just sitting there with her bare feet in the sand next to a pile of rocks that once housed and protected her large family. I remember the broken limbs sticking out of the rubble. The rest of the village worked to unbury her family, rock by rock, like a solemn ritual. They removed each body and lined them up next to the street—white sheets tucked over the dead bodies, the corners blowing upward in the warm wind. Doc bandaged Delaram's burns and cleaned her wounds, wiping her face clean. She sat there crying softly to herself, obviously in shock. Everyone in the convoy wanted to help (Mark and some others even started to help move the rubble so the villagers could get to the rest of the bodies), but there were insurgents in the hills north of the village. I could also sense their anger at us, the villagers. Shit like this happens, and we wonder why they don't want to cooperate. It was too dangerous to remain there. The captain gave the order to move out, and we rolled on. Delaram was older than she should have been, and there was this sad intelligence behind those eyes. After I took the picture, she told me her name and asked me what she was supposed to do. I had no answer. I just got into the Humvee, and we drove away. She was left by her home, now rubble, standing in clouds of dust kicked up by our convoy. We snaked our way back down the valley, driving on those horribly narrow dirt roads. She'll probably grow up to be an insurgent—vowing revenge—killing the next soldier she sees.

A fierce cycle that never ends. Mark would say it can't end and never will.

At the foot of the valley before the road opened out onto the flattened plain, I heard the explosion. Yet another IED. I watched the front of the forward truck leap into the air. Doc was riding shotgun with me, and we jumped out and ran ahead. There wasn't much we could do. The floorboard of the five-ton was driven up into the cab, flattening the driver. Somehow, the explosion had flung the private onto the road. His head was on fire, so Doc and I used our shirts to put it out—but he wasn't moving. I knew he was gone even before I saw those blackened sockets. I snapped a picture when Doc wasn't looking and slipped the camera back into *my pocket. We kept guard on the hills above, their shadows looming over us as the sun fell beneath the sawtooth peaks. The chaplain said a prayer. Mark stood next to me and cursed the chaplain and God while we prayed. Doc wrapped the bodies, and the captain gave orders to empty out the back of the truck and set it up with explosives. We rolled on down the road and watched as the remainder of the truck exploded into pieces—nothing left for the insurgents but the bent, burnt frame, like the bones of a dinosaur burning in the desert wind.*

I only got his last name—Pierson. I don't remember him much, but Mark told me he was a Christian and remarked that Pierson must not have prayed hard enough. He got pissed when one of the guys said Pierson was in a better place. Mark called him a "fucking moron." Five minutes later, I had to pull him up off the ground—another black eye, because Mark can't keep his mouth shut. Once again, Mark refused to go to the Doc or report what happened. He told me people don't want to debate—they want to fight—and he was ready to sit back and watch the whole world consume itself in its own stupidity and ignorance.

Some days I think he's right. But I must do this. I can't allow Delaram's experience to fall into oblivion. I can't allow these stories to become "nothingness," as Mark puts it. That's all I've ever done before, too busy with my own life and petty worries. I'll probably be court-martialed, and I worry when Mark tells me my pictures won't make a damn bit of difference. Perhaps not. Perhaps that's the faith I must cling to. Change is the only constant, and I'm well aware that man has brought death upon himself long before history was even written. But I know that I can be the instigator for a change to move forward from all this—once the world sees what I've seen. The world may move on, but Delaram's world has been annihilated, as was the world of those who knew Pierson. Those small individual worlds, existing as a universe to the person experiencing them, are the worlds worth defending, even if the mechanism as a whole continues to rage on and eventually destroys itself. Perhaps one life changed is a universal change of some sort (I can hear Mark laughing at all this). The perspective of one life given the freedom to define itself, rather than to be defined by its bleak environment, is worth the cost I will surely endure.

The entry ended. Blank pages followed.

Erin wept on the floor of her kitchen, curled in on herself like a sleeping child, holding Kevin's journal to her breast. Gabriel hid in the corner, staring curiously at his owner. Thunder sporadically overpowered her cries as rain mercilessly beat against the windows. An hour passed, and Erin couldn't cry anymore. Soon, the thunder, too, subsided. The rain continued. Gabriel came out from the corner and licked Erin's wet face, purring. Erin slowly sat up, scratching Gabriel's back. She gathered up the photos, stacking them neatly together next to the rest of Kevin's notebooks. Erin flipped through the rest of Kevin's journals, carefully studying each photo, reading her son's words. She then pulled the paper napkin out of her pocket, read it again, and stuck it in one of Kevin's notebooks.

Gabriel sat on the kitchen counter between the living room and the kitchen, his tail whipping back and forth. He watched Erin slowly push all of the furniture into the corners of the living room—she had to take two breaks while moving the heavy couch. Gabriel then followed Erin down the hallway and into the study, then back into the living room several times—almost tripping Erin twice—as she set up a laptop, a printer, and a scanner on the floor in the middle of the now-spacious living room. Erin grabbed the plastic container of memory cards and the rest of Kevin's journals, setting them next to her laptop. Erin sat on the floor cross-legged as she saved all of Kevin's pictures onto her hard drive, labeling each one. She scanned the rest of Kevin's photographs, laying each picture next to each other on the carpet. She began transcribing Kevin's journal entries. Erin juxtaposed the entries with the corresponding pictures, creating photo essays of her son's work. Erin's face was blue from the light of her computer screen as the night rolled on. Gabriel sat curled up next to Erin, breathing quietly—his legs periodically twitching.

The sun was at its zenith the next day when Erin finished typing Kevin's last entry. Though she hadn't slept at all, Erin didn't feel tired. She fed Gabriel to stop his meowing and grabbed some leftover pizza from the refrigerator. Erin sat back down on the floor in front of her laptop, holding the limp slice of cheese-and-mushroom awkwardly in her hand as she checked the prices for flights—there were only a few available. She checked her bank account online and worked the math in her head. Erin called her bank to transfer money from savings, asking them the exchange rate for the Dinar. She jumped back online and booked her flights: Lufthansa Airlines Flight 447 from Denver to Frankfurt. Lufthansa Airlines Flight 3518 from Frankfurt to Beirut. Middle East Airlines Flight 322 from

Beirut to Baghdad. Each stop had long layovers—Beirut an entire day. Total travel time was thirty-two hours and twenty-three minutes.

Erin finished her pizza and walked into Kevin's old bedroom. She hadn't been in there for months. For the first time, Erin looked through the boxes of Kevin's things sent back to her from the base. They sat in the corner of the room, collecting dust. By the time she had opened all the sealed boxes, the sun was resting again at the cusp of the horizon, ready to be swallowed again by the mountains. She found a few more journals with only a few entries.

Erin was once again in the middle of the living room, clothes folded and laid out in front of her. An open suitcase sat next to the clothes as she wrote out a list of other items she would need in a desert climate. The cat meowed and pawed the backdoor. Erin looked up and saw that the display on her cell phone was lit up. She answered without looking to see who might be calling.

"Hello?"

"Erin? Erin, is that you?"

Erin held the phone to her ear with her shoulder, asking who was calling as she continued to arrange a few remaining pictures in what she thought was chronological order.

"It's Pastor Knight, Erin. I haven't seen you at church for a while."

Erin let a few pictures drop from her hand, but only to look up at Gabriel, still pawing at the back door.

"That's because I haven't been to church, Pastor," Erin stated as she stood, stretching her legs. "How's the family?" Erin walked slowly to the back door.

"They're well. Emily is pregnant. I'm going to have another grandchild soon."

"This makes five. Congratulations."

"Thank you, Erin. But I called to see how you were holding up."

The cat jumped outside as Erin cracked the door. The grass in the backyard was still wet from the sprinklers, and Gabriel hesitated, shaking his wet paws with each step.

"Don't be silly," Erin said to Gabriel.

"I'm sorry?"

"I'm fine, Pastor Knight." Erin shut the back door. She walked back into the living room. "I appreciate your concern."

"I've known you a long time, Erin. I consider you family." Erin stopped. "And if there's anything you need from me—from the church—all you need to do is ask."

"Actually, Pastor, I do need to ask you something."

"Of course"

"It's about the Leviticus Alliance. I—" Erin paused, unsure what to say. "I once considered Victoria family."

The pastor cleared his throat. "It pains me no end, what Victoria did—what one of our own did."

"She did it by abusing the trust people had in her—the trust you and I had in her." Erin walked into the kitchen. The linoleum was cold against her feet.

"To be honest, Erin, I wanted to pull our sponsorship long before that atrocity. We spoke several times about how her speeches were becoming... vitriolic."

"But you didn't, Pastor Knight. And I stood right alongside her—even helped her with those hateful speeches." Erin shook her head, rubbing her temples with one hand. "No one did anything until it was too late."

"Don't blame yourself for what happened."

"I blame both of us, Pastor. I blame all those churches and religious groups Victoria boasted about—telling everyone how these institutions represented God, legitimizing everything the Alliance said. And we did nothing." Erin looked out the kitchen window. Gabriel was in the backyard chewing on blades of grass.

The pastor paused. "The church is run by man, Erin—easily corruptible. And Victoria was a wolf in sheep's clothing. God warns us of—"

"Yet God, unlike the rest of us, was well aware of what Victoria was going to do." Erin walked back into the living room and sat down on the floor in the center of Kevin's open notebooks and photographs. She began typing again on her laptop.

"Victoria did not represent God."

"In hindsight, no. But the people who were killed at that rally, some of them from our church, were doing what they thought God wanted them to do—and now they're gone."

"We cannot pretend to know God's plan, Erin. We can only have faith."

"Meanwhile, we ignore the suffering God allows. We do nothing." Erin glanced around at the pictures that circled her. A body missing its legs. A human jawbone on the side of the road, maggots crawling over the teeth. A small boy's legs crushed by a convoy, the mother in the foreground, spitting on the soldiers. "I've seen enough, Pastor. I'm tired of doing nothing. You told me once that God didn't want followers who ignored their doubts."

"Yes, at our last meeting," replied the pastor.

"Yet, He ignores our cries for help, our pleas for clarity. My own son died because God failed to make Himself clear to His children." Silence followed.

"You will be missed at church, Erin. And you're welcome for supper at our home anytime."

"I'll be out of the country for a few months—possibly longer," replied Erin. "But I appreciate the invitation."

"And if you need anything—"

"Actually, since you asked. What would you say to supporting a different kind of alliance?"

"A new... alliance?"

"Nothing like the Leviticus Alliance. It still needs a lot of work before I can even launch it." Erin looked around at some of the pictures that surrounded her. "It's going to be difficult to find the people I need."

"What will this foundation do?"

Erin paused. She picked up the unfolded napkin that was next to her computer. "Tell stories."

"Stories?"

"Delaram's story. Pierson's story. And the others."

"Who?"

"The stories of the innocents God ignores." Erin cleared her throat. "I'll call you with more details when I get back to the States. Until then, take care of the families at the church—and that new grandchild of yours." The pastor said goodbye and Erin hit the *End* button on her cell phone. She could hear Gabriel at the back door, scratching the wood, meowing to be let in. Erin stood. The cell phone in her hand vibrated. She looked at the New York prefix on the display. Erin opened the door for Gabriel just before she answered.

[XVIII]

[2014]

Steve was lying on a rusty cot, eyes closed tightly. He couldn't remember the last time he had slept soundly. When he did sleep, Steve would find himself naked on the floor of his cell, the cool concrete pushing up into his back. He would hear the tapping of a cane, and Steve would look past his bare feet toward the cell door. Mark would limp out of the darkness, his solid-white eyes staring straight ahead, unblinking, his head askew, revealing a large grotto on the side of his skull—spiders crawling out of the opening. Mark would stand there, jaw shut, methodically tapping his cane on the concrete floor, the sound echoing off the enclosed walls of the cell and growing louder in Steve's ears. The spiders, covered in thick, black fur, would dart out the opening of his son's head, crawling over Mark's pale face, eating away his skin, his muscles, his wide-open eyes—white skin giving way to red muscle.

Tap. Tap. Tap.

Then Steve would feel the furry legs on his own skin, the spiders slowly crawling up his legs, moving toward his abdomen. Steve's muscles would freeze as he lay immobile on the cell floor, his son standing over him.

Tap. Tap. Tap.

Hundreds more spiders would crawl out of Mark's skull, his now-empty eye sockets vomiting the ravenous creatures, some falling from his forced-open jaw. Steve would feel the sharp fangs slicing into his body, the sound of skin being torn away, his flesh slowly dissolving from the enzymes in the spider's saliva.

Tap. Tap. Tap.

The spiders would work their way up Steve's chest and neck—some chewing their way beneath his ribs and burrowing into his body. Steve would wake up yelling, clawing frantically at his chest.

Three weeks before, his disgruntled cellmate rose from his own bunk and beat Steve unconscious for waking him up. He was in the prison infirmary for two days before he regained consciousness. It was the only time Steve had slept soundly since he'd been at the prison.

He no longer had cellmates—segregation for his own protection. Steve couldn't even attend Sunday morning services. His right arm was in a cast since his former cellmates cornered him after the service, snapping his arm in two, pushing the broken bones through the skin. Steve's body constantly ached from lack of sleep. His eyes were always red, sunk deep into black circles hanging from his face. His eyes refused to focus when he tried to read the Bible. He relied on the chaplain to read passages to him on Sunday afternoons.

"Read verses on forgiveness, Chaplain." Steve always requested, rubbing his eyes with the back of his one good hand. The chaplain thumbed through his old leather-bound Bible, clearing his throat before reading passages printed in red, setting his hand on Steve's shoulder as he spoke.

A prison guard slapped the metal bars with his baton. Steve's eyes snapped open as his body jerked in his cot, smacking his cast against the cinderblock wall.

"Get up, ya fuckin' shit stain!" the guard yelled. "You got a visitor."

Steve squinted. The sun was at its meridian, yet its heat couldn't penetrate the cell, blocked by cinderblock walls. Steve rubbed his arm as he sat up. His cell door slammed open, and the guard stood impatiently, rapping his black baton on the side of his perfectly creased pants.

"Move it, fucktard. You got twenty minutes."

Steve stood and rubbed the back of his neck. He felt cold, even with thick drops of sweat slowly rolling down his neck, soaking his shirt.

"Who is it?" Steve asked quietly.

"I ain't your fuckin' secretary," the prison guard replied, his dark eyes impatient as he pointed his baton down the long corridor. A long scar ran from his mouth up the side of his left cheek. It moved as he spoke. "Another shit stain for sure, anyone actually wants to talk to you."

Steve walked forward, rubbing his eyes. His fingers were clean of grease, and he couldn't smell oil on his hands. He buttoned up his orange shirt, the name BRADFORD stenciled on the back in bold, black letters.

The guard slammed the cell door behind him, and Steve walked down the long corridor.

The small visitor's room was packed tightly with green plastic chairs and plastic tables of the same color. A soft light bled in through thin, wired windows across the top of the far wall. Most of the chairs were occupied, bodies on either side leaning forward, exchanging sentences in whispers. Steve rubbed his hands on his orange pants as he scanned the room.

A woman sat alone in the corner, her back to Steve. Her long, brown hair hung down past her shoulder blades. Steve shuffled to her, his cheap, standard-issue paper slippers scraping along the concrete floor. He stopped behind her. There was a notebook open on the table in front of her, bound in leather. Steve recognized the scrawled handwriting before she turned her head.

"Sit down, Father." Shannon said, closing the notebook and looking straight ahead, folding her hands over the journal.

A large, bald man with tattoos running the length of his forearms was seated at the next table. His orange sleeves were rolled up past his elbows, revealing red skulls with open mouths, surrounded by black fire. Across from the bald man sat a little girl with red pigtails that jutted out each side of her head. She was crying softly, her father's tattooed fingers wiping away the tears from her red, freckled cheeks. Steve squeezed past them and sat down across from his daughter, tilting his head.

"You grew your hair."

"Yours got thinner," Shannon replied.

Steve scratched the top of his head with his good hand as he stared at the closed notebook. "It's good to see you again."

"I can't say I feel the same way." Shannon narrowed her eyes. "I can't believe I was ever afraid of you—left you alone with Mark." Shannon looked at the notebook. "He blamed me, you know, for everything you did to him after I left."

Steve looked down, and then back at his daughter. "It's been years since I've seen you, since the trial. How have you been?"

"None of your damn business." Shannon leaned forward, looking at Steve's cast. "And you're not going to get any pity from me, no matter how many bones you manage to break."

"It's been difficult here. God has not made it easy for me."

"Let me guess. You've been seeing the chaplain, asking for forgiveness," Shannon continued, "trying to convince yourself you're not a hell-bound son-of-a-bitch."

"Your brother chose his own path," Steve said flatly. "As did you."

"You didn't murder me when I made my choice."

"No. I... I... didn't mean..."

"You're stuttering."

"We... we can all be saved... we can all be forgiven... if we chose to... to..."

Shannon tapped on the notebook with her fingers. "And those thirteen people at the rally? Did they choose to die in an explosion?"

"No. No. No." Steve closed his eyes and shook his head. "They didn't die because of me."

"Yes, I've heard all the lies before."

"The bombs," Steve continued, "they were only meant to scare people. They told me over the phone... no frag... but the injuries... multiple injuries consistent with frag... and outside of the specified blast radius..." Steve rubbed the back of his neck, looking up at the ceiling. "I didn't even place the bomb. Someone came and picked it up... too close... too close..." Steve looked at his daughter. "Why were there two of them?"

The bald prisoner with the tattoos was sitting silently, hands folded neatly in his lap, staring aimlessly at the now-empty seat in front of him.

Steve leaned forward. "I think it was them..." Steve stopped, looking around each of Shannon's shoulders.

"Them?" Shannon asked.

"They were trying to discredit her. She told me herself."

"You're speaking in pronouns, Dad."

Steve looked down at the table, speaking slowly. "Miss Richman. Victoria. She told me how we were just... words... words were no longer enough. Scare them. Cause a big controversy. Make the news."

"Right," Shannon scoffed. "It was all a big conspiracy to frame you, right?"

"I was... it wasn't me. I was... at home... with..." Steve trailed off.

"Fifteen minutes!" one of the prison guards yelled, hands clasped behind his back. Two more guards stood at the only exit, batons dangling from their utility belts.

"With whom, Dad? *Who* were you with that day?"

"I... I was with..." Steve trailed off again, looking puzzled.

"Don't bullshit a bullshitter, Dad. I learned from you, remember?"

"The bomb. It was supposed to be in a building nearby... under construction... empty..." Steve shook his head again. "No one was supposed to get hurt."

"People did get hurt, Dad." Shannon replied with frustration. "*Your* bombs were placed next to the stage, hidden in recycling bins."

"It wasn't me... I... I only made one..." Steve scratched at his chest. "Victoria asked me... the Leviticus Alliance needed more than words... I..."

"Yes, I know, Dad. You said all this in the trial. Victoria asked you to make the bombs. Her driver picked them up. The driver's testimony is the only reason they didn't electrocute your ass."

Steve looked puzzled, rubbing his scalp. "No. I only made... I only made one bomb."

"You really don't remember, do you? Victoria's driver? He turned out to be a member of some small extremist group. One of their members attacked Erin Zuelke a few months before the bombing in a parking lot."

Someone behind Shannon coughed. She looked over her shoulder and then back at her father. "You do remember the Leviticus Alliance was dissolved less than a week after the explosion—once they found out the truth about Victoria. The Alliance is now a distant memory." Steve didn't respond. "And Erin Zuelke? Do you remember who she was?"

Steve shook his head.

"She was the co-founder. Had a son in the military. We became good friends. Shortly after she was cleared of any wrongdoing, Erin flew out to the Middle East. She worked there for a year with other humanitarian groups—UNICEF, the World Food Programme... She eventually set up her own foundation, founded in memory of her son."

"Victoria had a son, too," Steve replied, eyes locked on the table in front of him.

Shannon ignored him. "Erin started lecturing in the Middle East, sharing the stories of the people in her son's pictures. One of her photo essays was even published in *Time*—a photo of a girl named Delaram on the cover." Steve shifted in his chair. "She was threatened I don't know how many times. Shot at. Once, she was almost kidnapped. I made her hire a bodyguard. Erin could have come back to the States to continue her work, but she refused. She said she wanted to remain in the trenches. She thought herself more effective over there. Told me she could find more of her own stories. It finally got her killed." Steve looked up. "Killed by one of the many random explosions in the public markets of almost every city in that region. She burned to death in one of the shops. It was on the news for less than a day. I adopted her cat."

"Why are you telling me all of this?" Steve asked.

Shannon sat back, wiping her face with the back of her hand, eyes blinking. "You go to almost any small village in that area, and they know Erin by name. She cemented into their collective conscious the stories from Kevin's photographs. Millions in the States know about Kevin's work, his story—they even know about Mark."

Steve remained silent for a moment, staring at the journal. He then leaned forward. "Why would they know about Mark?"

Shannon tilted her head. "I've taken on the responsibility of keeping a gallery of Kevin's pictures here in the States—right in the heart of New York City. I get letters every week from people who've seen the photographs, read the essays. Calls from universities and museums wanting to display Kevin's photographs." Shannon smiled. "In the end, Erin became the martyr Victoria tried to be."

"Lies!" Steve yelled, slamming his fists down on the plastic table. "Victoria Richman is a hero."

"Shut up!" the guard with the scar yelled, jutting his chin toward Steve.

"Victoria and her son," continued Steve, quietly staring at the table in front of him, "true soldiers. Both dedicated their lives to duty, to this country, to God. We live in an evil world that requires sacrifice, Shannon. An evil, evil world."

"It was your bombs that killed Victoria, Dad, not the evil world."

Steve closed his eyes, rocking back and forth in his chair. "Satan has many soldiers. They walk among us in disguise."

"And Victoria never even had a child." Steve stopped rocking back and forth. He opened his eyes. "Actually, that's not completely accurate," continued Shannon. "Victoria was pregnant once, but it was aborted. She was sixteen at the time."

"No. More lies. He was a good son. Fought in Iraq."

Shannon sighed, then continued. "After the bombing, all kinds of reporters dug into her history. Victoria was quite promiscuous in high school. They even found the guy who got her pregnant. He lives in Boston. A doctor who runs an assisted-living facility."

Shannon pulled out an article stuck in the journal. It was from the *New York Times*. As she unfolded it, Steve could see a black-and-white picture of Victoria in the upper left-hand corner. "Of course," Shannon pushed the unfolded article across the table, "being the head of a powerful religious foundation that pulled in hundreds of thousands of dollars from groups like the American Family Association, Victoria's abortion was something of a secret—its revelation caused quite a stir in conservative circles." Shannon opened the notebook, flipping through the pages.

Steve closed his eyes, pushing the article aside. "No. She had a son. He was a good son."

"What was his name?" Steve looked up at his daughter. "His name, Dad. What was the name of Victoria's son?"

"Ten minutes!" the guard with the scarred face yelled, now standing in an empty corner of the room, arms folded over his chest, looking at Steve.

Shannon leaned forward. "Don't you see? Victoria stole Erin Zuelke's story to manipulate you into helping her. Erin was the one who had a son, a son who died in the war." Shannon leaned in even closer. "And get this: Mark, your son, was with him when he died."

"I have no son!" Steve hissed, staring down at his lap.

"Quiet!" one of the guards yelled, pointing his baton at Steve.

"Really? Are you going crazy in here?" Shannon asked, making a small circle with her index finger near her temple. "You *did* have a son. His name was Mark Bradford. You shot him in the head, remember?"

"I have no son," Steve whispered.

"Yes you do, *Dad*. Unlike you, I don't hide from the truth. I have a *father*, like it or not. You have a son. You murdered my brother. Killed him like he was a rabid dog on the side of the road." Shannon began flipping through the journal. "Mark, your son. Your homosexual son."

"Shut up, you liar, you Jezebel," Steve replied with clenched teeth, his hands rubbing the back of his neck, leaving red marks on his skin.

"Now there's the father I remember," Shannon said, nodding her head. "Brings back a lot of wonderful childhood memories."

"It was a test. We will all be together again—a family again. But my faith must first be tested." Steve kept his head down, talking to the plastic table. "Like Abraham and his son, Isaac."

"Except Abraham didn't go through with killing his son, remember?"

Steve looked up, his eyes wide with fright. "Why didn't God stop me? Why didn't He send an angel to stop me from sacrificing my son?"

Shannon continued to turn the pages of the notebook, all of them heavy with ink. "Look here," Shannon said, pointing at an entry. "Mark was only a kid when he wrote this: 'Dad's faith only makes him stumble around in his own darkness.'"

"My faith is unshakable, Lord," Steve said to himself with his head bowed, eyes closed. "I am no hypocrite. I have carried out my duty. Our family will be together again. Please show me mercy, show me forgiveness."

"Keep asking God, Dad, because you'll sure as hell never get forgiveness from me."

"Five minutes!" the guard yelled.

"Tick, tick, tick, Dad." Shannon closed the notebook. "Time's running out for you."

"Surrounded..." Steve whispered to himself, shaking his head back and forth. "I am surrounded by deceivers of men." Steve closed his eyes. "Lord, deliver me from this den of lions."

"What was that, Dad? You're trailing off into theocratic *loco* land." Shannon snapped her fingers twice in Steve's face, then leaned back in her chair, pointing at the journal. "I always wondered where he came up with all that—especially at that age." Shannon narrowed her eyes. "Then I realized that he had the perfect specimen to study his whole childhood—we grew up in a thought experiment, run by a man who couldn't come to terms with his wife's death."

Steve shook his head violently. Shannon stood and pushed the notebook across the table, tapping on the cover. "I'm leaving this for you, and I'm never coming back here. I'm done being angry with you, Dad. I'm done thinking about what I could have done. I'm done with you. So, consider this my parting gift. It's a journal that Mark—*your son*—started when he was eleven. Read what's in there. Read it and try to convince yourself you have no son." Steve lightly touched Mark's journal, running his index finger along its spine.

Shannon started to walk away. She stopped and turned, staring at the top of Steve's head, his white scalp shining through thinning, gray hair. "By the way, Mark's murder put a spotlight on all the homosexuals kicked out of the military before the repeal of Don't Ask, Don't Tell. The government is extending full health coverage to those discharged because of the policy—giving reparations to some and reenlisting soldiers who want to rejoin, with their time in service intact." Steve looked up and blinked, his eyes red. "And it's all thanks to you, Dad," Shannon said. She turned her back and walked toward the exit.

Steve looked back down and slowly opened the leather-bound notebook to the first page. He saw his daughter's handwriting. There was a short quote near the top: *Act without hope. — Jean-Paul Sartre*. Below that, it read *Happy 11th birthday, little brother. — Shannon*. Mark's name was written at the top of the page in childlike penmanship. Near the bottom, a small gold cross without the gold chain was taped to the page. Steve shot up out of his chair and stepped back, knocking it over. The plastic chair bounced off of the wall and fell sideways onto the floor. The prison guard with the scar bolted toward Steve, taking three long steps before plunging the long end of his baton into Steve's side. Steve fell to his knees, holding his ribs, eyes watering as Shannon's figure was swallowed up by the dark hallway, black, steel bars closing behind her. The guard told Steve to *shut the fuck up* as Steve screamed, over and over, that he had no son. The remaining prisoners and family members sat in silence, a few eyes wide with fright, others narrowed in disgust. Steve began screaming for God to send him a sign, to send him forgiveness. The guard grabbed Steve by the back of his orange collar and yanked him up from the floor. Mark's notebook was clenched tightly in Steve's right hand as he was lead out of the room. There were a few nods of familiarity from others wearing orange shirts—nods that only the damned could understand.

Hours had passed since Steve was thrown back into his cell. Outside the sun had long since been consumed by the horizon, filling the night with ageless, distant suns, made dim by the lights of a nearby highway. A quarter-moon floated on a sea of black as it burned through the remaining clouds of a weak snowstorm that dusted the prison walls with white.

Mark's journal sat open on the floor of Steve's cell, its pages torn from the binding and crumpled into individual balls, strewn about the cold, cement floor like paper boulders from a massive rockslide. A small gold cross sat nearby. There was one page left in the book. A single entry: *Dad made a cake for my birthday today. It tasted bad, but I didn't tell him. He got mad again. This time about a stupid science book. Says he's going to pull me out of school again. He spent the rest of the night in the garage. I made some cereal for supper. He must really miss mom today. I think I remind him of her.*

Less than a foot above the open journal, Steve's bare feet dangled, toes purple. White sheets were wrapped around his neck, and his body swung slowly like a pendulum counting away the silent seconds. Steve's dry eyes were locked open, as if trying to peer through the cinderblock wall at the constellation Orion, the hunter prowling across a curved field scorched black by the now-hidden sun.

Remnants of Light   Mike Yost

Acknowledgments

This novel would not have seen the light of day without the unshakable support of my parents, David and Susie Yost, who have always loved me for who I am. My big brother, Paul, was always ready with a sharp wit that can cut diamonds and a sense of humor that makes the dead grab their bellies. You were the lifeline for all those years I spent in the closet, and I dedicate this book to you. My partner Dave has given me ceaseless encouragement and affection, and his numerous culinary creations have never failed to dislodge writer's block. My sister-in-law Robin gave me UNO and my irrational animosity for the color yellow. My ebullient niece Kelsey shared her contagious enthusiasm.

My editor and the staff at Whaley Digital Press returned numerous steadily improving drafts covered in red ink. Carson Reed kept slicing away at extraneous text—especially those pesky, prolific adverbs. Sam Henson has been my best friend since third grade and has better grammar skills than most writers. My good friend (and sister in another life) Sarah-Michelle Thompson went on all of the random road trips I needed in the middle of the night. Paul Goff was with me on the infamous MONDAY. Lisa Kuenning, Kara Kuenning, and Matt Kuenning have given me unwavering friendship. Martha Mendoza and Brandi Dean make me laugh—and make my night job bearable.

I would also like to thank Professor Emeritus Walter Nelson of Red Rocks Community College, who died in 2008. (I shouldn't have waited so long to contact him.) Professor Teague Bohlen cultivated the seeds planted by Professor Walter. Dr. Cynthia Wong introduced me to Borges, Kundera, and Ishiguro (among many others). Dr. Maria Talero gave me an insatiable—and unnatural—appetite for existential tomes. Dr. Gabriel Zamosc-Regueros gave me Nietzsche. Thanks to all the professors, students, coworkers, and strangers who have influenced me on this incredibly short journey we call existence.

Finally—to the fourteen thousand men and women of the armed forces who were unjustly discharged from the military for simply being who you are—you deserve better.

Printed in Great Britain
by Amazon